MW01628453

Hurricane Room

KIM SHERWOOD is a novelist and a lecturer in creative writing at the University of Edinburgh and was shortlisted for the *Sunday Times* Young Writer of the Year Award. She is the author of the highly acclaimed Double O trilogy, which includes *Double or Nothing*, *A Spy Like Me*, and *Hurricane Room*, as well as the award-winning novel *Testament* and *A Wild and True Relation*.

kimsherwoodauthor.com

Also by Kim Sherwood

Testament

A Wild and True Relation

Double O Novels

Double or Nothing

A Spy Like Me

Hurricane Room

A Double O Novel

Kim Sherwood

William Morrow
An Imprint of HarperCollins*Publishers*

www.ianfleming.com

HarperCollins books may be purchased for educational, business, or sales promotional use. For information, please email the Special Markets Department at SPsales@harpercollins.com.

hc.com

FIRST EDITION

Designed by Kyle O'Brien

Library of Congress Cataloging-in-Publication Data has been applied for.

ISBN 978-0-06-323661-5

Printed in the United States of America

26 27 28 29 30 LBC 5 4 3 2 1

Dedicated to the memories of
my mother-in-law, Vera Herrmann,
and my father, Craig Sherwood

Part I

Money

2004

ONE

Toxic

"You'll know him when you see him," M had told me. "You'll know the type."

I wondered just what type that was as I crossed a former concert hall now billed as the first professional strip club in Russia. Stepping aside for two women young enough to be my daughters, I followed them into Solaris Bar, where they might scream over subwoofers pumping Britney Spears's "Toxic," go bowling, or exchange venereal diseases with pinstriped *biznesmeni* for $150.

As a bouncer ushered me into a roped-off corner dominated by wood veneer and red velvet, I saw him.

The man I was looking for leaned with his back against the bar, elbow propped on the brass, one hand curled around a *granyonyi* glass, the other in his pocket. He wore a black wool dinner jacket with a single button, narrow silk-faced lapels, and silk-trimmed pockets. The jacket had straight shoulders, a clean chest, and a tight waist. No cummerbund or waistcoat. The shirt was clearly Turnbull & Asser's white-on-white waffle weave, paired with white moiré silk braces, which flashed as he took a sip of vodka. The bow tie was black silk, matching the stripe down each outseam of the classic Italian trousers, mid-rise and straight-legged. The shoes were black calf two-eyelet. Not patent, but shined to perfection. The man was mid-twenties. Tall. Slim, muscled build. Short black hair, a fringe that curled like a comma. A handsome devil, in a rather arrogant way. Yes, I knew the type. I could see why M had him tipped for the Double O Section. A chip off the old block, as my father might have said.

Berthing alongside, I ordered vodka with a pot of pepper and cast a line toward him in English: "First time in Moscow?"

A slow, sidelong look. "What makes you say that?"

"No pepper in your vodka." I decorated the surface of my glass with black ballast, which lumbered to the depths. "It's a trick the Russians taught me. You'll find fusel oil on the surface of badly distilled vodka. Poisonous. A little pepper takes the oil to the bottom. You get to like the taste and it becomes a habit."

"I avoid habits. As a rule."

"That's very funny, Mr. . . . ?"

The man sniffed. "The pepper could be poisoned."

"My tab is too long. Besides, haven't you heard? The circus has moved to the Middle East." I gestured around the bar, and further, encompassing the entire Cosmos. The biggest hotel in the country was a collaboration between Soviet and French architects, heralding perestroika, Gorbachev's attempt to galvanize the failing Communist economy by introducing a dose of capitalism. The dose worked like a virus; across Russia, managers looted so heavily shops went empty and gangsters killed each other on factory floors. Cosmos Hotel grew sickly and the Cold War grew old, leaving a twenty-five-story horseshoe known as Half a Cup by locals. One got the feeling it was a cup half-empty. Now I raised a toast to the TV over the bar, which showed explosions in Baghdad, red flares rippling the inky sky. "Here's to shock and awe."

It was 2004, over a decade before I would be given the assignation "M" and take my position in the throne room of MI6. I drained the glass. "My name's Emery Ware. Universal Exports."

The man watched me for thirty seconds, then reached for the pepper, freckling his own vodka before knocking the drink back. "James." He set the glass down with a bang. "James Bond."

We shook hands.

Bond said, "I'm attached to the British embassy. I've been here long enough to hate the weather. In London, April's a spring month."

"Whereas in Moscow, we're freezing our balls off." The standard coded greeting over, I tapped my glass. The barman, a stoned kid, reached for Russian Standard, better than the bootleg stuff they used to serve. I hadn't been to the Cosmos since the raves were known as Gagarin parties. The big thing then was Russian rap, too angry to be as absurd as it should have been: "Better hide your power in the daytime / when you are a mischievous Moscow playboy."

The only trouble was trying to hold on to a girl who offered no purchase but a pair of fishnets when the dance floor was coated in blood. Now the next generation of girls writhed onstage. But Bond's gray-blue eyes weren't fixed on them. "You don't look happy, Bond. Sorry to miss all the fun in Iraq? Or perhaps you're one with your generation and cast suspicion over the hunt for Weapons of Mass Destruction."

"I go where I'm told."

"That's not what I've heard." I lowered my voice. "M thinks you have what it takes to be a Double O but he's worried your temperament isn't cool enough. Sent you here to test your patience. And you're already blowing it."

A sharp look.

"Everything about you screams what you are."

Bond's right hand moved from his pocket to his left armpit, brushing the weapon concealed in the holster beneath his jacket, the unease of a Navy man more used to carrying a gun in uniform than out of it.

"That gesture, for starters, will give you away to the bellboy."

He snorted. "I'm not looking for a mentor."

"Shame. You need one. You're watching the watchers."

"Someone should," said Bond.

"Are you being clever?"

"Never knowingly."

"My point, *young man*, is that you are not watching the *girls*. Don't like women, Bond?"

That elicited a raised eyebrow. Bond nodded toward a cabal in the corner. "The hood receiving the lap dance is Mikhail Khodorkovsky, Russia's first oligarch. When Gorbachev legalized small cooperatives, Khodorkovsky turned 'non-cash' into real money and became a millionaire overnight. Next to him is Boris Berezovsky, Russia's second oligarch. He turned looting into an art form. By the time these two were done, the Kremlin declared the end of Communism and the end of democracy all in one decade."

"Spies and gossip columnists get a hard-on playing who's who. You want to blend in, watch the strippers. Better yet, take one to your room while you've still got your hair. Trust me."

"How do you know I have a room here?"

"Your girl told me."

"Yelena?"

I applauded. "He has a dancer already—what does he need my advice for? Not Yelena, son, the girl on your desk. I'm afraid she rather disapproves of you."

"That's only because she knows me," said Bond. "And she's not my girl."

"No after-hours fun in the stationery cupboard?"

"I mean she's not my *secretary*. She's operations manager," said Bond. "And I think she'd want it pointed out she's not a girl."

"Don't tell me I have a reconstructed man on my hands."

"I'm too young for reconstruction. Unlike some. What were you, back in the day?"

"*Back in the day*, I was 0013."

Bond straightened. "I know your reputation. If a man wanted to become a Double O, he could do worse than follow you."

"One of the few to survive the honor. Something for the record books. Speaking of, did you know that when you checked in here, you were very nearly the Cosmos Hotel's seven-millionth guest?"

In the mirrored ceiling, our doubles gauged each other.

"You've had people watching me?" asked Bond.

"Yes."

"To report to M?"

I left that alone. "The honor went to a tourist called Michelle Collins, if you're curious."

"That's why I let her cut in line. I don't need records."

"And here was me thinking you were playing the gentleman."

"I don't play."

"It's all a game. The Great Game where defeat comes at a great cost. You'll learn that one day. Jesus wept, I'm half-inclined to tell you to get out now."

Bond hunched. "That's what you'll tell M: get him out before he's in?"

"Suppose I were to tell M your bedroom door has been swinging. Suppose I were to warn him this young man is an ideal defector, who would ply his trade for any country that kept him in plentiful supply of good booze, bad women, and shiny toys."

"You'd be wrong," said Bond.

I laughed. "What a passionate defense. Intelligence is currency, Bond. What *sort* of legal spy are you, that's what the opposition wants to know. Not gay, like so many of MI6's defectors to the Soviet Union, blackmailed and desperate. But that doesn't mean the bedroom isn't a weakness for you. No longing phone calls to a girlfriend back home.

Putting up in a hotel—*this* hotel—instead of a nice townhouse with a nice wife. You're as available as a public lavatory."

"Are you inviting me to one?"

"You should be so lucky. I pay seven thousand dollars a month for a Stalin-era apartment on Kutuzovsky Prospekt because it makes my wife happy and my stepchildren popular at school. I'm past honey traps, and the FSB aren't trying to trap me. I'm trapped already."

"What number?" asked Bond.

"Children?"

"Wife," he said.

"Fourth, you cheeky sod."

"She's Russian?"

"Belarusian."

"Did you marry her for cover?"

At the far end of the bar, local gangsters with aspirational American accents did shots and beat their chests. Foreign students tired of their act tried to snag Bond's attention.

"Give it time. I used to be you. A good-looking young man with an easy smile who doesn't blink when a woman sizes him up. Wives numbers one to four will get to you yet. And if I were FSB I'd know how to get to you now. All it would take is a girl who puts up a little challenge. You'd be hers."

"You think I whisper nuclear secrets in my sleep?"

"Do you?"

He sneered. "*No.*"

"And what if a damsel in distress asked for your help, her beautiful golden hair spread over your pillow, her plump lips pouting? The help of a British spy, if only you knew one?"

"I'm nobody's knight in shining armor," said Bond.

"Can I have another reading on that line?" I filed away the irritation on Bond's face. "What else? Your wastepaper basket is filled with bottles."

"How do you know that?"

"Your cleaner. Maybe you're lonely. Maybe you're trying to forget something. No phone calls to family, so maybe it's inherited wealth that pays for your tailoring—parents dead, Bond?" That drew a wince. "Well, a healthy bank account is no weakness. Though vanity is: you dress better than any civil servant I ever met."

"Thank you."

"It's a low bar. But you're detail-oriented and your dress shows it. That's good. The bug in your room picks up the same little clicks and rustles as you check for listening devices every night. That's good too. Details will save your life."

Bond looked like he'd bit down on a lemon. "You bugged my room?"

"Of course we did. And you can bet the FSB have too."

"Where's your bug?" he asked.

"You tell me."

"Where's the FSB bug?"

"Not in the cistern or the bulbs you search so diligently, obviously. So, we add it all up. No dependents, no one to give you that extra measure of personal caution, but you do take professional cautions. You obviously work out. You're a straight, white man with money behind him, promiscuous, attractive. When you don't know you're being watched, your face is blank and your eyes are dead."

He gave a harsh laugh. "No need to spare my feelings."

"You're right: you don't have any. You're a perfect weapon and someone is going to use you. The FSB will have you on their one-to-watch list. And their wish list."

"It's nice to be wanted," said Bond.

"Isn't it?" I tried to work out his expression. Contempt? Self-loathing? Amusement? "Tell me why you want to be a Double O."

"I think I can be of service to my country."

"Excuse me while I find a tissue."

Bond shrugged. "Fine. I think I have what it takes."

"What does it take?"

"You tell me."

I twisted my glass as if aligning a kaleidoscope. "There are two types of professional murderers in the world. The first has a limited shelf life. Hitler had to rotate the men in charge of the gas chambers. Gave them nice little holidays."

"That's how you see yourself?"

"My father survived D-Day and liberating the camps to die as an agent for BRIXMIS in Berlin surrounded east and west by Nazis walking around as if the war never happened. What do you think?"

Bond spread his hands. "It's your analogy, I'm just standing here."

"Then stand to attention. The second type is a man-eating tiger. He gets the taste of it and finds he can't stop."

"A Double O is a tiger with a taste for death?"

"Not so much a taste. It's simply become a fact of life. He can't eat anything else now. *It's his nature.* And a very useful nature, too, for governments that need willing executioners. In some ways, we're not so different from SMERSH."

On the stage, a girl did something rather new and exciting with the splits, but Bond wasn't watching. He said, "SMERSH was the Soviet Union's murder squad directed at foreign spies. Bribery, torture, coercion."

"Do you think we draw our line in the sand so differently?"

He squared his jaw. "Yes. Your father must have thought so, too."

I gave Bond a beneficent smile. "I suppose he did, yes. M wants me to take you out for a spin, kick your tires, so to speak." I reached for the brochures spread on the bar. "Their literature is rather out of date. *Intourist greets you in Moscow—the capital city of the Soviet state and one of the most beautiful and comfortable cities in the world.* Unless you oppose Putin's new regime. Come on, young buck. I'm showing you the real Moscow."

Bond demonstrated his full height. "If it involves less psychoanalysis and more vodka, I'm game."

I studied him under the fake crystal chandelier. "Let's see if you can keep up with me."

TWO

Romeo

The space race was over. Other measures mattered now. Moscow had surpassed New York in number of resident billionaires. The Russian-language edition of *Cosmopolitan* topped European circulation, the pocket-size format poking from women's bags wherever you looked. A new branch of Papa Johns pizza opened at Prospekt Vernadskogo and served more people in a day than any other branch worldwide. On the outer ring of the city, gray Soviet blocks seemed to have their own weather system, permanently cloaked in dirty snow. But at the center, there were thousands of cars on the roads, all in a hurry, and for the first time ever some of them were Ferraris.

I swept Bond from the Cosmos Hotel to Old Arbat, where I tested his tradecraft down the crooked street. He scored one hundred percent, correctly recalling the sequence of the souvenir stand offering Putin T-shirts and miniature busts of Stalin; the Michael Jackson impersonator dancing with a bejeweled belly dancer; the antique shop selling religious icons for $2,000. A street child, who slept underground for the proximity to central heating, tried to loosen the Rolex Explorer 1016 on

Bond's wrist. He gently clasped her fingers before palming her a bunch of notes. So this hard-faced man was not hard-hearted. We passed a sushi bar that used to be a shop called Juice, one of the few places where for a handful of kopeks you could get a vitamin infusion to help you through the winter.

"What were you doing here, back then?" asked Bond.

"It was glasnost. You can't imagine those first trips to Moscow, after so many years daring to cross the Iron Curtain."

We dined at Cantinetta Antinori, the new offering from restaurant guru Arkady Novikov in a nineteenth-century building dripping with Russian and Italian flags on a shaded *pereulok* behind the Foreign Ministry. Novikov himself brought out the bistecca alla fiorentina made with beef from the Chiana Valley. He told us the meal was on the house.

"I trust I have your attention."

"Undivided," said Bond, appraising the 1999 Solaia wine, which would have cost 7,800 rubles. "But doesn't being known to every restaurateur in the world rather blow your cover?"

"Depends on the legend you've been given to operate under."

"What's your legend?"

"A liaison to the Department of Trade. In other words, a filthy rich Brit with import licenses and government connections. Here, the enemy already presumes you're a spy. It's what you *do* with that presumption." A shrug. "I make friends."

"Do the Russians know the truth about their friend?"

"My life as a Double O is dead and buried."

"How do you know where one legend ends and another begins?" asked Bond.

I heaved a sigh. "There is one eternally true legend—that of Judas."

"I didn't realize philosophy was on the exam paper," said Bond.

"Not philosophy, history. Those are the words of Comrade Joseph Stalin—worth knowing here. Ultimately, a spy always betrays someone: his country, his mark, or himself."

"While we're on history, I understand you're responsible for some of the most significant intelligence coups of those days. And kills." He seemed to hesitate. "The Stay Behind Slayer is taught at Regent's Park. A prime case of gut instinct, they say. How did you know it was him?"

"What do you see, looking around you?"

Bond scanned the Tuscan interior. "Something out of place."

"Exactly. It took them two years to import the stone alone. And that's how I identified the Stay Behind Slayer. Something out of place. Do you have the time? Mustn't be late for the ambassador."

Bond shook his sleeve out of the way and then froze, confronted by a blank wrist.

I slid his Rolex over the linen. "She had *two* hands, and you paid her for robbing you."

A strained smile. "As did you, I see." He slipped on the stainless steel bracelet. "What was it, then? The White Mice didn't catch whatever you recognized as out of place. But you *knew* you'd found your man."

"Boys who get their pockets picked by little girls are not permitted to ask questions of their superiors." I softened. "The Stay Behind Slayer is ancient history, a footnote in the Cold War. Now the US wants us to make nice. Russia is supporting Operation Enduring Freedom, of all the ironies, and we're to share intelligence. Of course, one wonders if such support is simply the Kremlin's attempt to win a pass for rape and pillage in Chechnya."

Bond considered that and found a through line I hadn't meant to cast: "You were in Berlin when the Wall came down, now you're in Moscow as it opens for business. Spent some time around useful men in the War on Drugs, too. Right place, right time, every time."

"Ambitions are important, James. No one will hand you what you want. You have to learn to take it." As I said this, Bond was distracted by a model walking past wearing a red dress that ended at just about her waist. She winked at him. "Not that you need instruction."

After dinner, we reported to Spaso House, where the American ambassador expected me for drinks. Peeling plasterwork revealed the "marble" columns were wood underneath. The portico was crowded with Russian diplomats.

I put my arm around Bond. "Welcome to the new age."

He said, "Tell Mother I died game."

My wife was already at the reception. She was closer to Bond's age than mine and spent the next hour flirting with him. When she spilled red wine on a white rug, I called for a taxi.

Closing the car door after her, Bond told me, "It might be time for Wife Number Five."

The window rolled down and Maria leaned out. "Divorce would cost him too much." Then she collapsed against the headrest and told the driver to take her somewhere fun.

"You want some advice, James?"

"No, but you keep giving it."

"Never marry your mistress. She knows all your secrets and you'll only disappoint her."

Where Old Arbat became New Arbat, a 1960s stretch in flashing neon, the Metelitsa club and Cherry Casino played host to hopeful pop stars singing to the seven hundred people who had all the money and connections needed to make them famous. Bond hit it big at blackjack, so I coughed up the $200 per head entrance fee at the British-owned Shangri-La, where he quickly made my money back, refusing to fold across the poker table from a Thief-in-Law. I was curious how the next minute would play as the gangster from the gulag squared up to the spy from Savile Row.

"The last man who beat me, I invite him and his syndicate to collect the money at my apartment." The Thief-in-Law bared gold teeth. "They never left. Would you like to come to my apartment?"

"I'm saving myself for marriage," said Bond.

"Huh?"

Bond slid the croupier a tip before requesting the winnings in thousand-ruble notes. He stood up. The Thief-in-Law did the same. They faced each other under a yellow lamp.

"I insist you come with me."

Bond looked at me. "Some men just don't know how to take no for an answer."

The Thief-in-Law wrapped a hand as thick as a boxing glove around Bond's wrist. His fingers probed the watch. "This real?"

"As real as the gold on the carpet."

"Huh?"

Bond's jab was so fast it might not have happened, but then the man choked with surprise, clutching his bloody mouth, and Bond stepped over the litter of gold teeth on the red floor.

I steered Bond to the cashier's cage. "Next time, de-escalate."

"He's alive, isn't he?"

We finished the night with vodka shots back at the Cosmos Hotel. Bond's eyes were veined as a river delta. He'd drunk twice as much as me, and I insisted on escorting him to his room in case the Thieves-in-Law wanted revenge. When a man with a tattooed skull barred our way, I kept Bond under my wing. The man faded into the cigar smoke.

"I don't need help," argued Bond as I opened his bedroom door. "Let them come."

"Until you learn to value your skin, I'll value it for you." I encouraged Bond to lie down. He looked much younger in the dayglow dawn filtering through the orange curtains.

"Sleep it off."

He mumbled, "I'm ready to go again . . ."

"I bet your father was proud."

Bond's breathing was growing deeper. "He didn't have the chance."

I took Bond's shoes off and set them side by side. "Mine neither. But life finds a way to make it up to us." I swept Bond's messy fringe to one side. "Maybe you'll make me proud."

Over the next weeks, I carried out an experiment. The most exclusive clubs operated what they called Face Control: if you didn't look attractive, glamorous, or rich enough, the bouncer turned you away within a split second. I urged Bond ahead of me in freezing queues. He was never turned away. Inside, Bond would take on my challenges: secure an invite to the next state reception from a woman who worked at the Ministry of Culture, or identify and tail home an FSB officer without being made. At Crystal, there were three categories of gamblers: professionals looking to win $300 a day; big players who bet at least $10,000 per game; and cheaters and police, both of whom expected to win dishonestly. The place was controlled by the Georgian Mafia. Bond was as good as the professionals. His interest didn't stay on the cards though, straying to men in their thirties to forties with a military look about them.

I was given to understand M sent Bond here to discover how the star prospect fared in muddy waters. But it struck me there was something I didn't know. He was looking for someone. For all my advice, Bond wasn't a schoolboy. He was ready to graduate. He obviously didn't have a photo and perhaps only the vaguest description, his gaze searching tough-looking hoods related to organized crime or the army. And they were everywhere.

When I took him to play golf at the Moscow Country Club—where all the men talked gear, taking to the new sport like arms dealers—Bond checked reservations for the restaurant. He didn't seem to be after a particular name, more a pattern.

At the second hole, I was already ahead. I offered small comfort: "Early days, Bond."

"It's always too early to start losing," he said.

"Maybe you need a bit of incentive. Two hundred a hole?"

"We could play for this." Bond tossed something onto the green.

I bent and picked up the stripped wires.

"Do you know the number one cause of apartment fires in Russia?" he asked.

"As a matter of fact I do. Exploding TV sets."

"Do you think they're all bugged?" he asked cheerfully.

"I wouldn't be surprised. Congratulations. What are your terms?"

"I checked the phone, the mirror, the fan, that's the only one I could find. I win, you tell me if that's the Russian bug or ours, and where I can find the other one."

"What do I get if I win?"

"My eternal admiration."

"I presume I have that anyway."

He bowed.

I won.

Sammy Kotwani, proprietor of the Imperial Tailoring Company, got Bond's measure in a room pretending to be a London club: burgundy-draped ceilings, paneled wainscoting, leather chairs. We shared champagne and curry with a media mogul and a politician. But despite his smooth tongue, Bond wasn't listening to the stream of valuable intelligence. As the clients thanked Mr. Kotwani for the mangoes sent to their homes, Bond's gaze was on the suits waiting on the racks. He was measuring someone himself.

Snow was finally melting from the streets the morning I followed Bond into his office, where his girl guarded the sanctum. She raised cool eyes from her computer, turning off the monitor as Bond threw the trilby pressed upon him by Mr. Kotwani toward the coat stand. It landed perfectly.

"Hole in one, Moneypenny." He took off his coat and hung it up.

"Beating Russians at golf is nothing to boast about, James," she said, rising to shake my hand. "Hello, Mr. Ware. I've heard a great deal about you from James."

I kissed her cheek. "You too, Miss Moneypenny."

Bond took up a seat on the corner of her neat desk where a file marked FOR YOUR EYES ONLY was stamped with the name of an operation: REMNANT. He said, "If my prowess on the golf course won't impress you, what will? Tell me and I'll pretend I've already done it."

"I'd be impressed if you turned up for work on time."

"I'll take the blame for that," I said.

"I'm here, aren't I?" said Bond. "Next to most of the drunks in this department, that's a record."

"I thought you weren't trying to get into the record books. But where Miss Moneypenny is concerned . . ."

"Where Ms. Moneypenny is concerned, it's also not the record books I want to get into." Bond turned his charm on her. "Just your good books."

"Die for the cause and I'll consider it," she said. "Now, if you've got the sexual harassment out of your system, we've got operational business to discuss."

"I'll leave him in your capable hands, Miss Moneypenny. Be good, son."

A smirk. "Don't bet on it." But it was performative nonchalance. Moneypenny's "operational business" had lit the same spark of deadly calculation in Bond I had seen as he measured the suits waiting to be collected from Mr. Kotwani's. James Bond was measuring someone for their grave. And the suspicion that I knew exactly who was a chip-chip-chip that grew louder and louder in my ears. Discreet inquiries among old Service friends told me Operation Remnant was the task force responsible for determining how explosives provided by NATO to Stay Behind Networks in the GDR had ended up in the hands of terrorists, used in a recent bombing campaign across Europe by terrorists on the far right. The suspicion was that someone had leaked knowledge of hidden weaponry caches left buried in woodland across East Germany. I remembered Bond's interest in my most celebrated kill, the Stay Behind Slayer, and sweat dampened my new shirt.

I returned to the Imperial Tailoring Company and riffled through the racks of bespoke suits. The largest was fit for a six-foot-seven man with arms as long as an ape's.

I swapped my SIM for a prepaid card and dialed a number by memory. "Does Mr. Kotwani tailor your suits?"

The voice on the end replied: "Good evening to you too, Emery. Yes, he does. Need an introduction?"

"Do not tell me you are in Russia."

"Arrived yesterday. Why, do you miss me?"

"You asked me to test the new prospect for the Double O Section. He's too stalwart to prove any use to you."

"What a nice word. You sound stressed, Emery."

"M led me to believe Bond was here for a bit of spit and polish. But I think he's probing me as much as I am probing him."

"How fun."

"He's *looking* for someone. The Stay Behind Slayer."

A pause. "You killed the Stay Behind Slayer in '86. Built your success on it."

"You and I both know that all I did was stage your body double's death. I told you it was a loose end that would come back to hang me. Or you. Are you behind the bombing campaign with NATO weaponry?"

No answer.

"There must be HumInt on a suspect matching your description. Bond and Moneypenny are after a six-foot-seven man. The connection between the explosives and the Stay Behind Network . . . MI6 must believe I failed to kill you. If they find you . . . or if I'm doubted . . ."

"That won't happen, Emery. This isn't the day for a hanging."

It was unclear exactly whose hanging he meant. If he was caught, would he talk? I needed my own insurance policy. That's when I decided to act on a long-held suspicion. I would use Bond for the Romeo sting. I gave Bond his mission: discover the details of an offshore account and get a look at the money inside. I identified the target: a bank liaison officer whose job was to land big fish, one of whom she hoped to marry on her way to better waters. Bond began by opening a safe-deposit box in the vault, giving him time to flirt with her and her time to register his suit, watch, passport, and bricks of cash. After a few lingering visits to withdraw cash, playing the enamored Romeo, he asked her to dinner. Dinner turned into breakfast. It was always her place, never his, the dutiful boy mindful of the remaining bug.

He waited until she invited him to meet her parents to tell her he needed help assessing a potential business partner, just a peek at an offshore account. Perhaps she recognized a trade when she saw it, perhaps not. Either way, she delivered all the details of the account including its contents and recent transfers, and her parents met a smooth-talking Brit who soon disappeared, leaving her with a diamond ring. I was certain it wouldn't be the last time we pimped this Romeo for England.

Afterward, I asked Bond if he saw anything ignoble in these activities. We were in a bar watching two naked women on a trapeze float over the pool table.

"What do you want from me," he asked, "history's first noble spy?"

"We are looking for what we are *always* looking for, James: someone who is a bit bad and at the same time a bit good. Listen to me, son. You have the potential to be something better than that. Better than us old warhorses. Though whether you have the taste for *better* remains to be seen." I wasn't certain why I had this sudden desire, to see him improve on me. Maybe it was a father's urge. Maybe it was nostalgia for my untarnished youth. "Perhaps you'll transform our reputation."

"We're not supposed to have reputations."

"There's nobility in you, waiting to get out, I know that much. Love and grief might do the trick. Or kill your humanity altogether."

"We're not supposed to have humanity," he said, straight-faced.

I shook my head. "What are they teaching you these days?"

"How to fuck good people over." He slipped me a piece of paper detailing a small fortune. "Looks like whoever owns this account is embezzling enough government money to marshal a private army."

Hiding the paper in my pocket, I leaned closer to him. "When we met, you acted as if I were a stranger. But you were waiting for me, weren't you? Watching the watcher?" He said nothing. I pushed: "Learned much?"

Bond transferred his attention to the girls, both of whom wore pink angel wings, scattering glitter over the players below with each arc. A wing brushed Bond's upturned face. "Yes, sir."

THREE

Wilderness of Mirrors

A day at the racetrack. James Bond got the best out of a Lada known as "a skip with a sunroof" while I timed his laps from the stands. On paper we were practicing his getaway driving. In practice we were boys with toys. The same couldn't be said of Miss Moneypenny, who climbed toward me with swaying hips, sporting a high-waisted pencil skirt in navy with a white blouse and aviator sunglasses, her ringlets exactly right despite the wind. Moneypenny was beautiful until she looked at you over her sunglasses with that direct, quizzical gaze, as if she found some irony in your presence. She transferred the same gaze to the track.

"Have I missed it?" she asked.

"It?"

"Whatever's supposed to be so impressive," she said, watching Bond gleefully neglect to apply the brakes as he took the chicane, shooting between points like a pinball.

"Then he still wants to impress you, our young man?"

She said coolly, "He doesn't know what he wants."

That I could believe. The question was whether I could be the one to tell him.

Bond pulled into the pit, jumping from the car and bounding up to us. Moneypenny put her handbag on the seat beside me as Bond approached.

"Ms. Moneypenny, I hardly dared to hope." He bowed over her hand.

"You said you had something to show me," she said. "Don't tell me that was it."

Bond smirked.

I sat back on the bleachers. Maybe here was the woman to challenge the young buck. She had her hooks in, that was certain, and I'd wager she'd have them in forever.

"Care to join me for a spin?" said Bond.

"I'm all yours," she said, picking up her bag.

"Careful," he said. "I'll believe you."

I watched them walk arm-in-arm to the pit, where the racing Aston Martin prototype DBR9 gleamed, ready and waiting. It was yet to debut at Le Mans. Bond opened the passenger door for Moneypenny, who swung her leg as if this were her childhood horse. Bond folded into the driver seat. The car shot out of the pit onto the track before you could blink.

I eased a device that looked like a hearing aid over my ear. I'd slipped a bugged Fire and Ice lipstick into Moneypenny's bag. It was her brand. The device was Soviet-era, and if she discovered it, she would blame the FSB. The dialogue unfolded against the muscular surge of the engine as Bond hurtled around the track at over 150 miles per hour. I imagined it as a surveillance transcript.

Bond: You look tense, Moneypenny.

Moneypenny: You don't look tense enough, Bond.

Bond: Tensed muscles get in the way of reflex. I'm half-asleep right now.

Moneypenny: That explains why you didn't get wide enough on that corner.

Bond: You're welcome to get into the back seat and drive from there.

Moneypenny: There is no back seat.

Bond: Then you're welcome to climb into my seat, as long as you don't mind me staying put.

Moneypenny: Your lap's too slow. [pause] The fastest time here is one minute forty-two. So we've got three or four minutes, given your speed, if you want to call it that.

Bond: Just for that.

I couldn't help but clap as Bond let the full throttle go, blurring past a historic single-seater. I heard Moneypenny laugh.

Moneypenny: Now you're showing me something.

Bond: I'll show you anything you want.

Moneypenny: Careful, I'll believe you.

Bond: A man can only hope. What have you got?

Moneypenny: Chatter says the target will arrive tomorrow night. I've booked us a room.

Bond: What did I do to deserve you?

Moneypenny: Nothing yet. But something tells me you're a good bet.

Bond: Be still my heart.

There was a rustle of fabric.

Moneypenny: It's still as a tomb.

Bond: Keep hold of me. It'll wake up.

The car slid home.

Afterward, Moneypenny refused drinks at the clubhouse. "If you'll excuse us, Mr. Ware, I've got to march James to a meeting across town."

Moneypenny and Bond were too smart to talk in the office—it was bugged and they knew it and everyone knew they knew it—and the device I'd slipped in her handbag stopped working after an hour. Clever girl. That left the old-fashioned way. I tailed them through Red Square, where tourists queued to see Lenin's waxy body and tried not to giggle under the stern gaze of armed guards, and the walls of the Kremlin seemed to pincer the church of Ivan the Terrible, whose onion domes swirled into points like flaming torches.

Bond utilized the GUM department store as Russian spooks utilized labyrinthine Harrods to shrug off surveillance, checking his six in windows and mirrors winking with the reflection of the cupola formed from 22,000 pieces of glass. I was reminded of the phrase used by James Jesus Angleton, the ulcerous Godfather of Spycatchers, to describe the mole hunt, mistrust, and paranoia unleashed after the revelation of Kim Philby's treachery. It was a line borrowed from T. S. Eliot, in fact—*a wilderness of mirrors.* There were doubles everywhere, and any lie could be the truth, and any truth could be a lie. There was no such thing as reality, only perception and interpretation, as good a description of spying as any. I followed Bond and Moneypenny through the wilderness of mirrors. Between them and their doubles, they would have lost anyone but me. I'd long made this wilderness my own. In the years to come, as I was promoted to Chief of the Double O Section and then to the role of M, my sense of self would overflow, mirrors on all sides, all of them offering me cover, until my self was merely a cover too.

Bond and Moneypenny were betrayed by protocol, taking exactly two buses and a tram to a place they'd never visited before: a chinoiserie tea shop in Chistye Prudy sandwiched between the old KGB headquarters and three railway stations. The rents were high and the cafés full of well-heeled students. Bond sat grimacing over a cup of what he termed *English mud.* He was too foreign, this orphan of the world. Too ready to be put to use and belong everywhere and nowhere. The traffic here was as bad as all of Moscow, and I pretended to circle the block for somewhere to park. They sat with their heads bowed, Moneypenny doing all the talking. There was a shared confidence there, as if the two were already old lovers turned best man or woman at the other's wedding. I was surprised to see them exit into the alley carrying overnight bags and climb into a dented Yugo.

There is a trick to tailing a car over 101 kilometers south without being made, a trick Bond hadn't yet learned. I know it was 101 kilometers because the destination was Tarusa, a town high on a bank over the Oka River. After the "Great Patriotic War," Stalin sentenced wounded veterans and dissident intellectuals to internal exile, decreeing these unreliable narrators must live a minimum of 101 kilometers from Moscow. Tarusa hugged the line. Since then, the town had thrived as an artists' commune, a hub for poetry and abstract expressionism and any other way you can say *fuck you* safely in metaphor. While I'm enjoying a professorial tone, let me describe Tarusa as a place of liminality and duality, a dividing line between center and excentric, city and country, future and past. It was in this borderland that Bond and Moneypenny seemed to have rented a tidy house in moldy clapboard with a vine-covered veranda framed by birch forest. Opposite, there was a much grander property, presumably their target's destination. I watched from the woods as the two played house. I pulled a fresh flip phone from my pocket, the cramped keys troubling my thumbs. I remembered the arthritic thumbs of the Wehrmacht officer as I dialed the number.

"Are you planning to visit Tarusa tomorrow night?"

"Why?"

"Bond and Moneypenny are waiting for you. Do you have your double nearby?"

"Always."

"Send him instead. I'll kill him. Put this to rest."

"You'll appear a failure, twenty years on."

"I've won bigger prizes since."

"With my help."

"And you've won prizes as big with mine. Stay away from Tarusa. Send the double." I told him the address.

"Listen to you, saving my life."

"You're my most valuable asset, Mora."

"Oh, Emery. Haven't you worked out by now that it's the other way around? Let the double kill the stalwart and the spare. Then kill him. Expect him before dawn."

I hung up. My cheeks burned. Chip, chip, chip. I reached into the glove box for my weapon. All I need do was let the double arrive a full twenty-four hours before Bond, the stalwart, and Moneypenny, the spare, expected the Stay Behind Slayer. He'd slaughter them in bed, or beds, whatever the case. Then I'd kill him, instant vengeance for a regrettable waste. No more sharp inquiries from Moneypenny. No more searching looks from Bond. Midnight came and went. Rain built like static. I massaged my chest, the cold getting in. Finally, I heard a snap of a branch in the undergrowth. I watched the shadow of the ex–Stasi enforcer cross from the woods onto the dirt track. He was nearly seven feet tall and had a circus weightlifter's mass. I could imagine the clean gunshots, a tap to head and heart. I would find Bond with brain matter pinking his pillow and Moneypenny with her well-ironed shirt spoiled.

I should have done as Mora directed.

But I didn't.

I climbed from the car and tramped through rotten mulch. The ex-Stasi man worked the lock silently and I followed his steps inside. The circus giant tunneled toward the bedroom. I toed off my shoes and crept down the carpeted corridor. After a long pause, he tried the door handle. I was just six feet behind him.

I checked my silencer was screwed on right, clicked off the safety, and eased forward, reaching for the man's arm and firing through his spine toward his heart. The blowback sprayed me. The weight of the falling body smashed open the door, and I crashed into the room on top of the corpse. It was like falling into a mass grave, a dream I had occasionally, and still do.

I was lifted up by Moneypenny as Bond kicked the gun out of the man's grip and banged the door shut.

"You really are watching me."

"Be grateful." I wiped blood from my cheek.

"I'll get you a towel," said Moneypenny.

"Then I'll be grateful." I collapsed into an armchair. My heart was beating far harder than it had for years, as if trying to get out of the sarcophagus inside my chest. Chip, chip, chip.

"How did you know?" she asked, returning to kneel beside me. Her hands were gentle as she wiped first my face clean, then my hands, removing all the trace evidence. For some reason it made me want to weep. I directed myself to stay in my role. I noted that she wore slacks with her shoes kicked off and her silk blouse half unbuttoned. Bond had stripped down to trousers and vest. Well, the room was warm.

"I received intelligence the Stay Behind Slayer wasn't as dead as I believed." A look to Bond. "Climbed out of his grave, in fact. I don't leave a job unfinished."

Bond's jaw worked. "You mean you didn't trust me to get the job done."

"Maybe I didn't want to be cleaning your blood off my hands. Oh, calm down, young buck. Look how thirsty he is for it. You'll get your two kills. I'm recommending you for the Double O Section. And you, Miss Moneypenny, to continue as his agent runner in the field. You've both impressed me these last weeks."

"Thank you, Mr. Ware," said Moneypenny. She considered the stained towel. "Your report said you shot the Stay Behind Slayer center mass the first time around, too. How do you think he survived?"

Panic filled me that she'd open the giant's badly tailored shirt and see no scars. "They made them tough back then."

She looked at the corpse sprawled on the carpet, the seep of blood from the shiny jacket. "And you never saw this man after that? Never had an inkling he'd survived?"

"I'm grateful to you both for helping me dot an i that I hadn't realized went unmarked."

"Wouldn't want a typo getting in the way of promotion?" she said.

"You've got my number, Miss Moneypenny. I could really use a drink. James?"

"Of course." He moved to a sideboard. "We were ordered to detain him, not execute him. What should we do with the body?"

"Oh, I have friends in all the wrong places. Nobody will blink. Afghan Rules."

Bond poured out a vodka. "What are the Afghan Rules?"

I said, "Anything goes."

I watched his steady hand, the grudging admiration twitch across his face, the calm pulse at his jugular.

Duplicity and betrayal are the cornerstones of espionage. As a result, espionage is a magnification of regular life, whether it's your extramarital affair or petty tax evasion. The distinction is that spies betray professionally. A Double O goes a step further. He kills professionally. This is a sordid business and before the twentieth century, spies were treated accordingly as base deceivers, necessary rats, and liars. It was writers who redeemed us. In Britain, authors whipped up fear of a German invasion until the government began to prepare for one, a prudent foresight come 1914. Spies were needed to win the war, and soon it was only the other fellow's spies that were rats and liars. Our own spies weren't practiced murderers, kidnappers, extortionists, and thieves. Of course not. Our writers told us they were gentlemen. As I accepted the glass from Bond, I took in the dark hair on his strong arms, his perfect shoulders, broad chest, hard chin, cold eyes, tousled hair. He looked like an illustration of a spy. He was the most useful thing of all. He believed his own fiction. And thus, he believed mine.

"Wait," said Bond. I paused with the glass to my lips. He turned to Moneypenny. "Did you remember to bring it?"

"He packs an exploding pen but not this," she complained, reaching for her handbag. Moneypenny pulled a little sachet from her bag. It was pepper. She sprinkled it over the three glasses.

"You've learned."

"I've had a good teacher," said Bond.

I smiled. "*Nostrovia*. Here's to your bright futures."

Bond slid one hand in his pocket, a picture of perfect confidence. He said, "The future."

2022

FOUR

Hurricane Room

The house in St. Petersburg was a black hole. Neighbors looked the other way when walking the dog. No post ever arrived. The site was air-gapped. The front door never opened. The windows remained locked, but sometimes heavily muscled men stood silhouetted behind the bulletproof glass, backlit by a chandelier. Occasionally, one of these men would smoke on the step, and children were taught never to smile or ask about their guns. On the third floor and servants' quarters, the windows were shuttered. The house had the same proportions and pleasantries as its neighbors: three bays across, dusky pink piping against a pistachio green façade, a gabled parapet. But beneath the skin, it was another beast, steel-reinforced and soundproofed walls transforming a minor royal's place in town into a prison.

The basement was an interrogation cell. The ground floor housed communications. Guards slept on the first floor and eked out whatever entertainment they could find from TV and poker on the second. Above that, there was a self-contained apartment, though self-contained wasn't exactly the right word. Contained by two barred and electronically locked doors and sealed windows was more exact. It wasn't uncomfortable. In fact, a lot of thought had gone into making the prisoner happy. But fine wine and fine furniture couldn't buy him. So the guards delivered a woman.

Anna Petrov wasn't just any woman. She'd been loved by this spy before, and the guards placed bets on how the spy would react when he came out of the shower and found her spread on his bed like an offering, after twenty-one months of solitary captivity. They knew his reputation. But he disappointed them. They hadn't counted on the spy's decency. Nor had they counted on Anna Petrov's resolve. She would not be used to break him. When the spy promised her that he'd give anything to secure her freedom, she reached into her pocket for a compact mirror she'd stolen, broke the glass, and slashed her wrists.

Cradling her, the spy yelled for help. A single guard rushed into the apartment and hurried toward Anna without thinking, the first mistake in twenty-one months. The spy disabled the guard, took his gun, and shot him.

None of this was audible from the street below, where Johanna Harwood—003 in the nomenclature of her department—was now knocking on the front door. She had been searching for the spy who had loved her too and now she was here, she wasn't going to let anything keep her from him.

Distracted by the confusion upstairs, a guard opened up by an inch. That was all Harwood ever needed. Give me an inch and I'll save a life.

"I work next door," she said. "Somebody here is using our Internet."

"We are not connected to the Internet. You are mistaken."

003 put her foot in the jamb. "It's happened three days in a row. It's slowing our connection down."

She could discern thickset eyes in the gap, nothing more. "You are not on our list of approved workers for this street."

Harwood heard a shout from inside and she followed her boot with her body, breaking the chain. She shot the guard in the stomach. He crumpled. The stairway was red-carpeted, as if beckoning her to put on a show, maybe her last. The next guard rushed from the comms room and she killed him with a double tap to head and chest.

Grabbing a key card from his belt, Harwood sprinted up the stairs. A fist seized her ankle and she tripped. Fingers closed over her mouth. She bit, she hit, she kicked. She broke the guard's neck. The key card worked like a wand on the third floor, where her reflection waited, splintered and stretched, in a mirrored ballroom. She tore across as three guards crashed after her, and the next set of stairs became a shooting gallery, deafening her as she exchanged shots in close quarters. Three more dead. Another door, five bolts, and a lock, and this time the card didn't work—Harwood returned to the bodies on the stairs, snatching keys from a man's belt.

The former servants' quarters smelled of lilies. Harwood advanced through a bright living room, toward an open bedroom door, where a pool of blood waited. Too much blood.

A psychiatrist asked her once, *How would you characterize your relationship with James Bond?* And she replied, *Let's just say, I knew him well.*

Johanna Harwood stepped into the frame of the bedroom door, where Anna Petrov lay dead on the parquet beside the body of a guard. It was Anna Petrov who had inadvertently provided the clue Harwood needed to find the man standing over her. James Bond glanced up, a gun hanging limply from his trigger finger. Anna's blood was a tidal pool dragged toward him as if by the movement of a celestial body; Harwood faced him over the ruin. An alarm sounded, panicked and persistent. Bond frowned, perhaps unsure whether the alarm, the open door, 003 herself, was all in his mind, or whether this silk-lined prison was part of the real world where the bells of St. Petersburg rang. A world he still occupied, and so did she. A world they shared again.

He wore black trousers with no belt and a red-spattered evening shirt unbuttoned to show his hammering pulse. His looks, handsome in a dark, almost cruel way by his mid-forties, were now purely dark and cruel, exposed by hunger and pain. The faint scar that once showed whitely down his right cheek had disappeared as a bone disappears in a graveyard, his face so thin his gums had receded. Silver streaked the black comma of his fringe. Those gray-blue eyes were blanks. He was an abandoned ship.

Anna's blood gained ground. The red line touched Bond's polished shoes. No laces.

"James," said Harwood. "It's me."

"I know." He moved the gun higher—or did the gun move him?

He pulled the trigger.

The gun in Bond's hand was a Pistolet Samozaryadny Malogabaritny, a compact self-loading pistol. Designed in 1969 with discreet dimensions, it had the potential to be a favorite with the KGB. But the slide-mounted manual safety wasted time and would have given Harwood a reprieve of a second if the safety wasn't already off. Another complaint leveled against the PSM was its stopping power. A man had been known to take a shot to the chest at twenty-five meters and keep fighting. But the 18mm cartridge was capable of penetrating fifty-five layers of Kevlar at close range, and Harwood stood six feet away without any shield at all. From the perspective of the bullet, Johanna Harwood's heart was wide open.

But the bullet passed by her ear in a localized thunderclap.

Harwood believed he'd missed. Somehow, at six feet, he'd missed. But then Bond launched past her, and Harwood turned to see the shot was intended for a remaining guard storming the room, but had only succeeded in winging him. Bond grappled for the man's gun.

She dropped to the floor. She checked Anna's pulse. Nothing. Leaned her ear to Anna's lips. Nothing. Harwood slipped on Anna's blood as she rounded a four-poster bed with a mirror mounted over the headboard, behind which, she was certain, a camera had waited for Bond to do what had made him famous. Returning from the en suite bathroom with towels, she stanched and bound Anna's limp wrists, the jangle of arteries like phone wires pulled from a crumbing wall.

"Stay with us, Anna, stay with us. Anna, can you hear me? Anna?"

Anna Petrov, Bond's former mistress and wife of a defector, led 003 to Bond, but not—she realized as she pumped on the woman's frail chest until sweat dripped from her brow onto Anna's tear-stained cheeks—not in time to save Anna herself. There was a faint victorious smile on Anna's lips.

Sitting back, Harwood wiped her forehead with a shaking hand—her whole arm juddering. Aftershock. Finally, she breathed. But a pounding filled the room, as if she were still pumping Anna's heart. Framed by silk-covered sofas printed with palms, James Bond was caving in the guard's skull with the butt of the gun.

"James. He's dead."

He ignored her.

"Bond. Stop. Stop."

She touched his sweat-soaked shoulder.

Bond jerked, scrambling away. He ended up on his haunches, tucked between a desk inlaid with tortoiseshell and a grand piano. He was as sinewy and spare as an anatomy maquette and shook as if someone were pulling his nerve endings. She remembered Bond telling her something Ernst Stavro Blofeld said after murdering Tracy, Bond's wife of a day: *I reduced him to human dimensions.*

"I'm sorry," she said. "I'm sorry about Anna. I'm sorry I couldn't reach you sooner. I've been searching . . . James, we've got to get out of here."

Nothing. Harwood knew that in the center of Bond there was a hurricane room, the kind of citadel found in the heart of a tropical house, a small, strongly built cell sometimes dug into the very foundations where a family could retreat when a storm threatened and wait for the danger to pass. Bond retreated to this internal sanctuary to wait out danger or pain; afterward, he'd step out and take a triumphant look around. But he'd been in a real cell for too long, and now he was locked inside his hurricane room.

"Do you hear me, James? I need your help."

He focused on her. "It was you." His grip tightened on the bloody gun. "You betrayed me."

Vertigo gripped Harwood hard and fast, as if the floor had opened up to reveal a glacial drop.

"You betrayed me," he said, "and now they've brought you here to trick me, like all their other tricks. You're a Russian agent."

"What are you . . ."

"Mora explained it all to me during our *sessions*. Rattenfänger isn't a private military company. They're not terrorists for profit. Rattenfänger is SMERSH reborn. We didn't destroy them. They simply evolved."

"But Rattenfänger has attacked Russia before . . ."

He got to his feet, leaning against the wall for support. "Misdirection. The brainchild of an absurdist theater director turned adviser to the Kremlin. Rattenfänger has set our streets on fire and started wars, deniably, profitably, and productively, splitting us apart. Colonel Mora is a Russian colonel. That's why they kept me here in St. Petersburg. But why I'm *here* is another matter. I am here because of you. You are Mora's agent."

Every muscle in Harwood's body tensed, a weight like she was strapping on armor. "Whatever you think," she said, "we have to *move*, right now."

Sirens sounded. He blinked—shutters in a hurricane. His gaze rested on Anna.

"She slit her wrists," he said. "They wanted to give me something to lose, and she wouldn't let them win."

"So let's make it count. Are you with me, James?"

His silence seemed to say: *For now.*

As she looted the bodies she'd left in her wake for weapons, ammunition, keys, Bond scrutinized the graying faces. What did he take from them? Evidence of her commitment, her determination, her trustworthiness? Or an elaborate deception?

In the comms room, they discovered a bank of phones and screens, and a steel door. Bond waved a pass taken from the neck of a guard at a pad, which flashed green, but then asked him for a code. He shot the thing. The door groaned open in a shower of sparks, admitting the reek of stale water and rat droppings. It was a tunnel.

"Wait," said Harwood. Her attention was on the phones, each one labeled, each one wired. "Marc-Ange Draco helped me infiltrate Russia. He told me he'd do anything to bring you home."

Bond just frowned.

Harwood picked up the landline for an outside line.

"Why aren't we using the tunnel?" asked Bond, as Harwood took point on the clamber into the attic.

"It leads northwest. That's the direction of the border with Finland. The closest route to Western powers. It's what they'll expect."

"Not least because you told Draco to meet us there."

"Exactly," said Harwood. "It will divert the heat and buy us some time to reach Archangel. Student dissidents there will connect us to smugglers in the port."

"You don't care you've directed that heat onto my father-in-law."

"Show me a fight he'd back down from for you."

He said nothing.

She offered him a hand but he pulled himself up the ladder with a grunt. Shuffling and hooting suggested a nest in the rafters. A portrait of Lenin stood propped on an ancient fuse box. The dormer window was locked, the padlock without a scratch. Harwood found an equally shiny key on one of the pilfered rings. She shoved the window open and slipped out onto the tiles. She could see for ten miles: the chain of rooftops, baroque, art nouveau, and Soviet, pastel pink and oxidized zinc blue, punctured by holy spires, the candy-striped dome of the Church of the Savior on Spilled Blood, Vladimirskaya's neoclassical bell tower. Bond gripped the sloping roof for balance, blinking in the flinty daylight. He took a deep breath, and she wondered if the compound of petrol, pigeon shit, and coming rain struck him as beautiful after all this time, because he almost smiled.

The world's most highly watched cities are in China, where there is one CCTV camera for nearly every two people. St. Petersburg has a competitive 13.49 cameras per one thousand people, just beating London. If a camera were pointed at Rattenfänger's roof, it would have filmed Bond and Harwood creeping over the well-maintained tiles. But there was a surveillance void around this house, so the two figures were, for the moment, phantoms.

"Tell me Moneypenny's exfiltration plan."

Moneypenny didn't have one, because Harwood was here rogue. "Later."

"Who's waiting for us at the collection point?"

She could say nothing.

"No backup. No exfil. No contact."

"Think where we are," she implored.

He stopped, scuffing grit under his boots, stolen from a dead man. "I know where I am. I want to know who you are."

Harwood checked the safety was off on her weapon. "This isn't the time."

"Why are you alone?"

Harwood twisted her engagement ring; the lapis lazuli stone was smooth and unspeaking beneath her probing thumb. "Nobody knows I'm here. I was ordered to give up hope."

"Hope of recovering me?"

"The medical opinion was that grief had made me unreliable."

"I'd be touched if I believed you."

She couldn't tell him yet the reason she hadn't been able to catch her heartbeat. "They said I'd deluded myself with comforts of finding you.

The analyst's opinion was that you were almost certainly dead already. The psychiatrist's opinion was that I believed there was a second mole, after I discovered the first, because I was in denial."

"So there are two moles, but neither is you?" he said cheerfully.

"I found the second: 000."

He snorted. "I knew a Cambridge spy was a bad idea."

"I told Joseph Dryden, 004, but I don't know if the message got through. We can't place a call to Regent's Park. Even if we found a way to get a signal past FSB, we can't trust the receivers."

"How convenient," he said.

"You can give me a lie detector test later. We've got places to be. You're about to become Russia's Most Wanted."

"And what are you to them, Johanna Harwood?"

She looked him up and down. When she spoke, it was a whisper. "Don't you know me?"

Helicopters pulsed in the distance. There was no time for either of them to fabricate or formulate. Tin roofing marked a change in the wealth of the district, sagging as they landed on it. Now, the countdown would start. If they had luck, police staffing the CCTV would mistake them for stalkers. That was the name for Russian guides who led tourists on rooftop walks, catnip for the Instagram age, but today no stalkers led influencers to pose with the city unfolding glorious and mummified behind, and no graduating students drank champagne from the sun-bleached deck chairs. There was only Harwood and Bond, using the intestinal span of head-height wires for purchase, crouching behind a vent as a helicopter buzzed overhead, whipping up dust. A homemade wire ladder signified a stalker's past freedom. Harwood hurried, finding a window wedged open by a brick.

"Quick, inside."

The growl of the rotors abated, replaced by the hum of overheated lights in a damp corridor. She called for the lift. Thin doors shuddered open. Bond looked around the cramped space, perhaps struggling to recall something. It was as if he found himself on a sound stage in the theater of the past, expected to play a role whose lines he'd forgotten.

Sitting opposite each other on faded, under-stuffed Metro seats, Harwood and Bond passed through stations made glorious yet awful by gilt murals that told stories of failed revolution: peace, land, bread. In between stations, the train was dim, neon strips flickering with every judder of the metal body. Still, it was enough for 003 to study Bond, who sat gripping his knees with white knuckles. His mouth was a hard line. Had she forgotten how to read him? No, not that. He'd never been a closed book to her before. And what did he see in her? She got a glimpse of it whenever the lights failed and she saw herself without mercy in the window opposite. They'd need new clothes. Something to disguise their faces. They'd need new selves entirely, if they were to get out of Russia alive.

That's when the train screeched to a halt.

FIVE

Out of Time

The carriage shuddered in silence. In the gloom, their fellow travelers were slippery shadows. Harwood stood up. Bond did the same and it seemed like he might take her arm, but instead his hand went to the gun in his belt, a semaphore he had trained out of her when she was young and he was whole. If he'd ever been whole. The hush was broken as the other passengers began to sigh and complain.

"They've put up a cordon," he murmured. "Shut down transport."

"We don't know that. They think we're heading west. It could be a red signal."

"We'll have to walk the track."

"We're too far underground," she said. "The City of Bones." The Metro had to be dug beneath marshland and the graves of serfs.

But he said he didn't care, moving toward the end of the carriage.

"Wait." She took his sleeve. "We can't draw attention."

"You want me to stay here like a rat in a trap?"

She felt his breath on her neck. "Why would I save you only to trap you?"

"You just described all of my relationships."

"You don't have relationships," she said, "only collisions."

"I suppose I shouldn't take offense?"

"No," she agreed. "They're your words."

The train lurched and continued on the tracks.

At one time, Admiralteyskaya was known as the Ghost Station. The deepest in the Metro, it had no suitable release into the congested living city above, so for years the arches on the platforms framed nobody. Now as the train shunted into the refurbished station, Bond was the first out ahead of the crowd, Harwood at his heels, telling him to remain inconspicuous. But her urging—the same he'd given her, teaching her to tail Sid Bashir around Paris, an embarrassingly obvious love triangle between 007, 003, and 009 in a place made for them—fell on deaf ears. So she followed him underneath the stained glass window and up the short escalator, where a mural of Neptune gazed down on them, and onto the main escalators: 125 meters long, an ascent from hell some called it, lit by columns like pillar candles. Nests of electric eyes raked them. Four policemen appeared on the other side, descending. Rattenfänger, the terrorist group for profit that had held Bond, translated as Pied Piper. If Rattenfänger was truly SMERSH reincarnated as Bond said and the Russian police were searching for them, it would mean they were Mora's rats. But they didn't turn. Still, Bond stepped out of line, taking the escalator two steps at a time. Harwood swore under her breath and chased after him.

Bond followed a family through the gates. Harwood did the same behind a man plugged into headphones. The metal detectors were a different problem. Both of them were carrying weapons. Harwood almost ran into the back of Bond—his whole body was tense, waiting. A school group flooded around them. The detectors wailed at phones, earrings, and penknives as Bond slipped through, Harwood in his stream.

The blue sky was blinding. Bond stepped into traffic. Harwood pursued him past cameras clinging to tramlines and street corners like limpet mines. The Hermitage lounged along the riverbank, an indulgent checkerboard of windows against Tiffany blue and buttercup yellow. During the Russian Revolution, Lenin's men stormed the palace, smashing and burning artworks. During the Siege of Leningrad, starving citizens stripped the silken walls and boiled the shimmering guts as soup, adding belts and shoes and any other leather they could find. In normal times, tourists would line the riverbank. Now, the souvenir stands were shuttered and had no worshippers. It was the same emptiness of Disneyland after midnight or an airport at lull. When the Double O's found signs of habitation, it was a queue clamorous not for bread but for designer clothes outside Au Pont Rouge, a department store in pale stone and polished teak with freshly gilded pre-Revolutionary signs of luxury in French.

Harwood said, "Western shops are closing. The sanctions."

"What sanctions?"

"The war," whispered Harwood. Saying the word here was enough to be arrested. Even holding up a blank sheet of paper with nothing written on it would draw police.

"What war?"

Of course. He didn't know. "Russia invaded Ukraine."

"When?"

"A few weeks ago."

"Have we airlifted out the Ukrainian president?"

"He refused. Told the Americans he needs ammunition, not a ride."

A flicker of a smile. "My kind of man."

Harwood said, "Mine too."

Bond removed his gaze from hers to look around the embankment—rushing cars, empty bistro tables, a mother urging three unruly children home. He drew a hand over his face. He struck her as a man out of time, awake for the first day in centuries; or a knight emerging from a vigil, but this wasn't the promised land. "So what's being done about it?"

"What do you mean?"

"What are we doing?"

"Supplying arms and intelligence."

"What are *we* doing?"

There was a familiar current to his voice, the first current of strength. But she couldn't meet it. She'd been rogue for a month. Before that, she'd been on enforced medical leave. And before that she was playing the role of a lifetime as an undercover agent. So she could only say: "Keep your head down."

Two armed policemen in riot gear ambled down the riverbank, studying shoppers through mirrored sunglasses. Harwood tugged Bond across the Red Bridge. They passed a bookshop, where George Orwell's *1984* was displayed on the bestseller shelf. There was more than one way to protest. But at the intersection of Malaya Konyushennaya and Nevsky Prospekt, they stopped in their tracks, confronted by the government's own protest. A sculpture took up the road like a checkpoint barrier: blocky letters reading ZAMESTIM. The Z was the neat capital of Zara. The *a* the friendly bubble of adidas. The M the golden arch of McDonald's. Epson, Škoda, TotalEnergies, IKEA, Milkyway. All brands that had pulled out of Russia since the invasion of Ukraine. *Zamestim* translated as *We will replace them*. Two teenagers lounging on the curb studied it with sneers. But most passersby avoided looking at the word. How close *We will replace them* is to *We can replace you*.

They kept to the shadows until anti-war graffiti began to break up the placid pastel façades. When they located a chemist, Harwood asked, "Any damage?" He looked at her dimly. She bought first aid supplies. Finding a shop whose window was obscured by mannequins and discount banners, Harwood changed in a broom cupboard with a sagging curtain for a door, the dusty mirror detailing her injuries. Her usually olive skin was washed out, the eyes Bond once called golden now ringed and dark, her strong eyebrows and cheekbones blunt as the line of her mouth, where laughter had long faded. The wild near-black hair curling at her shoulders was matted with filth. Her tall, slender frame was left buffeted and flinching. What are you? She stepped out wearing a knee-length mackintosh and a pink silk headscarf. Bond waited on the pavement in workman's boots, counterfeit Levi's, a navy-colored *vatnik*, and a cloth cap pulled over his fringe.

A bus carried them through an industrial district where arms manufacturers and disinformation trolls worked overtime. Lake Ladoga glistened in the distance. The bus would terminate at Kirishi, a town serving an oil refinery and a power plant, but they jumped off early on a road that ribboned through oat fields. Crops submitted to a cemetery, graves marked by Soviet stars, as the sun set in violent welts. Bond dragged his feet. Finally, they crossed the Volkhov River. They would catch the morning train to Archangel. The lonely hotel catered to workers: cheap single rooms with breakfast provided. Lit by a tasseled lamp, the woman behind the reception desk scowled at Harwood. "This isn't a place for that sort of thing."

"We'll take separate rooms," said Bond.

A laminated sign taped to the wall read rather grandly: *No Deserters. This is a Patriotic Establishment.*

Harwood found cold sausage, questionable cheese, and bootleg vodka in the petrol station over the road, which she spread out on the almost transparent bedsheet. They faced each other across the single mattress, Bond slumped in a plastic chair meant for patios, Harwood perched on the windowsill. The TV was tuned to the news: stiff presenters recited propaganda. Nothing about Bond or Harwood, yet.

Bond finally spoke: "That's what I did to Anna." Harwood looked to the TV, but she couldn't locate his subject. "A collision. I don't have relationships, I have collisions. I crashed into her and now she's . . ."

"Rattenfänger abducted and trafficked her, not you."

"I used her to get to her husband, Mikhail. A climate scientist who was flirting with defection. A Romeo op, M's orders. Funny, we call the target of a Romeo sting Juliet. Now she's dead, but it's not the end of a romance for the ages. Just wasteful. She was worth loving, if I . . ." He looked away, gained control of his voice. "I guess Mikhail is dead too?"

"They went on the run after your capture. He was found in a hotel bathtub in Sydney. She disappeared after that, but not well enough. It's Rattenfänger's kill, not yours." She took a reluctant bite of food.

"I used her to get over you," he said. "Now she's dead and you're here."

Harwood struggled to keep down the sour lump.

"You remember what we call the opposite of a Romeo and Juliet op, when a female spy is ordered to target a man?" he asked.

She felt like she was back in training: how to manage an unstable asset. "Yes. She's a raven."

"And her target?"

"A swallow."

"Right. Anna is dead and you're here to suck what Mora wanted out of me."

"I'm here because I went to the End of Everything to find you."

"Poetry, now?"

She bit her lip. "Rattenfänger is funded by a network called the Gray Group, coordinated by Lisl Baum." Lisl was the mistress of a gangster Bond had also used once, before Lisl became mistress of a criminal empire herself.

Bond said, "It was Lisl who cornered me in Barcelona, after you messaged me."

"I didn't message you in Barcelona."

He seemed not to have heard. "I hadn't seen her since the night we—" He broke off, and was quiet long enough for a bird to warn another of a raptor, and for the raptor to drag its shadow across the window. "As far as I was aware she'd gone straight. But when you called me away from Anna Petrov and Sid Bashir in Barcelona, it was Lisl waiting for me on the bench in Parc Güell."

Harwood said again, "I didn't send that message."

"It contained things you alone knew about our time together."

"You never kissed and told?" A barking dog made her turn, and she kept her face averted. "What happened on the park bench with Lisl?"

"She kissed me."

"That all it takes?"

"You would know."

Harwood waited a beat but it didn't help. "The Gray Group was a network of smugglers: art, diamonds, antiquities . . . The people trafficker they used was a man named Teddy Wiltshire."

"Was?"

"He had a talent. Disappearing people. He disappeared you. As well as countless women into the sex trade. He tattooed them with barcodes on the back of the neck. Partly ego. Partly inventory. He took photos. The barcodes contained destination addresses. I found him hiding in a radar station at the End of Everything in the Altai Mountains. That's where I discovered a photo of Anna. I scanned the barcode on the back of her neck and it led me to you."

"Did you kill Wiltshire?"

"Yes."

"Did it hurt?"

She said, "Yes"—without knowing whether she meant it hurt Wiltshire or her, Harwood herself almost strangled before blowing a hole in Teddy with a shotgun.

He said, "Good"—probably without knowing the same. "You did all that, then infiltrated Russia alone?"

"Yes."

"I suppose you want a thank-you. For rescuing a husk. You look at me as if you're cataloguing damage for a medical report."

She turned. "That's not how I'm looking at you."

"You don't want to get it all down? How about a debrief, Johanna?"

Harwood threw up her hands. "All right. What did Mora want from you? Intelligence?"

His eyes deadened as he retreated inside his hurricane room.

"Did you learn anything about their operation? Come on. I've got a catalogue to make."

"I remember you softer than this. Your tactics of persuasion were gentle, or gratifying. Never hard."

Her tactics of persuasion. Her performance reviews said that was her main asset to MI6. Her persuasiveness. Her perception. Her adaptability. Could it be that if you spent your whole life as a mirror, you forgot how to be yourself? Could it be that she was only ever a mirror to him, and now he hated what he saw?

"You don't want *gentle*," said Harwood. "Gentleness would kill you. You can't bear for me to see you weak. But that's not what I'm seeing. I know you want to believe in me. Otherwise you would've shot me in the head and left my body next to Anna's."

"What I *want* doesn't count," he said between gritted teeth. "I wanted you. I wanted to be the kind of man who stuck around. But you saw through me. I only wish I'd seen through you first. Maybe Anna would still be alive. She deserved more than whatever version of me washed up after *you* were through with me." His skin glowed red in the twilight. "I've always been attracted to women walking into water with heavy pockets. I suppose it's some urge to get you to turn around, or else an urge to follow. I've never cared to examine the thing too closely." His gaze turned almost dispassionate. "Are you walking into water with heavy pockets, Johanna Harwood, here in Russia alone for a relic like me?"

"It was my father who was suicidal," she said. "I'm walking out of the water with you. You wanted me. I'm right in front of you. I only need to know you're on my side and believe I'm on yours."

"That all it takes?" He fired her question back at her with a sneer.

"It depends," she said.

"On what?"

"On you."

"Me?" He laughed. "You want my confession? Here it is. Tiger

Tanaka asked me once why I seem to value my life less highly than other Westerners. A doctor told me it was patriotism, at the root: apparently I am a weapon animated by death or glory for my country. Sounds good, doesn't it? But I've had time on my hands, lately. Time enough to wonder if death and glory leave nothing behind"—he gestured like a magician revealing a trick, except the trick was his body—"no man to take out of himself. You start thinking about the face in the mirror when it's your only company. Not that I had a mirror, when they kept me in the cave. Only a dog bowl for meals, though I did use it to bash in a guard's brain pan once. It's the little things, in the end. But here's the punch line, darling. After twenty-one months, the face that looked back at me from that mirror was blank." He straightened. "My number is 007. My name is Bond, James Bond. But I don't know what that means anymore."

Harwood leaned forward. "*I know who you are*. You're the man who carved 007 into the rock face of a cell in Syria because you believed Moneypenny and I would go to the ends of the earth for you. And if we didn't find you, it was as good an epitaph as any. You're our man and you never stopped being our man. I trust that. So trust me."

Bond reared back. "You can't have found it. I carved my number into the cave *after* you were held in the compound in Syria. You can't have found it."

"We were in captivity at the same time. But I didn't realize it."

"No. Mora held you there when I was in Barcelona. He turned you. He showed me the video. You vowed to betray me. You sent the message. You led to my capture. So you can't have seen the numbers I carved in my cell after. You were released by then."

Harwood forced her voice level: "Moneypenny gave me a mission in Syria. It was to appear that I'd picked up a lead on your whereabouts and gone rogue to follow it. I would be captured and held. Then Sid would rescue me. Moneypenny wanted a woman inside Rattenfänger. My true mission was to hold out as long as would seem convincing to Mora, then pretend to turn. To gain his confidence, and ultimately discover the identity of the leak in MI6 that led to your capture. Through that, we hoped to find you. What we didn't know was that the false cover for my mission was very close to the truth. I did find you, only I didn't know it. I was held in the same Syrian base as you. We were probably walls apart. I followed my orders. I took the torture, and *pretended* to turn."

His eyes narrowed as if Harwood had tilted the whole sun at him. "I thought I heard you. Screaming. But Mora said it was a recording. If you were really there, he said he would have put us in a room together and made me watch while . . ." He stopped. "Mora would have used you to make me talk."

"Mora wanted to turn me and send me back into MI6 because he didn't trust his mole. When Sid and I returned to the Syrian prison site, it was to save a scientist called Dr. Zofia Nowak who specializes in quantum computing and artificial intelligence. Mora moved you when the mole tipped him off that we planned to infiltrate the site. After that, Mora didn't come to St. Petersburg and continue his interrogation of you because he couldn't. I took him into custody. When I was last in contact with MI6, he was being held indefinitely at our black site, and that's where he'll stay."

Bond shook his head. "But that would mean you and I were there together. And I could have . . ."

Harwood wanted to reach for his hand. "I don't claim to know what you've been through. But I had a taste of it. I saw your cell. There was nothing you could have done."

He flushed. "*Don't.* It might be that 000 is working with you, but *you* are the traitor."

Harwood spoke over B-roll of artillery shells rumbling on the news. "The traitor was Bill Tanner. He was listed as interrogating Mora during the Cold War in Afghanistan. But it was the other way around. Mora turned the tables. Bill betrayed us."

"No." Bond went to touch a tie that wasn't there. "Bill couldn't betray the Service. Bill could never betray me."

A sharp pain lanced her heart. "And I could?"

"I've known Bill Tanner since I first joined the Service. I've known you for as long as it takes to get you into bed, which isn't long."

"You've never judged a woman for that." She managed to rally. "You love a woman for that. And we were together for two years, if you want to give it a name, which you didn't."

"You hardly got your Double O status before you had two of us blinded: me, then 009."

"I'm a witch, then, am I? Mata Hari. Or Vesper?"

"Stop."

"Listen to yourself." She stood up. "You know it wasn't like that."

"Then what *was* it like?" Rising, Bond grabbed her by the arms. "Were we in love, Johanna Harwood?"

She did nothing to fight him. "I was."

"Not for long, though, hmm?"

"You had no intention of surviving beyond service as a Double O. I'd already watched my father kill himself. I needed someone who could dream of the future and mean it, even in a life like this. And then I met Sid. And he was joyful, and hopeful, and he had a dream of M giving me away in the community hall his mother painted. No one ever wanted me to be their home. I loved you, and I loved him. But he loved me back."

Bond let go. She almost fell, the TV steadying her.

He said, "I was a fool to ever trust you. Next you'll ask what Mora wanted me to give up. This is another mind game."

"*I don't care what Mora wanted from you*," said Harwood. "My mission is to pull you out of Russia alive. *You* are my mission."

"Whatever would Sid say?" His gaze dropped to her hand. "Where's your wedding ring?"

Harwood's breath tripped. She wasn't ready. "I don't have one."

"Another Double O catch your eye? Tell me it wasn't 000."

The venom in his voice was unknown to her. "I have no wedding ring because there was no wedding. Sid is dead. Mora killed him."

That wiped the bitterness from his face. The resulting blank was worse. Bond had mentored Sid. He reached for the remote and pressed mute. When it didn't work, he flung the thing, cracking the TV screen. Harwood winced. The presenters warbled and melted.

"How?" he barked.

"He stepped in front of a bullet meant for me."

"Why?"

Suddenly, Harwood couldn't see for tears. But she wouldn't cry in front of him. She said, "I'll sleep across the hall."

There was a communal bathroom: a shower with a stained basin, a sink ringed yellow, and a toilet with no seat. She tried to smooth her hair into something resembling order. Harwood wrinkled her nose. What was she doing? What were they, a couple on an ill-conceived honeymoon, the groom expressing his regret as cruelty, the bride weeping privately in the bathroom like a martyr? What, exactly, *was* this?

She had pinned everything on finding James, thinking it would return her to herself. She hadn't been able to save Sid, who believed that to save one soul was to save all of humanity. So she'd vowed to save Bond, in order perhaps to save her own humanity. Promised herself there'd be one man she didn't lose, after her father's madness; after Sid bled out in her arms; promised herself there'd be one price she'd refuse to pay. She'd given herself this purpose, this reason to keep going. *Find Bond*. And now she'd managed it, done the impossible. But it wasn't him. This man didn't believe in her. This man didn't know her, for all he said he did before firing. This man wasn't James Bond. She'd failed. And why had she hoped, in the first place?

There was a knock on the bathroom door. Harwood opened it, but instead of Bond it was a man whose hands were black with labor. His mouth parted at the sight of her, and then he moved his bulk into the bathroom, pinning her to the sink. He placed a rough hand on her bandaged arm.

Harwood said, "*Move*."

He flinched. Something in her tone, her expression, she supposed. Something that said she knew every shred of his nervous system and could easily turn him inside out. He stepped aside. So at least there was that. She was still 003.

Lying awake, watching the turning points of her life—from surgeon to spy—play out on the ceiling like cut scenes falling to the editing room floor, Harwood was forced upright by the hard sound of well-pumped tires on the graveled forecourt. She found Bond in the hall, about to knock on her door.

"Police?" she asked.

"Military."

A window looked over the rear of the building. It was barred shut.

The conversation taking place at reception sliced through the hotel.

"A couple," said the woman. "I think the man might be trying to escape the draft. Or, maybe, you know, there are those liberated Ukrainians at the camp up the road. Some of them don't have any gratitude. They show up here asking for help. I can give you the names of my neighbors who aid them."

"Thank you, Babushka. Just show us to their room . . ."

Bond tugged the bars. Nothing.

The bare bulb swung on its cord as four armed men wearing black balaclavas mounted the stairs. A bedroom door opened and closed again swiftly. The leader raised his rifle, pointing it squarely at Harwood, who covered Bond with her spread arms. She said in rapid Russian, "We are from the camp. We were told we have the right to leave if we want to."

The man said, "I doubt that. Papers."

"You know we don't have any papers. We were forcibly taken from our towns and brought here. We want to go home."

"This camp is your new home."

"The camp is a prison."

The man swung for her with his rifle. Harwood ducked under it and shoved her open palm under his chin, snapping his head back. Harwood tackled the next man around the waist, slamming off the wall with him as Bond picked up the fallen man's rifle and squeezed off shot after shot after shot.

Three dead. One unconscious, until Bond stood over him and put a bullet in his head. That made four.

Bond raised the rifle, muzzle pointing at Harwood, who almost lifted her hands in surrender. His attention was drawn to the hotel manager at the top of the stairs.

Bond's finger didn't leave the trigger.

Harwood told the woman to run if she wanted to live.

The manager screamed, turned, and clattered down the stairs.

Harwood and Bond darted across the car park into a rye field. Behind them, all the lights in the hotel flared. Someone yelled. Harwood looked back to see a finger pointing from a window. She plunged into the long, wet grain. Bond ran ahead of her like a man possessed, a man chased by demons in his dreams, a man who has long been out of time.

SIX

Scrub

A sign festooned in ivy read: *Shrublands. Gateway to Health. First right. Silence please.* The facility nestled in the South Downs seemed like a spa for bankers to passersby, and that was what it was until the Service took over. The Double O's called it Scrubs, borrowing from rhyming slang: Shrublands–Wormwood Scrubs–Scrubs. It was also what happened: your body, mind, and soul scrubbed from inside out until you were clean as a butcher's block. The road ran through a wide belt of firs to a mock-battlement entrance, as if this Victorian lodge were a castle in need of defending. Inside, a series of common rooms decorated like a forgotten military club gave way to bulletproof doors that required a security pass for admittance to the patient rooms, which bore the names of flowers and shrubs. Inside Hawthorn, Joseph Dryden lay pinned to a gurney by hospital corners. The monitor beeped uncertainly.

004's status had been critical on arrival, medevacked from Dubai after an explosion that stopped his heart for a minute. Now, he cut in and out of consciousness like a phone searching for signal, drawn to the touch of a doctor or a nurse, then lost again. He dreamt: a snow-covered hill red with blood, his men dead around him. Helmand in winter. But instead of the Taliban, it was 000 who stood in the center grinning, with Lucky Luke mangled at the traitor's feet. He woke with a start. His chest hurt. He could hear static. There was a radio on the bedside table, but maybe the problem wasn't the radio. Maybe it was his hearing aid. He was pulled back to Helmand, where an IED had fractured the base of his skull and lacerated the vestibular nerve beneath his ear, leaving him sensorineural deaf on one side. The shock wave that followed resulted in a mild traumatic brain injury, damaging the language center in the brain, turning speech into a wall of sound. Dryden had been medically downgraded from Special Forces and exited from the military.

That was when Moneypenny saved him. Dryden's close-cropped hair betrayed no sign of the microphone embedded in his right ear canal, or the brain-computer interface carrying sound to his language processing center, bypassing the cut nerve and the damaged tissue. The work of Q Branch. The device could read his brain waves, understand whose voice he wanted to focus on, and amplify that voice until its owner was whispering state secrets into his ear. The microphone streamed everything he said and heard to Q, a quantum computer, for processing. Dryden was never alone. The manual controls secreted inside his Garmin MARQ Commander watch allowed him to receive the voices of Q Branch—Aisha Asante and Ibrahim Suleiman—without anyone else the wiser. He was desperate for their voices now, but all he could hear was the staccato of gunfire.

But the touch on his arm wasn't ghostly and it wasn't clinical. It was soft and loving. When he opened his eyes, the light hurt. He made out Aisha Asante's outline and relief coursed through his body. She was holding her phone, playing him music, trying to pull him back to her shores. He swam eagerly. If anyone knew the answer to what was happening to him, it was Aisha, a graduate of Cambridge in quantum mechanics and then artificial intelligence. But she didn't look confident today. She looked scared.

Dryden reached for her. "You OK?"

She sat up, covering her mouth. "Am I OK?"

He reached up and wiped a tear from her cheek with his thumb.

She said, "We thought we'd lost you."

"It ain't so easy."

A shadow fell over Dryden's body. "Evidently." With effort, he turned to the doorway, where M's coat hanger body hung in the frame, his bald head a drooping hook. Sir Emery said, "Welcome back, 004. Thank you, Dr. Asante."

Aisha stood up, squeezing Dryden's fist. Then she passed M, who patted her arm before she closed the door behind her. Sir Emery's walking stick punctuated his steps. The cane was polished beech with a gold collar and decorative ivory head, the same white as his clamped knuckles. He sat with a grunt, crossing his legs to bounce his trademark Converse trainers. Dryden tried to pull himself upright, half at attention, at least.

"How's the pain?" said M.

"How long do I have to stay here, sir?"

He chuckled. "Dr. Akter will bore you with jargon, but the upshot is this. Blunt cardiac trauma. Your heart is bruised. You would have died were it not for the thief Moneypenny recruited—without my knowledge, I might add—who has now disappeared, rather conveniently, given Moneypenny's status."

Dryden swallowed. He heard the dry crackle like it belonged to someone else. "What do you mean—Moneypenny's status?"

"000 abducted Miss Moneypenny, after we were forced to release Colonel Mora and the Rattenfänger detainees held at the Americans' black site under the duress of a bioweapons threat that turned out to be false."

The monitor spiked. "What do we have on Moneypenny's or Mora's location?"

"Nothing. That's why I need you to recover *yesterday*, soldier. I am making you Acting Chief of the Double O Section. I need a show of force. We've had two moles uncovered at the very center of MI6: Bill Tanner and Conrad Harthrop-Vane. We're in a wilderness of mirrors now. Anyone could be a traitor and America doesn't trust us. I need an *exemplary* hero. I need you."

Dryden shook his head. "Sir, I'm not built for a desk. Especially not Moneypenny's desk. Let me into the field. She's my CO. I don't leave my team behind."

"I let you into the field, I turn you into another body pushing up poppies."

Dryden managed to straighten his spine. He remembered now—he'd been injured on his last mission, first a bullet from 000's sniper rifle, stopped by three inches of Kevlar and Johanna Harwood's voice on the phone telling him to take cover, then a close-range IED in Dubai. A bruised heart. Somehow that seemed ironic after one tour of Iraq, three tours of Afghanistan, and hundreds of individual missions as Special Forces.

"Did we get him?" he asked.

"000?"

Dryden nodded.

M sighed. "My prodigal son. No, we didn't *get* him. And I'm afraid I have worse news. Luke Luck walked out of the black site at Mora's side. I know he was your second-in-command and, ah, lover in Afghanistan. I'm sorry, son." M was surprisingly strong, forcing Dryden back against the pillow. "You're not going anywhere. We need you on the home front now more than ever, so listen to me. It's time to read you in."

"Read me in on what, sir?"

Sir Emery said, "Panopticon."

SEVEN

The Treachery Act

Moneypenny felt the tilt of the helicopter descending and knew her time was running out as surely as sand from a cracked hourglass. She didn't know where they were in the world but could hazard a few guesses: the air had grown frigid and the booms and moans had grown louder, an orchestra of ice. Even with the blindfold, she knew Conrad Harthrop-Vane had watched her steadily since they left the desert. 000's breathing was measured, his heart rate would be steady, the calm readiness of a Double O about to act. And the action was to betray his Chief. In the Second World War, the government passed an emergency law so they could hang those who betrayed their nation. The Treachery Act, it was called. She was in the mood for summary justice, but it wasn't on the horizon, so she wet her cracked lips and tried compassion.

"It's not too late, Conrad. You can make a different choice. Your father left you to fend for yourself with sharks like Mora. But your mother didn't. She would've stayed with you, if she could. She gave you that medallion you're wearing, didn't she?" His breathing shallowed. The zip ties around her wrists weren't tight enough to break with pressure. If she hadn't been under observation she could have used the pin of her brooch on them. Could she knock him off balance? "Your mother believed you were a good boy, and you'd turn into a good man. What would your mother want?"

There was a rustle, Harthrop-Vane perhaps taking off the headphones and mic so the pilot couldn't hear him reply. "It is too late. For you. You were captured thanks to your own failures."

"I was cornered by you and Lisl, so I offered myself as a high-value target. Stay alive as long as possible. Gather information. Find an advantage. I'm not a Double O like you, but I've had my training."

"Your training didn't help you see me, right there, picking off your precious Double O's."

"How many of your own team did you kill?" she asked. "009, Fairbanks. 0011, Mace. 002, Dumont. 0010, Savarin. 005, Ventnor. That's five. Should I expect to see Joseph Dryden and Johanna Harwood again?" She heard him click his tongue. "Or do you mean I didn't *see you*, and all your talents, and all your damage, and all the love I could have given you to help you become the man your mother wanted."

"Stop talking about my mother. You should have believed in me."

"I did," said Moneypenny. "That was the problem."

"As much as you believe in Bond?"

"Remind me—which of you is Rattenfänger's prisoner and which of you has been willingly working for them . . ."

"It wasn't them I was working for."

"Could've fooled me, Conrad."

He said crisply, "I did."

The chopper wobbled as it came to hover. The vibrations filled Moneypenny's bones, but it wasn't that which made her shake as hands came around her waist. The clip of a buckle, then the winch of a harness. Wind froze her cheeks as she was pushed toward a void of fierce nothingness, her toes edging over solid metal into air. She yelled as someone shoved her and then she was dropping toward the roar of waves. The hands that caught her were her best friends. She bounced off steel. The clip was gone, the weight of the harness lifting. Her burning fingers found the rungs of a ladder. She couldn't organize her feet, dropping with a smack. She heard Harthrop-Vane tell someone to be careful with her. Her stomach was a tombola of rising bile and sinking dread. Hope on, hope ever . . . She almost slipped but 000 kept her upright, his familiar smell close, a cologne of gun oil and mothballs. She heard murmurs, a whoop. The floor beneath her feet was rocking. Then fingers coiled around her arm. Moneypenny had the build of a woman who worked frustrations out at the Service gym: she was tall and strong and proud she couldn't be knocked off her stride. But the strength of the grip made her feel faint, and her bladder squeezed in response.

"Miss Moneypenny. How good of you to join us."

The blindfold came off and Colonel Mora overpowered her senses. He stank like a rat's nest and his body heat seared her. Mora's captivity in the black site had done nothing to diminish him: a giant with loose-hanging arms, head a shaved bullet, hands like enormous pink crabs. He wore combat boots and trousers, stripped to the waist as if this were a gladiatorial ring, or he was a barbarian chief. His chest writhed with a tattoo of the death's-head hawk moth, the symbol of Rattenfänger. Moneypenny knew from Sid Bashir's report that in their first encounter, Mora paralyzed 009 with a few jabs to his nerve endings and then sat on his chest, covering Bashir's mouth with his own, breathing in the agent's hyperventilation. Bashir said it was like Mora wanted to drink his soul. The terrorist leader was named after the Kikimora, a character from folk legend who entered a bedroom and sat on the helpless sleeper to give them the kiss of death. Preventions included reciting a poem, or blocking the door with a broom or chair—this last method seemed the more helpful, 003 had noted. Moneypenny felt prayer might be the best option right now.

She was in the officers' wardroom of a submarine. Mora was flanked by the men with no flags who made up Rattenfänger: dishonorable discharges, mercenaries, rejects, and capos. Mora and the detainees of the black site had escaped to a submarine: there would be no way for Q to pick them up on satellites. Could this be how they'd hidden Bond? She looked around with hope, but it wasn't Bond she found standing at Mora's shoulder. It was Luke Luck.

Mora turned to Harthrop-Vane. "Where is Lisl Baum?" His deep voice was snakelike, his tongue a red stump in the cavern of his mouth.

"Moscow."

Mora snorted. "Ever the survivor. Why did you bring this one here?"

Harthrop-Vane said, "She has valuable intelligence."

"Nothing I do not already know," said Mora. He looked Moneypenny up and down. "But I suppose we may as well have a little entertainment."

Terror choked Moneypenny. She had gone through a weekend of R2I before becoming an agent runner in the field. The course was a reduced version of the resistance to interrogation training taken by agents. The full experience included hooding, sleep deprivation, time disorientation, prolonged nakedness, sexual humiliation, and deprivation of warmth, water, and food. Unlike a Double O, she wasn't expected to retain dead silence beyond her name, rank, and serial number. That's what the L Pill was for. But that was during her days in the field. As Chief of the Double O Section, she'd long stopped carrying the cyanide capsule. She wasn't supposed to stray beyond her protection detail. She certainly wasn't supposed to go into theater to try to stop the terrorist threat that was bleeding out her section. She'd failed. So now she tried to remember that weekend at RAF St. Mawgan. But she knew it wasn't enough to withstand Mora, the man who'd broken and turned Bill Tanner, the man who drank pain. She'd give him everything. So don't try to resist him. Don't let it get that far. You're the boss. You bring two primary skills to the role: recruit and command.

Start with Luck. Moneypenny had embedded 004's ex-lover-turned-terrorist-turned-reformer in Rattenfänger and now he was glancing upward, perhaps listening to see if the chopper was still aerial. Was Luck still on her side? Could he get them both to the helicopter? Or was his finger near the trigger merely vigilance? Buy time.

"I have a subdural GPS device," she said. "MI6 will track my whereabouts. 000's brought destruction to your door."

Mora sniffed. "That true, son?"

"No, sir. She refused to have one implanted."

Mora said, "Don't trust Big Brother, Moneypenny? Well, maybe you were right. Your own has betrayed you."

"I'll trust 000 until he kills me."

Mora said, "How magnanimous."

"He's my agent."

"Shut up," hissed Harthrop-Vane.

"You could've shot me in the desert," she said, turning toward him. "But you don't want to see me hurt. It's not quite as satisfying as you imagined."

000 was about to slap her when he checked mid-air. Moneypenny watched his eyes. The man who had killed his teammates looked shocked at himself.

Mora said, "Developing a conscience, son?" He tugged her closer and brushed her ringlets from her face. "After all, she's practically your mother."

Moneypenny inwardly cursed. That was her route to Triple O's vulnerability and Mora already knew it. She said irritably, "He's ten years my junior."

"More like fifteen, *Miss* Moneypenny. I know. Where does the time go? One minute your agents fantasize about spanking you over your desk. The next minute the fantasy is more Mummy Dearest than Mother May I."

Moneypenny said, "I'm no older than Bond and you've all still got a hard-on for him."

She instantly regretted it.

He laughed, then gripped her throat.

"Wait," said Harthrop-Vane.

"The trouble with Conrad," said Mora, "is that no dutiful son likes it when Mummy and Daddy fight, even when he knows Mummy did a lot to upset Daddy."

Luke stepped forward—the phone on the bulkhead was buzzing. He lifted the receiver. "Sir, it's the communications room. They've picked up a signal."

Mora took the phone. He listened for thirty seconds. Then he ground out, "*Fools*. Signal Moscow to use the police and the army, whatever it takes." He shoved the phone into Luke's chest, then landed his blunt fingers on Moneypenny's left breast, finding the nerves clustered over her heart. She thought she was dying. But the blackness edged away, replaced by blinding light and the stench of Mora's rotten core, his mouth hovering over hers.

He hissed, "Your boy is loose, Moneypenny. Johanna Harwood found him and freed him. Wouldn't it be ironic if the fate of the world came down to a girl's crush?"

Moneypenny fought dizzying hope and dangerous despair.

"Don't look so pleased with yourself. Your value just went up. I think you'll find you would have preferred a quick end to my brand of suffocation."

"I can help recapture Bond," she said quickly, "if you let me out of here."

Mora snorted. "Bond didn't break in twenty-one months. I should've snatched you."

"Nobody knows Bond like I do. I'm the longest-lasting woman in his life. The only lasting woman. I was his agent runner in the field. I recruited 003. I know what they'll do next."

"Conrad here is very good at killing his teammates. He doesn't need your help." Harthrop-Vane's cheeks pinked. "But I do. You see, there are only men on this submarine, and I've been locked in your prison for some months. I have a great deal to work through. And you and I got very close during our interrogations." He smiled horribly. "I feel I can be myself with you." Then he raised his voice, telling the guard behind him to help her wash.

Moneypenny dug in her heels. "But you don't want Bond dead. 000 is a Double O killer and you don't want Bond dead. If you did you would've killed him yourself. You want something from him. Whatever it was, I'd bet he didn't give it to you. I know everything Bond knows and more."

The silence as Mora considered this was filled by cracking ice, the submarine not yet dived, a hesitation in the water. "You don't know everything. The location of M's War Book, containing vital information to be passed to M's Number Two in case of his death. That was Tanner, but I'm afraid M didn't even trust Tanner. And after Tanner hanged himself, you became Number Two, but he didn't *quite* trust you either. Do you know who M trusted to never flip, never betray, never stray? Of all the ironies, he trusted James Bond."

He was right: she didn't know where Sir Emery kept the War Book. But she had to keep him talking. "What do you want with M?"

Mora waved a hand. "Two adversaries with opposing ideologies locked in mortal combat, directing pawns against each other in the Great Game . . . that sort of thing. I want the password to Panopticon, contained in the War Book. But no matter. I have an alternative solution."

Moneypenny's stomach dropped. How could Mora possibly know about Panopticon? She knew the disbelief was written on her face and hated his chuckle.

"What's Panopticon?" asked Harthrop-Vane.

"Why not brief your agent," said Mora.

Moneypenny shut her mouth.

"Look at that resolution. Let's see who knows their geopolitics. Conrad, tell me about Five Eyes."

Harthrop-Vane frowned, evidently unable to see where this was going, and unhappy with that fact. "Anglosphere intelligence alliance," he said shortly. "Went public in 2010 but dates back to 1941, when US military intelligence officers visited Bletchley Park, where cryptanalysts had recently broken Enigma."

Mora said, "Nine out of ten. You lose one mark for imperialism. *Anglosphere* indeed. The 1941 Bletchley meeting was the foundation for a wartime agreement between the US and the UK, who dragged in her colonies. Why is it called Five Eyes, Luke Luck?"

Luck stepped forward. "Don't do context, sir."

Mora stroked Luck's cheek. "Spoken like the true foot soldier of history, anticipating his future as a footnote. The term 'Five Eyes' evolved as shorthand for AUS/CAN/NZ/UK/US Eyes Only—leave it to intelligence to be first unintelligible, then accidentally poetic. As British power faded, the US took up the role of colonial power, using the infrastructure of your empire for a landscape of surveillance. Britain is gripped by existential angst, desperate to prove to the US that she is still worth her seat at the table. Enter Q. Tell us what Q is these days, Moneypenny."

She held her breath. He reached down, probing the nerves in her armpit. Moneypenny's throat swelled, gorged on adrenaline. She squeezed her eyes shut, unwilling to cry, but she couldn't help it.

"A quantum computer? Yes, that's right, thank you for playing. A computer that processes information in simultaneous ones and zeroes, making calculations in mere minutes that would take binary code years to process. Combined, Five Eyes have satellite monitoring facilities stretching from Point Barrow on the Arctic coast to Kojarena in Western Australia. They have access to phone calls, text messages, Internet traffic, webcam images, emails, and billions of mobile locations tapped from subsea Internet cables all over the globe. Not only do they spy on their enemies, they are also very happy to spy on each other. The trouble is *all that data.* That's where the UK makes its bid for relevance. All the data gleaned by Five Eyes will be fed into Q. They call this new dawn Panopticon, a program to sift and sort this invasion of privacy until there's nothing private left. You have a good education, Conrad. Why do they call it Panopticon?"

Harthrop-Vane's attention lingered on Moneypenny. "Panopticon is the name of a Victorian design for a circular prison with cells arranged around a central well, from which prisoners can be observed at all times. The panopticon allows a watchman to watch prisoners without the prisoners knowing whether or not they are being watched. It's said that prisoners begin to police themselves, just as civilians will police themselves beneath the gaze of CCTV or when searching something on Google."

"Why does that sound familiar?" mused Mora. "Oh yes, that's right. You dropped me to the bottom of a very deep, very dark well, Moneypenny."

"I didn't drop you hard enough."

Mora clapped. "Tell us where the word 'panopticon' comes from, Conrad."

"A borrowing from the Greek, sir. All-seeing and all-seen."

"Full marks. Now give me a Latin borrowing for all-knowing."

"Omniscient."

"And all-powerful?"

"Omnipotent, sir."

"Yes." Mora sighed. "That's what Panopticon gives Five Eyes. Omniscience. Omnipotence. Real-time processing of live data, all around the world, every hour of the day. It comes online any day now. A great coup for your country, Moneypenny." He tipped his head. "I know you and M lobbied hard for it. Got down on the polished floor of the Pentagon and begged for significance. Congratulations."

"I was never told about this," said Harthrop-Vane.

"I wonder how much Mother didn't tell you," mused Mora. "I'd hoped Bond would give me the War Book, and thus access to Panopticon. But he's a stubborn boy. Happily, I've found another avenue of access to Q. Joseph Dryden."

Luke scuffed the carpet. "Send me into the field, Colonel," he said. "I can capture Bond. I was Special Forces. I can teach these private school boys a few tricks."

000 sneered. "I don't need help from Joseph Dryden's bitch." Luke stepped forward but Mora barred his way with a small shrug. 000 said, "I know your file, *Lucky* Luke. You were shit on the heels of your mother, who preferred sticking a needle in her arm to delivering the parasite in her belly. You were shit on the heels of your father, who preferred barrooms and back alleys." Luke tried to get round Mora but couldn't. "You were shit on the heels of the army to be stamped in the face of the enemy and forgotten about. You were shit on Joseph Dryden's heels on his journey to greener pastures. He forgot about you as soon as Moneypenny gave him a better life. And he was shit under my boots when I crushed his heart. Both of you. You were born to lose."

Now he'd let Harthrop-Vane wind Luke up, Mora released him with a glint of amusement in his eyes.

Luke raised his fists. "Try me."

Harthrop-Vane did the same. "I'd love to."

Moneypenny spoke up. "000, if you want to be a leader you need to learn some people skills."

Harthrop-Vane snorted in disgust.

Mora chuckled. "Conrad, you don't need assistance, do you? You've been waiting for this moment. Take the helicopter. You are never going to be *James Bond* to Moneypenny or M. But you can be better than James Bond to me. Bring me 007 and 003."

000 stood up straighter. "Yes, sir."

Mora turned his red smile on Moneypenny. "Any last words for your knight-errant before he enters the field of battle?"

Moneypenny steadied herself, settling her coolest gaze on Harthrop-Vane. "Bond is going to kill you."

Mora laughed, leaned down, and kissed Moneypenny, the stub of his tongue flicking against her own. She almost vomited. He tossed her into Harthrop-Vane, who caught her when she buckled. But when 000 whispered by her ear, it wasn't comforting.

"I'll bring James to you, but it won't be a tearful reunion. It will be you watching me beat him."

Moneypenny set her jaw. "Whatever gets you through the night, Conrad."

Part II

Ideology

EIGHT

Four Poisons of the Heart

James Bond once told Joseph Dryden that at Shrublands *the rooms are room-shaped and the furniture is furniture-shaped and that's the best that can be said for it.* He wasn't wrong. It was Dryden's last day and he was so eager to get through the checkup his palms itched. Dr. Akter wore a Mickey Mouse tie with his white coat and Dryden couldn't tell if this was supposed to be funny or soothing. He stripped down to his boxers. When Dr. Akter saw the many scars once again, some faint as the impression of invisible ink, others outraged as new tattoos, he said: "You do seem to have been in the wars."

"Just one long one," said Dryden.

Afterward, he pulled his clothes on while the doctor wrote notes like he was racing against a deadline.

"What's the verdict?"

"My primary concern remains your heart. You have to give the tissue time to heal. In my religion, we say the four poisons of the heart are a loose gaze, loose talk, too much food, and bad company."

"Sounds like the mess hall on a Saturday night. So what's good for the heart?"

"That's where my faith and Western medicine agree. A strict diet, and acts of obedience."

"Who am I obeying?"

"Well, a mullah would ask you to perform *dhikr*; seek Allah's forgiveness and invoke His blessing and peace on the Prophet; and pray at night. What I ask is that you *rest*, take light exercise, and please continue to attend mindfulness sessions. And remember, one digoxin pill every evening after dinner."

Dryden passed to the door, but paused. "Forgiveness for what?"

"That's up to you."

"I've killed a lot of men."

The doctor cleared his throat. "Did you do it to save lives?"

"It's not always that clear."

The doctor tidied up his notes. "Perhaps it's we who should ask forgiveness of you. When did you last speak with Dr. Kowalczyk about Operator's Syndrome?"

Dryden tugged his right ear. "What is there to say?"

Dr. Akter tapped his pen on the desk. "A lot. Operator's Syndrome is the name we health professionals have given the unique constellation of interrelated health and functional impairments within the special operation forces community. Those effects will change over time. Traumatic brain injury, endocrine dysfunction, sleep disturbance, chronic joint and back pain, headaches, substance abuse, depression, anger, stress reactivity."

"Suicide," said Dryden.

"Yes. Suicide. Marital and familial breakdown. Intimacy issues. Memory, concentration, cognitive impairments, visual impairments, hypervigilance. Inability to transition from military to civilian life. Existential crises."

"I'm great fun at parties."

"Except you don't go to parties, do you? You don't have a life outside operating. When you were medically downgraded in Afghanistan, your mild traumatic brain injury and hearing loss should have kept you from continued action. Before Moneypenny recruited you, you couldn't complete a grocery shop without a panic attack."

Dryden reached for the door handle, squeezing the thing.

"Careful. You'll break it."

His fist relaxed by a hair's breadth.

"For many ex-soldiers, jumping from a helicopter into live fire is simply more bearable than arranging a school pickup. It's what you know. That's why we're seeing so many veteran volunteers in Ukraine. You didn't have to face any of that. We kept you in the field. But there's only so long we can keep you there."

"I'm a better operator now than I've ever been."

"I'm not arguing. But eventually we ask the body to pay debts we can't cover. M is offering you meaningful retirement from action."

"I don't want it."

"What's left for you?"

"I've got to find my team."

"And then?"

"Then Moneypenny will be back in her chair and I'll be out in the field."

"At what cost?"

Dryden's jaw jumped. "It won't be me who pays the price."

"You mean Conrad Harthrop-Vane. Nothing travels like bad news."

"He killed my brothers and sisters. He bruised my heart. He betrayed our mission. And I'm going to kill him for it."

"Are you sure you don't want to kill him because he's reminded you of your mortality?"

"I died twice. It didn't stop me. And Conrad Harthrop-Vane is going to pay because he's everything that's wrong with this system."

"He's your shadow," said Dr. Akter.

Dryden released a long breath through his nostrils. "I used to think he was Bond's shadow. They're a lot alike. And nothing alike at all."

"He might be James Bond's reflection. He's your shadow. Do you know how to burn away a shadow, 004?"

Dryden shook his head.

"Turn on the lights. As bright as you can."

Dryden thought of the light Panopticon was about to shed over the world, burning away any shield to a person's inner thoughts, inner heart, inner soul. And he was asked to defend it. But Panopticon might bring back Moneypenny. In the aftermath of the explosion in Masdar City, 000 and Lisl Baum escaped with Moneypenny held captive. Q tracked the plane as far as American airspace, and then it disappeared: from air traffic control, satellites, everything. Even Q couldn't find it. Riddle me that . . . Aisha and Ibrahim told him Panopticon would provide the answer. Dryden bounced on the balls of his feet. They'd keep Moneypenny alive. A high-value target like her. And Luke Luck was with her. The one love of his life. Lucky Luke who'd been imprisoned in the black site despite all of Dryden's pleas to any higher power he could reach. He's not a terrorist. He's not a villain. He's a decorated war veteran. You can take my word for it, can't you? So much for that. Panopticon might give him Luke. It might deliver 000.

"Thanks, Doc. I'll pray every night."

Dr. Akter watched him go and thought to himself, I actually believe him. But he couldn't say it was a prayer for anything good.

NINE

Want

The train pulled on the lonely line cast north through swamp forests from Moscow toward the Arkhangelsk Oblast. Harwood and Bond paid for a private first-class berth in cash, jumping aboard as the whistle blew. They lay on opposite beds, one pace this way and three paces that. It might have been as many miles. Harwood had longed to rest her head in the dip between his chest and shoulder; longed to feel his arms around her; longed for his breathing beside her in the night. Now that breath was here, but it echoed like a cold sigh from a meat locker. When the pattern changed and she thought he was asleep, she rolled toward him, studying his blank profile in the moonlight.

"My father was a spy," she whispered. "I found out a few days ago and I wanted to tell you. When I was a child, he'd tell me enemy agents had poisoned him. We thought he was delusional. And he was. Paranoid schizophrenic. My mother gave me his camera and there was a roll of film in it with a shot left. I used it to take the photograph of Wiltshire's laptop, the image of Anna's barcode, before the laptop died. So I guess my father helped me. It's a nice thought, after all those years I spent trying to help him and failing."

The train jerked, a cradle in a storm. His breathing didn't change. Harwood was about to turn over when his voice arrested her.

"You didn't fail," he said. "You loved him and you were loyal. You were there for him when being there meant watching him kill himself. You were never one to flinch. You followed Anna down a path most people don't want to think about because it's the stuff of nightmares. You didn't fail."

Harwood found her voice. "You sound very certain."

"I know—" He broke off.

She knew what was meant to come next. *I know you.* But he didn't anymore. That's what Mora had achieved. The chill cloaked them once again, and Harwood thought that was all they would exchange, until overhanging trees belted the train and the thwack-thwack-thwack had Bond lurching upright, pinning his back against the cabin wall and tucking his chin to his chest.

"You're safe."

Bond grunted. "You should've killed Mora."

"I wish I had."

"I suppose it wouldn't look good on your résumé," he said, "killing the boss."

Harwood sat up. "Did I follow Anna through hell to find you, or did Mora set the whole thing up? If I didn't know how effective his interrogations were, I'd have hit you by now, James."

Bond tapped his fingers on his taut stomach. "C'est la guerre." He cleared his throat, but still the words were compressed, as if he had a limited supply of oxygen to give them. "Mora asked if I cried when my parents died. No one's ever asked me that. The usual break-you-to-make-you stuff, dismantling the puzzle of my life, scattering talismans and totems." He was quiet for a moment. "My mother collected ceramics on summers away. Devonware crockery. There was one saucer, painted with scenery of a house in a valley, a river, and trees. After she and my father died, I spent hours studying it. That valley looked peaceful. The saucer was inscribed with four words around the circumference: *Hope On Hope Ever.*"

That was the title of his poem for the numbers station, used to call or identify agents clandestinely over shortwave radio. The poem was written by a Victorian, Gerald Massey. Harwood remembered the words.

HOPE on, hope ever! Though to-day be dark,
The sweet sunburst may smile on thee to-morrow:
Tho' thou art lonely, there's an eye will mark
Thy loneliness, and guerdon all thy sorrow!
Tho' thou must toil 'mong cold and sordid men,
With none to echo back thy thought, or love thee,
Cheer up, poor heart! Thou dost not beat in vain,
For God is over all, and heaven above thee—
Hope on, hope ever.

The iron may enter in and pierce thy soul,
But cannot kill the love within thee burning . . .

Bond beat his fist into his palm. "Hope on, hope ever. I repeated those words in my cell, remembering the drone of the radio in my numbers station tutorial with Q, remembering the house in the valley on my mother's saucer, remembering Moneypenny's calm in any crisis, always there for me. Hope on. Hope ever. But Moneypenny never came for me. Neither did Felix Leiter, René Mathis, M, Marc Ange-Draco, or Tiger Tanaka. Neither did you."

"I'm here."

He shrugged that off. "I realized, eventually, Moneypenny must think me dead, or else Q could not locate me. I decided to use the cyanide capsule in my mouth. Dulce et decorum est, and all that jazz. Mora must have seen my determination, or resignation, because he pulled the capsule out with his fingers."

Harwood touched her jaw.

"I willed myself to die." He rose, turning in the tight space. "Die, die, die, die, die. But there it was. That old wellspring. My *famous will*, which would not let me go, no matter how I tried." His eyes latched onto her, gray-blue yet ablaze. "Hope dies eternal."

"You're not alone anymore. You've never been alone. M, Moneypenny, René, Felix, Marc-Ange, Tanaka—they're desperate to find you. You have a family. It's right in front of you."

"Bill Tanner was family. Bill Tanner had my back."

Harwood got to her feet. "You've never been a man who believed in the old boy network or the word of a villain over his own senses. Did you hear me screaming for help in that Syrian mountain, or not?"

"I heard you screaming for me. At least, I thought . . ."

"Then who do you trust? Yourself? Or Mora?"

"Myself?" He said the word as if it were foreign to him.

Her fingertips grazed his knuckles. She skirted her hand up his forearm, feeling new scars, the shirt rolled to the elbow. "Who do you trust?" she said. "Him, or me?"

His hand clamped on hers. "I saw the tape. Mora asked if you agreed to betray me. You said: *I do.* Ironic. Sid never heard the words."

Harwood held her breath. "It won't work. You can't intimidate me into confirming your worst fears. *I can't be intimidated.*"

He pressed in. There wasn't anywhere to go except backward. She fell onto the mattress. He leaned over her, not allowing her any movement. Harwood wrapped her legs around his waist, drawing him closer until her pelvis met his, eliciting a grunt of surprise.

"What do you want?" he asked.

"You're the one pinning me to the bed," she said. "What do *you* want?"

The question was a whip. He pulled away, twisting in the box of their compartment, his fist bouncing on the window, which rattled, plastic and tired. "I lived my life by wanting, once. Wanting to win. Wanting to beat the other man. Wanting the woman. Wanting to please M—first Sir Miles, then Sir Emery. But in that cell, there was nothing to want. Nothing to seduce, nothing to drink, nothing to eat, nothing to defeat." Bond studied his empty hands. "I lived my life by moving, once upon a time. I recognized foreign coastlines with greater ease than I recognized British beaches. I am at my best in no-man's-land. I even proposed in an airport and God help me, Tracy said yes. But in my cell, there was no moving, beyond one pace this way and three paces that." He traced the steps. Moonlight slatted across his shirt in prison bars. "I lived my life by giving. Body, wits, faith, loyalty. But in my cell, there was no one who wanted what I could give, only what I could never give. I am not a traitor, I told myself. I am not a traitor and never will be, no matter who betrays me." His gaze stuck on her. "Nothing to want, nowhere to go, nothing to give. There was just—*being*. There was just—*me*."

She said gently, "Being you is most men's fantasy."

"Then let them do it. I don't want it anymore."

She breached his body heat. "None of it?"

His gaze raked her.

A bang at the door. Bond shook himself, calling out in Russian to ask who was there.

It was the conductor, a babushka with a tremulous voice. "Are there any women in your carriage?"

Bond drew a hand over his mouth. "Yes."

"Then lock your door. The train is making an unscheduled stop. We are taking on soldiers."

Bond stared down at Harwood.

She whispered, "Could be they've run out of military trains for transportation so they're using civilian."

"Risking staying onboard . . ."

"This train will take us clear through to Archangel. We have to risk it."

"There is no *we*."

Harwood straightened the black woolen dress she'd stolen from a washing line. "Then I'm going to the restaurant car. Alone."

"The soldiers—"

"I'll take the Russian army over that look on your face."

The restaurant car was in the middle of the train; beyond it was the kitchen, and then six cars carrying soldiers. The carriage was decorated in faded patterned fabrics. Harwood assessed the first-class passengers. The real money in the north belonged to shipping, gas, minerals, and plantations, and those people didn't take the train. Her company was university professors, scientists, low-level forestry and agriculture management. Walking to the end, she took the table to the right of the kitchen door, tucking herself into the corner with her back to a faded poster advertising the northern lights, and the emergency cord. At the table in front of hers, a father and son played a word game.

A waiter with thin wrists poking from his shirtsleeves asked whether she'd like Stolichny salad, Georgian-style chicken, or venison with vegetables. She decided salad was the safest bet, and added a glass of wine. In the dark square of the window, Harwood tied her hair with the pink headscarf and rubbed some color into her cheeks, though she could hardly feel the tips of her fingers. It was as if they belonged to somebody else. Harwood tested her trigger finger. The joint moved.

At the far end of the carriage, the door opened. Harwood watched with a clenched stomach as a reflection materialized in the window. But it wasn't Bond. Her hand flew beneath the table to the gun strapped to her thigh.

Conrad Harthrop-Vane used his heel to close the door behind him, keeping one hand inside his jacket as he scanned the compartment. 000 found her and a grin that belonged on a voodoo mask spread over his pale face.

The waiter now carried toward her a wobbling pat of potatoes, eggs, pickled onions, canned green peas, and beef tongue congealed in mayonnaise. Harthrop-Vane took the seat opposite, a few inches of wood and fabric separating him from the boy behind playing hangman. If she fired, the boy would die too. The waiter recited the menu and 000 interrupted him, saying venison would do. The waiter asked how he liked his steak.

"Bloody, with a glass of red."

Harwood glanced at the table across the aisle, where a man with a gray beard and scratched glasses read a paper. At the table ahead, two women in their mid-forties studied a laptop, discussing some figures. Too many civilians. Too much exposure.

000 said, "When I was told a woman matching your description bought two tickets, I hardly dared hope."

"You've come a long way on a little hope," she said.

"You too," he said.

She gave a tight smile.

"Aren't you going to eat that?" he asked.

"I've lost my appetite."

"Where's Bond?"

"Not with me."

"*Two tickets*, remember?"

"He bought two tickets as well, heading south. Safer to split up."

He bit his lower lip. "How disappointing. Still, M will be so relieved to know you're safe. Tell me Bond's destination and we can have him picked up."

Harwood kept the gun rigid on her knee beneath the table. Her free hand toyed with a knife on the linen. As far as 000 knew, she still believed he was on the side of the angels. She'd gone AWOL while he was a trusted member of the pack. He didn't know it was her who discovered 005's body in the Altai Mountains, her who warned Joseph Dryden, if Dryden ever got the message. She turned the blade over, reflecting the little lamp on the table into his eyes. But *she* didn't know if Dryden got the message, she didn't know the status of the Double O Section, and Harthrop-Vane would.

"M sent you to find me?"

"He's been very concerned. The team missed you."

"You seem to have done all right. No major terror attacks on the news. You must have stopped the Gray Group funding Rattenfänger's next strike."

"I'm expecting my knighthood any day now. And you—infiltrating Russia alone. They said it couldn't be done. But you dragged Bond out of his prison."

"How do you know that?"

His nostrils flared. "A thing like that makes waves. Q reads waves."

"Speaking of Q—where's Joseph Dryden?"

"Don't tell me you'd prefer he rescue you?"

"I don't need rescuing. But yes, if it came down to it—I'd prefer 004." She enjoyed his wince.

"Why's that?"

"He doesn't expect a knighthood."

Harthrop-Vane put his left hand to his heart. He was a right-handed shot, and that hand was beneath the table. "Ouch. All right, you got me. Felix Leiter knew it too. Of the four reasons to become a spy, I'm in it for ego, that's what he said."

"When did you see Felix?"

"Our causes aligned, hunting the assassin known as Trigger."

Harwood tried to remain expressionless. She alone knew Harthrop-Vane had been using Trigger as a cover to pick off Double O agents and their allies, and though Felix believed it was Trigger who took a near-deadly shot at him on the mission to save Zofia Nowak, it was really 000. So if Felix had thrown his lot in with Harthrop-Vane, it meant he'd trusted the man who was out to destroy them all.

"And where is Felix now?" she asked.

"We entered a Central American jungle together on the trail of Trigger. He never exited."

The train faltered, a little jump.

Harwood said, "You should take more care."

"He insisted on staying down there to bother the natives when we didn't turn anything up."

Harwood rocked with the sway of the carriage. "There are only four reasons?"

"MICE. The old Cold War adage. Money, ideology, compromise, ego. Yours is ideology, the way I see it."

"What do I believe in?" Harwood glanced at the clock over the door. Come on, Bond, stop licking your wounds, come and lick him.

"You don't want to sew up the damage after it happens, you want to fix things before they get broken. You told me that once."

"I suppose that sounded terribly naïve to you."

"Not as naïve as your effort to save doomed men from themselves."

She took a sip of wine. "I don't remember you being this insightful, Conrad."

"I don't remember you calling me Conrad."

"Maybe it's all this talk of dead fathers. I pity you. I always have."

His jaw jumped. "I rather hoped you'd be impressed, me swooping in to find you in the middle of Russia when no one else could."

"I'll leave the applause to Moneypenny."

"Yes. Well."

Harwood's scalp crawled. "What are her orders?"

He looked mournful. "She's a little tied up at the moment."

The wine burned in her throat. "What about 004?"

"Out of action."

"That doesn't sound like him."

The waiter approached the table, tripping as the train rattled. Neither Double O moved to catch the plate. That confirmed it: 000's hand was on his gun under the table, and now he knew hers was too, his gaze snapping to her locked arm. The plate of venison clattered, spilling a red droplet on the tablecloth, followed by a bigger drop from the glass. Harthrop-Vane told the waiter to take it off the bill and the man bowed, retreating.

000 stabbed the venison with his fork. "Call this bloody?"

"I'd be happy to add some, Conrad."

He laughed. "So it's like that."

"005 told me to see you through the gateway."

He sniffed. "Then it was you who tipped off Joseph Dryden to take cover. I've replayed that moment a hundred times. If he hadn't stepped behind the bookcases, the shot would have killed him. Don't look so pleased. He still walked into an explosion."

"Did he walk out again? Or is he like Felix, *not exited*?"

Harthrop-Vane sighed. "Bond really isn't on the train with you? I'm disappointed. A chance to look James Bond in the eye as he realizes he's no better than a myth."

"The strength of England lies in myth," said Harwood, reciting Mora's words from a Barbican rooftop what felt like a lifetime ago. The door to the kitchen opened over her shoulder. "The strength of Sherlock Holmes, Winston Churchill, Scotland Yard. The strength of—"

"Me," said James Bond.

Conrad Harthrop-Vane paled. A hasty sneer did nothing to recover his sudden choke as he stared up at 007.

"I know we've met," said Bond, "but you'll have to forgive me—I don't seem to remember your name." A snarl escaped Harthrop-Vane. Bond slipped into the seat beside Harwood. He looked over the table. "At least it's not red wine with fish. There's a child sitting behind you. That's the only reason 003 hasn't taken the shot. But the father's on his last guess and the boy's about to draw the noose."

Hissing filled Harwood's ears—the train window buzzed with static, the dust of bauxite mining, and then the cloud was gone and floodlights revealed machinery moving over shallow scars in the landscape, as if the world had ended but the diggers kept extracting anyway. A muffled boom made them all tense: dynamite lifting the earth out there in the dark.

Harthrop-Vane said, "The rear six carriages of this train are filled with Russian troops."

"I suppose that answers *you and whose army.*" Bond turned his smile on Harwood. "Rather playground, isn't he?"

"Some men just don't grow up," she commented.

"You don't say." He clicked his fingers. "I remember now—it's Double O Nothing, isn't it?"

Harthrop-Vane purpled. "Mora doesn't think so. He bet on me to beat you."

Harwood said, "Mora is in prison. I put him there."

Harthrop-Vane sighed. "It didn't take."

Bond blinked twice, shutters falling in a hurricane.

Harthrop-Vane pointed his fork at Bond's chest. "I'm going to enjoy burying you."

Bond gave a one-shouldered shrug. "I might be a myth. I might belong to a bygone era. But if you're my replacement, I think I'll stay out of the grave a little longer."

The father and son stood up noisily, searching for a lost pen, picking up a fallen scarf, joking with the waiter. Bond slipped Harwood's knife under the table. The train was taking a curve around the foot of a hill that waved blackly with pine, hiding Plesetsk beyond, the intercontinental ballistic missile site turned cosmodrome, protected by boreal forest and the Severnaya River and kept secret until the end of the Cold War.

Bond said, "Now."

Harwood pulled the emergency cord. Bond leaned forward and Harthrop-Vane howled—Bond must have stabbed him under the table. Harthrop-Vane's gun went off, but the shot went wide, puncturing the paneling to the kitchen. There was a thud, then a belch of flames kicked open the saloon doors. Harwood was wrenched sideways into the window, which cracked but held.

The train was jumping the tracks.

It was a confluence of events. Harthrop-Vane's bullet had ruptured a propane tank beneath a lit stove, releasing gas in a sudden explosion that plunged the tank itself through the rotting wooden floor of the carriage, striking an inadequately maintained joint bar, where a decades-old fracture now split as the brakes went into action around a curve. It only took a second for the train to wobble on the bend, and gravity took effect. The whole thing came peeling off the track, casting the train across the bauxite field, scraping fourteen sparking carriages over open-pit surface mines prepped with ANFO—ammonium nitrate and fuel oil—ready to detonate.

TEN

Move

The train had left the track behind but was still moving, rolling around and around as it jerked and walloped across the shallow pits. You could hit ANFO with a hammer and it wouldn't go off. But the drilled holes flooded with fuel were daisy-chained to detonators, and the train now dragged at the cords. At any moment the detonators would go off, the ANFO would be set alight, and the train would be engulfed as easily as tinfoil shrinking in a flame.

Johanna Harwood lifted her head—her hair was sticky with something. Blood. Glass grated her scalp. Burning filled her nostrils. People were screaming. She was lying on the cracked window, which was now the floor, and now the ceiling. Bond had Harthrop-Vane by the throat and the two men were lifted, then dropped, as the train made another rotation. Harthrop-Vane landed on top, pounding punch after punch across Bond's jaw. Harwood wiped her face, looking through the prismatic window at the tumbling world.

The six carriages beyond the kitchen held the army, and were heading first into the mine.

The six carriages behind the dining car held civilians.

She had to decouple the train.

Harthrop-Vane found a steak knife in the detritus. He slashed at Bond's chest, but Bond seized his arm, fighting for the blade.

Harwood pulled herself along the windows to the door. The connecting passage was a wind tunnel that deafened her. The emergency hatch in the floor flapped open. She wormed her head through, reaching for the red-hot iron hook holding the carriages together. She had only a minute to achieve this before the train flipped again. Harwood drew her sleeves over her hands and gripped the hook in one hand, lowering a leg to kick at the chain with her bare foot, her shoe lost somewhere. She kicked with all her force, once, twice, three times, the ground spitting rocks at her, the howl in her ears worse than a torpedo, and then the hook budged.

The civilian carriages barreled away, stopping at the edge of the mines, safe.

An explosion almost broke her neck as she clung to the underside of the careening carriage. She wriggled her way back inside. The train was now sliding on its back, making the ceiling the floor, where Bond used a teaspoon tucked into his fist like a short dagger, combating the slashes of Harthrop-Vane's knife. Sparks flashed between the two men. Harthrop-Vane's blade sliced Bond's stomach. Bond swerved and Harthrop-Vane stumbled forward. Bond grabbed him in a headlock and drove him into the kitchen, where fire leapt for both men, and beyond them the carriages holding the army scraped across the mine pits, blasting dynamite that smacked the kitchen, separating them from the rest.

Harwood followed Bond and Harthrop-Vane into the kitchen, met by the pop-pop-pop of shattering glass and clattering saucepans and a live wire from a kettle zipping through the air. White heat came from every side, and then the rear end of the carriage popped open like the lid of a jar shaken up too much.

Bond landed a boot in Harthrop-Vane's stomach, then a knee in his chest, getting a hand to his throat, but Harthrop-Vane had hold of the wire and was about to jab Bond's chest. Harwood yanked the plug from the wall, slipped beyond Bond, and wrapped the wire around 000's neck, strangling him from behind. The three staggered, a six-legged monster, toward the fiery mouth where the next train car used to be, and then a depression of air sucked Harthrop-Vane outward with Harwood tethered to him. She couldn't see if he'd been thrown clear or fallen underneath the train and dragged into the burning pit. The exploding earth swallowing the train was about to consume her, when Bond caught her around the waist.

007 and 003 trembled on the jagged edge of the car, dancers failing to hold a pose, as the carriage kept gliding over the gaping wound of the mine and finally sighed to a stop. Acrid smoke ate the oxygen around them. Through the tattered metal fabric of the train, they saw planes and helicopters buzzing overhead, dispatched from the cosmodrome.

Harwood laughed. In the midst of it all, she laughed.

He smiled at her.

Then his smile fell. "Mora is free."

A jet hared above them. Harwood grabbed hold of Bond's lapels and dragged him through the gash of metal and wood as sparks turned to columns of flame. They jumped to safety, teetering on the rim of the pit.

The only thing to do was move. Put distance between themselves and the train, which would funnel the search efforts toward the Archangelsk Oblast, cutting off their escape route. Keep moving. They double-timed through the night, arriving at the Northern Dvina River by daybreak, where they stole a motorboat. The river wound through a factory district, where they abandoned the vessel, taking an off-road UAZ from a dilapidated warehouse. Bond got the engine going and they bumped onto dirt tracks, the radio switched to the news. As the sky grew dimmer, they heard the bulletin. Wanted: a British man and woman, possibly on foot or using stolen vehicles. The man is six feet tall with dark hair and gray-blue eyes. The woman is five-nine with dark, curly hair and hazel eyes. They will most likely speak Russian, but may also assume other identities. This couple are Western spies intent on destroying the Russian way of life. They are armed and dangerous. There is a reward for their capture, dead or alive.

"*Smiert spionam*," said Bond. "It's been a while."

When the engine died, Harwood and Bond continued on foot, far-off hills purplish in the sunset. Hunting birds swooped and dove in sudden bursts of death. Rain began, fat drops that got into their clothing. The road climbed out of a valley toward a village. A lonely sound came from the center, where three men shared a bottle of bootleg alcohol on a bench. Harwood and Bond tried a few empty homes: nothing in the kitchens but dust and animal droppings.

A tidy fifteenth-century monastery with a bell tower stood away from the village. The door was unlocked. Harwood's feet were burning, joints stuck fast, the balls stiff as marble. The monastery was painted with icons, like a comic strip telling the story of good and evil. An altar beneath a heavy gold cross. Pews worn soft. Flagstones up the nave carved with skulls. In an office behind the vestry, Harwood found candles, matches, and a blanket. She discovered a half-empty bottle of wine and two communion cups. Laying the blanket before the altar, she lit three red candles and then spread out the food they'd managed to scavenge. Pulling off her wet jacket and caked boots, she folded to the floor with gratitude.

Bond watched all this from the aisle, clasping and unclasping his hands. Finally, he sat down beside her. In the guttering light, the pain on his face was smoothed away, as if here, maybe, was the Bond she used to know.

"Perhaps the gentleman would like to sample the wine first?"

Bond popped the cork and sniffed the unmarked bottle. "If I'm not mistaken, a nineteen seventy-two Château Mouton Rothschild."

"Just the thing for tonight's menu: a dinner of locally grown beets, fish smoked with our own wood chips, and for dessert, we offer organic cherries, carefully handpicked and selected for you by blind nuns."

"Blind?"

With one hand, Harwood held her pink scarf to her eyes; with the other, she pressed the cherries to her nose. "No other senses can be permitted to interfere with our life's purpose."

"I see," said Bond.

"Said the blind man." Through the silk, she watched him coming closer. He stole the cherry from her fingertips with his lips.

"Delicious," he said.

Harwood lowered the blindfold. "You're having dessert first."

"You should always have dessert first," he said.

"Why's that?" she asked, breathing in the smell of him, earth and sweat and cherry juice.

"A man could be killed before he gets through the main course."

"He could," she agreed.

His gaze flickered over her body. "You're wet through."

"So are you."

"We should get dry."

"We should."

His fingertips touched her cheek. Then dropped to her lips, which he traced, as if trying to remember something.

Rain danced on the roof.

"Johanna?" he said.

"Yes?"

"Were we in love?"

She whispered, "Yes."

He leaned forward, and his lips touched hers.

Bond jerked back as if electrocuted. He retreated to the corner of the blanket, seeking the edge of a map. He'd told her once there was nothing more lowering than a woman asking in the morning, with lethal insight, "Feeling better now, honey?" But it never stopped him finding comfort in the arms of nameless women. She wasn't sure if it was a compliment or an insult that he wouldn't find comfort in hers, even if he couldn't trust her.

Then she looked into his black pupils and remembered that when Mora waterboarded her, she'd transmuted the sensation into swimming with Bond in the Ionian Sea. When Mora blasted her with noise, she danced with Bond to the strains of a symphony orchestra floating from the windows of a Budapest conservatory. When Mora spiked her adrenaline, she was taking a hairpin corner at 170 miles per hour in her Alpine A110S with Bond beside her. Had he used the same technique to survive, and now it was working in reverse, dragging him back to that torture?

"James?" Harwood reached for him. "You're safe. You're safe with me."

"No I'm not," he whispered, and the words were weights signifying too high a cost.

Bond got to his feet.

Harwood followed.

"I can't do this," he said. "I can't know if—I saw the video. I watched you vow to betray me. Almost anyone at Mora's hands would have. I can understand that. But I can't forgive it."

She swallowed. "I was following Moneypenny's orders. It was all to find you. It was an *act*, James."

He shook his head. "Then you're too good an actor."

Tears stung Harwood's eyes. She pulled the gun from her harness, swiveled the thing, and gave it to him.

Bond took it, looking at his own hand as if it were moving unbidden.

"All right," she said. "You believe you can't trust me. You believe I betrayed you, that I'm betraying you right now. Kill me."

Bond's jaw twitched.

Harwood waited. Faith pounded in her veins.

"I can't," he said. "But I can't be with you, either. Mora is free. I'm going to find him and do what you should have. This is the end. Our end."

Harwood stood alone at the altar as James Bond walked away into the night.

She listened to his steps disappear. She listened to the silence that followed. When was she last in a place of worship? Sid's funeral, a mosque in Bristol. She stared at the gold cross before her now. This would almost be absurd if it didn't hurt so damn much. Sid's last words were a question: Was she a traitor? He'd died with that doubt. A doubt she planted to go undercover, to become a triple agent and save Bond, the man who went missing on a joint mission with 009, leaving Sid with so great a guilt he called off the engagement. Maybe that wasn't true. Maybe there was a second at the end when Sid believed in her. But a second wasn't enough. It wasn't a lifetime.

And now here, again, the man she loved didn't know if he could trust her. Because she was too good an actor. She who'd spent her life acting in the service of others. To pacify her father. Acting for the Secret Service, for Britain, for Moneypenny. Acting for men who needed her to play whatever role was missing in their lives. Mother, lover, healer.

Too good an actor.

It was the ultimate insult to one who acted because it was what she was told was needed from her, her greatest value, her mode of survival.

It was the ultimate form of perception.

He'd seen her, and she didn't like what he'd seen.

Harwood reached into her coat and removed the wad of her father's negatives, which she'd exposed after taking the photograph of Anna's barcode, just before the train journey to St. Petersburg, during which she'd slept as if dead. She'd not had the chance to look through them yet. The film hadn't seen the light for thirty years, she guessed, holding the strips up to the candlelight. They played like a comic strip too. She held them closer. Yes, that was Bill Tanner in London, ruddy and haunted, perhaps back from Afghanistan and his first meeting with Mora.

Were these surveillance photos from a life spent watching? What would her father make of his daughter's life, spent watching for the needs of others? And who was Charles Harwood watching? The negatives told a story of men at lunch, prostitutes on beachfronts, nightclubs . . . The seedy and the desperate. He was a photographer. That's what she thought, until her mother told her he was really a spy, and she realized the fracture in her relationship with her mother came not from Harwood abandoning the medical path her mother prepared for her, but from following her father's doomed path as a spy. She thought of her mother's words: *After what they did to your father.*

Harwood pocketed the negatives and reached for the wine.

Self-pity is a most unattractive quality. That's what her grandmaman used to say. And she was right. Harwood wiped her mouth, palm coming away gritty and red. Sleep tempted her. A deep, un-remembering sleep.

Something jolted Harwood back to consciousness. She wasn't sure what. But as her eyes lighted on the cross, she thought of vows.

A Hippocratic Oath, which she'd sworn when training as a surgeon.

A license to kill, which she'd undertaken as a Double O.

A promise to herself, which she'd made when all was lost.

You came here to bring back Bond. You gave yourself a mission. You are going to see it through.

She stood up as the sound fully reached her. The thing that had woken her. The rotor of a helicopter. Harwood reached for her gun—her holster was empty. Bond had walked off with her weapon. She extinguished the candles with her fingers and went to a stained glass window. Through the colors, she could see a spotlight in the sky, hoovering the earth for clues. Did they have thermal imaging? Did they know she was in here already? The helicopter settled overhead, pinning its spotlight on the church. The dangling figures of men rappelled from its body.

A priest hole—was that a thing in Orthodox monasteries?

Should she run for it?

Maybe they didn't have thermal imaging. Maybe they were simply canvassing the area.

Harwood snatched up the blanket, bundling the food and the bloody cherries. She hurried into the office, burying the blanket in the drawer where she'd found the wine. The wine! Harwood dashed to the pew, stabbed in the cork, and gripped the bottle by the neck. With her other hand, she pulled her knife from her boot. Then she looked around a last, desperate time. There was a cupboard filled with priests' robes. She backed inside, letting the velvet cover her with stifling, mothy hands.

A man's voice on a loudspeaker made her jump. First he spoke in Russian, then in English. "Be warned we are setting fire to this church. If you are citizens of Russia, come out with your hands raised above your head. You have nothing to fear. If you are spies, you have a choice between death by fire or firing range. We have you entirely surrounded. Make the choice quickly."

The crash of glass, followed by three explosions, *bang bang bang*. Then an intake of breath, and *whoosh*. Harwood pressed her eye to the cupboard door. Fire raced up the aisle, enveloping the pews, the velvet over the altar, the rafters. Harwood covered her mouth with the sleeve of a priest's frock. Think, damn it, *think*. There was no window in the office. The exit was through the main body of the building, which was rapidly becoming no exit at all. But if she went out there they'd kill her on sight—and that was if she was lucky. Could she count on help? She wasn't sure how long she'd slept: Bond could be miles away. And if you were one of ten people still living in the abandoned village and saw a military helicopter hovering over a burning monastery, would you do anything about it, or would you simply turn over in bed and pretend to go back to sleep? Unseeing meant surviving here. There was no cavalry coming. And the fire was making the decision for her. At least she could buy seconds of confusion.

Harwood struggled into the robe of a priest. She put her father's negatives and the knife inside the pocket. The gown came with a hood. She took a diver's breath, drew it over her head, and ran toward the danger.

She burst from the church on fire. Two men tackled her, rolling her in the grass. She heard one shout that it was a priest. At that, the men let go as if scalded. She had enough time to look up and see she was ringed by military vehicles and men in Russian uniforms. And between their legs was a path into the woods. Harwood stabbed the nearest man in the leg. He doubled over with a shriek. She wormed between knees, boots, grabbing hands, found an inch and took it, racing into the wood under a spray of bullets.

Harwood ran for her life. The helicopter was so low its engine shook her stomach. Branches whipped her face, clawed her arms, shredding the robe. She was racing downhill—the very first glimpse of dawn nestled down there, a blush on a river. The searchlight kept her in its gaze. Vehicles crashed through the trees. Men on foot. Dogs. Keep running. Just keep running.

A bumper bit her legs. Harwood jinked left. The car swerved with her and hit a tree. The UAZ toppled, churning mud. Harwood jumped onto the upturned bonnet, reached into the open window, and tore an assault rifle from the hands of the passenger. She filled the car with bullets and then jumped down, firing behind her wildly.

The river was beyond the forest, indigo in the early light. Harwood burst from the tree line as an Alsatian leapt for her, snapping at her priest's hood, searching for her neck. She rolled, thrashed, pulled. Finally, she got free of its jaws and splashed into the river. Strong currents pulling her. Get to the other side. The dog leapt after her, then barked in panic, swept away. Vehicles slid to a halt at the riverbank. The water was pulling at the robe. She couldn't get it off. She beat with her legs furiously. Grasping for something, anything, she found a tangle of roots. Harwood pulled herself to the bank. The river was too deep for the vehicles, but the helicopter was still airborne. She'd lost the gun in the struggle with the dog. Forget it. Forget about the helicopter, too, its burning eye on her.

Ahead was a stretch of open fields. Bullets spat either side of her—they seemed to want to miss. Thank God for small mercies and *run*. She crossed the field in zigzags, remembering that her father used to take her to school this way to avoid imagined snipers, helping her avoid the spotlight of the helicopter now. But it was reaching for the earth in front of her, juddering to ground. And the iron belly birthed a line of armed men.

Harwood looked back. The ground complement had laid a temporary bridge over the river and were bringing up the rear.

Think.

Think quick.

She had a false passport in her pocket, belonging to a Turkish national. That wouldn't explain her presence here. She took it out and crushed it beneath her boot. What else? Anything that could identify her? Her father's negatives. She dropped the sodden robe. Anything else? She pulled off her engagement ring, stamping Sid's lapis lazuli into the earth, and sank to her knees after it, raising her hands over her head.

ELEVEN

Give

The clearing in the forest was a near-perfect hole, an aperture burnt through a map. The river and trees formed the circumference, and inside a circle of headlights illuminated Harwood hanging from a tree by her zip-tied wrists.

"Tell me your name again."

"Natalya."

"Why were you in the monastery, Natalya?"

"The novice said I could take refuge there."

"I'll bet he did."

Cackles. Harwood tensed herself against it. Her shoulders were ablaze. The unit was a dozen strong. The leader was a heavyset bald man with the coolness of many campaigns behind him. He was neither incensed by her costly escape attempt nor excited by her capture. He was just doing his job. It was a quality that chilled her.

"Well, we'll know soon enough. Hold her still."

A man held her from behind. The leader approached her, so close she could see his laughter lines. He dug into his pocket. A blade? No, a phone. The flash stung her.

"You take a pretty picture, Natalya, or whoever you are. Let's verify your identity with base . . ." He thumbed in a number and pressed send.

A skinnier man with a shock of blond hair spat. "They send us out to hunt and don't even give us a picture of the quarry. We're no better than these dogs to them, Caspar."

"Quiet," said the leader—Caspar.

The pack of Alsatians were on chains now, growling at Harwood. The blond man took the leash of the closest dog and let the animal lunge for Harwood. She recoiled as far as she could. You trained for this. She remembered the strong arms lifting her out of the sensory deprivation tank, marking the end of the R2I course. It was Bond. A Double O always "rescued" another after interrogation training, a method devised to create a lasting trust between agents. But now the dog snapped at her feet and Bond was nowhere to be seen.

"Stop, Peter. She's supposed to be with a man. Maybe it isn't her. We must wait for further instruction. In the meantime, call in a roadblock ahead."

Harwood said quickly, in the best Russian she'd ever mustered: "I'm not whoever it is you are looking for. My name is Natalya. I ran away from my husband. Please, listen to me."

Caspar considered her with mild interest. "OK, if you want to give us a show. Why did you leave your husband?"

"He beat me."

"And we'll find evidence of this on you, I suppose?"

"Yes."

Caspar wagged his head. "All right. But you asked for it. Strip her."

Harwood willed herself somewhere else as eager hands tore at her dress, as the cold wind rasped her bare skin. She wasn't here. She wasn't afraid. She was waking up in James's bed, the most sinfully comfortable mattress she'd ever experienced, waking up to the smell of eggs and coffee, and his amused voice calling from the kitchen, asking if she ever planned to get up . . .

"You have poor taste in men."

I've heard that before, thought Harwood. She was left in her black briefs. Caspar studied the bruises and wounds of the past two weeks. The red ring around her neck where Teddy Wiltshire strangled her. Scarlet ribs. Blue toes.

"Please," she said, allowing tears to flow down her face. "I was trying to escape my husband. Please . . ."

Peter said, "Maybe she's telling the truth. Look at her."

"Never believe a woman's tears. Why did you run from us, Natalya, if you had no reason to fear us? Aren't you a patriot?"

"I thought my husband had sent the police after me. He's done it before. He tells them I'm mad."

Caspar searched her face. "Could it be you are so unlucky as to escape a brute, and run into us? Tell us the name of your town. Your street."

There was a framed map of the region hanging in the novice's office. Harwood summoned an address at the very edge.

"What is your husband's name?"

"Alexei."

"When were you were married?"

"Six years ago."

"Your mother's maiden name?"

"Zaitseva. Please, my arms. Please, cut me down."

"Do you have children?"

"No."

"Why not?"

"I can't."

Peter chortled. "That's why her husband beats her."

Caspar shrugged. "Who knows why men do what they do."

They were buying the narrative. "Please, I can't bear it, my arms . . ."

Caspar looked at his phone. "Damn signal is weak. You are right, Peter. They keep us in the dark, then leave us waiting."

Harwood began to sob.

"She's just a stupid housewife," said Peter.

Caspar waved a hand. "Let her down. Stop her crying."

Two men lifted her to the ground. Harwood buried her face in the soil. She was a few feet from Peter, who held his weapon loosely, banging the muzzle against his knee. But her arms were still bound.

"A stupid housewife, or a well-trained spy. Which is it? Why don't they answer? How many people do they have to ask? I'm tired of this," said Caspar. "There's one way to find out for certain."

His knee landed heavily on the small of Harwood's back. She froze. She heard him undo his belt. His fingers grasped her hair. The men began to clap in unison. Harwood shut her eyes as tight as they would go. She wasn't here. She was in James's bed. But there were twigs and dirt in her mouth. She wasn't here. She was on a beach. What beach? Anywhere. White sand. Calm sea. She wasn't here.

Caspar paused. "What was your mother's maiden name?" His men booed.

What had she told him before? She couldn't think of anything. Couldn't even think of her own mother's maiden name.

His fingers dragged at her briefs. He got himself into position.

You're trained for this. They trained you for this.

Clarity burst into Harwood, the clarity of a surgeon opening a heart. She was the calmest she'd ever been in her life.

She whimpered, "Zaitseva. Please. Don't you have a sister or a daughter?"

Caspar clicked his tongue. He sat back, dropping her head in the dirt. She heard him doing up his belt.

"She's telling the truth."

"That's it?" said Peter. "You believe her?"

"I know the sound of fear."

"Even so. Why not have her, while we're here?"

"Her husband's probably given her syphilis."

"Doesn't bother me," said Peter. "I've already got it."

More howls. Harwood rolled onto her side, covering her face. Through the crack in her fingers, she saw Peter swinging his gun.

"Sir, your phone. There's an answer from headquarters."

Caspar reached for it. "Another way to waste my time, most likely." He looked at the photograph on the screen. He flushed.

Harwood lunged. She seized Peter's gun with her bound hands and pulled with all her strength, sending him staggering. She had the thing, even if she couldn't quite hold it straight. Her first shot was at Caspar, clipping his thigh. Then she fired indiscriminately, backing toward a humming vehicle as a dog leapt for her and brought her down.

Peter's boot landed on the muzzle of the weapon. He kicked the dog aside, then stamped on Harwood's hands, pinning her to the ground.

Caspar wrestled the gun free from Harwood's desperate hand. "She is the spy," he panted. "Get me a first aid kit. Peter, they want the man. She must know where to find him. Make it hurt, but don't kill her."

"Wait!" shouted Harwood in English from the ground. It was like a magic spell—for a moment, everyone in the circle froze. "I'm a surgeon. That bullet has nicked your artery. Look at the amount of blood. I can keep you alive."

Caspar looked down at his leg, first with annoyance, then with a pale flush that traveled down from his forehead.

"Let the men see to it, they have field kits," said Peter.

"You need more than that," said Harwood.

"How do I know you're a surgeon?" said Caspar.

"The femoral artery has multiple sections. There's the common artery, which supplies blood to the tissues in the abdominal wall, the groin, and your tiny dick. You want to fuck again? There's the deep artery, supplying the femur, hip, buttocks, and deep tissues. Then there's the superficial artery, delivering blood to the lower leg, including the muscles at the front of your thigh and part of your knee. Want to be able to walk? The main femoral artery is four centimeters long. It's made of tunica intima, media, and adventitia, gossamer-thin layers and blood vessels that burst more easily than a balloon. And yours just went *pop*. You want to die here?"

Caspar grasped his thigh. "What do you need?"

"A med kit. Free hands. And a coat. I'm freezing."

Caspar chuckled.

He sat on the hood of a car. He let her use scissors to slice his trousers, which were thick with blood. She was tempted to let the scissors do what the bullet had failed to do—or would have been tempted if Peter wasn't pressing a pistol to the back of her head. She barked an order for water to be boiled, and it was followed. She cleaned and sterilized. She said she needed a torch on the area, and one was provided. The spell was lasting. Apart from Peter, and the revolver to her head. Apart from Caspar watching her every movement. She dipped the artery forceps in the boiling water, and then dug into his meaty thigh.

"That hurts," said Caspar.

"That's life," said Harwood, earning another chuckle. She pressed gauze to stop the flow.

"After you've sewn me up, you know we'll do whatever it takes to get his location out of you."

Harwood said, "This is a little fiddly, if you don't mind."

He grunted. "You're a brave girl, that's for sure. We were told you were traveling with this man. Why aren't you with him?"

"I can see the bullet. Bite down on something."

"Where is he?"

"He left me," said Harwood, getting the bullet in her grasp.

"That wasn't very chivalrous."

"Haven't you heard?" she yanked the bullet. "Chivalry is dead."

Caspar said, "Son of a whore, this hurts . . ."

"I could do a better job if you took these handcuffs off."

"I am not a fool twice," said Caspar. "Sew me up, girl."

"If you're very nice, I'll even leave my initials."

Peter struck her behind the ear with the butt of the pistol. Light exploded in her skull.

Caspar barked, "For God's sake, she's holding a needle near my balls!"

So she was.

"You could save yourself some pain and me some time," said Caspar, sweat on his forehead. "Tell me where he is. You will eventually. So why go through it all, huh? I can see from your body you've been through enough."

"My body agrees," said Harwood. "But I don't know where he is."

He shook his head. "Brave girl." Then he pounded the hood of the car, taking his pain out on metal that folded under his fist.

"It's almost over," she said. "Someone bring him vodka and painkillers."

A desultory search. The excitement that they'd captured an English spy, then the fact that she was stitching up the boss wearing pretty much only a coat, combined with Peter's slow and detailed narration of exactly what he was going to do to her body when she finished playing nurse . . . it was too much anticipation, not enough delivery. They would want another show soon. And she was out of tricks, down to her last stitch.

So buy time. Keep buying time until you find an opening.

Peter was saying: ". . . You'll see, you'll be begging—"

"OK," she said. "OK. Stop talking, will you? We agreed to split up when we heard the chopper. Less conspicuous. He doubled back on our tracks. I'm closing. Pass me more gauze and some butterfly tape."

Caspar grabbed her chin. "I wonder if you're telling the truth."

"If he was still in the area, don't you think he would've attempted a rescue by now? I'm telling the truth. Let me close the wound."

Caspar released her. "Take the helicopter and two cars. He should be within a tight radius if he fled when we arrived. We'll stay here." He sucked his teeth as the needle bit. "I'm not paid enough for this anymore."

Peter nudged Harwood. "Are you done?"

Half the men were moving off. That left five here, including Peter and Caspar. Except that made eleven in sum. There were twelve men before. Had one gone out on patrol?

"Yes," she decided. "I'm through with you."

"Then while we're waiting," said Peter, his hand creeping around Harwood's body, "why don't we have some fun, Caspar?"

Caspar shook his head. "I'm in no state. Tie her up and gag her."

"She shot you," said Peter. "Lied to you. Made a fool of us all. You're going to leave that unanswered?"

Harwood saw Caspar's gaze shift to the men watching. This could go one of two ways. Either he asserted his authority by telling Peter to follow orders. That was if he felt it was Peter threatening his authority. Or if it was her, a woman who deceived him, shot him, and then had the power to keep him from bleeding to death, if it was her that threatened his authority . . .

Caspar said, "You've been patient, boys. You'll take turns. But remember. We keep her alive. Peter, you first."

She was still holding the sewing needle and her hands were bound in front of her. Peter removed the pistol from the back of her head. He went to pass the weapon to Caspar. Harwood jabbed out quick as a viper. The needle scraped open Peter's jugular, spraying Caspar and Harwood in blood. Peter staggered back, clutching at the gushing wound. Harwood snatched the pistol. She held it to Caspar's head.

"What's your mother's maiden name?"

Caspar burbled something incomprehensible.

Harwood smiled. "*That's* the sound of fear."

She fired.

Caspar's skull blew into a red cloud.

Harwood dove behind the car as the spell broke and gunfire shook the forest. The soldiers who'd moved away were running back. She checked the gun. Five more bullets. She raised her head and squeezed off three shots. That left nine men. Or eight, in fact. Where had the twelfth soldier gone? Harwood fired off two more rounds. Six men left, no more bullets.

She was pinned between the car and the river. She could jump, try and swim for it, though every limb hurt and her hands were bound. She was rising when a dog landed on her back. Harwood wrestled with the animal as shots whanged into the car, interrupted by a scream.

One soldier missing . . .

Harwood kept fighting with the dog, using her arms as a shield. The teeth were almost through the wool of the coat.

She heard another scream, then yells to take cover, followed by an explosion that smacked the air out of this satanic circle, breaking its hold.

The dog's teeth were in her hair. Harwood found the gun and crashed the butt into the skull of the animal. The dog skittered away, barking.

Then a soldier appeared around the rear of the vehicle. He grasped her ankle. Harwood fired—no bullets. She swung the gun at him like a club. They rolled in the mud. She got a hand in his hair and forced his face into a puddle, drowning him in an inch of dirty water.

The dog landed on her back. She couldn't hold it off anymore. But then it was gone with a yelp.

Hands on her: shaking, panicked hands. "Johanna? Johanna?"

"It's not my blood," she said.

"That's the answer we were after," said the owner of the hands in a thick voice. "Go to the front of the class. Let me see your arms. You ought to know better than to play with stray dogs."

"If I'd learned that lesson, I'd have never played with you . . ."

A gentle laugh. "Bull's-eye, Ms. Harwood. Now, we're going to get you up. You've taken a few knocks, but you're OK, aren't you? Been through a shock, but nothing you haven't survived before. You've got more mettle than sense. Tilting at windmills. Coming into Russia after a hopeless case like me. But windmills don't stand a chance before you, do they? All right. Let me see back here. Some bruising around the thighs.

Bruises fade. Bruises fade. What's this? Did you take a blow to the back of your head? That's OK. Just stay awake. This way . . . Are you with me, Johanna? 003, stay with me. I need you alert. You've had a trauma to the head and you've got to stay awake."

James Bond was rubbing her hands. Everything hurt. She was wearing a khaki sweater, men's trousers, woolly socks far too big. That's funny. She was sitting in a helicopter. It was on the ground. Wires dangled from the GPS screen. Bond was leaning through the open door, his feet still on the earth, like Clark Gable by Vivien Leigh's bed. It was raining heavily, plastering his hair to his skull. Why did he look so worried? Behind him was a scene of carnage. She saw Caspar's headless body displayed on the hood of the car. Oh yes. That's right. He shook her.

"No you don't. I need you with me."

She focused on him. "You came back."

A nod.

"Why?"

"I forgot to tell you something," he said. "I'm going to buckle you in, all right?"

"We can't take off yet. Up the hill. You'll find a priest's robe. In the dirt, there's my engagement ring."

"Johanna . . ."

"I can't leave it here."

He bit his lip. "Fine. Take this gun. I'm going to start the engine. *Stay awake*. Any trouble, you take off. But don't leave me bloody stranded, all right?"

Her teeth were chattering but still she said gamely enough: "No promises."

The next thing she was conscious of was the rattling of the helicopter lurching into the air.

"Come on, Johanna. What's the sixty-second element on the periodic table?"

She wore large headphones. So did Bond, who was at the controls.

Her father's negatives were in her lap, gritty with mud, but no ring. She'd stamped them into the earth side by side. "Samarium."

"I should've picked something I know."

Harwood rubbed her throat. Bond passed her a canteen of water. She drank half, letting her heart rate slow.

"You couldn't find my ring?"

He shook his head. "The rain."

The scene below was getting smaller, as if it had never happened. Nothing did happen, she told herself. You stopped it happening. You trained for this. You delayed, deceived, bought time, saved your body for the most part, and gave up nothing real. If this were an exercise, you'd receive full marks. So put it out of your head. Cut that scene from the script and crumple it up. Toss the ball of paper in the fire.

Harwood lifted her eyes to the blue sky. What a beautiful day.

She leaned toward James. "What was it you forgot to tell me?"

He moved closer. Lifted the headphone from her ear. She turned to him, so they were cheek to cheek, as if swapping whispered thoughts at the back of a theater.

He said: "Thank you."

TWELVE

Hope On, Hope Ever

The dacha was in a tree-lined valley by a river. Bond circled the house three times in the helicopter before determining it was empty. The helicopter fuel was in the red, the day growing late. There was a smile on his face as he began the descent.

"What is it?" asked Harwood.

He nodded toward the house. "Hope on, hope ever."

Harwood and Bond covered the helicopter with fir branches and tarpaulin they took from a boat that bobbed and knocked against the stilts of a jetty leading from the dacha, whose intricate timber-lace façade had been mounted onto white stone and glass. The security was more illusion than anything else, an alarm with a code Bond disabled in thirty seconds. When they opened the front door, they were greeted by the smell of anticipation. A sanctuary kept spotless by a local cleaner, awaiting the return of its owners. There was even a fully stocked larder, which they tore into while dripping mud onto the tiles. They saw each other as if looking into a mirror, grinned, and said they'd better do something about themselves.

Harwood followed Bond up mango wood stairs without risers to a bedroom that occupied the entire top floor, one wall of glass letting onto a balcony that looked down at the river. A breeze chasing through the corridor of the valley stippled the water. An emperor-size bed thick with brocaded pillows and velvet blankets faced the view. Bond and Harwood glanced quickly at each other, as if this were a school trip and she'd snuck him into her room. There was an en suite where a walk-in rain shower with fluted glass took up half the bathroom. Cotton dressing gowns, his and hers, hung from the back of the door.

"You know what I want?" said Bond.

"An alarmingly cold shower, followed immediately by an alarmingly hot shower, and then an enormous breakfast."

He grinned. "That's *exactly* what I want. Care to join me?"

"Not for the cold part, thanks, you madman." She took the shorter dressing gown and returned to the bedroom, but left the door open, so if she wanted she could have turned to see him strip. But she didn't. She passed to the far side of the bed. She didn't want her borrowed clothes to touch the sheets, so she tugged off the woolly socks, the rucked-up trousers, the scratchy sweater and stuffed them in a basket. She heard the shower go on. Harwood considered the dressing gown, but she didn't want to get blood or dirt on that either. So she sat naked on the blankets. The mattress dipped gently. The river was half blue, half-muddy, perhaps disturbed by something, or simply reflecting the clouds sliding into the valley as the sun grew low.

"For those scared of a little cold water, the shower is now hot."

Harwood turned. She could see his outline through the fluted glass. Her stomach tensed—excitement, fear, longing, defensiveness. But need won out and Harwood crossed into the bathroom. She placed a hand on the brass, and slid the door back.

Bond stood facing her under the flow of the shower, reminding her of a swim they'd taken in a Jamaican lagoon, how he stood under the waterfall, taking its weight on his shoulders, and how she'd stood in the shelter of his body, arms around his waist, his heartbeat thudding against hers. She did the same now, feeling new scars under her hands. Bond's arms came about her waist. He laid a soft kiss on her forehead. Then he was lathering his hands with soap, easing the grime and blood from her neck, her arms. She followed the same pattern down his body. When she crossed a new sign of injury, a mark of harm, she saw his eyes change like the river, clouds passing overhead, but he didn't stop her. Instead, his mouth found hers. She kissed him, and he drew her to him with a sudden urgency that she met with equal hunger. He lifted her by the waist. She wrapped her legs around him.

"James," she said. "James."

"Yes," he said. "Yes."

Now she put on the dressing gown and got inside the white cotton sheets with the velvet blankets and indecent number of brocaded pillows. James told her she looked like a terrible tsarist before the fall so she ordered him to be a good serf and bring her some coffee, which he did on a tray with all the food he could find. He lay beside her naked, eating more than she'd ever seen a person eat in one sitting, until all she could do was laugh. He told her it wasn't kind to laugh at hungry peasants and she agreed, feeding him caviar on her fingertip, which he took demurely, before taking her whole little finger in his mouth and sucking it clean. The food was forgotten.

Afterward, she lay naked on his bare back across the bed, her head turned on his bicep to watch the river, her legs intertwined with his. A bird bigger than any she'd ever seen—it must have been an eagle—turned in circles, seemingly content to thread an infinity loop from one side of the valley to another. A wave of gratitude passed through her. She kissed his ear.

"You're real," she said.

"Are you sure?" he said. "I've had this dream before."

Harwood smiled into the crook of his neck. "Me too. What made you come back?"

A beat. "I know you. I might not know myself, but I know you."

There was a marble fireplace downstairs, big enough to accommodate a tree trunk and already laid. They sat before the flames on a sofa made for six, Bond's head on Harwood's lap. She'd kept the dressing gown. He wore linen trousers he'd raided from a walk-in wardrobe. Firelight gleamed on his scarred chest. On the mirrored coffee table the pair of guns were doubled.

"We could stay here forever," he said.

"Rattenfänger will know there are a limited number of places we could reach with our fuel level."

"All right. A life on the run. As long as I've got you and an endless supply of caviar, I'll survive."

Harwood said, "You don't ask for much."

"Give me the simple pleasures."

"Simple pleasures?" said Harwood, topping up her glass with champagne.

"Well, I'm not complaining it's Shampanskoye instead of Bollinger."

She filled his glass. "It's admirable how you manage such hardship."

"Thank you for noticing." He sat up to clink and take a sip. Then he lay back down on her lap, balancing the glass on his stomach.

She said, "We could, you know."

He kissed her bare thigh. "Could what?"

"Stay here. Or somewhere like it. If we make it out of Russia alive, we could remain hidden. Live however we like. Be happy."

"Sold," he said, looking up at her, "to the girl with the golden eyes."

She snorted, shaking him gently.

"Where shall we go, then?" he asked.

"Somewhere like this. Somewhere peaceful, where nobody knows us."

"Mr. and Mrs. Somerset," he said, and then the mischief on his face faded with a memory. "Maybe you'd better pick the name."

"How about this. You'll be James and I'll be Johanna."

"Much better. Will we fashion disguises? I could grow a mustache."

"No you couldn't."

"I grow a commendable mustache, I'll have you know."

"It doesn't mean you should," she said. "I still want to recognize you, after all . . ." Something tugged at her memory. "Do you have my father's negatives?"

"Yes." He drew them from his pocket, finding the frame of the barcode tattooed on the back of Anna's neck. "I wish I could kill that bastard Wiltshire a second time."

"I made the first time count."

He stroked the negative. "When I met Anna, I was determined to prove I didn't give a damn you'd chosen Sid. Anna met the worst version of me—the best Romeo ever pimped for England, in M's words. What else is on here?"

"Surveillance photos, I think. There's something about them, I'm not sure . . ."

"What was your father's vintage?"

"Tanner's. He's there. I suppose my father might even have overlapped with you and Moneypenny, when you first joined up."

"I don't remember a Harwood."

"It seems nobody did. No Service pension. Maybe they don't provide support if the injuries are mental. They simply watch your daughter until she becomes usable. Moneypenny upcycling the broken pieces . . ."

"You're not broken. You never were." He tapped the negatives. "You didn't tell me what happened to Bill."

Harwood caught up the end of the dressing gown cord and twisted it in her hands. "Mora turned Bill Tanner as the Cold War came to an end, which means Russia has had a man inside our security services ever since. At least, until last year. He hanged himself. I'm sorry, James."

The logs caved in with a hiss of smoke. He stood up, keeping his back to her. His fist softly met the marble mantelpiece.

"Do you really believe it was Bill who gave Lisl Baum my number in Barcelona, and told her what to say to lure me out there?" he said.

"What did her message say?"

He shifted. "It seemed to be from you. But it could have been things I'd told Bill, I suppose."

Harwood wanted to ask more, but didn't. "My mother said my father took a photograph that condemned him. Tanner is in these negatives."

Bond held the negatives to the light of the fire. His whole body stiffened. He reached for a gilt silver magnifying glass on the mantel. The fire whispered, then cracked. Rain beat at the windows. An animal howled. Bond's hand was shaking.

"What is it?" asked Harwood. "James?"

"I know who betrayed me. I know who betrayed you, and Sid. I know who betrayed your father." Bond faced her. "And it wasn't Bill Tanner."

Harwood accepted the negatives and the magnifying glass, warm from his grip. It took her a moment to interpret the inverse image, and in that moment her entire life turned upside down and inside out.

M.

He stood under a bough of spring blossom speaking with a man who, now she looked closer, could have been a twin for Mora.

"I don't understand," said Harwood. "What is this?"

"I watched M kill this man in Moscow in 2004," said Bond, his voice like the first crack of an earthquake. "He was supposed to be the Stay Behind Slayer, 0013's greatest kill in Berlin before the Wall fell. He told me and Moneypenny that he hadn't seen this man since that night in Berlin. That he must have *missed.* He said he was glad to have the chance to tie up a loose end. But this is a photograph of him having a *chat* with the fellow *after* he was supposed to have killed him in Berlin. He's holding a newspaper. The front page is the Wall coming down. He lied."

Bond looked down into the fire, his eyes distant and fixed far beyond the flames.

"Twenty-one months of my life, breathing Mora's air, to protect M. I didn't see it before but I see it now. This man is Mora's body double. Mora was the Stay Behind Slayer. M was supposed to kill him in '86 and didn't. I was supposed to kill him in '04 and M stopped me. M saved his life. Since then, there must have been a rupture of some kind. Mora wants M's War Book. I resisted. Twenty-one months of hell to protect the man who damned us all."

Harwood stood up and had to reach for the arm of the sofa to stay balanced. "We need to get out of Russia. We need to warn Moneypenny. Rattenfänger will be watching Archangel and M will be watching MI6 comms. But there has to be another way. Tiger Tanaka would help us, if we could get to him."

Bond turned gray-blue eyes on her that glinted with tears.

Harwood laced up stolen walking boots tightly over black jeans, then put a thick coat on over a cashmere polo. Her fingers weren't working properly. Bond came down the stairs wearing black trousers, a gray cable-knit roll-neck, and a padded jacket. He'd shaved and brushed his hair, though the comma still fell over his forehead. She remembered Tanner telling her what tipped them off when Bond returned from the dead after disappearing in Japan and being subjected to brainwashing in Russia, years back. Appearing in London, he hadn't gone to his flat but checked into the Ritz. Tanner said it was "stage" Bond. There was something staged about him now: groomed, perfect, polished, no sign of shock or betrayal. He could have walked out of a men's catalogue. Like nothing could ever touch him.

"You look like your old self," she said.

He spared a glance at a mirror, but then averted his gaze. "Are you ready? It's a long walk to Japan."

Harwood took a last look over the dacha. "I'm ready."

THIRTEEN

Last Man Standing

Joseph Dryden considered himself a caretaker. Though M had made him Chief of the Double O Section, Dryden put the word "Acting" in the title. Leaning on Moneypenny's chair behind Moneypenny's desk, Dryden gazed out of Moneypenny's window onto a rain-swept Regent's Park. He was supposed to consider this a promotion. But he wished Moneypenny would walk in right now and take her seat. Fresh out of the hospital, the bruises on his face and hands were nothing compared to his heart. And while he was wishing for things, he wished Moneypenny had thought to install a punching bag in here. He'd been a champion boxer in the army and was still built for it, carrying a heavyweight's load. He took some short swipes at the air. In the frame of glass over Monet's water lilies, he was only a man with navy shirtsleeves rolled to his elbows shadowboxing absolutely nothing at all. Dryden adjusted his pale gray tie.

He imagined what Lucky Luke would say: "Look at you, dressing for the cake eaters. Come on. Loosen up and we'll have some fun . . ."

Are you a caretaker, or a gravedigger, slowly burying the Double O Section? 004, last man standing, leader of his own merry band of one, preparing to give Five Eyes a tour of Q Branch like an estate agent. Today Panopticon would come online. Tomorrow there would be champagne at Bletchley Park.

The first thing Dryden would change was the name: Panopticon. As a soldier, he knew the best chance of mission success was reliable intelligence. So the initiative to feed data collected by the Five Eyes global surveillance system into the fastest computer in the world made strategic sense and would be a coup for the UK. But trusting any government with this much power took a leap of faith. His father had faith. His father's father was born in Jamaica under colonialism and served in Britain's navy during World War II before immigrating to the "Motherland" with the Windrush generation. Born in 1950s Notting Hill, Dryden's father spent his life rising through the ranks of the London Underground. He told Dryden that if they see how hard you work, they won't be able to keep you down. When Dryden started hanging around petty drug dealers at school, it broke his father. He didn't live to see his son sign up and rise through the ranks himself. Dryden's mother had no faith in the system. Working as a journalist on the *West Indian Gazette*, she grew to expect letters from the KKK and harassment from the government. She'd been brutalized by police since she could walk. Distrust toward the system is the sanest attitude to take in this world, his mother said, when he turned up at her door not dead, interrupting an argument between her and the pastor from the Baptist church. She was refusing to plan his funeral. Didn't think her son was so harebrained as to get killed now he wasn't even in the army, but working for an NGO. He told her she was quite right but to stop making the young pastor cry.

A knock on the door was muffled by the green baize soundproofing.

Phoebe Taylor said, "They're approaching."

The public face of MI6 was four and a half miles away at Vauxhall Cross, opened back in 1994 after Century House, the previous MI6 headquarters, had been deemed unsafe. (The fact that a glass tower on top of a petrol station had ever been deemed safe was a rather embarrassing quirk.) Even the architect of the new Vauxhall building, Terry Farrell, hadn't known its purpose. Farrell insisted on giving windows to the circular room at the center, until the anonymous client was forced to come clean: we can't have windows because it's a shredding room, the opposite of a Panopticon watchtower. Quickly dubbed Babylon-on-Thames, MI6 Headquarters was a postmodern Mayan temple, a frog done in Lego bricks, crouching over two moats one had to cross to even reach a door. Built in the spirit of visibility, Vauxhall still had some secrets the public—and the UK's enemies—didn't need to know. It wouldn't pay, for example, to build Q in a spy headquarters searchable on Google maps. So the powers that be decided to install the quantum computer beneath the Regent's Park office, where Britain's deadliest agents ate lunch. Bob Simmons operated the lifts of Regent's Park. The pad responded to his left palm print. His right arm ended at the elbow, a war wound. He stayed on his feet all day. It was said he could read the building like weather. So when Dryden stepped onto the lift, he asked Bob what was in store for him today.

"Holding your tongue, I'd wager."

"Feel like taking my place?"

"Not on your life, sir."

"What did we say about this whole *sir* thing?"

"Right you are, 004."

Q itself was a dangling golden chandelier kept in a soundproof, bulletproof, bombproof glass chamber bored into the ground. Hugging the sphere were offices and labs with glass floors and glass doors. Dryden entered Aisha Asante and Ibrahim Suleiman's lab with a knock at the door.

"Vibrations!" said Ibrahim. "You'll disturb Q!"

This ritual meant more to Dryden of a morning than his first cup of tea. Ibrahim ran an exasperated hand through his spidery hair. The son of Iraqi interpreters to the British army, he'd joined up himself as an engineer before training in biomechanics. He was responsible for one half of Dryden's interface.

"Ready?"

Aisha spun around in her desk chair. The sleeves of her neon green blazer were rolled up six times, a sure sign of nerves. She tried to fix them now. "I haven't felt this tense since my finals. I used to get this sensation in exams as if I were slowing down in time, but everything else was continuing on as normal, the clock in the exams hall ticking down the minutes, leaving me behind without a word written."

"That part sounds like all my exams," said Dryden.

"The well-being officer said it was called tachysensia. After a disastrous exam, my father—he was still working as the head caterer at Oval cricket ground—he ambushed me with a sports psychologist, who provided me with what she called a bag of tricks to combat panic triggered by fear of failure. What worked best was standing in nature and looking up at trees, saying aloud *Awe and wonder, awe and wonder, awe and wonder* . . . until time and my body snapped back together. Today I walked to work repeating *awe and wonder* to myself. Seriously spooked the kids doing the local school run."

"You should try my method," said Ibrahim. "Vomiting in the loo."

"Just remember you're both the smartest people in the room," said Dryden. "In fact, remember you're the smartest people in any room and you'll be fine in life."

Beneath the Regent's Park building, a tunnel threaded sewers, buried rivers, and the Tube to connect with the public-facing building at Vauxhall Cross. Dryden squared up to the blast-proof doors, flanked by his scientists, and stitched on his best smile. The steel barriers shuddered open, admitting M alongside the intelligence leaders of America, Australia, Canada, and New Zealand. The Five Eyes.

Dryden drew himself to attention. "Welcome to Regent's Park."

M stepped over the threshold, coordinating handshakes and introductions, making every use of the laughter lines creasing his handsome face. "Gentlemen"—he bowed to New Zealand—"and lady, you're in for a treat. Joseph Dryden is a fine example of why we will always need the human touch, even in our brave new world. And Dr. Asante and Dr. Suleiman are the best that brave new world has to offer. This feels rather like Christmas, doesn't it?"

Dryden stepped aside as M ushered Five Eyes into Q Branch. There would be a vague public recognition of new commitments among Five Eyes at Bletchley Park tomorrow, a symbolic location where nothing of importance would happen. Down here, it was Chatham House Rules: anything said would go unrecorded and would never be attributable. Panopticon had been in the works for years, but with the betrayal by 000 and the escape of Mora from a black site operated by Five Eyes everyone was looking for someone to blame and nobody wanted to trust anyone else. M's wilderness of mirrors. There was still a chance the US could pull out, even at this last moment. *Charm them*, M had ordered Dryden, so with a grin he told New Zealand, concerned by the abrasions on his face, that she should see the other guy.

"That is precisely what would make us feel better. But it seems Mora and Rattenfänger have disappeared." She considered Q. "And your supercomputer can't find them."

Aisha said, "That's why Panopticon is so important, ma'am. Currently, Q has immediate access to UK spy satellites and any other systems we can, um, pry open. But with ready access to the stream of data from Five Eyes, Q will pull data from every possible avenue. Artificial intelligence is already revolutionizing military decision-making. Public intellectuals worry about lethal autonomous weapons systems, AI-powered drones that can target civilians with certain racial features or protest placards. And they should be worried. But we should worry *even more* about the data."

New Zealand inspected Q's gleaming tentacles. "Why should I worry about the data?"

Ibrahim joined in: "AI is used to *assist* with data but it's also *dependent* on it. The question of data integrity, quality, and veracity is absolutely key, but nowhere near enough scrutiny is being given to those questions versus the AI capabilities themselves."

Canada said, "Swarms of drones do sound a lot more dangerous than . . ."

"Data poisoning," said Aisha. "That's what we call it. The process by which AI sifts through data and comes out with a conclusion is known as black box decision-making because it's opaque, too complex for us to understand how it reached its outcome. So we'd better make sure it's using good data to get there. We're in an information war—a war for the very idea of truth. We need as much reliable data as we can get our hands on. Panopticon offers that because of Q's processing power. We will be able to provide the data our militaries and governments need to make fast, clear-headed choices. All the more necessary, given the growing threat of the Axis of Cyber: Russia, China, North Korea, Iran, all very happy to use cyber warfare as a primary weapon."

Dryden tugged at his right ear. In some ways, he was an extension of AI itself, and the idea of data poisoning made him feel like a layer of his skin was being peeled off.

M joined in: "We've enjoyed a twenty-to-thirty-year lull in which terrorists represented a greater threat than rogue states. But now Iran and Russia have engaged us in hybrid warfare. We will continue to see a rise in sabotage, arson, cyberattacks, and proxy violence through paid terrorists and thugs. That is not to mention attacks from parties beyond the control of rogue states, like Rattenfänger, who will attack any nation, from Russia to America, and use any method for their own profit."

America said, "Like the recent bombing of the BBC."

"Or similar attacks elsewhere," said M, "by groups spanning from far right to religious fanatics. The bioweapon scare is a prime example. Rattenfänger knew the right buttons to push. A roll mat, ventilation holes, and a satellite phone discovered in a shipping container. Someone who didn't show up for work. A suspicious package. It's our playbook and they ran it, convincing the PM and the president to release Colonel Mora. Naturally, I do not question the wisdom of our leaders. Ours not to reason why. But if we can be manipulated so easily, we need Q to sift what our Five Eyes see and tell us what is true and what is false."

"And what if something happens to Q?" asked New Zealand.

"We have given every assurance—"

"Then you'll be happy to reassure me again."

Aisha said, "What happens in this room is entirely hidden from the world. We don't even have security cameras down here. Our own black box. The only way to access Q from outside in the case of an emergency is M's unique code, which is kept locked in the War Book."

"War Book?" asked Canada. "We weren't told about that."

Aisha winced, but M hummed, leaning on his cane. "The War Book contains my security code, my nuggets of earthly wisdom, my years of innocence and experience. Only my Number Two knows its location."

America looked around. "Didn't he off himself in this building after a security breach?"

M drew himself to his full height. "I would ask you to treat Bill Tanner's name with the respect his service record demands. Ours was a long history, the sort that bores more *junior* men, who have grown up with the War on Terror, to whom joes and Check Point Charlie and dead drops are the stuff of legend, or worse, schoolboy history. But what do we have to show for your War on Terror? A world in chaos. A power vacuum where there should have been a superpower. Identity wars and culture wars and information wars. No winners, only losers. You might do well to listen to a veteran."

"You can't keep a jack-in-the-box, so why should we trust you with this gold?"

"Mora was our jack in *your* box." M clapped Dryden on the back. "The Double O Section will recover Mora and destroy Rattenfänger using the power of Panopticon. That's a guarantee, gentlemen. And lady."

Australia rocked on his toes, making Ibrahim wince. "Wasn't it a Double O who abducted your Chief of Section?"

"000," said Dryden. "Conrad Harthrop-Vane."

"You don't inspire confidence," said America. "You knew 000 when he was a boy, M. How did this happen?"

M punched the floor with his cane. Ibrahim covered his mouth. "The same attributes that made him a perfect weapon for us make him a perfect traitor. The same could be said for any of *your* higher-profile 'whistleblowers' and chat room spies. I wonder, for example, where we might find Felix Leiter."

"We're not under the microscope here."

"Perhaps you should be."

America held up his hands. "Given recent circumstances, gentlemen—and lady—I'd move to delay turning on the Christmas lights. We'd feel more comfortable keeping our current arrangement, with the NSA sifting data and allotting access."

"The current arrangement is slow and unequal," said Dryden. "Panopticon can interpret data in minutes that would take other computers a century. This is a game changer."

"I recognize that. I am simply not confident the UK is the home for it."

Dryden said, "You want confidence? I've died twice and I'm still standing."

America's lip curled. "Knocked down seven times, get up eight, something like that?"

Dryden's jaw twitched. "Something like that. And I'm going to keep getting up until I've put 000 in the ground."

M said, "004 here was injured in the line of duty in Afghanistan. The IED damaged his hearing, but Q Branch developed a hearing aid that connects 004 to Q. The first in future augmented soldiers." Dryden noticed all but New Zealand took a step away from him, as if he were a mutant. "With Panopticon, Five Eyes will put immediate actionable intelligence into the hands—even the minds—of our soldiers all over the world. It's a new dawn, gentlemen. And lady. You came to us in '41 because the cryptanalysts of Bletchley Park had cracked Enigma. This is our field. So let us till it and you enjoy the fruits."

New Zealand said, "This isn't the time for second thoughts. We are losing. We came here to do something about it."

Canada said, "Hear, hear. Let there be light."

Australia said, "I can never remember if that's the first thing God did."

"In the beginning was the Word," said Dryden, "and the Word was with God, and the Word was God."

M opened his arms. "Today, the word is data. Dr. Asante, Dr. Suleiman, please."

Dryden nodded to Aisha, who moved to the central screen, Ibrahim lining up next to her in front of a red keyboard, like two piano players taking either end of the scale. Behind them, Five Eyes and Dryden watched a silent symphony take place. There should have been fireworks. There should have been an earthquake. Icarus should have fallen, wax wings melting, the attempt too far, the power too great. But all that happened was a series of ones and zeros flowered onto the screen with the rambunctious hunger of spring after a long winter.

"Panopticon is online," said Aisha.

Q seemed to shine a little brighter, but it was simply the reflection of jangling watches, rings, and jewelry as Five Eyes applauded.

FOURTEEN

Loose

Your boy is loose, Moneypenny. Replaying those words, almost tasting them, Moneypenny forced herself to eat the steak tartare. She was vegetarian. Her stomach also hurt from taking a pounding with a bar of soap tied up in a sheet. An old hazing trick. *Your boy is loose, Moneypenny. Johanna Harwood found him and freed him.* It had been days but felt like years since her capture. It was the unpredictability that got to her. She was allowed to roam the kitchen, the doctor's office, and the crew's quarters forward, not that she wanted to. Mora called her his free-range chick. She ate with the "officers," seated at Mora's right-hand side. She was treated with a vague but not ill-mannered respect. Veterans solicitous for her opinion, curious about the perspective from the other side. And did she have a preference for cinema night? Did she know how to play five-card draw?

Then a switch. She might be making a cup of tea when a man would pin her against the counter and scald her hand. If she reached over the table, they might slam her head into it. Crude cruelties from childhood, meted out to them by parents or superior officers. Barking, cheering, and then afterward: normal service resumed. Did you want the salt, Moneypenny? Or were you reaching for the pepper? Down here, there was no way to know if 000 had captured 007 and 003 yet. It was a waiting game and in the meantime they enjoyed her humiliation, a bit of relief to break up time in the dark. If she stayed in her bunk, refusing the temptation of the unlocked door, they brought the torments to her. Mora didn't seem to want information. She'd locked him in a hole and had many of these things done to him and now it was his turn. All this told her something. Another word for unpredictability is hubris. She wasn't an agent, merely a runner in the field and then a Section Chief. An administrator. He underestimated her. Let him. She'd already poisoned one man, and broken another's bones during a struggle. But it didn't help. There was one thing she was yet to find. A way out.

Your boy is loose, Moneypenny. Johanna Harwood found him and freed him. Wouldn't it be ironic if the fate of the world came down to a girl's crush?

Moneypenny muddled egg into the red mess and ate from a gold fork. Down the table, Luke Luck was shoveling in steak tartare as if there were no tomorrow. He was her best chance. At least, she prayed Lucky Luke was still on her side. They hadn't been able to talk. The mercenary who'd sought to humiliate her in the shower was found knifed the next day, seemingly an argument over drugs, but Luke was in the scrum. She'd given him this mission. Ordered him to embed himself in Rattenfänger, an outfit he'd worked for by proxy and then betrayed for Joseph Dryden. No one here knew of that betrayal. They thought he was loyal. They thought he was bitter and angry and lost to a headlong dive into hell. Luke shoved the empty plate away, took a shot of whisky, and called for a deck of cards and someone to suck his cock while they were at it. He certainly looked like someone taking a dive into hell.

"Your game will have to wait, Luck," said Mora. His hand closed on Moneypenny's wrist. Sometimes the switch flipped for no reason. "I have another in mind."

The tablecloth was green baize. Moneypenny stared, unblinking, at the coarsely woven wool as Mora dismissed all but Lucky Luke. Green baize covered Moneypenny's door in the Regent's Park office of the Double O Section. The material had been there since Sir Miles Messervy was resident. The baize remained once Sir Miles finally admitted he could not run all of MI6 and the Double O's at the same time and Sir Emery took over Regent's Park, before he took M's chair at Vauxhall. The coarsely woven wool was threadbare by the time Moneypenny was promoted from Bond's runner in the field to Chief of the Double O Section. To her, it was the cloth of billiard tables and gun cases; the dividing line between kitchens and parlors; it was the playing fields of Eton, where boys like Bond were exhorted to play up, play up and play the game. Green baize covered the door of Number Ten and the table of the Cabinet Office. It signified a place where men made decisions that determined other people's fortunes and fates. She'd always had it in mind to scrape the baize off her door and replace it with modern soundproofing. She just hadn't got round to giving the order. She wondered if she ever would as Mora told Luck to guard the door. Luck stood at attention across from her, his gaze over her head.

"Do you know what day it is, Miss Moneypenny?"

She dragged herself straight in her chair. "It's *Ms.* Moneypenny."

Mora twirled his knife. "The day Panopticon comes online. MI6 has been rightly concerned about cyber warfare, ensuring that the most sensitive areas of Q are protected by quantum encryption. That includes the neural link in 004's ear."

"Did Bill Tanner tell you this? Or 000?"

Mora ignored her. "Accessing Q is like being a tourist in North Korea: once you're through the first door, your every move is scrutinized and controlled, and every level of access comes with its own challenge. The discrete AI that handles 004's slice of Q requires a great deal of bandwidth and very low latency, however. This means there is a one-time key embedded within Dryden's hardware. An entangled quantum pair. A chink in Q's armor. If the hardware in Dryden's head were linked, say, with our own AI, we would be able to impersonate his mind and exploit the Double O access that he enjoys. Think of it like a string with a can at both ends. If I whisper in Joseph Dryden's ear, Q will hear me."

"That's impossible," said Moneypenny. "Any data Dryden sends to Q arrives with a unique sound file for analysis, which Q *must* receive before accepting the data itself."

"Quite," said Mora. "As such, the sound file itself is considered 'clean,' allowing us to infect the safety precaution and inject poison into Q's bloodstream."

Steak tartare rose in Moneypenny's esophagus.

"Knowledge is what's at stake in every Great Game of spies. I will see everything Panopticon sees. I will hear everything Panopticon hears. I will know the secrets of the East, gleaned by the West, and I will know the secrets of the West, gleaned out of brotherly love and paranoia. The power to blackmail presidents, ambush armadas, premeditate troop movements, the fly on the wall in nuclear power plants and the fly in the ointment on stock exchanges. I will breathe your air but you will never see me."

"How will you access 004's neural link? Since we're chatting."

"Ha. Since we're chatting. All I need do is hook his neural hardware up to X."

"X?"

"X is our very own artificial intelligence system."

Your boy is loose. "And where is X, on a map, for instance?"

Mora wagged his colossal finger. "That would be telling."

"You plan to send false data to Q?"

"While we see the truth, the West will see our version of the truth."

"Disinformation," said Moneypenny. "To what end?"

"Once we have 004, we will drop a little poison into Q's ear where it will fester. As you know, the swiftest route for Russia to penetrate American naval defenses is to sail from the Arctic through the North Atlantic Ocean. Standing in between is the UK with her nuclear submarine base. With a little disinformation, verified by a handful of Russian subs flirting with the receptors on the Greenland–Iceland–United Kingdom SOSUS barriers, Panopticon will convince Western powers that Russia's fleet is steaming toward them, drawing NATO submarines away from their usual patrol to cover the Atlantic Bridge. This will leave British waters without subsea defense. Ninety-five percent of global Internet traffic passes through a mere two hundred seafloor fiber-optic cables. There are as few as ten global choke points where these cables come ashore. With your coastline naked, we will lay mines and blow up every single cable linking Britain to the rest of the world. Do you know what happens when the Internet turns off, Miss Moneypenny?"

Sweat itched under her arms. She said, "On day one, businesses will cease to function because they no longer have access to banking or phone networks. After a week, the national grid will go down because power plants and electricity substations rely on the Internet to work. Gas pipelines will shut down without any power or Internet coordination. A national blackout will upset the regional balance and likely spread to Europe and beyond. There will be no fuel, so no food transportation. Riots. No police or army, because no fuel. Hospitals will have stopped working, too. There will be mass death. No transport, no aviation. We'll be a plague island." Moneypenny took a breath, which seemed to stick somewhere between her windpipe and her stomach. "But to hook 004's neural link to X, you would need to lay your hands on him, wouldn't you?"

"Lay—what a coy way to put it."

"And he'd need to be alive for X to learn how to imitate his mind."

"You're smiling, Moneypenny. Has anyone ever told you that your smile is most disconcerting?"

"I am reliably informed it is distant, ironic, and quizzical."

Mora grunted. "Tell me what's so *quizzical* this time."

"If the success of your mission depends on capturing Joseph Dryden alive, I have every reason to smile."

"Your faith is touching," said Mora, "but misplaced. Luck, I am sending you with a team into the field. After Panopticon comes online, there will be a public Five Eyes summit at Bletchley, which will suffer a drone attack." He turned back to Moneypenny. "The summit will be guarded by your pet assassins."

Moneypenny was afraid the calculations on Luck's face would show, so she said, "Double O's are not assassins. They are agents with a license to kill. There's an important distinction: judgment."

"Very noble, I'm sure. Of course, 004 will want to save the day," said Mora. "He likes that sort of thing, I'm informed. But it leaves him terribly exposed, don't you think? Breadcrumbs will lead 004 to Segovia, where Luck and a wet team will collect him."

"Dryden doesn't mind a bit of exposure. He doesn't thrive in the dark, unlike some. And if you bring him here, he'll rip what remains of your tongue out."

Mora rose, seized the back of her head, and shoved her face through crockery into the green baize. He picked up the coffeepot.

Your boy is loose, Moneypenny.

Your boy is loose, Moneypenny.

Your boy is loose . . .

When the lights snapped on, Moneypenny was in her own bed. She pressed a pillow over her head, expecting blaring noise to follow. But it didn't. She sat up to see Luke Luck entering her bunk room. He was holding bandages and burn cream.

"You shouldn't be here," said Moneypenny, wary but hoping, hoping.

"I'm here because of you." He sat down beside her. "And there's nowhere I'd rather be. Well, maybe that stretches things a bit."

Moneypenny rolled her head back on the pillow. "I'm glad to know you're still in there. You play the part so well, I was beginning to wonder."

"Me too."

"You have to reach Dryden before anyone else on the team. Do you know where we are?"

"Patrolling the Arctic. I don't know the location of X, though."

"What else have you picked up?"

"A name. Zofia Nowak, some scientist. I think Mora has her somewhere."

"Zofia . . ." She was a genius in quantum mechanics and artificial intelligence who Rattenfänger had targeted in the past. But Dr. Nowak was supposed to be in hiding under the protection of CIA agent Felix Leiter—though since his disappearance in Central America, Moneypenny didn't know the scientist's status. Rattenfänger must have grabbed her after removing Leiter from the equation. "Tell Dryden this: Zofia Nowak has been captured by Mora. Find Zofia and you find his base of operations. But it's imperative Dryden sends a tactical team. *He mustn't come himself*, it's exactly what Mora wants. Got it? Now go."

"I can't, not with you here."

Moneypenny fiddled with the tub of cream. "I'm not your mission."

"You're my CO. I should stay here with you . . ."

She took his hand. "Listen to me, Luke. You're my soldier and you'll walk the lines I give you."

"I've heard that before." He sounded weary.

Moneypenny gently pushed up his olive green sleeve. The needle marks were like the marching beat of red ants. She gave a mother's stroke. "Pick a number."

"Huh?"

"Any number. Humor me. What's your lucky number?"

"Five."

She took him by the hands and turned him to face her. Moneypenny drew a cross over his chest. "I anoint thee 005."

"What's that, like a blessing?"

"In a way. The Double O Section was born in World War Two as an intelligence commando unit that accompanied forward troops making an attack with the brief of capturing documents, ciphers, enemy gear—before it could all be destroyed. The first mission was Operation Sledgehammer. Agents were sent behind enemy lines with permission to kill in order to protect their mission. That makes us something of a curiosity today. Across MI6, all operators are protected under Section 7, which offers immunity to agents involved in bugging, bribery, murder, kidnap, and torture as long as their actions have been authorized in writing by a secretary of state. The difference is, we don't need individual permission. Our agents carry a license to kill at all times."

"Sounds more like a curse than a blessing." Luke's expression was somewhere between appreciation and comedy and pain. "I accept. I'm a born loser, like the man said, here for a scrap. But I can knock down, chew up, and spit out any man you like on my way down."

"That's what I want to hear. Only, this time, maybe you could rise up. Everything depends on 004 remaining out of Mora's hands. Do you understand, 005?"

"Yes, ma'am. Good luck."

"And you."

He winked. "Born with it."

Moneypenny used a shaking hand to rub her burnt arms. Maybe she backed the wrong horse when it came to Harthrop-Vane, but she wasn't a fool for believing all this time that Johanna Harwood would find Bond, and one day 007 would walk back through her door. That meant she wasn't a fool to place her faith in an addict who had fought for both sides, either. 005 would get the job done.

Her door groaned again.

Mora greeted her pleasantly. "Good morning, Miss Moneypenny. Where did you get the cream?" His hands closed on the tub. "Here. Let me do that for you."

If you're going to walk through my door, James, for God's sake, don't leave it too long. Moneypenny grabbed Mora's index finger with all her strength and pulled. It wouldn't snap.

Mora hissed: "Oh Miss Moneypenny. Redoubtable, dependable, Miss Moneypenny." His laughter was a death rattle. "We have surfaced to allow Luck and his team into the field. We picked up a message. It would appear 000 failed. Bond and Harwood remain free."

Your boy is loose, Moneypenny.

"I am most unhappy. Wouldn't you like to make me feel better?"

Your boy is loose, Moneypenny.

FIFTEEN

Bletchley

At the height of Bletchley Park's code breaking mission during the Second World War, nine thousand people worked on the estate, calculating the cribs and menus that would help the world's first computers crack the German Enigma code for analysts who would give dispatch riders intelligence that could save a fleet or stop an attack on a city. Each office in each hut in each section was a cell that operated without knowing what the neighboring cells were doing. Information was pushed by broom through chutes from one hut to another. Paper cascaded from violent pneumatic tubes. Phones were wired to call a twin on the far side of the compound. You might star in the Christmas play or bunk with the voice on the other end of that line, but you'd never discuss it, never ask, never tell. Loose lips sink ships. Careless talk costs lives. Keep calm and carry on.

Now a museum, Bletchley Park remained inscribed in the codes of the last century, the street sign for Sherwood Drive written in a modernist sans serif typeface. The clean and uncluttered lines of the low huts belonged to the same mid-century moment and the flaking window frames were still painted military green. By contrast, the Victorian mansion at the center of it all looked like an indigestible gingerbread house, possessing enough fairy-tale charm to pick up the past. It seemed you might hear the arguments between mathematicians, linguists, crossword setters, and chess champions once gathered here: the "odd bods" and "men of the professor type"; the chatter of typists and card punchers; you might meet the women who'd taken a first at Oxford in languages but were refused a diploma and equal pay, the secretly gay men, the refugees; you might feel the ache of Wrens who stood for twelve hours a day in a room as black, reeking, and noisy as hell, brushing and tweezing and cross-referencing these early whirring computers on which everything depended. The tennis court might yet echo with a rally. The pond might busy itself with lovers' boats. But today, the ghosts of the past had something other than broken codes, broken hearts, and broken bodies to reenact. A gigantic sign had been erected on the lawn reading EMERGING TECHNOLOGY AND SECURING INNOVATION SECURITY SUMMIT.

The repetition of *securing* and *security* seemed to call for an editor, in Joseph Dryden's view, but perhaps AI hadn't mastered *style* yet, or maybe it was deliberate overdetermination, because security was indeed everywhere. For 004, wearing a three-piece suit and polished dress shoes rather than a bulletproof vest and desert boots was still alien, and he felt the contrast all the more surrounded by uniformed and non-uniformed police, mounted patrol officers, and drone pilots monitoring the skies. As Acting Chief of the Double O Section, he was here as a delegate rather than protection. Still, he stood to the side of the ballroom, giving him a clear panorama from the stage—where Aisha and Ibrahim were delivering a talk on threats to innovation—to the audience, beginning with Five Eyes themselves, then government officials, business leaders, and academics, to the windows, through which he could trace the orbit of drones across a clear sky.

Ibrahim had detailed the promises and dangers of using artificial intelligence to manage the sheer volume of data produced by contemporary surveillance with his hands in his pockets and his attention fixed on the coved ceiling, his expression one of dismay at the oak and linenfold paneling. He wasn't made for daylight, Dryden thought, but Aisha made up for it, bright in a pink suit with matching nails. She picked up the baton with a quick breath, steadying herself. She glanced at Dryden.

He signed, "Smartest in the room."

She gave the slightest nod. "I want to end by reflecting on the achievements made here at Bletchley Park. There is a plaque in the entranceway with a quote from Shakespeare. It's from *Henry V*: *The King hath note of all that they intend by interception which they dream not of.* By cracking the Enigma machine, the code breakers at Bletchley Park intercepted German military plans and shortened the Second World War by *years*. Today, we live on a planet ringed by over seven thousand satellites, many of which will remain in geostationary orbit for billions of years after our extinction. The language of the Internet is misleadingly cozy. We talk about the 'cloud' and the public could be forgiven for looking up at those satellites and imagining a cloud of data floating up there with them. But the majority of the world's Internet runs through cables as thin as a hose along the ocean floor, with a handful of choke points where transoceanic cables converge and come ashore. Those satellites are the eyes of intelligence agencies and taps on those Internet cables are our ears."

Dryden watched M in the front row, who was batting his cane between his metal knees. The other four of the Five Eyes were trying to catch his attention, wondering where this was going, but he was ignoring them, waiting for Aisha to continue with an expression of grandfatherly tolerance.

Aisha said, "This meeting of the abstract and physical—metaphorical clouds and physical undersea cables—is akin to the contradictions of late modern warfare. When the abstract and open-ended War on Terror was first framed, many feared a forever war. The global militarization of our friends and allies"—America stiffened in his seat—"and the globalized nature of terror has created a world where violence can erupt anywhere, whether a field in Afghanistan, a home in Gaza, or the Underground in London. This has been dubbed *the everywhere war* and its hallmark is that we are always at war, but no one is certain whether to call it war or not. This extends to cyberspace, a perfect site for the everywhere war because the Internet is everywhere."

The press were stirring, sensing this was now very much off script.

"You've probably heard the story about the first message to be transmitted over the Internet. It was supposed to be 'login' but the system crashed after only two letters had been sent. So the first word sent over the Internet was 'lo.' As in *lo and behold*, the Internet isn't secure. The fault lines were there from the very beginning."

Nervous chuckles.

"Quickly in its development, the advanced surveillance and communication systems offered by the Internet became primary weapons and targets in modern warfare, with the prospect of 'switching cities off' now a real possibility. Civilian and military infrastructure, those very real cables under the sea, are in danger from a battlefield with no front. In cyberspace you are surrounded, as we are physically surrounded by the infrastructure of the Internet. We have gripped the planet in a vise of surveillance from the skies and the seas, allowing us to intercept threats to our safety. But the more we rely on this vise, the more we sacrifice human freedoms and decision-making, the more vulnerable we become to attack on a system we can't do without. We are capable of knowing everything about any person on any given day on this planet by methods which they dream not of. But *we* can dream it. We can create intelligence that surpasses our own. That means we can dream a different future, too, where these technologies are put toward creating a just, equitable, and livable future. One day, I'd love to stand up and give that speech. Thank you."

Dryden's applause was the loudest in the ballroom, though the academics did a good job making up for the slow clap of the spies. Lunch was served in the original canteen with a British favorites menu that drew polite grimaces. Afterward, the Five Eyes and government officials trooped onto the lawn, where group portraits would be taken. Dryden stood in the shadow of the mansion with M, watching the national press wrangle egos in height order.

"I suppose you gave permission for that postscript?" murmured M.

"Yes, sir," said Dryden, watching Aisha and Ibrahim huddle by the lake with the tech people from Silicon Valley.

"Very rousing."

"Yes, sir."

"This deadpan routine won't work on me, soldier."

"No, sir."

M chuckled. "You have your doubts about Panopticon?"

"Give me a target and point me at it, sir. I'm keeping Moneypenny's seat warm, that's all."

"You are in the unusual position as a Double O of having one living parent. Call me sentimental, but wouldn't it be nice if she didn't outlive you?"

"I don't have a death wish, sir."

"You don't?"

"No. I just know my life isn't worth more than my mission or my team."

"Spoken like a true Double O." He tapped his cane on the gravel. "And perhaps the last."

"We also have 003 and 007," said Dryden. "Until we're told otherwise."

M sighed. "It's the hope that kills, son."

"Not in my experience, sir."

"No?"

"No. It's the bullet that hits you . . ." Dryden looked from an Authorized Firearm Officer cradling a carbine assault rifle to mounted officers coming around the lake. Why had he said that? Something felt wrong, that's why. He watched the drones crisscrossing an invisible dome drawn by the pilots steering them from Hut 3, where Enigma messages intercepted from the German army and air force had been combed for clues. The drones were following a tight formation, apart from one. That was what had snagged Dryden's attention. A shadow out of place on the lawn. A single drone was passing over the lake toward them, sights aimed at Five Eyes and the government ministers now cracking awkward jokes about the everywhere war while juggling champagne and cake.

"Get them to the bunker," said Dryden.

M followed his gaze to the lone drone. Then he turned to the men wearing bulletproof vests and earpieces behind him and repeated Dryden's order.

"You too, sir," said Dryden, waiting to see M turn toward his protective detail before he strode through the Five Eyes and down the slope toward the lake, over which the drone was hovering. Dryden reached for the weapon in his shoulder holster—you can take a boy out of the army . . . There was a moment in which all the noise surrounding him dimmed as the message from security spread and the drone watched and waited. Dryden reached Aisha and Ibrahim and told them to get to the drone pilots and provide backup.

"Backup?" asked Ibrahim.

That's when the drone above started firing.

Dryden tackled Aisha to the ground, covering her body while tufts of grass and soil exploded around them and his hearing aid softened the sonic blows to his brain. Dryden reached out, grabbing Ibrahim's arm, but the younger man wriggled away, running toward a member of the catering team who had been hit and was already dead. A police officer covered Ibrahim, firing rapid rounds, and the drone responded.

"Get down!" shouted Dryden, rising—but he was too late. A round went through Ibrahim's shoulder.

Dryden saw a mounted officer hit ten feet away. His horse danced and screamed. Dryden scrambled to his feet, scooped up the machine gun, grabbed the reins, and hauled the horse around, swinging into the saddle and charging toward the lake. The horse splashed into the water, urged by the press of Dryden's heels as he leaned forward like a jouster and squeezed off round after round at the drone, which stopped its wild spray to twist and turn on him.

He waited for the drone to fire back, for bullets to cut through him like the clouds cutting through the blue sky. But the drone didn't fire. Dryden pushed the horse until he was nearly under the target, which was now spinning wildly, trying to defend itself against the police drones. Dryden hit the body. The rogue drone exploded over his head, a falling star that curtained him and the horse in diamonds.

He turned, searching the scene of panic and destruction. Aisha was holding Ibrahim in her arms. Her hands were bloody.

SIXTEEN

Going Dark

A daylight attack on Five Eyes by a police drone in full view of the press will provoke chaos and renewed efforts to find me and Rattenfänger using the powers of Panopticon, but we remain invisible beneath the ice shelf. Naturally, the drone is programmed to avoid Joseph Dryden, Aisha Asante, and Ibrahim Suleiman, vital components to our endgame, especially as we must rely on Q Branch to assess that the only way to hijack a police drone is to buy the code. I wonder if Dryden will reach that conclusion as quickly as Moneypenny would have. He doesn't really seem like the brains of the operation, more the brawn. I suppose you didn't want him for his mind, Luck. Ironic that it's his brain I need.

Aisha stood up as Dryden entered Q Branch. "Have you heard—"

"Ibrahim is still in surgery," said Dryden. "We won't know anything for another three to five hours, but the doctors think he might lose use of his arm. I know. The best thing we can do for him is find out who is responsible for this and bring them to justice."

"You mean kill them, right?"

Dryden smiled. "What happened to a livable and equitable future?"

"Don't test me," she said, sitting down and blowing out her cheeks.

"Yes, ma'am. What have you got?" Then he looked over at M, who entered leaning heavily on his stick.

"No injuries among Five Eyes," he said.

"That's what matters then," said Aisha.

M looked from Ibrahim's empty seat to the remnants of the drone laid out on the lab table. "You tell me what matters, Dr. Asante."

She wiped her nose. "Yes, sir. The police discovered a relay transmitter on the rooftop of a derelict building beyond the fence, which would allow the enemy to pilot remotely."

"From how far?" asked Dryden.

"Could be the other side of the world. The simplest way to hack a drone is to jam the original radio control source and pretend to be the source yourself with a stronger signal, right? But jamming the signal only works for off-the-shelf products. For a secured police drone, you would need the code the drone expects to receive with its instructions."

Dryden turned to M. "Inside job?"

M's brow wrinkled. "Humans are always the weakest link."

"It depends who's doing the programming," commented Aisha.

"On machine or man?" asked M.

"Both," said Aisha. "We should look at the company that services the drones."

Dryden nudged the drone. "Find me that weakest link."

And it will be a matter of moments for Q to discover the bribed technician and follow the money to Segovia. M will wish to send a local team, but Joseph Dryden will think this is all too easy. He will have suspicions. And he will not want to send anyone else into harm's way. After all, he's a hero.

Q crunched the bank accounts and social media of employees at the company subcontracted by the UK government to service police drones and produced the weakest link: a man deep in gambling debts with a lump sum in his current account. Almost too easy, Dryden said. Not everyone's a criminal mastermind, said Aisha. The transfer originated from a lawyer in Segovia, a Castilian mountain town. M said he would dispatch S Station but Dryden didn't like the smell of it, any of it. So Phoebe Taylor booked him on the next flight, and that evening Dryden drove a Land Rover Classic Defender V8 through the arcade of the Roman aqueduct that soared over Plaza del Azoguejo. When his brown Palladium leather boots hit the stone, the warmth of the Mediterranean evening immediately suckered his pink shirt and tan chinos to his skin. Dryden craned up at the aqueduct, two rows of arches constructed from unmortared granite blocks stringing together mountains on either side in an extraordinary balancing act.

004 will be directed to the home of a prominent lawyer. Now, this is important, so listen carefully, Luck. The house is built into a shelf of the mountainside. To the left as you exit the house is a sheer cliff. To the right is a drop into the valley. Our forces will come from either side, rappelling down the cliff, and climbing the valley. The garden will be a shooting gallery.

As "a new client with a large deposit," Dryden was directed to the home of the senior partner, a former ducal residence. He followed cobbled streets that sloped to a fortified door surrounded by carved stone detailing the pain of saints and martyrs. Dryden rang a brass bell. The lawyer was expecting a new client, and he heard footsteps immediately. A maid answered.

He stepped into an open-roofed courtyard with Moorish tiles and a well. Passing, he saw pennies at the bottom, spent wishes. He followed the maid through columns to a stairwell painted with gold leaf, entering a parlor where every wall was packed with paintings. He thought he spotted a Picasso but there was no time to check because he was ushered out of doors and into a garden, where a terrace overlooked a tree-lined verdigris green pool.

The lawyer unfolded from a seat behind a table where two glasses waited beside a sweating champagne bucket. Dryden extended a hand but the man simply walked past him and into the house. That's when Dryden noticed a body slicing through the pool.

You are bait. You won't mind my being blunt, Luck. 004 has proven a challenging opponent in the past. We want him distracted. He either loves you or hates you. Either way, he'll want to fuck you.

Dryden stepped to the iron balustrade, his hand creeping to his gun, but he stopped mid-motion when Luke Luck climbed out nude, tucking a towel around his dripping body as he took the steps to the terrace. Dryden was rooted to the spot, watching as Luke poured them both a glass of champagne. He smelled of copper and minerals, ancient history. As Dryden accepted the flute, Luke brushed a kiss against his cheek and took the gun from the holster, setting it on the table.

"Miss me?"

You have no idea—did Dryden say that aloud?

"I know you'll have a lot of questions," said Luke, taking a sip and then setting the crystal down with an extended note. "I had to take my chance and get out of that hellhole, Joe, but I was never with Mora or any of those bastards."

Dryden found his voice. "Is that right?"

"I guess I've caused you a lot of stress," said Luke with his shit-eater grin.

"You could say that."

Luke's hand drifted to Dryden's belt buckle. "I look forward to making it up to you."

Dryden let Luke's fingers move, studying every part of him, until he saw the glint of the earpiece in Luke's ear. He scanned the terra-cotta rooftops for the ambush, but there was not a single shadow out of place.

Disconnect him from Q Branch as quickly as possible.

"Are we alone?" asked Dryden. Sunshine poured through Luke's blond hair and sparkled on his wet skin, threatening to blind him.

"Are you asking me or Q Branch?" asked Luke, brushing his lips over Dryden's right ear.

"Both," said Dryden thickly.

Aisha's voice appeared in Dryden's mind, a strange intrusion as his heart hammered: "Nothing on satellite, we're searching."

Luke's hand splayed over Dryden's chest. "I hear you got your heart broke."

Dryden was about to snatch Luke's wrist when the man's fingers formed a circle over Dryden's heart very deliberately. *O.* Then another. *O.* Then he extended all four fingers and his thumb. *5.*

005.

Luke crooked his finger and tapped on his own chest. The communication was trapped between their bodies, hidden from overwatch or listening ears.

Dryden dared to smile.

"I perform better without an audience," said Luke aloud, tapping Dryden's Garmin MARQ Commander watch. "That's how you turn off the voices in your head, right, mate?"

Dryden nodded. "Going dark," he said, and Aisha's protest was cut off. He ran his hands down Luke's sides, where the flesh goose-pimpled at his touch. He tugged at the towel as Luke pulled at his shirt.

In the tangle, Luke signed against Dryden's stomach: "Moneypenny at stake."

Dryden allowed himself to be guided toward a sun lounger. He lay down, pulling Luke after him, scanning the trees, the drop over the terrace into the valley, the mountainside with the fairytale castle. Luke unbuttoned Dryden's shirt, and as his lips traveled down Dryden's chest, his hands signed rapidly against Dryden's twitching thigh: "Ambush. Exfil now."

Dryden grunted. He tangled his fingers in Luke's short hair and pulled him upright. "You want to make things up to me? Put some clothes on. I perform better without an audience, too. I'm booked at the Hotel Real."

"If you say so, boss," said Luke with a wink, reaching for a pair of jeans folded on a chair.

Keep him in the garden, keep him busy, keep him disarmed.

Dryden tried to calm his pulse as he stood up, reaching for his gun. Luke was studying the mangled scar tissue over his heart. He closed his shirt. But Luke's eyes widened. Dryden glanced down. There was a red bead playing over his chest. Luke seized him in a kiss and turned them both around. The sound of impact was a sound Dryden had heard a thousand times in Afghanistan.

We will use a sedative. It is imperative he remain alive.

But blood wasn't bubbling at Luke's lips or slugging from his chest. Dryden held him up, checking his back. It was a dart.

Poison?

Luke's hands were reaching for something—reaching for words. He spelled out letter by letter as his eyes slipped out of focus: Z-O-F-I-A-N-O-W-A-K. Sweat soaked his face.

"Hang on," said Dryden. "Wait, wait . . ."

Luke shook himself, as if trying to throw off a great weight. He struggled onto one elbow, reaching for the gun in Dryden's hand. He croaked, "Find . . . find . . ." Then he sat up and pushed Dryden aside, firing every round in the chamber. Dryden looked around, seeing a man in full tactical gear and a black balaclava dance with bullets. As he jerked, the man's index finger found the trigger of the weapon in his hands, and bullets shredded the champagne bucket in an explosion of ice. Blood spattered Dryden. He looked down at Luke, who clutched his guts with a look of surprise.

"No," said Dryden. "No."

"Don't go," Luck breathed. "You have to listen to me, you can't go . . ."

But another two men were rappelling down the hillside into the garden. Dryden rolled, scooped up the M16, and fired, clipping one, but before he could take aim again another man climbed over the wall and landed in the garden. Dryden got Luke in a fireman's hold, feeling the heat of blood on his back, and jumped onto the table, climbing the ivy to reach the rooftop, clattering over the tiles. A bullet whipped past his leg. They weren't aiming for his head. Dryden slid down a roof, stopping himself and Luke just in time. The street was five stories below. The next rooftop was a jump away. He couldn't make it with Luke.

Dryden carried him to a stack of chimneys and laid him in the dust. "Wait here." Luke was grasping his stomach, which was rising and falling sharply, blood spilling from his fingers. "I'll send help. *Wait for me.*"

Dryden took a look back at his pursuers—five men—and to the edge of the roof. He jumped.

Suspended in the air between heartbeats, he hit the other side with a groan, hauled himself up, and carried on running. He kept leaping toward the aqueduct.

He fumbled with his watch. "I need medical help to the rooftops, find Luke on overwatch, gunshot to the guts."

"Are you OK?" asked Aisha. "Your heart rate—"

"Get help to Luke!"

"On it," said Aisha. "Dryden, listen—Q combed through the drone's programming and it was programmed to miss you, me, and Ibrahim. They want us alive, I don't know why. But Five Eyes are asking questions about you and your link to Luke and Rattenfänger. Now it looks like you planned this with Luke."

"What?"

"Five Eyes want you to come in. They've ordered Q Branch to enter lockdown. There are orders to detain you."

M's wilderness of mirrors. If 000 was a double agent, so were the rest of them. No one could be trusted. Well, that cut both ways.

"I'm not in the mood," snapped Dryden. "Find me Zofia Nowak."

"Nowak?"

He hurdled onto the town wall, clambering up the steps to the Roman aqueduct until he was at the very top, almost losing his balance as the clouds above and the buildings below seemed to swap places and his heart kicked. But he wasn't alone. The wet team pursued him into the gulley where water had run for thousands of years. It was twilight, and tourists below posed for selfies as pops of light far above illustrated the firefight.

Of course, the team may find it necessary to maim 004.

Dryden looked over the edge. He eased a toe into the air, checking his six, and jumped as the oncoming man fired. Dryden twisted in the air, throwing out an arm and catching the granite block, hugging the column, then scaling down and dropping into the arch. He tried to catch his breath, but his chest was constricting.

But he isn't at full strength. His heart, poor thing.

He heard a scuffle above as a man climbed down—Dryden reached out, grabbed his ankle, and yanked, hauling the assailant into the air. He fell to the square below with a thud. Dryden heard screams and watched the crowds outside the restaurants scatter. Another whisper of grit, this time from both sides of the arch, and two men appeared to Dryden's left and right, trying to find space with him on the blocks. He raised his left arm, knocking the man's gun out of position, and jabbed with his right elbow, catching the other in the chest and then shouldering him into space. Another scream. Dryden twisted, headbutting the visor of his new friend, which shattered. Dryden wrestled the man for the gun, using the strap to wind him up, choking him until the man dropped to his knees and Dryden could kick him off the edge, snatching the gun.

Everything depends on seizing him. I will not accept failure.

But then a hand covered his mouth with something that stank and Dryden almost vomited, the oxygen in his lungs suddenly burning. He staggered to the edge—if he had to go over with the attacker he would. But the man held on to him, as if trying to save his life and render him unconscious at the same time. Sirens filled the plaza but the sound was growing distant. His heart was bursting.

I understand a lot of water has flowed under the bridge between the two of you. He swam and left you to drown. This is your chance to pay him back for that, Luck.

The hand disappeared. Dryden almost fell but grabbed onto the column in time. He turned. There was a bullet in the man's skull. Dryden looked to the landscape of roofs, finding the form of Luke Luck luminescent, prone over a rifle he had just used to save Dryden's life, where his head now sank.

SEVENTEEN

Desconocido

"Are you happy? Have we treated you well?" The same questions might be asked by a concierge or a hostage taker. Here, the voice came from a man holding an iPhone, which he pointed at migrants daring to cross the Darién Gap, ten thousand square miles of choked, mountainous rainforest and marshland strangling the border of Panama and Colombia. The Darién Gap was not officially a war zone. Officially, it was the "controlled flow of migration." But there were more sexual assaults on migrants here than assaults on women in occupied zones, and municipal workers in white hazmat suits resorted to mass graves for the bodies the jungle didn't swallow. The body bags were labeled DESCONOCIDO, *unknown*. The dead came from South Asia, the Middle East, Africa, and the Caribbean, families who paid cartels to take them to America. Every time America made migration harder, the cartels profited. They filmed people on day one of the journey across the Gap, when they were still optimistic. "Are you happy? Have we treated you well?" The videos appeared on YouTube and TikTok, luring more people to risk the journey.

Aisha Asante tasked Q to search the videos for Dr. Zofia Nowak.

Luke Luck was comatose in a hospital in Spain with a discreet guard. Ibrahim Suleiman was recovering from surgery at Shrublands. Q Branch was in lockdown. That left Aisha alone—and unmonitored. Dryden had refused the order to come in. He was technically AWOL, though Aisha still felt tethered to him, following his order to find Dr. Zofia Nowak, the one person in her field Aisha considered her equal.

After the Double O Section had rescued Dr. Nowak in Syria, Felix Leiter housed her in a California desert military base that legally couldn't exist because it sat on Native land, as America explained to Aisha, and as a place that didn't exist, the base couldn't commit crimes like forcing workers to burn highly classified and toxic materials used for radar-absorbent coatings on stealth airplanes in open pits, and therefore no case could be brought against them, and the Shoshone Indians couldn't challenge the US occupation of their territory—because, once again, the base doesn't exist, got it? But if it *did* exist, America allowed, Dr. Nowak had been in witness protection there under Felix Leiter's supervision. Why do you want to know? Oh, just wondering . . .

The idea of witness protection was to provide the subject with a comfortable environment where they could blend in and find employment. Dr. Nowak was given certain "puzzles" by the US government to keep her busy. As long as the puzzles were in the line of solving the climate crisis or keeping a pandemic at bay, rather than hacking foreign powers or protesters, it seemed to suit her. She kept hellebores in the garden, a favorite of her grandmother's, whom she could have no contact with now. Her only contact was Felix Leiter. At least, that had been true before Leiter agreed to join Conrad Harthrop-Vane's hunt for Trigger. As it would turn out, that hunt was really 000 searching for himself in the jungle, like so many gap year kids before him. And he'd left Leiter there. Officially he was listed as MIA. Unofficially, America said they considered him KIA.

America admitted it had, let's say, *misplaced* Zofia Nowak shortly after Felix's disappearance. The last trace on her server showed her trawling satellite footage of the Darién Gap, Felix's last known location. But Zofia didn't have Panopticon. Working under the theory that Zofia might have gone physically looking for Felix, Aisha had tasked Q with scouring data from Panopticon, raking through any social media video, CCTV footage, and satellite images around. Though Panopticon couldn't find Felix, it did give her footage of Zofia working her way south from California, snatched from ATM and doorbell cameras, bus shelter tapes, and now a TikTok short taken on a boat in the Darién Gap.

"Are you happy? Have we treated you well?"

Behind the smiling mother clutching her toddler on a rocking motorized canoe, Zofia Nowak hunched over her rucksack.

"I've got her!" Aisha stood up. She stabbed the comms button on her desk. "Dryden, we've got her. Last known coordinates . . ."

Dryden was resting on a stump in a campsite that consisted of hammocks stretched between trees like ligaments, a tarp shading firepits, and a rainbow tapestry on the dirt floor, sewn from shredded tents and discarded clothes, trodden into the earth by 100,000 people across a year. He heard Aisha's words, rubbed his face, and drew his burner phone from his pocket, bringing up the map. Around him, people sat dazed, hugging each other or broken limbs, trying to find privacy among the bucket showers and toilets, or counting out the last of their money to pay two dollars to use the Wi-Fi hotspot so they could ask relatives to send more money, allowing them to buy the chicken and rice cooking in blackened pots or pay for a porter to carry a relative who had fallen on the rocks. Zofia's last known position was another half-day trek.

"Take me off Q's radar," he told Aisha. "M's right, this is a wilderness of mirrors. We don't know who we can trust, who set me up in Segovia. This must be an inside job. I won't sit in a sweatbox while this threat is out there. I'm going to find Zofia Nowak and get answers. Going dark."

"Be safe," she said.

"You too."

He tapped his watch, ending comms. The ensuing silence was like ducking under the sea and then finding a wave rolling overhead: he didn't know which way was up. The truth was he needed Q Branch far more than Q needed him. Next to him, Dryden's Indigenous guide watched him carefully. He was a teenager with bullet wounds starring his bare chest, courtesy of the Panama border guards. Dryden was traveling in the wrong direction, as Zofia had done, seeking to penetrate deeper into the rainforest instead of escape it. This put him in the same category as explorers, engineers, missionaries, colonialists, and orchid hunters, all of whom had been beaten by the isthmus, which had also beaten the Pan-American Highway in the 1930s, the one gap in a road that stretched from Alaska to Argentina. About a decade ago, guerrillas killed a Swedish tourist they suspected of being a spy, and Dryden wondered if his guide was turning this idea over in his mind as Dryden pointed on the map. But the guide gave a philosophical shrug, as if to say, *Die where you wish*.

Dryden got to his feet. He rummaged in his pockets for dollars and pressed them on a woman nursing a silent baby. She stared at him, then hid them under the baby's blanket, burying her face in the baby's neck.

Dusk was coming. Slick branches sucked at Dryden's clothes and mud pulled on his boots. He could hardly see the path. He was walking in the steps of jaguars. They came to a ravine, where a tennis shoe and torn clothing and roll mats littered the edge. Red ropes clung to the rocks, navigating a way down. The guide turned to Dryden and asked a question. It wasn't *Are you happy?*

"I'll go alone," said Dryden. "Thank you." He pressed money into the boy's hands.

One step forward. Two steps. Three . . . Dryden let his body carry him, listening to the chatter and screams of the jungle and the roar of the water below, as he climbed down the ravine, his fingers biting the rocks, following the frayed rope that marked out safe passage. One step forward. Two steps. Three . . . If he were to fall into the river from this height it would be like hitting concrete. It's not the fall that kills you.

Once he'd descended midway, he edged onto a plateau where a tree trunk bridged to the other side. He thought there was no way it could bear his weight, but when he looked across he saw a man carrying two children across the makeshift bridge. Dryden put his hands out, waiting and willing. He called out that he was there so that the man wouldn't flinch when he finally glimpsed him in the half-light. Dryden accepted the toddler and five-year-old girl, setting them on firm earth. The man clapped him on the arm and continued as if this were a normal meeting. Maybe here it was. Dryden stepped into nothingness and edged across the ravine.

Ascending, he found coverage once again—he was nearing another Wi-Fi hotspot. Landmarks that had been whispered secrets were now on Google Maps. He was approaching the camp. This one was an actual compound with high earth walls and a tiny airstrip, where a flying shoebox rusted. Dryden settled into the undergrowth and watched as the gates opened and closed for migrants. The guard shouted they should have their money ready, it would speed up entry. As a large group gathered, Dryden got a good look inside. Huts, a kitchen, wooden platforms with showers and toilets. And in the center of it all, a bamboo cage. The gates to the compound closed before he could see what, or who, was inside. He would wait until nightfall.

The rainforest crowded the compound, wanting to reclaim the space. Dryden hauled himself into a tree, praying that its occupants would think he was a big cat as he crept onto a heavy branch that sagged over the wall. He didn't sleep. He didn't dare, listening to the rustle and calls of creatures he couldn't identify.

From here, he could see men gathered around a few fires; a mud building with barred windows; a large, deep pit, which was empty, whose purpose he couldn't fathom; and people sleeping under tarps. There were two figures in the bamboo cage, and no one slept anywhere near it. Every young man was carrying a gun.

The canopy was finally louder than the drunken laughter. Dryden slithered down the branch, dropping softly to the earth. He walked on the balls of his feet, moving from shadow to shadow. Behind a shower rigged from the trees, Dryden dropped to a crouch. He had a good look at the cage now. Fires painted the bars in orange and blue. Inside, a man lay on the dirt floor, running his left hand through his straw-colored mop of hair. They'd taken away his prosthetics, leaving him without a leg beneath the left knee and no right hand. It was Felix Leiter. Dryden closed his fist in quiet victory. Next to Leiter, a woman stood, rattling the bars, shouting. It wasn't Zofia Nowak.

EIGHTEEN

The Pit

Joseph Dryden willed his hearing aid to amplify the voices inside the cage over the babble of the rainforest and the low murmurs of migrants and cackles of the cartel soldiers. The woman was shouting that they'd made a mistake and Rattenfänger would give them hell to pay for it. There were three armed guards in front of the cage, who gave each other nervous looks, edging away. It seemed to Dryden they wanted distance from the woman, who similarly paced as far from Leiter as the cage allowed, as if desperate to categorize herself differently.

She called: "Rattenfänger will kill you for this."

One man spat over his shoulder, "You shouldn't have tried to help the American spy to escape!"

"I didn't!"

"That's not what he said."

Leiter looked half-starved. She didn't. She was tall, with long, straight hair, which fell to her mid-back and shone like molten gold. In profile, she was pale and beautiful, if you went for that sort of thing.

Dryden thought of Luke's blond hair matted with dirt and blood, his blue eyes drugged and panicked. She shook the bars. Dryden realized her left hand was missing a trigger and middle finger. So this was Trigger, the assassin 000 had used as cover, blaming her for his kills. James Bond had been ordered to eliminate her once, orders he bucked because he did go for that sort of thing. When Bond realized the cellist he'd been idly watching through a sniper scope while waiting to kill an assassin was the very assassin he was tasked to take out, he aimed for her left hand instead of her heart. It was the end of her days as a cellist and a sniper. She faced court-martial for failure in Russia and fled.

The CIA said Leiter had followed Conrad Harthrop-Vane into the Gap because a crook in Tangier told him Rattenfänger sent radio messages for Trigger to Panama, where another crook told Leiter the sniper who nearly took out his heart lived in the Gap. He thought that if he found her, he'd get his hands on an essential component of the Rattenfänger apparatus, bringing him one step closer to finding Bond.

Trigger gave up rattling the cage and turned on Leiter. Dryden's hearing aid brought their hushed voices to him as if on the wind.

Trigger said, "Tell me why I haven't killed you yet."

Felix Leiter said, "My winning personality."

"Don't flatter yourself."

Leiter raised himself on his elbow. "Hey, *you're* the one playing friendly neighborhood assassin to the cartel, I'm just their prisoner. I asked for your help the honest way. I told you there was a psychotic British agent using your code name to pick off Double O agents, muddying your reputation and drawing Russia's attention to you."

"You know nothing at all about Russia."

"I'm a CIA agent, I could give you any level of protection you want. Suburbia instead of life in a jungle with killers."

She sneered. "You know nothing at all about women."

"I know you were content to leave me to rot in a cage without an arm and a leg and hardly enough food to survive. You were content to let them lure Zofia Nowak to this compound and then hand her off to villains."

Dryden cursed inwardly. He looked around for a way to get Leiter out. There were fifty armed men between them and the gate.

Leiter was still talking. "I don't run as fast as I once did, and that jungle was no limp in the park. So when I managed to escape they caught up to me, and I told these gentlemen we're in cahoots. Now we're in this godforsaken jam together and cahoots it is, honey. I'm a former marine, a CIA agent, and a Station Chief. You want to get out of here? Let's lend each other a hand."

"Can't make it alone, Mr. CIA?"

"I *could*," he said, "but I'm not alone, and neither are you. So as long as I'm breathin' and you're breathin', honey, how about a little détente? On such treaties kingdoms were made."

Dryden heard her teeth grind. She said, "I had a kingdom. Your friend exiled me from it, and then you exiled me from my Elba."

"I'll be sorry tomorrow, promise."

She shook her head. "You know nothing at all about the jungle. I've lived in it since a British Double O took my hand off."

"I lost mine for the same man. 007. He's my friend and he's missing."

"And now so are you."

"I ain't missin'," said Leiter. "I know exactly where I am."

Another shake of the head. "You know nothing at all. The biopirates are going to feed you to the snake, and I'll enjoy watching every second."

"Shucks, darlin', I didn't know you cared."

Dryden looked around. Biopirates meant flora and fauna smugglers, but he didn't see any snakes, and he didn't want to. The three guards were facing the gate, the only way into the compound. He crawled forward, nostrils filling with rot, edging to the rear of the cage. The bamboo was thicker than his thigh and the gap between the bars would only admit his hand. But the cage was on a dirt floor.

"Leiter," whispered Dryden.

Trigger turned sharply, looking from Dryden in the shadows to the guards. Leiter stiffened, then stretched, turning languidly. The sharpness of his chin and cheekbones gave the impression of a cowboy on the edge of consumption. He shuffled closer, rubbing his leg as if in pain.

Dryden put his fingers through the bars. "004."

Leiter smiled and seized what he could of his hand. "Glad to know you, pal, you don't know how glad. Where's the cavalry?"

"I am the cavalry."

Leiter eyed him. "Well, you're built like a tank, God's own armored charge, so maybe you'll do. What's the plan?"

Trigger watched them, arms crossed over her chest.

"The bamboo is too thick to cut but it's driven into the ground. I think I can dig under it, then push it in, and you can squeeze out. There's a plane on a short runway outside the compound. Quick, clean, quiet."

Leiter nodded. Dryden pulled a knife from his boot, and another from his belt, passing one through to Leiter. Trigger leaned her shoulder against the bamboo. Dryden didn't like the look on her face. He started digging.

Leiter turned to Trigger, murmuring, "Wanna help? Between you and me we got two good hands. We get out of here, we can put them together and clap."

"Let's not," said Trigger, turning to the guards and raising her voice. "There's a British spy here! They're trying to escape!"

The sleepiness of the compound was shaken instantly, the guards wheeling around, the cartel soldiers leaping up from the fires, the civilians scattering to the edges.

Quick and dirty it was.

Dryden got to his feet, told Leiter to shield himself, drew his gun, and fired at the bamboo until it shattered. Then Joe "Door-Kicker" Dryden did what he was famous for in Afghanistan and kicked the rest in, grabbing Leiter under the arms and dragging him out. But then a weapon pressed into the back of Dryden's head. That meant there was a hand close enough to grab, which Leiter did, throwing the cartel soldier off-balance. It was a scrappy fight in the dirt and it couldn't last, a gang pulling Dryden one way and hauling Leiter another. The only satisfaction was seeing Trigger kicked to her knees, three men covering her with old rifles. They were scared of her, but they weren't convinced as she protested she had just proved her loyalty.

Dryden gasped as someone kicked him in the ribs, knocking him to the ground, smashing his watch, and then there were too many legs to count and Dryden just rolled with it, trying to protect his head. He could turn the neural link to Q back on with a voice command, but what good would it do? Call in an air strike on a compound full of civilians? And the CIA would just detain him anyway. Moneypenny needed him. He had to find Zofia Nowak. That was his last thought before someone stamped on his head.

When Dryden came to consciousness, he was lying with his arms and legs bound on the floor of the cage, Leiter beside him in the same condition, and Trigger kneeling with hands behind her head. She was staring at him with hatred. There were four men inside the cage with them, arguing. The door was open. The sky was light.

"We should tell Rattenfänger," said one of the men.

"You want more demands from them? We gave them the scientist. A CIA agent and a British spy, we can sell them for a lot."

"They'll find out. They know everything."

"They saddled us with Trigger in the first place. They're too much trouble."

Trigger said, "I've lived here among you as a friend!"

The man nearest smacked her. Instead of going down she used the rebound to pop up and twist, slamming her elbow into his nose and breaking it. The man screamed, blood spraying everywhere. Well, Dryden could respect that, but it didn't do much good, as another man stepped forward and clubbed her to the floor, before panting: "We should just kill them all."

"Let's have some fun at least. The pit."

There was a pause, a shared smile, as this idea circulated.

"But we can't film it this time. They'd see."

"Fine. Some fun for us. I bet the British spy lasts longest."

"How long?"

"Him? Three minutes."

"Three minutes? You're crazy!"

The bets came thick and fast. Trigger was arguing with everything she had but it wasn't working.

Dryden turned to Leiter, using his shoulder to nudge him. "What's the pit?"

Leiter spat blood before saying: "Snake pit. Ain't you glad you came to my rescue?"

"I'm looking for Zofia Nowak."

"She came looking for me. I coulda cried. They turned her over to Rattenfänger. There was nothing I could do, but brother, I tried."

"Do you know where Rattenfänger would take her?"

Leiter shook his head. "I'm real sorry, pal."

There was a commotion in the compound, people cheering and battling to get a good view around the pit, others wanting to leave, massing by the gates. The door to the hut opened. Two men emerged, carrying a basket.

Dryden said, "Have you seen them do this?"

"To an informant."

"How many snakes?"

"Just the one," said Leiter, "but one is all it takes. A golden lancehead pit viper. The biopirates brought it from Snake Island. Rumor says sixteenth-century pirates introduced it to the island to guard their gold. Scientists say rising sea levels after the last ice age cut the island off, triggering a separate evolutionary branch. The snakes are the only population. No predators, no ground-level prey, the snakes took to the trees and developed an even faster-acting venom to instantly kill migratory birds that stop to rest in the canopy. The island is prohibited territory apart from scientists guarded by marines. But the biopirates risk it anyway, for the black market value. If that snake bites you, your internal organs melt inside a minute."

Leiter grunted as the guard above him kicked him in the back.

"Any weaknesses?" asked Dryden.

Leiter shook his head.

Dryden clicked his neck this way and that. "These snakes are rare? Monitored by scientists?"

"Sure."

"Are they biochipped?"

"I'd guess so. They're an endangered species, only exist on that island."

"Do you know if the biopirates take the chip out?"

"I doubt it, no one wants to even touch the thing."

He was right: the cartel soldiers were using long grabbers to take the viper out of the basket and drop it into the pit, the meter-long animal thrashing and hissing.

Leiter looked at him. "Tell me you got some clever Q gadget, some snake repellent spray, up your sleeve."

"Not exactly," said Dryden.

There was no time to say anything more because two cartel soldiers hauled Dryden to his feet and dragged him, fighting, from the cage toward the pit. Leiter and Trigger were pulled after him. The cartel lined them up near the edge. The pit was six feet deep and six feet square. The snake was circling, staring up at the people ranged around the edge shouting and wagering folds of money.

"Her first!" someone shouted.

Trigger dug her heels in as two men drove her toward the pit. She was using her elbows, knees, teeth, anything to slow them down, but there were only a few inches to cross.

"Wait!" called Leiter. "She ain't with me! I lied!" There were jeers: no one believed him. "I'll go first!"

Trigger stared at him as she strained with every muscle to keep herself upright.

Leiter shrugged. "I'm from Texas. I ain't afraid of snakes."

"I'll do it," said Dryden quickly. "I'll make you a bet. I'll last five minutes. If I do, we live."

The man nearest to him laughed. "Five minutes?"

"That's a guarantee."

The volume increased as new bets were placed on this loco spy's bravado.

"All right, five minutes, we pull you out, and you all live. For today. Tomorrow, we do the same thing. And the next day. There isn't much fun in the jungle."

Dryden nodded. "Give me a weapon."

"Now he wants new terms."

Laughter and boos.

"A rock. Come on. Where's the fun if I die inside thirty seconds? You'll lose your bet. You bet three minutes."

The man sucked his teeth. "Give him a rock."

Dryden's binds were cut, and a rock was dumped at his feet. He picked it up, facing the pit, and drew the sweet heat of the jungle into his chest, expanding his stomach, the oxygen easing through his autonomic nervous system. He took a step and looked over. The snake fixed on him, body shimmering and twitching, ridged eyes narrowed to slits, tongue probing and tasting.

"Calling home," said Dryden softly. They were the key words needed to reawaken the link. Someone shoved him. What if Aisha wasn't on station? "Calling home," he said again as his toes edged over the side of the pit. What if she'd severed the comms because Fives Eyes were pressuring her for his location? Dryden sat down, as if he were about to slip into a pool. His own Snake Island. "*Calling home.*"

He jumped, landing with a jolt that went through his body. The snake reared backward, coiling like a spring, head following him like a mirror. Dryden raised the rock. "Aisha? Are you there?" This close, he could see every tan cell slithering as if independently, dragging its heavy muscle over the dirt. Was it his imagination or were the fangs glistening? Sweat stung Dryden's eyes. Above, men were screaming and hooting.

The viper lunged. Dryden stepped back smartly, lashing out with the rock, and the snake backed off a little.

"Thirty seconds gone!" someone called.

That was it, thirty seconds? The snake came again and Dryden's back hit the earthen wall of his grave as he swiped with the rock, catching a glancing blow on the body, which was surprisingly firm. But it didn't make a difference, the viper springing forward, head going right for his jugular. Dryden smashed the thing with the rock, sending it flying. He backed into the corner. He could hear Leiter pleading but didn't spare him a glance, keeping his gaze locked on the snake's beady eyes. It was bleeding.

Great, you've made it mad.

"Calling home!" barked Dryden.

"Dryden? Can you hear me? I don't think the signal is getting through the canopy—"

He could have cried. "I'm facing a golden lancehead viper. I think it's biochipped. Can you do something with my hearing aid?"

Nothing. Maybe his signal hadn't reached her. The snake was coming at him low now, eyeing his ankles. Above, someone shouted that it had been a minute. The snake darted and Dryden dropped, pinning the thing beneath one knee, but it was worming and beating, head lashing at him, venom flying. Dryden averted his face as he tried to bring the rock down but it squirmed away. He held up his arms.

Then Aisha's voice found him, calm and steady. "A biochip reacts to radio waves. I'm commanding your neural interface to send a signal that will fry it, conducting electricity through its nervous system. It will be disoriented for ten seconds. *Now.*"

Dryden dropped his guard. The snake began sputtering like it was boiling from the inside out. He moved to the tail, trying to avoid the gyrating head and flying venom, took the rock in both hands, and fell to the floor, pounding and pounding at the middle of the body, until the spine broke, and the snake slumped.

He sank back. His hands were wet.

"Dryden? Dryden?"—it was Aisha.

Dryden looked at his palms, waiting to feel the venom. At least it would only take a minute. Above him, men were celebrating wildly, as if he were one of their own. He'd slain the monster. Dryden smiled, wiping his face—the wetness got onto his cheek. It was blood. It was just blood.

"I'm all right," he panted. He looked at the broken snake. "Thanks, little sis. I've got Leiter but Nowak isn't in sight."

"Are you out of danger?"

Dryden looked up at the baying men. Out of the frying pan and into the fire. "Go dark. No traces."

A rope was thrown down to him.

"Dryden, isn't it better to be detained than—"

He got to his feet unsteadily, still clutching the rock as he murmured, "There's a traitor in Five Eyes, has to be. They detain me, they'll kill me. Moneypenny needs me. I have to find Nowak. Look after yourself."

"You too, big brother."

Dryden took the rope and climbed out, falling on top of the rock as if he were totally exhausted—which he was. A hand went to his shoulder. Dryden turned and swung, clubbing the cartel soldier around the head. There was shouting, threats to shoot Leiter, chaos as people tried to collect bets and others tried to clear the space and get a shot at him as he ranged around with the rock like a madman.

Then gunfire sprayed the circle. Dryden looked back. Trigger had used the chaos to get free and was unloading a clip into the cartel. She grabbed Leiter under the arm and helped him run. Dryden picked up a fallen gun and followed, sprinting across the earth. He bumped into a boy with a gun, who tried to keep ahold of him, but Dryden set the kid aside and hurtled through the gates. Gunfire followed. Leiter was winged, a bullet slicing through his side, but Trigger kept him upright, and then staggered herself, a bullet finding her thigh.

Fifty paces to the plane. Dryden wrenched the door open and squeezed into the cockpit. The runway was shorter than any he'd ever seen and he wasn't a pilot. Trigger was helping Leiter into the body of the plane.

"Why'd you do that, darlin'?"

"Because you might be the only thing in this jungle that's just semi-toxic," she said, checking his wound. Dryden told her to stanch the bleeding from her thigh but she ignored him.

"I knew I'd charm you eventually," said Leiter raggedly.

"You know nothing about women," she said.

"Maybe you know nothing about men," he said. "Real men, anyway."

"And you're a real man?"

"Every last remaining inch o' me, honey."

Dryden gunned the engine and barreled toward a wall of trees, which were shredded by gunfire, bullets thumping into the body of the plane—and then they were airborne, beating through the branches until he could reach out and grab the stars.

NINETEEN

Cotton Burning

As far as five time zones from Moscow, and the same size as Germany, Buryatia had one of the highest concentrations of military bases in Russia. The population was one million, about half indigenous Buryats. Their language was endangered. So were their people, forced to bear the brunt of conscription. Soon, Ukrainian spies would blow up a train inside Severomuysky Tunnel carrying aviation fuel on the railway linking Buryatia to China and North Korea. Following the sabotage, Russian authorities will order trains to pass over Devil's Bridge instead. The Security Service of Ukraine will anticipate the move, blowing up the thirty-five-meter-high bridge just as a train carrying fuel crosses. A source inside will say: "Russian special services should get used to the fact that our people are everywhere. Even in distant Buryatia." For now, Devil's Bridge was intact, blood-red steel coiling out of the mountains to curve across the valley, supported by three-legged concrete pillars rising from the fir trees. Harwood stepped onto the bridge as the cloud of nighttime's cold, beached in the gorge, rose as spray.

"No vibrations," she said. The bridge carried three tracks separated by a ballast of sand and crushed stone bordered by a walkway, where she now trusted her feet.

Bond stepped after her. "I wonder what it would take."

Harwood followed his gaze to the bolts and nuts connecting the brace to the rails. "Haven't you derailed enough trains?"

He grinned. "Never."

"You can bet they're maintaining these tracks to transport weapons."

"Everything fails," said Bond. "It's only a matter of time."

Harwood turned to him. "Even you?"

This time his voice was soft. "Never."

The first blush of dawn highlighted how much his face had changed, the mortician's pallor of captivity replaced by weather-beaten bronze after crossing from smog-heavy cities to undulating, treeless plains and sprawling pine forests into desert. She pressed her lips to his gently. Electricity passed through her. The grit beneath her boots was vibrating.

Bond pulled back. "Good to know I can still make the earth move."

"Wouldn't want your confidence to suffer. Let's go."

The crown of each pillar supporting the bridge was boxed in by a steel cage, with a ladder for engineers. Harwood threw her legs over, grasping the top rung, then making room for Bond. They hung from the bridge, the structure shaking like a dog trying to cast off fleas as a train screeched to make the curve. It was freight, as they'd hoped. There would be two guards, one front and one rear, with no walk-through. Harwood lifted her head and saw the flatcars carrying Russian Tigr military vehicles shudder around the bend and onto the bridge.

Bond counted: "One, two, three . . ."

The Double O's vaulted onto the bridge and grabbed onto the chain of the nearest car.

The pressure could have torn Harwood's arm from the socket but she held on, scrambling around the camouflage-painted Tigrs. She wedged herself between the electric winch mounted on the engine block of the 4x4 behind, and the swing doors of the armored hull in front. If needed, they could roll under the flat-bellied chassis, which offered a clearance of sixteen inches for IEDs. But she hoped they could sit like this, watching the mountains slide by like rear projection.

Bond settled beside her with a wince, holding his ribs.

"Any damage?" she asked.

"You'll have to be more specific."

She laid her head on his shoulder. Bond's arm came around her. Four thousand miles of stealing cars, horses, and boats; jumping on trains; marching, marching, marching; four thousand miles of near-misses and there but for the grace of God go I: fistfights and bribes, persuasion and concealment. There were points when she thought all would be lost by chance—army training maneuvers where nothing was marked on a map, police rousting a village for conscripts, gangsters fighting over turf. But somehow, with each mile, Bond had solidified. Purpose renewed his step. Revenge sharpened his eye. Harwood patted her pocket for the negatives. That season in Moscow had been Bond's chance to kill Mora and save Sid, himself, her, years in the future. It was Bond's chance to see through Ware's legend. But he hadn't. None of them had.

Bond's hand closed over hers, covering the negative.

The train followed the curve of Devil's Bridge across the abyss, picking up speed to barrel through fir trees. Blue-shrouded mountains massed from the mist. A boomtown turned ghost town hugged the tracks, corrugated houses whistling with wind. The Baikal Amur Mainline—known as BAM—branched north from the Trans-Siberian Railway to form a loop on a blank stretch of map, built on permafrost in the shadow of avalanches by forced laborers in the 1930s, then prisoners of war, a toll of 400,000 dead for four hundred miles. It wasn't completed until the end of the century.

The Northern Muya Range grew razor ridges as the day cleared. Then they were plowing into the Severomuysky Tunnel—flipping from light so bright it shocked your irises to no light at all; from pine to concrete dust; a loss so sudden, it was how Harwood hoped death would come. Don't let it be slow. Don't let it be the stretched starvation of her father, whose suffering her mother said traced back to what he shouldn't have seen: to the negative in her palm.

Then just as suddenly as the darkness of Russia's longest railway tunnel swallowed them for ten miles, it spat them out in sight of the Muyakan River. Earthquake damage collected boulders along the tracks like a child building a dam on a beach. They passed closed factories and perfectly preserved railway stations with nobody in them. The BAM Zone—as it was known—seemed to exist for the BAM Zone. An ouroboros.

The train would carry them to Severobaikalsk at the northern tip of Lake Baikal in under three hours. They were here to catch a spy. Harwood and Bond had reached the edge of Russia alone, but to cross into Japan they'd need help. Buryatia was key to the invasion of Ukraine because of the weaponry supply lines. The Double O's knew there would be a partisan group intending to sabotage those lines who might be persuaded to assist MI6. The challenge was to identify the handler. Members of the cell wouldn't know each other, in case one was arrested. The handler would have a singular overview. It had to be someone with reason to travel, a person who could innocently come into contact with a useful cross-section of society: an invisible worker on the BAM.

Rancid char on the air hit Harwood: a wall of yellow-hearted flames fringed with gray towers of smoke. The permafrost that once supported the tracks was melting thanks to climate breakdown, pushing up the heads of woolly mammoths and saber-toothed tigers, exposing swamps whose dead trees formed the perfect peat for wildfires. Ancient viruses sparkled in the atmosphere. Harwood buried her face in Bond's chest, and then the heat of destruction on the back of her neck was gone, and she opened her eyes on Lake Baikal.

The ring of mountains looked small compared to the largest freshwater lake in the world, a 395-mile crescent that reached oceanic depths, crystal-clear ice overlaying black bubbles like patterned lace. It was the season of *rasputitsa*, the thaw. Beyond the fifteen-foot waves frozen in place, the water was pearlescent, stirring free, the blue of dreams. Twenty-five million years old, the lake was self-purifying thanks to microscopic shrimp. But now those shrimp were eating the runoff from a vast paper mill, hydroelectric dams, and the industrial corridor that supported the army and Bitcoin farming, poisoning the olmu fish they fed, which in turn poisoned raptors, bears, the planet's only freshwater seal, and finally humans who have prayed here for as long as there have been gods. Not so much the dog eat dog world of Darwin, but dog eat dog that recently dined on arsenic. At last, Severobaikalsk came into view, set on a plateau above the northern shore. Harwood wondered what poison they'd encounter there.

The hinterland shacks were from the days of the work camp, adapted from old railway cars. In the empty lap of the hills, the first sign of planned life was the station, which gave the odd impression of a skate ramp, the roof curved with all the optimism of sailing into a brighter future. The population, close to 25,000, was declining every year. Ninety percent were Russian Orthodox, ten percent Buryat. This was not a place where strangers went unnoticed—unless you had something to do with the railway. The Double O's jumped off the train before it came under surveillance, weaving between buckled fences and birch trees to reach the depot, where Bond shrugged into the black jacket of a shunter driver, and Harwood opted for the long coat of a conductor.

She smoothed his lapels. "Once more unto the breach, dear friend."

A half-smile. "Cry God for Harry, England, and Saint George."

Walking six feet apart, 007 and 003 proceeded up Leningradsky Avenue toward the main square. There were more shop window posters proclaiming the success of the war here than in the cities close to St. Petersburg. Separated from the lake by a pine forest, high-rise buildings constructed from prefab panels locked together like the shields of an advancing army. The Palace of Culture had been built under Communism to provide railway workers with a social club, a cinema, restaurants, and a library. Harwood mounted the steps a little behind Bond. When he pushed into the bar, the swinging door revealed two women in white shirtsleeves glancing up from their tea. Harwood caught the door as both women looked Bond up and down before exchanging views behind the menu. Bond took a corner table with his back to the wall. A waiter hurried over. Bond grunted that he wanted a vodka.

Harwood ordered coffee from a gray-haired barwoman who asked if she'd just pulled in. In reply, Harwood asked if it had been a busy day. The woman said it was quiet but there would be a good number for the card game. Harwood nodded. In the mirror over the bar, she saw Bond sweep the room with his gunmetal eyes.

The game was poker. Bond joined by tossing a roll of notes onto the table, not so much money it was ostentatious, not so little he'd prove no good if his luck turned. Harwood watched him enter the ring: the way these men hardened by a land of exile instantly made room with a nod, not the grins of sharks, but the warmth of recognition. What did they think they understood about him? That he'd endured a long, hard winter on the railways? That he'd endured something, that was certain. He threw the first hand, then won the second, immediately buying a round. Then he maintained a steady success, a pacemaker in a race. The leader was a heavyset man cloaked in the orange jacket of an engineer. He crumpled the cards, staining them black with the grime of the day. It made it easy to see he was cheating. The man to his left was too drunk to notice when his own card disappeared on the next deal, replaced by a sooty slip. Bond's eyebrow twitched.

The engineer talked too much—to cover his cheating, perhaps? His complaints—the lack of women, the long hours, the shitty mud of the thaw—drew confidences from the other players. At least you weren't on the latest shipment of fuel from North Korea, the army treat us like serfs. You want women? Go talk to the Chinese girls on Olkhon Island, tell them you're a shaman, tourists love that. At least you're paid—I'm a firefighter and I live in a fishing shack on the lake just to bring home a little extra, except I don't have a home! Good at winning indiscretions—that could make him the man they wanted. Except he was too brash to run a spy ring.

The door dinged. A woman wearing a colorless quilted coat over the white shirt and waistcoat of the BAM tea ladies, with a square scarf tied over her bald head, crept to the bar. She was Buryat. She whispered that she'd like tea. She sat with her back to the card game but her attention drifted over the mirror, lingering on Bond. Harwood ordered *gruzinchiki*, fish rolls fried and rolled in dough, sliced, and served with melted butter. There was no wedding ring on the woman's thin hand. Her right-hand coat pocket was heavy, like she had two phones.

They were after someone invisible. Like a Buryat tea lady dying of cancer with no family and absolutely nothing left to lose.

Harwood pulled her phone from her pocket, a cheap burner, and toggled the Wi-Fi on. She scanned the networks in the room. Most had names like Telefon123 or Vlad'sTelefon. There was one called SuckMyD1ck and she'd bet anything it belonged to the engineer, who was now baiting the table with a wad of money. Bond cast his own crumpled notes into the pile.

"Raise," he said.

The table followed or folded. The engineer asked if anyone had heard about the Buryat soldier spreading lies about the army, trying to persuade good Russians to defect to Ukraine, a story so absurd Harwood almost laughed. *Psst, hey you, want to defect?* But it solicited more serious stories about discontentment in the tank division. The tea lady's hand strayed to her pocket, where she seemed to weigh the sagging load.

There was one Wi-Fi network called Namgar, a Buryat name. The tea lady was the one Buryat here.

The dish arrived and Harwood thanked the god of spying that it was huge. She turned. "I'll never finish this alone. Would you like to join me, Namgar?"

The woman flinched.

"We met on the BAM before Christmas," said Harwood, putting out her hand.

Harwood was what Hollywood casting agents and MI6 alike called ethnically ambiguous: a mixture of French, French-Algerian, and Northern Irish. She watched Namgar try to decipher her now, possibly wondering if she was a mix of Russian and Buryat.

"I was in hospital before Christmas," she said.

"That's right, you were going in for treatment. How are you now?"

That cemented it. Namgar clearly never told anyone on BAM about her illness or anything else. That meant this stranger was creating a reason to talk. If you were a handler for a partisan group, you'd want to know why.

"A little better now. Thank you, I haven't eaten."

Behind her, Bond said softly: "Call."

"Me too." Harwood told the bartender they'd be in the corner.

As Harwood carried the tray over to a corner where dusty potted plants would shield their privacy, the engineer hit the table with his fist, making the glasses and ashtrays jump. Bond had won, deploying his usual tactic when something or someone didn't seem right to him: light the fuse and see what happens. He moved to touch his collar, then stopped—Harwood wondered if he'd been reaching to loosen a bow tie.

The engineer sucked his teeth. "Who invited you to play? Are you even a member of this club?"

"I was born with club membership," said Bond. "Can't you tell?"

Bond's neighbor clapped him on the back. "Born in a railway shack? Me too. Next round on you, brother, yeah?"

"Make mine a double."

Harwood settled with her back to the wall. Namgar sat at a right angle to her, keeping her shoulder blades to the panels too. Bond was in Harwood's eyeline between the palms. He kept one arm under the table, and she saw he was drawing a pattern on his knee. A circle with a cross through it. Locked on target.

"You're not from here," said Namgar.

"I mainly work on the Trans-Siberian, but with things getting busier on the BAM they keep moving me back and forth. Your treatments were in Irkutsk, I remember? You must be glad to be home."

The woman's lips parted. "Yes, that's right."

It was a guess there'd be no cancer ward here, and Namgar would have to travel to the Paris of Siberia, nearly five hundred miles south. "When did they release you?"

"When they realized there was nothing more they could do for me."

Harwood touched her teacup. The mirroring that MI6 so prized filled her eyes with tears, a flash of sympathy, and she wondered if it was genuine or not. She thought it was. *You're too good an actor*. "I'm sorry."

Namgar adjusted her headscarf. "We talk about vital circuitry, on the BAM. The components needed to keep a train running even if the driver dies. I suppose my vital circuitry is broken."

"But you're keeping the train on the tracks."

"For now."

Harwood went all in. "I saw more wildfires, coming in. It could be cotton burning."

Namgar stiffened. Ukrainians used the word "cotton" to refer to sabotage implemented by Ukrainian Special Services in Russia and the occupied territories of Ukraine. It came from Russian media and officials describing the growing incidents of sabotage with the word *khlopok*, which meant both "blast" and "cotton" in Russian. Namgar's hand returned to her heavy pocket, her finger dipping, then thinking better of it. "I don't remember meeting you, if I'm truthful. But my memory is bad these days. What service was it?"

"British."

The card table broke out in talk. Bond sat with a quiet smile. The engineer was red in the face.

Namgar twisted a colorful ribbon wrapped around her slender wrist. "Perhaps you have me confused with someone else."

"I hope not," said Harwood.

A whisper: "Why?"

"I remember you saying you have family around Baikal. I don't know the area so well, but I'm told now's the time to see the lake, before the ice melts. I could use a guide."

"A guide?"

"Yes."

"Is there anywhere you'd especially like to see?"

"Sakhalin." It was the island that almost stitched Russia to Japan. "We need to send a message to friends, who can pick us up there."

Bond got to his feet. So did the engineer.

"I could ask my cousins," said Namgar. "But it would cost you something. Come to the sacred cave at Cape Ludar. Sunrise."

"What should I bring?"

Namgar glanced at the mirror over the bar, which showed the back of the engineer's chunky head, and Bond's rebuilt physique and faint smirk. Harwood wondered what the woman saw in Bond's quiet, deadly control. He could be a villain, if you didn't know better. Namgar said, "My cousins would accept a show of good faith, instead of cash."

"Troubleshooting," suggested Harwood.

"Something like that."

"What's the trouble?"

"That man. He's always so loud."

Harwood said, "Does he come here often?"

"Yes. And he's always getting people to *talk*."

Harwood had found their Ukrainian spy. Bond had found her Russian counter-spy.

Bond pocketed the cash. He looked in the mirror for the first time. She drew a finger over her throat, before fiddling with her scarf. He nodded.

"It looks like he'll come to a bad end," said Harwood.

Bond asked the barwoman for directions to the nearest thermal spring. He made no attempt to lower his voice, and her reply was equally clear. She told him the café and swimming pool would be closed now, but you could use the springs day and night. Bond nodded his thanks and left without a look to Harwood. The engineer hung back, but then someone laughed at him so he followed Bond with a curse.

As the door swung shut behind him, he sent a text.

TWENTY

Vital Circuitry

For ancient Buryats, Lake Baikal was a source of life, which broke to the surface in hot springs. The nearest springs to Severobaikalsk reached fifty degrees Celsius, a temperature surely possible only in the devil's cauldron, so the Buryats named it Goudzhekit: Devil's Place. Still, Namgar bathed there whenever she could. The waters of Goudzhekit were said to heal the nervous system, circulatory system, musculoskeletal system, and the endocrine system. Vital circuitry, Harwood thought, as she walked through the taiga forest, the last of the snow crunching beneath her boots. Frosted huts lining the ski slope glittered in the starlight. Between them, the black hulk of mountains seemed to tear strips from the fabric of the universe.

She'd taken a taxi to a nearby guesthouse, not wanting to register the same destination as Bond with the local rumor factory. Now, she eased her gun from the small of her back and crossed an empty children's playground. Finally, she rounded a wooden lodge with a hand-painted sign for hot springs. The back was fenced off, a high partition to protect bathers from the wind. That left the main door, outside of which an empty taxi was parked. Bond must have paid the driver with all his winnings for a loan. Harwood tried the door of the lodge and found it was open. A shuttered ticket window greeted her with an honesty box. A sign pointed to the changing rooms.

Harwood could feel the heat rising. She dumped her coat. The wooden boards groaned, so she toed off her boots. The benches were empty. One cubicle had the door shut. She eased it open, finding Bond's clothes folded on the bench, and an empty weapons holster hanging from the hook. *Come and get me*, it seemed to say.

She heard a thud, followed by a grunt. Harwood took the steps outside, descending into vapor, which she realized was only partly mist—columns of it were frozen, the breath of life sculpted in ice. Another step and the vapors cleared and she saw Bond naked waist-deep in the spring, holding a man's head under the foaming surface.

He looked up. "Won't be a minute. He's just taking the waters."

"I hear they're lovely this time of year." Harwood sat on the bottom step, easing her feet into the steam.

A tidal wave as Bond lifted the man out. The engineer's face was pink. He roared, trying to wrestle free from Bond's grip, but he couldn't.

"Last chance," said Bond. "Tell me what you know, and who you report to, and I'll let you go. Or you can drown and boil to death at the same time."

"OK! OK! I've been sent to find Ukrainian terrorists. I think the handler is a man in the BAM card game, but I haven't found him yet."

"And to whom do you report this grand total of nothing?"

"Until meeting you today there was nothing to report!"

"I'm flattered. Who do you take orders from and how do you make your reports?"

Nothing.

Bond plunged him beneath the surface again. The great man writhed and wriggled in his grip. Harwood leaned back on her elbows, gun balanced on her knee.

"OK! OK! I take my orders from Vladivostok."

"A name."

"I don't know! It's not FSB, it's a man high up in Rat—" he broke off.

Bond's grip released. The man struggled away, coughing water.

Harwood stood up, gun level now. "Rattenfänger?"

The engineer looked between the both of them, unsure what to be more afraid of: the secret he'd divulged, or the two spies in front of him. Harwood cocked the trigger. He nodded.

She said, "A name."

"I don't know."

"How do you communicate with him?"

"Phone."

"What does his voice sound like?"

"He speaks through someone else. There's always a delay. It's like he doesn't want anyone to hear him."

The sound of Sid biting off Mora's tongue came to her. "What's the phone number?"

He recited a Vladivostok number.

"Have you been there?"

"Once. It's a big gray building on the Morskaya Ulitsa facing the harbor near the railway station."

Despite the heat, Bond turned gray.

Harwood adjusted her grip on the gun. "If you speak on the phone, why did you go to Vladivostok?"

Sweat froze on the man's face. "I met him once."

"He was there?"

"Yes."

"Why would he want to meet *you*?"

"I'm the chief agent in Siberia. He told me security in this region is more important than I might think. He told me if I failed . . . That's all

I can say. He stayed in the shadows. But still somehow, when you're near him, you feel like you're near death."

"You are," said Bond.

"Not here," said Harwood. "This is a source of life."

A frown, and then Bond, naked, dragged the engineer out of the pool and hauled his scarlet body across the changing room floor, through the doors and into the snow. Harwood followed. The hiss of broiled skin meeting ice, a shriek, and then the engineer was on his feet and attempting to run, slipping and sliding.

"He's close to the partisan network," said Harwood. "They want him dead. In return, they'll help us."

Bond nodded, putting out his hand. She passed him her gun. He fired.

The man collapsed, a red splash on shimmering ice.

Bond lifted the body into the trunk of the taxi and swept snow over the bloodstains. Then he turned and walked back into the lodge, moving like an automaton, until he met the steam and sank into the water.

Harwood stripped off her layers. To rescue Bond, she had first summited the Altai Mountains to the End of Everything, the meeting point of Russia, China, Kazakhstan, and Mongolia, in search of Rattenfänger's people smuggler. The highest peak was considered the entrance to the afterlife. The shamans in the mountains were conductors between the world of the living and those who had moved to a better world. It was known as a "power place," where the scientifically impossible happened. On her climb, she bathed in a thermal spring, where the heat told her she was still on this side of the gateway. Now this heat made her heart toll like a church bell, her skin sing, her nerves fire. She was vitally alive. She had cheated death, stealing Bond from its jaws. She was no longer alone. But how long could it last?

She walked into Bond's arms, which closed around her with every muscle tensed, as if locking something out.

He murmured beside her ear: "A source of life?"

"The water's meant to heal you," she said. "Make you stronger."

"You make me stronger," he said, tangling her curls in his hand, mouth moving to her throat, then down her body.

Harwood held on to him as the heat surged between them and around them and froze in the night air, captured like a word uttered between sleeping and waking but remembered forever.

TWENTY-ONE

Choices

"Why are Rattenfänger so interested in the furthest reaches of Russia?"

The only sign that Bond heard Harwood was his fist tightening on the steering wheel.

"Why would Mora be in Vladivostok?" she asked.

Nothing. She could smell blood leaking from the boot of the car. She cracked a window, letting in the evergreen forest and sweet wood smoke. The unpaved road was purple in the pre-dawn, a line plowing through meadows that unrolled to distant steppes. Bond's silence wasn't the controlled quiet to which she was accustomed from him. It was the quiet of someone who couldn't hear your questions, because they weren't here at all. He was back inside his hurricane room. A blur of movement drew Harwood's attention, but it took a moment to process what she was seeing: a wild horse jumping from the long grass into the road, where it reared and then brought its hoofs down in challenge to the car.

"James!"

The engine balked as Bond hit the brakes and the taxi jerked to a stop.

The horse lowered its head, locking eyes with Bond, who held his breath. Then the animal shook its mane, as if disappointed, and jumped out of the headlights and into the darkness.

Bond spoke through gritted teeth. "When I lost my memory after blowing up Blofeld's castle in Japan, the one thing I remembered was Russia. It seemed important in my life." A low laugh. "Vladivostok—I kept thinking I had to get to Vladivostok. So I crossed Sakhalin and reported for duty in Vladivostok. Imagine the delight of SMERSH. They took me to a big gray building on Morskaya Ulitsa. I was given to a doctor who was considered a world expert in brainwashing. When I turned up in London, drugged out of my head, I nearly murdered Sir Miles Messervy. Emery Ware must have known exactly what they were doing to me back then. He wanted M's chair. What better way than to hasten Sir Miles's exit from the stage at my hands? All these years, I considered Ware a mentor. A rather debauched father figure, I suppose, but I was out of fathers and he seemed to volunteer. The irony is that when I confronted Sir Miles under the haze of Russia's brainwashing, I accused him of using me for most of my adult life as a tool. And that's exactly what his successor has done."

"He's poison, James," said Harwood, touching the negative in her pocket. "The only thing to do is draw the poison out. But we have to make it to Japan first."

It felt wrong to bump a taxi up Cape Ludar, where the remains of an ancient Mongolian fortress reached through the marsh tea like bone through a wound. They climbed past the weather station and emerged into the open, a spit of mountain pine overlooking Lake Baikal. Namgar stood facing the Sacred Sea, its colors giving life to her cheeks. At the cough of the engine, she turned. Harwood opened the boot. Namgar looked inside. She nodded. Harwood slammed the thing closed.

"Come with me."

She led them to the weather station, a battered concrete box bristling with antennae. On the floor, surrounded by rat droppings, there was a glass cube, inside which green circuit boards crawled with wires and golden chips, borrowing power from the automated sensors.

"We communicate via the Tor network," said Namgar. She drew a laptop from her satchel.

Tor used the onion protocol, making it impossible to snatch messages in transit. The way it had been explained to Harwood in training was to imagine you want to send a letter privately. You slip the letter inside an encrypted envelope, then pass the letter through any number of hands, with each hand stuffing your envelope inside another. The envelopes are identical in size so no one knows how many stops your letter has taken before it reaches the destination. DARPA designed the system and today it was used by criminal enterprises, intelligence agencies, and civilians who didn't want to gift their private data to surveillance capitalism. As interception was wildly tricky, state actors targeted the destination or source machine instead. First and last stops were the weakest link. Hiding a message to Tiger Tanaka from both Russian and British eyes—Mora and M—meant trusting the security of Namgar's network and Tiger Tanaka. Harwood was prepared to bet on both.

Still, once Bond connected the laptop to the Tor dark website, used by the Japanese PSIA, he did not type out his numbers station poem, but an ill-formed haiku:

YOU ONLY LIVE TWICE:
ONCE WHEN YOU ARE BORN
AND ONCE WHEN YOU LOOK DEATH IN THE FACE.

Harwood said, "You never wrote me poetry."

He raised his eyebrow at her and added a line: DUE HOME MOSCOW FRIDAY 1300 APRIL NO PARTY BAD LUCK.

"Will he know you mean Dué Post on Sakhalin?"

"He knows I hid out there when I crossed last time."

"And you think he'll realize 1300 isn't a time, it's 0013?"

"Combined with April in Moscow he should. Tanaka knows our case files better than we do."

"All right. Send it."

His trigger finger landed on the enter key.

Outside, Namgar told them to ask for Sasha at the seasonal settlement on Cape Zavorny. "He will take you by hydrofoil to Olkhon Island, about halfway down Lake Baikal. On the island, you will meet a friend of ours. He will arrange passage for you to Sakhalin. I will make the taxi disappear. No one saw you?"

Bond said, "No one."

Namgar nodded.

Harwood said, "Thank you."

Namgar turned to catch dawn breaking over the mountain. "This is a sacred place. It is supposed to make your innermost desire true."

Bond turned his back, walking to the edge of the cape.

Harwood said, "Has it worked?"

"Maybe. Good luck."

"You too."

Harwood hugged herself as the wind picked up, watching Namgar drive into forest that closed behind her. She followed Bond to what felt like the edge of the world, sitting with him there, her legs dangling. Below, the cliff face was decorated with petroglyphs from the Bronze Age.

What would she say if she were making a report on the challenges an agent would face trying to recruit this man? He'd been catastrophically betrayed by those who were supposed to most care for and protect him. She was reminded of her own reaction as a child when her mother left her to the care of her elderly grandmother and paranoid schizophrenic father. It took her years to speak, until she was forced to speak in order to care for her father, and she hadn't stopped caring for others since.

Confronted by Bond's silence she was tempted to retreat into her own hurricane room, to finally abandon caring for the other, and care purely for herself. Except she didn't want to find she'd always been on her own.

Just then, Bond cleared his throat. "Do you remember what I told you on Devil's Bridge, that I never fail?"

"Yes."

He closed an eye against the sunburst. "That's what I tell women who look at me the way you look at me—when I want them to look at me the way you look at me."

A half-smile. "I know."

"You do?"

"Yes." She laid her hand on his thigh. "But that's not why I look at you the way I do."

He turned to her. "I know."

Those words knocked back and forth between them. *I know. I know.* At night, harboring beneath a lone dwarf pine in the desert or a blanket of furs in a barn, he was still visited by nightmares, his fists ready, heart pounding like he was drowning. Harwood would wake him with her voice alone: "It's me, James. It's me." His shoulders would drop as he said, "I know."

It might be that *I know you* was even more intimate between spies than *I love you*.

She kissed him, leaning her forehead against his. "Do you ever think about our long-term"—she laughed as he winced—"*objective*, as Double O agents?"

"World peace," he said drily. "Or did you have bigger ideas?"

"I was born with bigger ideas. What's your innermost desire?"

"I can think of a few . . ."

She tangled her fingers in his. "Other than that."

His voice was quiet. "To kill the man who tried to break me. And then kill the man who betrayed me."

"And afterward?"

He pulled back. "That was always our trouble, wasn't it? I couldn't envision an afterlife, while still alive. What's your innermost desire? Are you wedded to this life?"

"Interesting verb choice. I want justice for Sid. I want justice for my father. I want—I want to find out who I am, when I'm not performing. It was my capacity to adapt and persuade that MI6 wanted. You said I'm too good an actor."

"I didn't mean . . ."

She shrugged. "Yes you did. I want to find out what happens when I stop acting. If I have value when I'm not playing a role."

"Value to MI6? Or to me?"

There was no way to dissemble here, nowhere to hide. But she also didn't have the courage to confirm or deny.

He seemed to take her silence as an answer. "I don't—*value*—you because of an act. What? You don't believe me?"

"When I was a teenager, my mother warned me to beware snake charmers. When I met you, I climbed right into the basket."

He leaned away to examine her from a distance. "You think I'll break your heart?"

She met his gray-blue eyes. "You have form."

His smile wavered.

Harwood brushed his knuckles. "A man makes his own luck. A woman makes her own choices."

He paled, perhaps at the memory of his last words to Sid Bashir as they discussed their mutual feelings for her; perhaps the realization that Sid had shared those final moments with her; perhaps her choice itself, and all the reasons she made it.

Harwood and Bond followed an old mining road next to a river swollen with ice melt, picking sour berries and pine nuts as they went. This seasonal settlement existed on the memory of a Soviet quartz mine beside a lagoon. Sasha greeted them with clear alcohol that tasted of fir. He led them to the hydrofoil station.

It was more than ten hours over Lake Baikal's frozen waves. As they grew closer to shore, a strange armada shimmered on the horizon: Lexus SUVs drawing doughnuts on the white-on-black ice, hip hop thumping, roofs open for Chinese tourists who rode face-to-face with selfie sticks. Sasha told them it was for TikTok.

"What's TikTok?" asked Bond.

Orange cliffs towered over palatial ice formations, where vans queued to deposit hundreds of people to join the hundreds of others skating and cradling fish soup heated by fires built on the ice itself. The sandy shores of Olkhon fluttered with the holy poles of the Buryats tied with ribbons in every color. Local guides swept the ice and set up tripods, before which people jumped to get the most desirable shot.

At a Chinese restaurant, Harwood and Bond ate dumplings in a steamy window booth. It wasn't the waiter who delivered the bill, but a man with a mop of graying hair and a mouth hidden by the high collar of his fleece.

"Follow me."

He took them to an old Soviet ambulance. Driving over ice to the mainland, they circled the yellow cloud hanging over Irkutsk and then swung away from the Mongolian border. It was a twenty-four-hour drive, stopping to bake fish over a fire. When the road ran out, they were met by Buryat herders on horseback. Bond was given a chestnut stallion. He mounted and pulled Harwood up behind him. She circled his waist with her arms and buried her face in his collar. They rode into the sunrise, steering clear of the road to Vladivostok. They did not share a language with the nomads, but there was shared food and fire and that was enough. They passed shrines winking with stones and coins. They lay under the stars. Bond was asleep when Harwood whispered by his ear: "I want you to know, in case this is our last night. I choose you."

TWENTY-TWO

The Prison Without a Roof

Under the tsars, Siberia was known as the prison without a roof. Now they were one step away from freedom: crossing the Tatar Strait to reach the former gulag of Sakhalin Island, where they must invisibly travel a distance twice as big as Belgium, standing forty kilometers from Japan's northernmost island, Hokkaido. But that step seemed the most uncertain of all. Development in offshore oil and gas fields meant the strait was busier than ever and bristled with security, and the ferry connecting the island to Japan had been terminated.

Fishermen trawling for giant red king crab took Harwood and Bond around the Chestye Islands, uninhabited but for slaty-backed and black-tailed gulls, which dive-bombed the boat for the gigantic crabs. From the rocks, sooty guillemots opened black beaks to reveal hungry orange mouths. The rusting ribs of wrecked ships shivered in the gray sea. A navy patrol came close enough to make eye contact. Bond didn't blink. The crab boat rounded the mountain-backed dark sand beaches of Sakhalin, putting Bond and Harwood ashore onto the western coast, which glittered with amber.

Bond said he remembered the island like a dream that visits occasionally throughout your life: the architecture caught between Russian and Japanese rule, part Eastern, part the concrete prefab of all Russian provincial cities. These townships were so unused to strangers that when they passed through the shadow of a tower block, the young mothers sitting on tires in a Khrushchevka yard under the flap of laundry froze, bubliks half-dipped in tea, cigarettes halfway to lips.

The Russian mainland was a narrowed eye watching from the horizon. They walked the high, precarious path above Voevodsk Chasm, a mine pit turned prison yard; here, convicts and exile settlers had gathered to watch hangings over a hole where the wheelbarrow men worked, shackled forever to their labor, sleeping, eating, and dying with wheelbarrows bound to them. Now the shaft was overgrown with waving grass, and the lay-by was used for barbecue. Harwood tensed when she heard steps behind them. She glanced back. They had a stalker, a man with his hood up.

"He's picked the wrong people to mug," said Bond, but he didn't sound convinced.

On the beach below a child tried to fly a kite but there was no wind. In the gray chop, the coast guard idled, and Harwood saw glass glinting on deck, as if someone were watching them through binoculars.

"Could the FSB agent have sent up a flare?" she asked.

"I checked his phone."

"He could have deleted a message . . ." The coast guard wasn't moving. The man's steps behind maintained the same distance. The big gray building on the Morskaya Ulitsa facing the harbor near the railway station occupied her imagination. "Do you remember what they did to you in Vladivostok?"

"Some things are better left forgotten."

Before Harwood could reply, a helicopter whipped the long grass into a frenzy, buzzing over them and out to sea before wheeling back around, the pilot peering down at them. Harwood grabbed Bond's arm. Bond looked back at the stalker. As he did, another hooded man stepped onto their path ten feet ahead. Harwood squeezed Bond's bicep. Her free hand drifted to the small of her back, where her weapon waited.

"I'll take the helicopter," said Bond.

Harwood nodded.

"Three, two . . ."

On one, Harwood pulled her gun and shot the man ahead of her and then turned and shot the man behind, as Bond drew his weapon, sighted, and squeezed off six rounds at the helicopter, shattering the glass, chipping the rotor, and finally killing the pilot, spinning the glass dragonfly like an ornament until it shattered on the ocean.

"Go, go, go . . ."

They double-timed over mass graves sinking into marshland, passing torture cells that resisted time's passage. The score lines of coal tracks separated the beach from a bare, sharp hill, the path knotted with weeds and clouded with mosquitoes. At the end, the wooden cottages that once glorified the prison governor, priest, and officers stood peeling. The coast guard was joined by three other ships. But the searchlights couldn't find them through tangled machinery long since stripped of copper and gold, "hedgehogs" meant to tear out the bottom of invading ships in wartime. Dogs hunting for food scattered at the sight of them. And then the road ran out. A stone track corkscrewed through the taiga, carrying them past a cemetery with more unnamed hillocks than named stones. Dué Post stood alone on the promontory.

Now it was a race between the circling hunters and Tiger Tanaka.

TWENTY-THREE

You Only Die Twice

The Hotel Okura was built for the 1964 Tokyo Olympics, combining Western modernism with decoration by Japanese artists and potters to create a mid-century icon and one of the most luxurious hotels in the world. When it was demolished and rebuilt in anticipation of the 2020 Olympic Games, there was fear that the checkered green carpet of the lobby, the distinctive hexagonal dropping lamps, the patterned lattice-work windows, the clusters of tables and chairs designed to look like plum blossoms would all be sacrificed to a bland Instagram-friendly canvas. But there was no need to worry: the son of the original mastermind led the redesign, crafting a replica of the carpet, remaking the lamps from the originals, and re-creating the atmosphere of sixties Japan with paper shoji screens and low chairs around lacquered tables. Entering, one had a sense of stepping safely back in time. But over reception, a massive digital clock read world times. It was a little after 8 p.m. in Tokyo. In London, M would be at one of his clubs for lunch.

One hand in his pocket, half-turned to scan the lobby, Bond told reception that he and Harwood had a booking under Hazard. With a commendable effort to ignore the state of their clothes, the woman said their adjoining rooms were on the thirty-third floor of the Prestige Tower.

The "fisherman" who picked them up from Sakhalin had given them tickets for the bullet train. Boarding on Sapporo island, they had sat opposite each other in first class in silent thought. Now they rode the lift with the same distance. Bond passed her a key card.

"There's a bar on the top floor," he said. "Starlight Lounge. How about a drink, after freshening up? I always liked you in starlight."

"Charmer," she said.

"Is it working?" he asked.

They entered separate bedrooms. The blinds were raised on a panorama of pulsing neon. On the table was a platter of sushi, a pot of green tea, and a bottle of Japanese whisky. In the wardrobe, Harwood found a range of clothes exactly her size. She'd forgive the security breach. In the bathroom, she even found her shade of lipstick. Tiger Tanaka seemed to understand that coming back in from the cold meant picking up a character for which one might need crib notes.

Harwood stood under the power shower until the water ran clear from her body and her feet could support her no longer. She ate everything off the platter in her dressing gown and then flipped through the hangers. There was a strange tightness in her stomach, as if this ending were a beginning, their first mission all over again. She remembered Moneypenny's instructions to pick Bond up from the Pera Palace Hotel in Istanbul. She had kept the engine of her Lotus Exige running. He swept from the revolving doors into the bright day wearing a lightweight gray suit and skipped down the stairs toward her.

She heard his hand land on the roof of the car and then he bent down to greet her through the open window. There was a moment of assessment. Then he said: "I feel better already."

"Don't like playing with others?" she asked as he slung himself into the low seat.

He smiled. She felt that smile deep in her body. "Depends on the game."

"Well, today's game is cat and mouse, only the roles are up for grabs. We're chasing them, they're chasing us"—*they* were arms dealers—"and the winner is whoever ends up on top."

He raised an eyebrow. She grinned before darting out into the traffic.

"Nice little car," he said. "I bet she runs well on the track."

"Do you race?" she asked.

"I've been known to test the traffic laws."

Just then, a stretch of road opened up ahead and she pressed the demure button reading SPORT. The whole car seemed to leap forward with the power of a rocket and the nimbleness of a dancer. Inside, their bodies rattled and swayed with the twisting velocity. Outside, the car would seem as serene as a swan on water.

He said, "I think I'd enjoy keeping up with you."

She told him: "You're welcome to try."

He laughed easily but his eyes glittered. "Challenge accepted."

Yes, she knew his reputation and yes, she flirted with him anyway and yes, after the shooting in Taksim Square where she performed emergency surgery on a child with nothing but a biro and a steak knife while Bond returned fire with deadly accuracy she invited him up to her room and yes, she disregarded the advice of older and wiser women in the Service who told her he cheats and acts surprised when you're hurt and yes, she did commit while telling herself she wouldn't and yes, she did hope for a future and yes, when she realized it was not in his makeup to worry about his own safety, only his objectives, she saw the danger to herself of watching another man she loved die in her arms and yes, she went through the painful motions of him and her and Sid and yes, all the while M must have been thinking this was a *very* helpful distraction. M, who promised to give her away at the altar. M, who must have appreciated life's ironies when Moneypenny recruited the daughter of the spy who once almost caught him. M, who sent Sid to die in her arms.

The excitement of that day racing through Istanbul belonged to another person. But she felt a little of it as she selected a dress with a split-leg jewel-colored sequined skirt and a sheer black sleeveless body, and a sequined clutch bag to match. Harwood took the lift to the forty-first floor. The doors opened to a wraparound twinkling tiara of skyscrapers and pale clouds streaking the black sky, which seemed much closer than the flow of shining traffic far below.

The Starlight Lounge tunneled toward a black marble bar, burnished gold by the hanging lights. Harwood's heels clicked over the herringbone floor as she walked into his spotlight. James Bond stood clean-shaven with his back against the bar, one elbow on the brass rail, one hand in the pocket of his mohair-blend midnight blue trousers with black silk stripes down the sides, which matched the black silk bow tie and facings on the midnight blue wool jacket lapels, worn over a textured white shirt with cocktail cuffs. The swell of the dinner jacket reminded her how much strength his body had regained since St. Petersburg. His eyes never left hers, not until she was beside him, and then he sighed, bowing to her dress.

He said, "I feel better already."

"I've heard that line before."

"How's it aged?"

"Better every time." Harwood slipped onto the barstool. "Have you ordered?"

"I was waiting for you."

Her lips twitched. "I'll follow your lead."

He returned her knowing smile with something between self-mockery and mischief, and then turned to the bartender, a silver-haired man in white tie.

Bond said: "Vodka martini, shaken not stirred. For myself and the lady."

"With pleasure, sir."

Bond held up a hand. "Three measures of Gordon's, one of vodka, half a measure of Kina Lillet. Shake it over ice and add a thin slice of lemon peel."

The bartender did not betray any displeasure at being instructed on how to make a cocktail in one of the best bars in the world, but he did execute the three-cornered hard shake with his elbows raised and a soulful concentration that seemed to express his tested dignity. The hard shake prevented the ice from simply crashing one end to the other, and sounded like a train going too fast over points on the track. When he poured, there was a dusting of perfectly circular ice. He slid the martini glasses toward them and retired with the practiced professionalism of a man who has starred in *The Mousetrap* for a thousand performances.

Harwood clinked her glass against Bond's but didn't drink, watching him take a sip first.

He closed his eyes. "So there is a God."

Harwood laughed. The drink warmed her from the inside out.

"If we could meet again . . ." Bond began, but stopped, looking at her over the glass. "If I'd known then . . ."

She shook her head. "There's only today."

"Today." He drew closer to her, brushing her curls behind an ear. "If there was only today, I'd want to tell you—"

There was a discreet cough. The Double O's looked around to find a young man in a tidy black suit. "Sir, madam, your host will see you in the Imperial Suite at your pleasure."

"Thank you," said Bond, moving away. He knocked back the martini.

Harwood did the same, taking his arm as she rose from the barstool. He walked with his arm inside his jacket, resting on the butt of his Walther PPK, which she glimpsed as they entered the lift and climbed the tower. The doors opened onto a lofted living room decorated in pale wood and marble. They were greeted by a big square figure with a wide gold-toothed grin, long dark lashes, and graying hair.

"Bondo-san!" Tiger Tanaka folded Bond into thick arms.

When Bond extricated himself from Tanaka, he'd let go of the gun. "Hello, Tiger. Trust you to put yourself up in better digs."

"Do you insult my honor, Bondo-san?"

"And it only took me ten seconds."

Tanaka gave a booming laugh, but he maintained a hand on Bond as if afraid he might float away. He turned to Harwood. "And you must be the famous Johanna Harwood. René Mathis informed me you'd suffered enough of us old men wringing our hands in despair. You were going to bring him out alone. And you did." Tanaka bowed.

"Luck was on my side."

He wagged his head. "I call it tenacity."

"I call it bloody foolish," said Bond, moving into the living room where he unbuttoned his jacket and sank into a corner sofa, "but she seems to think I'm worth it."

"I'm happy to revise that opinion," said Harwood, sitting beside him and crossing one leg over the other, revealing the gun strapped to her thigh.

"I am pleased to see you enjoyed my gifts," said Tanaka, waving a hand over them both. "Now we will have sake and tell each other epic tales."

"When did you see René?" asked Harwood.

Bond turned to her. "When did you?"

Tanaka passed them ceramic cups. "You must know, Bondo-san, first she won Felix Leiter as a devotee, then she converted René to her cause, who gives me to understand she next recruited Marc-Ange Draco, and then me, calling on me through 004 to make an incursion into Chinese airspace to rescue a woman and clean up a bloodbath. You would make a good Section Chief, Harwood-san."

"You didn't tell me that," said Bond.

Harwood almost said, *You didn't ask*—but knew it wouldn't be fair. She hadn't told him the lengths of her journey because she didn't want him to know the lengths she would go to for him, as if that weren't already evident, a self-defeating act of self-defense. So she asked Tanaka instead: "Do you know Dryden's status?"

"I regret I must tell you disturbing news. Moneypenny was captured by 000 after Mora and his men broke out of the black site. Joseph Dryden was made Acting Chief of the Double O Section, but MI6's analysts believe he went rogue. It is conceivable 004 was working with 000."

Harwood said, "No it isn't." She opened the snap on her clutch bag. She passed Tanaka the negative.

He moved to see the frame under a lamp. "What am I looking at, Bondo-san? This is Sir Emery, I can tell that much."

"That's Emery Ware meeting with the opposition, a body double for Mora, who he claimed to have killed as 0013. M is a double agent and has been since the Cold War. I need to get back to the UK without him picking me up on radar. Can you help?"

"Yes, of course . . . You plan to extract him from MI6?"

Bond nodded. "I don't know who I can trust there."

"You are safe here, far from MI6 and Five Eyes, but it will be a challenge to smuggle you into Britain. A challenge I shall relish, Bondo-san. But I fear you are picking a battle you cannot win, even you, against all of Britain's security."

"Can you put me on a flight tonight?"

"Yes, I can arrange for you to travel as a diplomat . . ."

Harwood said, "Don't you mean us?"

Bond said nothing. Tanaka looked awkward. Harwood's joints were suddenly sore and swollen. She kicked off her high heels and dug her toes into the rug.

Bond looked to her bare feet. "Uh-oh."

"What?" she asked.

"Don't think I've forgotten: your shoes come off, the gloves come on."

Harwood turned to him. "I don't need gloves for you. Your jaw isn't that hard."

That same jaw clenched. "Try me. You're safer here. I'm going alone."

Harwood stood up. "No you're not."

"You should stay with Tiger—"

Harwood scooped up her heels and stalked toward the lift.

"Where are you going?" he called.

She curled her lip, facing him. "Are you alone or not? Make up your mind."

Bond muttered a curse. "I don't want anything to happen to you."

"You'd have to stop my father lifting his camera for that."

He stood up. "Then learn a lesson from him and stay out of the firing range!"

"It's where I belong, like you!"

Tanaka raised his hands like a referee between sumo wrestlers. "You are both of you too eager to run headlong into danger. In this way, you are a perfect match. Surely two deaths are enough without tempting another, Bondo-san?"

Bond loosened his collar. "Don't look so worried, Tiger. You only die twice."

TWENTY-FOUR

Black Box

Q Branch was in lockdown. Aisha Asante was the last person in the laboratories and offices. Dryden was off radar and off comms. Ibrahim was at Shrublands, groggy after surgery, and they weren't sure what level of motor skills he would have left. Closeted in silence, she felt she was slowing down in time, but the clock was ticking on as normal, just like in the exams hall, as Q fruitlessly searched the data provided by Panopticon in search of Rattenfänger. Five Eyes said they had expected more and Aisha could hear her heartbeat, so slow and loud. She remembered the advice of the Oval cricket ground sports psychologist: gazing up at trees, saying aloud, "Awe and wonder, awe and wonder, awe and wonder . . ." So she rode the lift up through the building and spilled out into Regent's Park to march around the boating lake to London Zoo, finally slowing down at the fences enclosing the penguin house. She repeated "Awe and wonder, awe and wonder . . ." as the penguins slid into the pool on fast-forward. Until finally she realized she was dripping wet—it was raining—and she was back in her body.

Did you get this far in your career and persuade Joseph Dryden to rely on you by being second best? No, so grab the bat and step up.

Aisha marched into her office, wriggling out of her muddy trainers. She and Ibrahim had a no-dirty-shoes-on-the-reinforced-glass policy and she'd worn her spare pumps on a date the other night only to forget them at the guy's flat. Her socks were damp, so she pulled them off too, then chucked her blazer after them, standing barefooted in her culottes and vest over her computer.

"Let's see what you can do."

She scrolled through the most recent notifications from Panopticon. An alert from Japan caught her attention. The country was a key hub of international electronic cables, with ninety percent of the world's Internet traffic passing through its waters. With proximity to China, North Korea, eastern Russia, and East and Southeast Asia, there was discussion of inviting Japan to join the Five Eyes alliance. But for now, it fell outside the Five Eyes agreement not to spy on each other so there was an NSA tap on a subsea cable choke point known to come ashore and carry data to servers belonging to Japanese intelligence. Without Panopticon, she never would have had the data so swiftly, if at all, the NSA routinely keeping material to itself. But now she clicked to see why Q had flagged the package, finding two digits that had rung a bell inside the black box: 00.

She read the message in its entirety:

YOU ONLY LIVE TWICE:
ONCE WHEN YOU ARE BORN
AND ONCE WHEN YOU LOOK DEATH IN THE FACE.
DUE HOME MOSCOW FRIDAY 1300 APRIL NO PARTY
BAD LUCK.

Aisha translated the message into Japanese, but that didn't offer much, other than the fact that the first three lines didn't make the right syllables for a haiku, though they almost did in the original English. So she'd guess the poet was an English speaker. The Double O was a military time meaning 1 p.m. But wasn't it strange to mention a month and time but no date? Bad luck could refer to Friday the 13th, if that was supposed to mean the time and date of the sender's arrival in Moscow. She returned to the first three lines. Searching online offered no matches. She asked Q to search through case files. Also no matches. Maybe the answer lay in the intended recipient.

She muttered, "Who are you speaking to . . . ?"

"Are you talking to me, Dr. Asante?"

"We're in lockdown—" She turned, finding Bob Simmons in the doorway with concern shining on his face. "Oh, Bob, I didn't realize it was you. Everything OK?"

"Just wanted to check on you, miss. You've been down here a long time by yourself."

"I'm fine," she said. "I don't want to leave in case . . ."

"In case Dryden needs you again?"

A cheeky shrug. "In the meantime I'm decoding riddles."

"You'll be wanting dinner, then?"

"Huh?" Aisha turned to her computer. Maybe it wasn't Britain's case files she should search.

"It's nearly teatime."

"I'm fine . . ."

But at some point a plate with a sandwich, crinkly chips, and a cup of tea appeared beside her elbow, and she must have consumed them because the plate was empty a little while later. She was searching through packages grabbed from the same server, data Japan's intelligence agency sent for backup to a secure center. Secure once it reached the data center, anyway, but not secure on the ocean floor.

Aisha looked up. The clock said it was one in the morning. There was another empty cup beside her. She remembered now: Bob had brought her coffee. Q chimed with a result. Aisha pulled the screen toward her.

She was looking at a transcription of a diary found on the body of a man who had attempted to assassinate Tiger Tanaka and—Aisha stood up.

"James Bond," she said.

She shook out her hands. She was suddenly sweating. She went to call Dryden, then remembered he was dark. She told herself to calm down. The dead man had kept detailed notes of his surveillance. She read through Bond and Tanaka's debate over cricket versus baseball, the cultural merits of Japanese brothels, and the similarity between ninjas twisting sharp nails into knots to defeat barefoot pursuers and devices used to puncture the tires of jeeps in Iraq. When she found a conversation about poetry, she almost cried "Eureka!" The dead man wrote: "Subjects compared merits of Western and Japanese poetry and TT asked JB to write a haiku:

YOU ONLY LIVE TWICE:
ONCE WHEN YOU ARE BORN
AND ONCE WHEN YOU LOOK DEATH IN THE FACE.

This was a message from James Bond for Tiger Tanaka.

Aisha seized the red phone on her desk, which was linked to M's office. He answered with a clearing of the throat, as if he too were enduring a long, silent night and needed to shake his body back into time. Well, this would help. "Sir, I've found him. I've found him!"

M said, "004?"

"No—I, um, haven't been able to get him back on Q. . ."

"Then who have you found?"

"James Bond. 007. He sent a message to Tiger Tanaka in Japan. He's resurfaced, sir."

There was silence on the other end.

"Sir?"

"What does the message say, Dr. Asante?"

"I'm working on it, sir. It seems to be some kind of code."

"Let me know."

She hung up. Now she had a reference point for the code: James Bond's life. She plugged MOSCOW and APRIL into Q, asking the supercomputer to trawl through Bond's case histories. She was given more than a thousand hits. Aisha's shoulders dropped. She began to scan each one. She had to narrow it down somehow . . . "Due home Moscow" was strange, wasn't it? Moscow wasn't Bond's home, though it had been when he was attached to the embassy there, records she opened now.

"That's it . . ."

He had arrived in April 2004. But what could that signify now?

She looked back at that time: 1300. Wasn't that a strange inclusion without a date? She added it to the search parameters within files relating to Bond's stay in Moscow.

The only significant 13 was 0013, Sir Emery Ware, now M, also stationed in Moscow at the time. If you reversed 1300 you got 0013. Aisha wanted to punch the air.

The doors opened. Aisha turned to see M framed against the red light. "Sir, I was about to call you—I've worked it out! Did you come down in the lift? I didn't hear you."

"I used the tunnels," said M. "What have you worked out, Dr. Asante?"

She turned her back on him, pointing to the screen. "Bond has sent Tanaka a message about you, sir. He met you in Moscow in April, when you were 0013."

"Yes." He rattled his walking stick. "That's right."

"He says he's coming home and he doesn't want a party—he means he wants to keep it quiet, I think. I don't know why. He says something about bad luck. Friday the 13th is bad luck. But you're 0013. So he wants Tiger Tanaka to know that *you* are bad luck—wait . . ."

A sigh. "You really are much smarter than everyone else here."

There was something mournful in his voice. Aisha turned her head, meeting his watery eyes as he closed in behind her. He was drawing something from his walking stick—it looked like a sword, as if this were a corny Regency movie. She was so tired she was seeing things. She was moving too slowly in time, but the blade was moving far, far too fast. Aisha heard herself gasp. She looked down. The sword erupted from her chest. M's hand closed over her mouth.

"I'm sorry, my dear. You were too smart for your own good."

She clutched his arm, trying to yank his hand away, call out for Bob Simmons. She was being lowered to the floor—he was cradling her there. She couldn't budge him. She screamed for help but the sound was swallowed by M's palm. She could taste his sweat. She could taste her own blood. The trees moved in the breeze. The penguins slipped down the slide. Awe and wonder. Awe and wonder. Awe and wonder.

Part III

Compromise

1986

TWENTY-FIVE

Sarcophagus

Berlin before the fall. Meteorologically, the prevailing winds had come from the west. Politically, the wind blew from the east and it seemed the Wall would never come down. Incoming planes hopscotched with the airstream, jumping east-west-east-west over the mad zig-zig of the Wall. From above, you noticed how the Wall shone like a mirror in the low afternoon sun; on either side there was a replica television tower, a zoo, a convention hall, a sports stadium, and a grand avenue, Kurfürstendamm in the West and Unter den Linden in the East. A mirror city.

If Paris smelled of coffee and onions and Moscow of cheap eau de cologne and sweat, Berlin was boiled cabbage and cigars. I had earned my spurs here more than a decade earlier with Bill Tanner as my junior running mate. Since then, I'd made my way through Vienna, Prague, Bangkok—but Berlin was the Capital of Spies and for a man of my generation, it was Mecca. Returning in '86, I could have knelt down and kissed the cracks already appearing in the new asphalt of the Tegel landing strip. I was nearing forty-five, the life expectancy of a Double O, or mandatory retirement. It was from this city the orders issued that led to my father's death. It was across this city the world carved up power. Everyone who was anyone was here. It was in Berlin that I'd make a name beyond 0013. I could taste it.

My mission was to eliminate a SMERSH operative targeting the Stay Behind Operation. Early in the Cold War, NATO troops were outnumbered and feared a Warsaw Pact attack. If the Soviets rolled over the border, Stay Behinds drawn from military units specializing in long-range reconnaissance, surveillance, and target acquisition would rapidly deploy forward and allow Warsaw Pact troops to bypass them. Using pre-reconnoitered hide sites and caches of arms, ammunition, and radios, they would create a demolition belt to bottleneck the enemy and provide intelligence and support to Stay Behinds drawn from the SAS, who would infiltrate into East Germany, Czechoslovakia, Poland, and Russia herself. These Stay Behinds were part of NATO's official order of battle, but there was another variety created and run under the auspices of the CIA and MI6: civilians prepared to organize resistance, sabotage, and intelligence gathering. This civilian Stay Behind Network amounted to a clandestine, irregular army, whose very existence was a closely guarded fact. And now someone was picking off civilian Stay Behinds in West Berlin.

Intelligence said the SMERSH operative was using the freedom of SOXMIS, the Soviet diplomatic liaison given freedom to spy in the West, to acquire and eliminate his targets. The theme was reciprocity, as the British did the same inside the Soviet zone. Both SOXMIS and BRIXMIS would push their luck and "stray" into restricted areas in order to win intelligence that might help keep the Cold War cold. Three-man vehicle-borne patrols carried out ground and air reconnaissance, taking photographs of weaponry, troop movements, tech. The patrols were 24/7, 365 days of the year, and there was no end in sight. It was the job of the British Royal Military Police 19 (Support) Platoon, otherwise known as the White Mice, to deter SOXMIS from straying too far.

Six frustrating weeks into my mission in Berlin, with two more Stay

Behinds murdered in their homes, the White Mice received a call from the West German police about a SOXMIS vehicle too close to London Block, the headquarters for BRIXMIS in the Olympiapark, originally built for Hitler's Olympics. I didn't expect this stop to yield anything more helpful than the others: the West German police would pull over a Škoda; the driver and two other men inside the SOXMIS vehicle would refuse to speak, crossing their arms and staring stonily ahead; they'd stick a sign in the window: CALL THE ROYAL MILITARY POLICE. The White Mice were the only people with the jurisdiction to handle this particular hot potato.

So two West German police vehicles would front and rear the SOXMIS car after covering it with a blanket to prevent the spies taking photographs. Then the White Mice would turn up, speak in German or Russian with the senior Soviet officer, making sure to be polite without fraternizing. They'd obtain identity papers, carrying them back to the patrol car, where they'd get on the cumbersome Tech Aid phone and call base. A SOXMIS liaison officer would turn up and give their own chaps a slap on the wrist, then the White Mice would escort SOXMIS back to the Soviet-controlled zone.

Meanwhile, 26 Liaison, the covert boys, would check the area for dead letter drops, trying to stop whatever roll of film or map SOXMIS had gathered from working its way back East.

But as I followed the White Mice officers over wet grass to the heavy SOXMIS vehicle that day, the blanket was thrown off like a curtain rising in a theater, and I was surprised to see there were four men in the car, not three.

Seated in the rear beside a sheepish officer gripping a camera, a long-limbed, over-muscled man with the look of a prison brawler squeezed into uniform stared dead ahead. His head was shaved. Stubble glinted on his jaw. The sun was low, keeping him mostly in shadow, but when I crossed the spotlight in the sky, the man glanced up with the speed of a flick-knife. His age was indeterminate: he could have been eighteen, he could have been thirty. Experience had weathered him and exuberance lit him from within. He grinned at me, as if the two of us were sharing a great joke. The grin reached the man's eyes the way lava reaches an unlucky town. I had faced death many times in the field, but I had never known a chill like this.

Back at the White Mice vehicle, I gripped the blue siren as if holding on for dear life. It was the same siren the German police had: we found it made the East Germans working for SOXMIS flinch. New overlords, old fears.

"That's him," I said. "That's the man I'm looking for. The Stay Behind Slayer."

The officer on the Tech Aid covered the mouthpiece. "Sir?"

"I can feel it."

"Can't arrest him on a feeling, sir. Whatever we give the Reds, they give us fivefold over in the East. We pull him out, tomorrow a BRIXMIS vehicle will be rammed or shot."

"He's on his way to commit murder."

"Well, he won't get the chance now, sir. We'll escort the vehicle back over."

I willed myself to see it like a game of chess. "Get me BRIXMIS on the phone, I want to speak to a Chipmunk in the air right now."

"I can do that back at base, sir, I'm not supposed—"

"Please."

The RMP pulled a face. "As you're in the family, so to speak. Been wanting to tell you. Everyone still talks ever so highly of your old man."

"Thank you."

Finally, I got through to a Chipmunk plane: RAF officers on "flight training" carrying out aerial surveillance of the Soviet zone. "We're sending a black Škoda SOXMIS over Checkpoint Invalidenstrasse. I want you to follow it. Keep track of anybody exiting the vehicle before it returns to base. There's a monster inside, nearly seven feet tall, shaved head, large build. He's the target. Alert the nearest BRIXMIS. I want to know every movement this man makes."

Why had SOXMIS come so close to BRIXMIS headquarters in West Berlin? No Stay Behinds lived nearby to target. It was almost like the SMERSH operative wanted to be caught.

From that day on, BRIXMIS tracked the target around East Berlin. He made no further excursions West. There had been no ID on him. He didn't seem to be a Party functionary. He split his time between brothels and bars. Until one night BRIXMIS lost him on Karl-Marx-Allee. The tiled façades of the monumental boulevard—built after the Second World War in a Stalinist production of ancient Greece—were peeling, and shelters had gone up over the shops and restaurants to stop tiles falling on pedestrians. The target ducked under and never emerged out the other side. But the BRIXMIS drivers were the best in the business and they soon picked him up again in a trackside cluster of ruined factories, a startling figure striding over icy concrete, silhouetted black against spray-painted walls tumbling into technicolor landslides of rubble. Then—he was gone. Last seen near Checkpoint Oberbaumbrücke.

If he'd chosen that point to make it over the Wall, it would put him in Kreuzberg, where the head of a civilian Stay Behind Network lived. The BRIXMIS driver said it was almost like the target had been flirting, daring someone to find him. So that's exactly what I did.

Once a central district, Kreuzberg was surrounded on three sides by the barbed wire shadow of the Wall, relegating it to the outskirts. The Death Strip with its border fortifications kept Kreuzberg and Mitte, West and East, capitalism and Communism within shouting distance of each other but worlds apart. Rents and property prices had plummeted, houses crumbled. The working class, artists, students, and immigrants moved in, transforming the ramshackle streets into their own center. As I got closer to Checkpoint Charlie, a strange thing happened: my ears popped. It was a vacuum and nothing could live here. And yet life did go on, border guards watching children play in a kindergarten in the East. There was even a viewing point, wooden stairs and a little platform, from which West Berliners could wave to family on the other side, and tourists could gawk, pointing at the car barrier, the skeletal white ribbon of tarmac lit by rake-like posts, the concrete watchtower, Stalin's lawn and dragon's teeth, the signal fence, the hinterland wall. Beyond it all, German shepherds waited for someone to chase, and soldiers watched the tourists right back. And beyond them, people appeared preserved forever in the windows of apartment blocks as if in a surveillance photograph. Rising behind it all was the famous Television Tower.

I reached Kreuzberg as evensong played from the copper treetops; rain painted the pavements in puddles, reflecting the Shell petrol station occupying a bombed-out slice of flats. On a stretch of grass stubbornly growing before the spray-painted Wall, caravans formed a commune and kids played as parents cooked over fires. Punks and Turks jostled me. The Stay Behind lived in a wedge of a building above a beerhouse.

I caught the door for a mother managing a double pram, and then slipped inside before it closed. The stairwell smelled of piss. As I climbed I thought of a tattered poster I'd seen in the American guard tower: "SOLDIER . . . WHY ARE YOU IN BERLIN? TO SHOW THE BERLINERS, YOUR ALLIES AND THE COMMUNISTS THE BEST SOLDIERS IN OUR ARMY. TO PROTECT U.S. LIVES AND PROPERTY. TO HELP THE WEST BERLIN POLICE TO KEEP LAW AND ORDER. TO FIGHT LIKE HELL, IF NECESSARY. FOR U.S. RIGHTS AND A FREE BERLIN." A cat lunged from a windowsill hissing. I batted it away. And why are you in Berlin, 0013? *To fight like hell, if necessary*, seemed a good summation, and it always seemed to be necessary. But for what? The Wall had been up since '61 and showed no sign of coming down. Who was the winner here?

The door to number 21 was ajar. I pulled my weapon from my coat and screwed on the silencer. I nudged the door with my toe, creeping across a cork floor, brushing through an avalanche of fur coats into an open-plan living room–kitchen with the latest furniture from Sweden. The window was open, letting in the smell of frying sausages and petrol. A grunt and clatter brought me up short. I rounded the geometric-print sofa, and for a split second froze.

The target crouched over the supine figure of a man in his seventies, whose stick-like legs emerged from loose corduroy trousers, his slippered feet squirming and his straw hands scrabbling, because the hulking agent of SMERSH was covering his mouth with his own as he knelt on his chest, seeming to kiss the life out of him.

I cocked the trigger and pressed the gun to the back of the enemy's shaved head.

A long sniff as the man sat back, leaving his victim gasping.

"Stand up slowly." I tried German: "*Stehen Sie langsam auf.*" Russian: "*Medlenno vstan'te.* That's it. Now move into the center of the room. Turn to face me. Get on your knees and interlace your fingers behind your head. Slowly. *Medlenno. Koleni. Ruki.*"

There was a moment's pause before each order was followed, as the man from SMERSH seemed to pore over every detail of me, from the grip on my gun to the make of my shoes. I kept the weapon trained on him and leaned over to check on the old man, who was on all fours now, purple and hacking. He crawled to the armchair, grasped a glass of lager, raising it with arthritic knuckles to his white lips, losing half down his baggy shirt.

He gasped: "*Danke.*"

I told him to stay there, I'd get medical help. I was reaching for the Bakelite phone on the console when the devil kneeling on the Egyptian rug said in English accented by the Urals: "You'll regret saving his life."

My hand was on the receiver, but I didn't lift it. "Why?"

"He is a Nazi."

A glance was enough to catch the panic flushing the man's cheeks from bone white to brick red.

"That's not in our file."

"It's not in a file you've seen," the devil corrected. "Ernst here joined the SA in July 1933 and from 1941 to 1942 served eagerly with SS-Infanterierregiment 10. He was responsible for murdering partisans and thousands of Jews in the Ukraine and elsewhere. He transferred to the SS-Gebirgsjäger Division 'Prinz Eugen,' fighting partisans in the Banat, where he committed atrocities that would keep you from sleeping ever again." Ernst's eyes were flashing left-right, left-right as if reading the devil's speech on tickertape. "By June 1944, Ernst had achieved the rank of Hauptsturmführer. When MI6 and the CIA first set up the Stay Behind Networks, they turned to German army personnel—radio operators, little men. They found them poor recruits. Gestapo, SS, and Wehrmacht on the other hand were all too eager, and considered experts on the Communist threat. Ernst approached your Western services with a rather sweet love letter, promising to devote to you his versatile experiences in the economical, propagandistic, political, and military fields. He even wrote out his curriculum vitae. In detail. He promised to fight alongside the white races against those colored Commies. And you paid him one million marks to set up a network of thirty thousand tamed Nazis. You can see quite a bit of that money went on the latest fashion and gadgets. A lot of it went to girlfriends and pals. Cigarettes, whisky, a thousand marks a month to members. All very cozy. But of course, he over-recruited and recruited wrong and word got out. Caches of explosives and ammunition ended up in the wrong hands. Networks could name each other. All very embarrassing for Whitehall and Washington. So he was cut loose and ended up here, having failed to reclaim his place in the security apparatus of future Germany."

"The Soviets rounded up pet Nazis, too. Am I supposed to blush?"

"It might interest you to know that Ernst liked to play both sides. The CIA lapped up what they called his *racial fanaticism* because it attracted other Stay Behind recruits, and let us be honest, fit rather well with their own race theories, too. But Ernst was never a true believer. He simply wanted power back, so he also kept the Stasi happy, as a precaution. A young BRIXMIS agent named Francis Ware found out, so Ernst had to take care of him. You were told your father died in a BRIXMIS car crash. That's not exactly a lie. But it was only a crash inasmuch as I can make death by poison look like choking."

Ernst gripped the arms of the chair and lurched upward. I swung the pistol on him. "Sit down!" My gun equivocated between the old man and the devil on his knees. "That's why you led me here?"

"Yes."

"I'm simply supposed to believe you?"

"You can see the truth in Ernst's face."

My gaze snuck to Ernst, who wrung a quilt in his hands. "And you want me to buy you've been targeting Stay Behinds because they're Nazis and you're a man of justice? The last Stay Behind you killed was a teacher in her late twenties. The one before that a journalist born in '45."

A long, rumbling laugh from the cavernous chest. "I am not a man of justice. I am a man of death. As are you. I led you here, Emery Ware, with your license to kill, so *you* can have justice for your father."

Again, Ernst flinched from his seat. Again, I barked at him to sit still. My toes wiggled inside my shoes, a sign of life, that I existed here and now, not listening to my mother cry at night. "Who are you?"

"They call me Mora."

"You're SMERSH?"

"For now."

"What does that mean?"

"Did you know that when we train police in Russia as marksmen, we play a sound effect of bullets to provide a sense of reality? We have no ammunition left. We've lost thousands of men in Afghanistan. The unions are organizing in Siberia. When the explosion occurred at Chernobyl, the state made no announcements for two days. But people in Moscow were already talking about it. Rumor had spread. We have never before known people to speak openly on forbidden subjects. It is the beginning of the end."

My arm was starting to ache from pointing the gun. "So the West has won."

"The game isn't so short as that. I am more interested in what comes next."

"Now it's *I*, not *we*."

Mora relaxed onto his heels. "It could be *us*."

I sneered. "You've got the wrong man. I'm no traitor."

"That's not what Fräulein Marlene told us."

I backed up and folded onto a sofa, forming a triangle with Mora and Ernst. "I didn't tell her anything. I was just a young agent in Berlin for the first time, showing the ropes to an even younger agent. OK, maybe I was showing off . . . We got drunk in the Resi and a lady called me on the telephone system. There was a phone on each table . . . She told me she was lonely. A pneumatic tube system carried souvenirs and trinkets about the bar. She sent me her knickers. My friend bet me a bottle of whisky I wouldn't go through with it. I did, like a fool, but when I discovered she was an East German agent I reported it to my superiors, and paid for it with chicken feed assignments for a year. I was inexperienced, not treacherous."

A smirk. "She told SMERSH you were very experienced, where it mattered."

I heard myself swallow on a dry throat. "She was SMERSH? Why didn't she try to kill me?"

"A boast won you a stay of mercy. You told her she was lucky to run into you, because you were going to be a very big man one day. You could get her over to the West. Her whole family too. Unusual for a young Double O with a sterling reputation to have career aspirations. And you've kept hold of both, from what we hear: the standing and the ambition. But the clock is ticking. Soon you'll be forced to retire, and then what? A Double O rising in the ranks of leadership, it's not been done before. Trained killers train other killers or take to alcoholism in the country. You'll need to stand out. 0013 already has a reputation for ruthlessness. You're famous even in Moscow. You have the right accent and the right connections for MI6 to embed you with the 'businessmen' who'll make the world go round in the next decade. Drugs, guns, oil, minerals. But you'll need a competitive edge, as you capitalists have it, intelligence your peers in the same circles can't gather. I can help with that."

"You? You're a child"—even as I said it, I asked myself why I was entertaining the devil. And even as I asked it, I told myself this was an intelligence opportunity. Our training taught us to recognize serendipity. When an opportunity presents itself, don't stop for a risk assessment: trust your gut, your judgment and wisdom and experience, and seize it with both hands. Here was a young gun in SMERSH who wanted to share intelligence. *Share* intelligence—where had that thought come from?

It was as if Mora were listening to my designs. "And in return for intelligence that could save lives, hasten the end of the Cold War, and send you up the ladder, all I'd ask for is access to what you see, what you hear, what you think. My own SOXMIS in the land of Her Majesty's Government. Take the temperature for me. Whisper in my shell-like ear."

I snorted. "Where did you learn English?"

"A prison."

"Which prison?"

"Siberia."

"You were born to exiles?"

"A wheelbarrow man and his own daughter. They died, however. I was raised by a Hungarian professor of English literature who'd been rounded up after World War Two to pad the prisoner of war numbers and forgotten about in the tundra. He taught me English. Until I killed him."

"Why?"

A shrug. "He realized he was never getting home. He asked me to do it. He'd been a good teacher but an unkind man. Understandable, I suppose. He expected a bullet. That seemed dull to me. I enjoyed making his death last."

Bile clogged my throat. "What are you?"

"A nightmare. The failures of the twentieth century made flesh. A fairy godmother here to make your dreams come true. A peasant from the wasteland. I've been called it all. I'm much more interested in what I'm going to be. Russia will soon belong to the dogs and you won't be concerned with us anymore. Oil is the future battleground. China is flexing its muscles. But we will make our return to the world stage with terrible thunder." A smile. "America will have you on a leash. You hardly matter now. You'll matter even less once the threat of nuclear war in Europe wanes. Do you want a seat at the table? SMERSH will adapt. A private army of sorts, with international recruits and backers. The benefits of your globalization. Acting in the shadows for Moscow but very far away from her. Until we are strong enough."

"For what?"

Ernst lunged for the phone. I kicked out, catching the man a glancing blow to the head. Ernst rolled over, fingers filling with blood spurting from his scalp. He moaned.

"Oh dear," chuckled Mora. "Hurting a prisoner. That's not very gentlemanly."

"I never claimed to be a gentleman." I stood over Ernst. "You just presumed I was."

Mora grinned. "Exactly the pragmatism I admire. Aren't you tired of playing cat and White Mice? A two-way channel. We share intelligence for the mutual advancement of mankind—but mainly the mutual advancement of you and me." His face turned demure. "I'm a very good secret keeper."

Ernst grabbed me by the ankles. And before I knew what I'd done, I lowered the gun from Mora and fired straight down at Ernst, a clean shot to the head, which sounded with a muffled whisper then a thud as the skull split open on the cork.

I waited for the wave of revulsion, the sickness to my stomach at what I'd done, executing an unarmed man without orders, using my license to kill for personal reasons—but all I saw was a dead Nazi who murdered my father and widowed my mother. And nothing happened. The ceiling didn't cave in. No SWAT team charged through the door. I was like a diplomat driving away from a hit-and-run. And the only witness was Mora, who now clambered to his feet, towering over me by five inches.

Mora said, "I realize this may feel unreal. But don't worry. I have it all on tape, if you ever need to jog your memory."

On tape? Perhaps I did feel faint.

"I've been using British ammunition," he said.

"Hmm?"

"When I've shot a Stay Behind, it's been with your bullets."

"Yes, I've noticed that . . ." Was all this truly happening?

"Like I said, we've been aware of your potential. But nobody acted on it. Killing the Stay Behinds was my idea. My superiors still believe we'll invade West Germany and roll on to Paris and then London, so I could convince them it was worth the bullets. They do not know my true intentions and they do not see what's coming. But I do. And it's you."

He put out his hand, big and sharp-edged as a cleaver. I felt unsteady on my feet, so I took it. Afghanistan Rules, after all. Anything goes. Like killing a Nazi on the Western payroll.

MI6 did believe Ernst was the latest victim of the Stay Behind Slayer, as Mora promised, my bullets matching his. Three murders since my boots were on the ground. "We can't have you failing," said Mora silkily. So he produced a circus performer turned Stasi enforcer resembling him, whom I tracked to the villa of a Stay Behind in Spandau. I "saved" the industrialist who lived there and chased the giant into the black forest, crossing the Albrechtshof rail tracks that divided West Berlin from East Germany. Conveniently, the Eastern guards were looking the other way. Shots were fired in the dark. There were no witnesses. I took a photograph of the body. In reality, the body double covered himself in red paint. I would have preferred to kill him, sensing that Mora was happy with a loose end he could wrap around his new friend's neck. But Mora explained a body double was hard for him to come by and a sacrificial goat might prove useful in the future.

There was an embassy dinner in my honor. That was the start of a golden road. I was made Head of Station in Berlin. I was still there the day the Wall came down. I even joined the "wall-peckers" who brought hammers and chisels to chip away the graffitied blocks. Hawkers spread East German weaponry out for sale on blankets as the chip-chip-chipping carried into the night. I remembered reports on the cleanup of Chernobyl. Scientists wrapped in Sellotape for protection had located the nuclear core melted into the hellish bowels of the imploded structure. They poured concrete over it. They called it the Sarcophagus. I imagined a concrete shell pouring around that conversation in Kreuzberg, the concession, the compromise. The hammers kept working. Chip, chip, chip. But the sarcophagus held.

2022

TWENTY-SIX

A Death in the Family

The battered Cessna fought the air currents over the rainforest. Joseph Dryden, no pilot, was glad when Felix Leiter dumped himself into the neighboring seat and checked over the instruments. Behind them, Trigger let a waterfall of hair curtain her face as she strapped her bleeding thigh.

Leiter croaked, "003 not with you?"

"AWOL after Bond."

"Naturally." Leiter was glad some things could still be counted on. "If a hospital is in your immediate plans, I'd appreciate it, before I lose another limb."

Dryden nodded.

"How'd you find us?"

Dryden said, "I was looking for Zofia Nowak."

"Rattenfänger has her," said Leiter. "There was nothing I could do."

Dryden wiped his forehead. Fuel was low and the sun beat on the metal carcass of the plane. He didn't have a next move. He'd need Aisha to task Panopticon with searching for Zofia again, even if it risked bringing Five Eyes down on him. He said, "Calling home."

Leiter turned to him. "How does that work? Voices in your head?"

"Except I'm not imagining them. Calling home. Come in, Aisha. Calling home." Nothing. "I don't understand, she was there before . . ." He boxed the radio. "Reckon you can get this thing operational?"

Leiter nodded, going to work with one hand.

Maybe Aisha was being reprimanded for helping him. He shouldn't have left her in a difficult spot, but he knew she'd never back down. And he wasn't about to be detained by Five Eyes in the black site where they'd stuck Luke while Moneypenny needed him. A voice far in the back of his mind asked him if he wasn't more afraid of being trapped behind a desk than he was of being trapped in the black site.

"Got it," said Leiter, passing him the radio.

"All right, I'm going to use my numbers station. You keep radio silence, OK?"

"Why?"

"Wilderness of mirrors."

"Ah, old James Jesus Angleton. Paranoia running rife since 000's betrayal?"

"They don't trust me anymore," said Dryden, aware how stung he sounded. He'd almost added: *after everything I've given.* He tugged his right ear. "Mistrust in the system is the only sane attitude to take in this world."

"All right, I'll keep shtum." Leiter passed him the radio.

Dryden clicked it, trying to recall the lines. He'd never needed them before. Clandestine wasn't exactly his style. "Maintain your post: that's all the fame you need; for it's impossible you should proceed. Already I am worn with cares and age, and just abandoning the ungrateful stage: unprofitably kept at heaven's expense, I live a rent-charge on his providence." The plane kicked and rattled. Leiter tapped the fuel gauge. "You, whom every Muse and Grace adorn, whom I foresee to better fortune born, be kind to my remains; and oh defend, against your judgment, your departed friend." Leiter pulled a map out from a faux-leather pouch. "Let not the insulting foe my fame pursue; but shade those laurels which descend to you: and take for tribute what these lines express; you merit more, nor could my love do less."

The radio hissed, and then Ibrahim's voice came through. "Base receives you, go to channel 812." He sounded strained—but perhaps that was the static.

Leiter turned the dial.

"Secure," said Dryden. "Ibrahim? What are you doing out of hospital?"

There was another hiss, then Ibrahim's voice slipped through. "It's Aisha. She's de—"

The muscles in Dryden's face seemed to seize, his jaw jumping. "Say again? Does Aisha need me?"

"Dead. Inside Q Branch. Stabbed. She's dead. 000's code was on the tunnel door. We don't know why his code still worked. She's dead, Joe. There was no one with her."

The plane rocked. Leiter grabbed hold of the controls. Trigger had to scramble aside as Dryden fought to the door, opening it. Trigger got her arms around his chest. 004 hung over the edge, wind on his cheeks.

"I'm going to kill him," said Dryden.

"Who?" said Trigger.

Dryden bit out: "Conrad Harthrop-Vane. 000 breached the castle."

Leiter called, "Get that door closed."

Trigger tugged on the rusted hinges, which screamed, finally relenting against the blast of the wind. Then she leaned over Leiter's shoulder and whispered, "What's happening?"

Leiter said, "A death in the family."

Dryden said again, "I'm going to kill him."

Trigger turned to him. "I can help with that."

"He uses you as cover."

"Yes."

"You let him."

She lifted her chin. "Yes."

Leiter twisted around. "Hold up—"

"It was the only way to keep my life," she said. "Now I want it back. He uses my communication network. We can get him through that."

Eventually, Dryden gave a single nod. "Just give me something to aim at."

Trigger said to Leiter: "Panama, the Colón Free Trade Zone."

The Perspex window emblazoned with peeling lettering advertising a defunct perfume brand offered an unpromising view of the Free Trade Zone. Folk hauling merchandise from shipping containers into shops selling America at a discount; cranes over a half-constructed cruise port with duty-free shopping set to replace the nearby empty mall, whose escalators still ran but whose businesses didn't after the owner landed on a sanctions list; near-constant traffic to the city's morgue. Leiter sat in the humid office, watching all this go on as it had when he was here last, believing he'd prized the location of Trigger out of the manager with Conrad Harthrop-Vane's help. Joseph Dryden stood in the corner, his face wiped blank.

The door to the outer office clicked. The manager found his secretary missing and was shouting over his shoulder as he came into his office. Then he saw Trigger behind his desk and shut up. Trigger drew a hand through her golden hair and cupped her chin in her palm.

The man patted his stomach as if it were in danger, looking from Trigger to Leiter, and then rested his hand on the butt of a gun stuffed in his belt. "My American friend, you enjoy your trek through the Gap? You seem to have left a couple of things behind."

Leiter wrapped his hand around a scuffed walking stick and thumped the floor. "Easy come, easy go, friend. Seeing as you helped me find Trigger, I thought we'd come and thank you." He nodded toward her. "I'd drop your shooter."

Beneath Trigger's hand on the desk there was a short-nosed pistol.

"Trigger?" The man released his gun, dabbing at the sweat building between his open shirt buttons.

She nodded.

"I didn't help him! There was another man, a pale white man, he said the right code—I was doing as he said!"

Trigger tilted her head. "The gods are asleep and do not watch."

"Yes! That's it!"

"Do you know its origins?"

His eyes slid sideways to Leiter.

"It's what looters say when they steal from temples on holy days," she said. "Because there's no one around. Just like nobody will see what happens to you today."

He stepped back. He was close to bumping into Dryden. "How do I even know you are Trigger?"

"Your shoes are a size too big," said Trigger. "Compensating for something?"

"I demand—"

There was a blur and smoke filled the room. The manager hopped up and down, howling and clutching his foot. Falling to the floor, he wrenched off his boat shoe with a sob to find his toes were intact. Trigger spun the gun on her finger and winked at Leiter.

"I have performed my job loyally, passing on messages for you!"

"They weren't for me."

"Huh?"

"The pale man used me as an alias. The messages weren't for me, they were for him. I want to find him. You'll put an urgent communiqué through. Use the words *Ot volka bezhal, da na medvedya popal.*" She spelled it out for him as he crawled to his laptop. "Tell them I do not appreciate the cartel trying to feed me to poisonous snakes. I have killed them all and the American spy." The manager gurgled. "The system will tell you where the message has been sent. That's what we want to know."

"OK. OK." He dropped into the client seat. He was muttering. Dryden stepped forward with a creak. The manager hunched, typing faster.

Leiter shifted on the windowsill, then said: "Your urgent code is: *I ran from the wolf but ran into a bear.*"

"So?"

"You're right, I'll never understand Russians."

"It is like saying—out of the frying pan into the fire," said Trigger. "And before you start, I know that's the permanent state of weather in Texas."

"I have sent it. It can take a while for a reply to come."

Trigger said, "Got any tequila?"

"Mezcal. In the drawer."

She unscrewed the cork and drank with a sigh through her body. She passed the bottle to Leiter, who took a swig and grimaced. "That's poison."

"Better than snake venom."

The computer beeped.

Dryden pointed. "What does that mean?"

"I messaged the radio station in Tangiers. They sent the message to the pale man's satellite phone. He is in the Arctic. A place called Pyramiden. That is everything you wanted? You'll leave now?"

Leiter stamped the ground with his stick. "When he gave you the code—the gods are asleep and do not watch—you figured he was walkin' me into an ambush, huh?"

The manager spread his arms. "You cannot expect me to risk my life for a CIA agent."

"How'd you know I'm a Company man?"

"It is practically tattooed to your forehead, friend."

Leiter said, "That so? Let me get this straight. You're more afraid of Rattenfänger than the CIA?"

He licked his lips. "I am more afraid of Rattenfänger than anything."

"So when we leave here, you'll likely get on the horn and report the whole thing up the chain."

The manager's face fell. "No—no. I say nothing at all. I do not want trouble."

"Trouble's already here," said Trigger.

"Please! This is not my war, I am an honest businessman. OK, maybe not so honest, but this is my world, huh? I'm not in your world. If a few spies get killed what is it to me?"

Dryden's hand closed on the back of the man's neck, and Leiter had to scramble out of the way as Dryden drove the manager into the window, popping the Perspex and dangling him out the frame, his hold on the man's belt the only thing keeping him from falling six stories.

"Whoa!" shouted Leiter. "Cool it, bud!"

Dryden called down: "Are you going to report this?"

A shriek: "No!"

Dryden let go, the manager slipping by inches, then tightened his fist again. "You sure?"

"Yes! Please! Yes!"

From the desk, Trigger said: "Drop him."

That raised Dryden's head. He turned to look at her. Dryden pulled the manager inside and hurled him across the room, shattering a wall of shelves. Then he walked out.

Leiter said to Trigger, "You see a fuse and have to light it, huh?"

"It's already lit," she said, looking down at the crumpled manager. His hand was inching toward the gun in his waistband. "I wouldn't."

He went for it.

The report of a bullet ate all the sound in the room. Trigger holstered her weapon.

Leiter watched the manager clutch at the hole in his chest. "Stupid bastard," he said.

Trigger swept from the room but Leiter stayed.

The manager reached out. Leiter took his hand, giving him company for the minute it took for him to die.

He caught up with Dryden on the docks. 004 was breathing in fumes, his lifeless gaze on shipping containers used either as torture chambers or to export cane sugar.

"It's my fault," said Dryden. "I never should have left her."

Leiter said nothing.

"She was the best . . ." Dryden bowed his head. "You and Trigger should get to a hospital. You look like a scarecrow."

"Don't flatter me, I'm struggling to resist your walking slab of handsome act as it is." That got half a smile. "And where would you be going, 004?"

"Pyramiden."

"I owe 000 a bullet, too. Anything I can do to help? Let me at least scope the place out for you."

Dryden tilted his head, as if listening to a distant voice. "Can you do it without raising alarms? I won't let anything stop me killing him."

"I can make discreet inquiries. And I never saw you."

"Thanks."

"Thanks for the airlift." Leiter took his arm. "But let me tell you something, from one veteran to another. I know Trigger is the walking wounded and I'm several levels beneath that, and I don't want to be dead weight. But I don't like you going alone. If you have a friend out there in the cold, I'd call 'em."

The faint smile widened.

TWENTY-SEVEN

Midnight Sun

In the Cold War, cities crowded with human beings made up the epicenters of espionage: Vienna, Berlin, London. Today, intelligence has been overtaken by techno-espionage and the epicenter is somewhere humans can hardly tread. Dubbed the New Ice Curtain, the Arctic Circle was warming faster than anywhere else on the planet, revealing a new Northern Sea Route that would enable whoever controlled it to extract trillions of dollars' worth of oil. The number of Russian spycraft in the region had trebled—and that was only the intercepted planes. But Pyramiden, an abandoned 1920s Soviet mining settlement on the archipelago of Svalbard, remained strangely peaceful.

From the perspective of spy satellites, Pyramiden was a ghost town patrolled by seven Russians armed against polar bears. Why they patrolled a shuttered settlement was unknown. Pyramiden was located at the gateway between Russia's nuclear submarines on the Kola Peninsula and NATO powers, huddled in a valley between the Nordenskiöld Glacier to the south and a fjord spreading from Greenland to the west with mountains all around. One of those mountains rose in the shape of a pyramid over the peeling Palace of Culture, an empty hotel, a rotting primary school, and crystalized apartments. A bust of Lenin watched over the whistling parade ground. His red granite skull seemed impossibly dense, even swollen, boxed by the wind. In summer the ocean was still too choked by ice for boats. Darkness wouldn't fall for months. This was the land of the midnight sun.

In normal circumstances, a submarine approaching a place like Pyramiden would call for help from a nuclear icebreaker and a harbor tug. But American satellites whizzing overhead every thirty minutes would notice that. So the Rattenfänger submarine was left to seek the perfect polynya—a stretch of open Arctic water amidst ice, a Russian word for a Russian problem—navigating beneath inverted ridges that plummeted 150 feet, then flirting with thickness of no more than ten feet.

For the men aboard, the hours-long zig-zig beneath the ice grew more and more maddening, the word from the navigator remaining the same: "Heavy ice, heavy ice." Moneypenny wasn't sure whether to feel dread or hope. Could whatever waited for her on the surface bode any better than this sunken prison? Until, finally, there was no avoiding finding out. "Thin ice! Thin ice!" And then: "Clear water!" The pumps burred. The submarine rose like a balloon. Water rushed into the tanks. The submarine hesitated, suspended. A periscope darted up along with the ESM antenna. Nothing within five miles. Three minutes later, the submarine was sleek on the surface of the Arctic Ocean, caged by the gnashing teeth of the ice pack.

Mora escorted Moneypenny onto the sail, his fist clamped on her arm. She found she was grateful, despite the pain, because he kept her anchored in the face of the gale driving across the bridge at more than sixty miles per hour. The force deafened her and ice stabbed her cheeks, the rest of her swaddled in wool and oilskin, which would save her life but also make her unidentifiable to any satellite that happened to capture their emergence. Even when the wind relented, there was the boom and crash of the ice itself, settling million-year-old grievances. The sun bouncing off the twisted ridges of ice blinded her. She didn't think she could withstand a minute of this, but she wasn't given a choice.

By the time the low-lying blocky Soviet architecture of Pyramiden became visible through the static of ice, she no longer cared what awaited. The tortured metal frames of dead industry lay around like skeletons in an elephant graveyard. She had asked Mora to pinpoint X, the artificial intelligence system he planned to train using Dryden's neural interface to hoodwink Q, on a map for her. For that, he would need a large data storage center. As more of the world moves online, more cold server farms are needed to store photos, messages, emails, banking, DNA tests: memories shed like dead skin and never swept. The trouble was how to keep the servers cool. Heat dissipation could crash every Apple device in the world. It could cripple a nation. There were different solutions. Microsoft packed servers into "submerged oceanic facilities": shipping containers sunk to the seafloor. China had a different answer: caves. Moneypenny peered up at the pyramid-shaped mountain of ice and realized she had reached the endgame. The cloud under the mountain.

The question was whether Luke Luck had succeeded in delivering his message to Joseph Dryden. If not, she'd find Dryden here, ready for dissection, and Mora's plan would be set in motion. Submerged and running silent, Mora also didn't know what to expect. Had 004 managed to evade capture? Were 007 and 003 still free? Or would 000 have succeeded in crippling the Section?

The submarine crew piled into the hotel where a bar keeping the guards happy waited to serve them. But she wasn't offered any relief. Mora's fist never strayed from her arm, and she was dragged through the snow toward the Palace of Culture, flanked by four of the crew, and the submarine's doctor. Mora marched her down a corridor with anemic potted plants and a black mold ceiling. He kicked open a swing door, pulling her into a ballroom with murals of wartime glory, where 000 waited at attention before a throne built for the master of ceremonies. Half his face—his perfect face—was melted away. She could smell the burnt tissue. When he swallowed, she could see the ligaments and muscles stir beneath his crisped skin. It looked like he'd thrown himself onto a grenade, though she knew he didn't have that noble bone in his body.

000 drew himself to attention. "Colonel. Moneypenny."

Moneypenny thought he might even be relieved to find her alive and intact. She put concern into her voice. "What happened, 000? You're hurt. Was it 007 . . . ?"

Mora looked around. "I do not see 004."

"Luke Luck's team were unsuccessful."

"Unsuccessful," repeated Mora. "Unsuccessful. And 007 and 003?"

"Tiger Tanaka . . ."

"Unsuccessful?" echoed Mora.

"I almost had them."

"Almost." He let Moneypenny go to pace the groaning boards. "I can't bank *almosts*, son."

000 winced, edging back on his heels.

Mora was framing himself as 000's father, and Moneypenny had framed herself as his mother, her route to reaching him. Very well. She said softly, "Your face, Conrad. You need a surgeon. Can you feel anything?"

His mouth, half-charred and twisted, twitched. "Not a thing."

"Is that right?" whispered Mora, sniffing the air by Harthrop-Vane's cindered cheek. "Mmm. All that time bottled up beneath the ice, I'm hungry. What did happen to your pretty face, son?"

"Bond. A train. There was an explosion."

"Where is Luck?"

"Comatose at Shrublands."

Mora growled.

"He seemed to help 004. I told you not to trust—" Harthrop-Vane cried out as Mora's knee jabbed him in the back, sending him staggering to the floor.

Mora raised a colossal boot to stamp onto his head.

"Wait!" said Moneypenny.

Mora paused. "He betrayed you and still you want to save him."

"He's my agent."

From the floor, Harthrop-Vane's ragged breathing hitched. Then a whine filled the room. It was a phone, which Harthrop-Vane reached for now with one hand, the other spread in surrender. He checked the screen. "A call on the comms system. Our asset in Panama."

Mora stepped back. He collapsed into the throne. Moneypenny watched as Mora stretched. Luck must have succeeded in warning Dryden. The question was, When would the cavalry arrive? And would 007 and 003 lead the charge? She had to hold out a little longer, that's all. Hope. She savored the sensation, no matter how dangerous its flicker on her face.

000 climbed onto one knee. "I ran from the wolf but ran into a bear. That's Trigger's urgent code." A drop of grease and blood splashed from his cheekbone onto the screen. He read the message, then climbed to his feet, though no permission had been given. The pulse in his neck jumped. "Our asset is dead. His second-in-command says it was Trigger, working *with* Felix Leiter and a six-foot-four black British man. 004. They were using the comms system to find me. That means they now know about Pyramiden." 000 looked up from his phone. "If Luck had succeeded in helping Dryden, he would have told 004 to stay a thousand miles away from you. But 004 is searching for me, and he knows I'm your soldier. So Luck must have failed in his mission. And now Dryden knows where you are. Trigger and Leiter were wounded. They've checked into a local hospital. 004 left without them. He's alone."

Moneypenny fought for a different interpretation. She felt faint.

Mora brought his hands together slowly, a single clap. "He's a team player. If he's isolated, he'll seek support before attempting to infiltrate a place like this." He steepled his fingers. "Your pet thief, Moneypenny. I wonder where she got to . . ."

The doctor steadied her. "If you need a sedative, Miss Moneypenny . . ."

"Stay away from me." She faced Mora. "What do you get out of this?"

"You forced my hand," said Mora.

"Me?"

"Since the collapse of the Soviet Union, I've run Rattenfänger for the Kremlin, spreading destabilization in the West. But between you and me, I've never had much patience for orders. You thought I was merely a colonel. You've never been able to discover who runs Rattenfänger. Now you know. I am king and holy father, and I want more. You forced me out of the darkness, detained me, photographed and fingerprinted me. I am not content to be a warmonger from the shadows and you've kept me from the light. The Kremlin is distracted with the Ukraine and the army is unhappy. This is my moment. But I do not wish to take over an isolated country against a unified West. Poisoning Panopticon will change all that. I will hobble the West and become lord of the Arctic—and thus, lord of the world. Russia will be mine. The West will be mine. I will win the everywhere war."

Moneypenny raised her voice over the rattling windows. "You won't. I won't allow it. 007, 003, and 004 are all free."

"So am I," 000 told her, "and I've beaten them on every test you've ever put me through."

"Yet they're loose and you're missing half a face," snapped Moneypenny.

000 sipped the air, as if anticipating a delicious taste. "Bad news out of Regent's Park, I'm afraid. I hate to be the one to break it to you. 004 is suspected of working with Rattenfänger. He's gone dark. He fears he cannot trust anyone at home."

Moneypenny fought off the doctor's attempt to steady her. "Why?"

"Aisha Asante was murdered inside Q Branch."

Moneypenny acted before she knew she was moving, lunging toward 000, swinging the steak knife Luke Luck had smuggled her. He caught her wrist and twisted until she dropped the knife with a yell.

"It wasn't me!" He laughed, but then the laughter died. "It wasn't me, Moneypenny."

"Like hell it wasn't," she panted, "you two-faced bastard."

Harthrop-Vane dragged her close enough to feel his frayed skin. "M isn't who you think he is."

Mora said, "Now, now, Conrad, that's need-to-know."

Wait. No. Wait. Moneypenny felt a wave begin at the tip of her skull and sink through her body, reconstituting her insides. 000 released her. Moneypenny staggered. Staggering. Staged. Meaningless words swirled around her.

The doctor put his arm around her waist. "Here, let me give you a shot, you're in shock . . ."

"Stay away from me." She began to fight. "Stay away!"

Mora's applause echoed around the ballroom.

TWENTY-EIGHT

A New Legend

Rachel Wolff had a very good fake ID with a whole life attached to it. In spycraft, this was known as a new legend: a mocked-up history with full online presence, even a paper trail. It wasn't hard to achieve if you had the right connections. A passport was purchased from an addict or a homeless person, someone vulnerable with only their selves left to sell. All the better if they looked a little like the customer. Then a narrative was constructed. This narrative, to Rachel, was like peering through Alice's looking glass into a life unlived.

If, instead of emigrating from Serbia to Britain after surviving the Holocaust, her grandfather had chosen New York. If, instead of attending the Beth Hamidrash Hagadol Synagogue in Leeds, she'd been a member of the Brooklyn Heights Synagogue. If, instead of having a diamond thief for a father and a con woman for a mother, her parents were schoolteachers in Brooklyn. If her parents hadn't been murdered by a war criminal turned diamond dealer. If a spook called Moneypenny had never visited her grandfather's jewelry shop and offered Rachel the chance to have her vengeance. The chance to wipe her slate clean and be a hero.

The whole thing could have been a dream, and didn't that seem more likely, more realistic, than the idea of Rachel as some kind of hero? Still, she'd liked the feeling, while it lasted. This current taste of normal life, this glimpse through the looking glass, left her cold. Left her, in fact, casing New York's Diamond District for neglected back doors, bank vans with running engines, hagglers who forgot to shut their suitcases. Not that she'd try anything, of course. She wasn't that stupid. Rattenfänger could be looking for her, as well as the UK police for diamond theft. She was bored, she told herself. Homesick, even, for her grandfather's shop.

She was standing across from the black marble frontage of the House of Diamonds, watching a YouTuber lose situational awareness as he showed off to his phone about a bargain, when the fine hair of her short crop stood up. Rachel scanned the windows. No one on the street stood out as wrong, or too right.

She decided to follow the YouTuber, a watch dealer confusingly wearing a New York Knicks snap-back hat and a vintage Chicago Bulls hoodie, with an Oris Aquis Date Diamonds on his wrist. He was talking to a selfie stick, and Rachel followed him onto Sixth Avenue, watching his screen for those behind her. The usual crowd was outside the 47th Street Diamond Exchange. She was clear until Bryant Park, where the branches of trees streamed skyward like inverted jellyfish. There was an Asian man with glasses and a bowl haircut sitting at a kiosk having coffee. Hadn't she seen him exiting a bank two blocks back?

Rachel crossed the park to where the New York Public Library beckoned reassuringly, a pale palace in marble. She rounded the building to the Fifth Avenue entrance, trotted up the stairs, nodding hello to stone lions Patience and Fortitude. In the gift shop she bought an NYPL T-shirt and cap. She changed in the toilets, then took the stairs to the Rose Main Reading Room. The room stretched two city blocks: free of columns and lined with books, it offered no hiding places. Rachel found a corner seat and pulled a book off the shelf. It was a dictionary of criminology. Smiling at that, Rachel buried her face, pulling her cap down. She watched the three entrances. The Asian man with glasses made no reappearance, but there was a mousy student she may have seen on Sixth Avenue . . . Rachel watched the student plug in a laptop and lose herself in work. Watched her for so long that she had to stretch her neck, looking up at the ceiling, which was painted with a mural of blue sky and blushing pink clouds, the kind of sky you'd find over Mount Olympus, or in the moment between life and death.

Paranoid, *moi*?

Still, Rachel waited until a staff member with a trolley paused to answer someone's question. She stood up and took the trolley, pushing to the exit with her hat pulled down. She left it there, darting into the lift. On exit, the Asian man with glasses was there on the phone. He didn't notice her.

A zigzag through the Garment District. The same white van kept reappearing reflected in the windows of the brick warehouses. She lagged at a boutique and let it get ahead of her. The back window of the van was half-obscured by a toolbox, as if the interior was converted with shelves, typical for tradesmen. But only half-obscured. Enough clearance for a camera. Rachel kept her hat down and stayed in crowds.

She reached the famous green awning of B&H at West 34th Street and Ninth Avenue. The photo and video store sold everything from cameras to drones with gadgets whisked across multiple floors by a conveyor belt system. Rachel stopped at the counter where a bearded man with white shirtsleeves, a green waistcoat, and a yarmulke was tutting over a broken laptop.

"Busy here today," she said, glancing at the mirror behind him.

He heaved a sigh.

"Shabbat just a few hours away, at least. Nothing will blink or beep at you for twenty-four hours."

At that he lifted his eyes. "Small mercies. What can I do for you?"

"Do you have a white noise generator?"

"Yes."

"Could you show me how it works?"

With a shrug, the man called it up on the system, and after a minute a box whirred on the conveyor belt overhead—he plucked it off with the dexterity of a card croupier. The unboxing was done with the same detached professionalism.

"It is very simple. On, off. It emits a noise-cancellation barrier of up to 150 feet."

"Great." Rachel switched it back on. But she whispered anyway: "Can you tell if my phone has been injected with malware?"

"Did you click a link you shouldn't?"

Rachel gave a winning smile. "I think I've been StingRayed."

He said, "A StingRay is layman's talk for an electronic surveillance tool that simulates a cell phone tower but with a much stronger signal, forcing phones to connect with it—then it can take your international mobile subscriber identity, intercept calls, scrape data, and place malware in your phone. It is used from airplanes and vehicles by the US police and military against drug cartels and other criminals. Are you those things?"

"It's also used without a warrant against protesters. A van is following me. I'm an activist. I think it's got my phone but I want to know for sure. My big brother says I'm paranoid."

"Well." The man shrugged. "Let's see if he's right." He rebooted her phone. "Now we check the shutdown log in the sysdiagnose archive."

"I never did master Yiddish."

He chuckled. "Well, I would say try Duolingo, but this phone has spy malware on it that can track your location and listen to you even when you're not making a phone call. So perhaps it's best to buy another."

Rachel drew her hands back from the counter, as if a Geiger counter had told her the phone was radioactive. "Good idea."

"And perhaps this phone could spend the day riding our conveyor belt."

She grinned. "Great idea."

The man showed her to the staff exit. She wanted to hug him. There was no van waiting outside. She skipped across the street into a vintage store, where she swapped her NYPL outfit for a Leatherman jacket and a beanie. She hustled to the High Line, a disused elevated railway line transformed into a public park stitched into the western flank of Manhattan.

For the first time that day, Rachel detached her pocketknife from her keys and kept her hand on the blade in her pocket. She listened for helicopters. Between 25th and 27th, the path took her into the treetops. A photographer raised her hackles, but he was searching for an Edward Hopper look into a series of windows where normal life went on. At the 17th Street and Tenth Avenue overlook, the steel beams had been replaced by a glass-fronted balcony, where people watched the traffic. She idled there, checking off passersby. A young white man wearing a T-shirt with the NASA logo, but instead of NASA it read BOWIE. A black woman in her thirties wearing a beret and Dr. Martens boots. No one she'd already seen today. She followed the concrete planks past crab apples and alumroot, asters and sedges, glorious goldenrods; through dumpling steam at the open-air food court where trains used to deliver flour to the biscuit factory; past vines that parted like curtains to reveal the redbrick meatpacking plants below. No white van rumbled on the street.

She took the stairs at 14th Street and walked a strip yet to be touched by money, crumbling low-rises occupied by a taxi company and a storage facility. A white van was parked in the forecourt, but it was a different make and model. The Hudson surged into view. She set her aim on the Hudson River piers where, between rotten wood splintered by Hurricane Sandy, concrete piles supported concrete tulips to create an undulating park. She crossed onto the manmade lily pad and bought an ice cream, because, why not? Then she settled on the steps of the amphitheater, looking out to Hoboken. Ships trifled with the scaly water. That couple, weren't they indecently giddy? And that man in the puffa jacket, what was he hiding under there?

The couple left arm in arm. She picked up an abandoned newspaper. Rachel was an expert safecracker, so the cryptic crossword was defeated in no short order. The man in the puffa responded to the shouts of his children in the playground and moved off. As she wrote in the last answer, her neck pricked.

Someone on silent feet had just sat down behind her. Why hadn't she taken the uppermost level? No time for self-recriminations now. Rachel looked in the reflection of her watch face. A sixty-something-year-old man sat directly behind her, shirt open to reveal a hairy, wiry chest. There was a whole amphitheater of seats to choose from. Rachel gripped her knife. Maybe he was lonely. But the gray grizzle on his cheeks covered a tan. A lonely traveler?

"Excuse me," the man said. "Do you have the time?"

No use pretending she didn't have the time. The question was how much time did she have left?

"It's gone three," she said.

Rachel saw his shadow move. She twisted. As she did, she heard a step, but she didn't have time to think about it, because the man's hands absorbed all of her attention: the swollen knuckles, the light hair, the purple freckles, the ring with a protruding needle that was jabbing toward her neck. Rachel knocked his wrist with one hand, raising her penknife with the other, but the fist with the poison ring was about to close on her forearm.

That's when the man coughed and seemed to faint.

Rachel looked up to see Joseph Dryden lay him down on the bench. Blood slipped from the man's mouth. Dryden took Rachel's newspaper and waved it over the paling face.

"Anyone watching?" asked Dryden.

Rachel swallowed. "No."

Dryden dumped the newspaper over the man's face. He took a bottle of Brooklyn craft beer from his pocket, splashed it over the corpse, and left it at his feet. Then he took the man's wallet and a device that looked like a hi-fi remote.

"What is that?"

"It's blocking the CCTV cameras. He didn't want any witnesses. The ring contains poison. You wouldn't have felt the effects for a few hours. He didn't want anyone to know he was ever near you."

"What did you do to him?"

"Punctured his lung," said Dryden, sliding the stiletto blade up his sleeve.

StingRayed, Rachel thought. She wiped her forehead. "I missed you, killer."

"You too, kidder, you too."

TWENTY-NINE

Field Commission

On the Lower East Side, redbrick façades formed a game of snakes and ladders, with factory casement windows for squares and fire escapes forming hissing ZZZZs stenciled by the low sun. A neon arrow at the corner beckoned tourists to Katz's Deli, where waiters would berate them as they pretended to be Sally—*I'll have what she's having*. A few doors down, Russ & Daughters was selling bagels like there was a run on lox. The walls around the vintage market bursting the seams of a derelict site were painted with a mural of Bugs Bunny, who snickered at boutiques selling white shirts for over $100. This neighborhood was a place to see and be seen. The Ludlow Hotel offered a reassuringly solid sanctuary among the noise: the limestone fireplace burning despite the hot weather, marble floors, a Moroccan chandelier. Rachel Wolff followed Joseph Dryden to the stairs. She was tired from a day of being prey and wanted to ask him why they were climbing four flights, but knew the answer: a lift announces your arrival. His suite was done in dark wood with brass accents. She made use of the bathroom: a mosaic floor shimmering like the scales of a fish, a mirror lined with bulbs that said *Showtime*. At the green marble sink, Rachel wiped away the layer of sweat coating her face to find she was grinning.

Dryden waited on the balcony, which had a view like a diorama, old New York stacked in front of the financial city, former factories turned into loft apartments, rooftops littered with vents and deck chairs, weed plantations, spray paint that philosophized in thirty-foot letters, asking: WHY? Responding: WHY NOT? Instructing: EVOLVE.

"You've done well staying invisible," he said. He opened a beer and passed it over. "Not even a single police report. You must be going mad."

"Until today. You look good. No lasting damage?"

"Nothing physical," he said, clinking her bottle. "Thanks to you."

Rachel felt a blossom of pleasure. "Are you here because you knew I was in trouble?"

"I'm sorry to say I brought the trouble. Somehow, the opposition knew I was trying to find you and didn't want that to happen. Because of your particular talents, I imagine. I'm here because I need your help."

"Who are the opposition?"

Dryden hunched his shoulders. "Say we were attacked in this room. Where are your weapons?"

The bedside tables were lumps of petrified wood, too heavy to budge. There was a notepad with black paper and a white pencil, sharp enough to stab someone. A welcome pack held together with a pink paperclip, which she could use to pick a lock as easily as scratch someone's eyes out. "Stationery."

"What about the bathroom?"

"Well, for one thing, that's the nicest hotel bathroom I've ever seen, and I've stolen from some nice hotel rooms."

"For another thing?"

"The bulbs are exposed. You could electrocute someone, or crush the bulb in a towel, then scatter the shards on the floor. You've got beer in the minibar, maybe a bottle of wine. They make good clubs." On the street below, the cars were so small they could be Tonka trucks. "Or you could chuck someone off the balcony."

"There's always that."

Rachel relaxed in the chair, perfectly poured plastic. "Why are you testing me?"

"Because I need your help with something too dangerous for a simple diamond thief."

"Fuck you."

"Elegantly put."

"Who broke you into Free Port?"

He ran a hand over his closely cropped hair. "This isn't that. This is the cold server farm of Rattenfänger. I need the help of a Double O with the talents of a master thief."

Rachel picked at the label on her beer. "You told me you have to kill two people in the line of duty to be awarded Double O status."

"Forensics reported that the diamond Janus and the thief Marko were both killed by the same gun, and it wasn't Moneypenny's. They couldn't figure it out. It was you, wasn't it?"

She looked into the setting sun. "I had to do it."

"I know."

"What happened to Moneypenny? When I couldn't contact her afterward, I disappeared."

"MIA. I've been made Acting Chief of the Double O Section in her absence. Rattenfänger has abducted a computer scientist called Dr. Zofia Nowak. Intelligence tells us Rattenfänger has a base at Pyramiden, a former Soviet mining town in the Arctic. Satellite imagery shows a mountain the shape of a pyramid. At night, there's a glaring cloud of color over the mountain. Energy discharge. We think there's a data storage center inside."

"Can't afford an Apple subscription?"

He snorted. "I need to get inside, shut it down, and rescue Nowak. I'd take good odds we'll find Moneypenny there too, and 000. I have an account to settle with him. Rattenfänger have enough troops to mount a small-scale war. I need backup to get inside and backup to get out alive. I need you."

"So what—you're offering me a field commission?"

"If you want it."

That same rush of pleasure, as if she'd been picked first for the team.

Dryden continued: "It's not an easy life, or a long one. There's a mandatory retirement age of forty-five. Most agents don't make it. You have the possibility for a life here in New York. A normal life. I'm not forcing you. I'm not offering anything. I'm here because you have the skills, talents, and courage of a Double O, and I could use your help. But it's your choice. What do you want?"

Rachel answered, before she could stop and consider: "I want my life to mean something."

Dryden offered his hand.

Their fingers intertwined for a moment of peace, and Rachel considered them: the trigger finger that killed, the fingertips that could read the trembling dial of a safe. "Can I choose my number?"

He chuckled. "004 is taken."

"Any others?"

"003 and 007, well . . . they're current unknowns. We don't use six. Eight is on medical leave. And nine—we've rested that. You want to pick anything up from your apartment?"

"No."

"I thought you'd say that. There's a suitcase by the bed with kit for you and a set of throwing knives."

"I thought that was yours."

"Mine's the duffel bag."

She looked around. His was basically a gym bag. "Let me guess, you have a tailor in every port."

He gave her a deadly serious look. "Yes."

"Are you carrying a gun?"

"You tell me."

"Not under your jacket."

"It's in the bag."

"Why not keep it on you? This is the land of guns and opportunity, after all."

"I don't need to give a cop a reason to stop me. If they look for a reason."

"Did you carry it into the country?"

"Nope."

"Why not?"

"Because only law enforcement can do that on planes."

"Which you are. But not today."

He tilted his head.

"Or maybe you're still enforcement but the law is letting you down," she said. "There must be a reason you've rung my bell. You gave me a lot of numbers and none of them are active. What's happened to your team?"

A fire engine howled down the street. Dryden smoothed his purple tie down his pink shirt. "You know the origin of the word 'decimated'? I remember learning it in primary school."

"I didn't go to school in England," said Rachel. "I moved from Novi Sad after my parents died when I was fourteen."

Dryden nodded. "Our schools are obsessed with the ancients. Greece, Rome, Egypt. I couldn't stand it. I hated school. Always getting in trouble."

"You mean you weren't always Superman?"

"It was the army that taught me discipline. I was never like Aisha . . . Anyway. Ancient Rome. Decimation. If a regiment failed the empire, Roman command would line them up and execute every tenth man. Decimate means to destroy every tenth."

Rachel touched his elbow. "And that's what's happened to your team?"

"I'm the last man standing. But I've been told to come in and endure interrogation questioning my loyalty after they let death inside my castle."

"Disobeying orders, a stand-up soldier like you?"

His eyes twinkled. "Sometimes a leader has to make a decision in the field."

"And that decision is me?"

"You're the best play I've got."

"Stop, I'll blush."

"You're a con woman, you can control when you blush."

"True."

Dryden pulled on his right ear. "We passed the hotel bar. Who was the best mark?"

"White guy in his late twenties talking to a blond woman around the same age. They didn't know each other. He was telling her that he studied art at undergraduate level, but now he's doing a master's in finance. She asked him why the change. He told her, I guess I'm interested in the art of money."

Dryden shook his head. "I didn't hear that, and I've got superhuman hearing. Literally. So he'd be your target?"

"No."

"Why not?"

"She asked him if he was staying in the hotel and he said he lives around the corner but comes to the Ludlow to use the Wi-Fi. He obviously has money somewhere, but I'd guess it's his parents' and they keep him on a tight leash after his experiments in satirical video art. He can't afford Wi-Fi. Didn't order a drink. Ate her oysters. She's the mark."

"Who was she?"

"You know who she was. Why are you testing me?"

"Humor me," he said.

"Her lanyard said UN. Not all assets sparkle. Information runs the world. Why are you testing me?"

"Because you haven't trained as a Double O. We train hard so we can fight easy. We train hard so that when things go sideways, we know: I've been colder than this, wetter than this, hungrier than this, more scared, more banged up, more tired. I'm taking you into a situation I can't control and you haven't been trained."

"Moneypenny didn't see a problem with that."

Dryden opened his hands. "Moneypenny's tougher than me."

"Then why are you here?"

"I'm all out of options."

Rachel stood up. She faced him with arms crossed over her chest. "You do know how to flatter a girl."

"*And* I believe in you."

She looked at her trainers. "You *do* know how to flatter a girl."

"Not really. Never had to. I just say what I mean."

"Maybe that's why I like you," she said. "You don't lie. Growing up with the Chevaliers, lying was like breathing. We were thieves. We lied to survive. Secrecy was everything. The Rachel who went to school and played with the other kids and made dresses with her mother, she was a legend. Nothing was real. And now I'm living in another legend. I'd like my own name to mean something. Rachel Wolff."

"It will," he promised. "Pick your number."

Rachel thought of the hands of the blind man's watch, the object for which Moneypenny had sent her down this tunnel, a diamond-encrusted relic from the eighteenth century. It could be read by touch. There were two turquoise beads at twelve o'clock, known as a double one, to let the feeler know when they were passing into afternoon. She'd stolen the blind man's watch, smuggled the timepiece into the pipeline, and followed it out the other side, except instead of profiting, she'd risked everything, killing to stop a bomb going off and putting herself in danger to protect Dryden. It was the first time in twenty-something years she'd risked herself for someone else.

She said, "How about 001?"

"First on the call sheet, huh? I like it. All right, 001. It's go time."

THIRTY

The Eye of the Needle

The officer at the switchboard lifted the receiver, listened for a moment, and then flicked the switch to hold, saying to his neighbor, "I've got someone claiming to be Johanna Harwood. Right code number. Says she wants to speak to M personally."

A shrug. "Any oppo could know that much. Put her through to Liaison."

The Liaison Section was the first cog in MI6's defenses against hoaxes and hacks. It was an elaborate machine, sifting through those members of the public who desired access to MI6. The eye of the needle was narrow. There were other people in the building who dealt with the emails, and others who scanned letters for anthrax and parcels for explosives. Liaison dealt with counterfeit people. The officer told the voice on the end of the line to wait a moment. When the call was passed to Captain Walker, a former prisoner of war interrogator from Military Intelligence, it was up to him to keep the subject talking for three minutes as the call was triangulated and a voice match performed.

Walker was perky. "Hello, who am I speaking with?"

"This is Johanna Harwood, 003. I need to see M."

"I'm afraid I don't know an—Emma, was it? Are you sure you've dialed the right number?"

She repeated the number of the outside line for the Service. "Tell M it's Harwood."

"Yes, you've got the number right. But I can't place this Emmet you want. This is a big department. Could you tell me a little more about the person you're after?"

"This is an open line."

Captain Walker had to give credit to her confidence, whoever she was. He asked the caller to wait, playing particularly grating hold music while he called the head of his section. "Ma'am, I've got a woman on the public line claiming to be Johanna Harwood, and she wants to see M. I know this isn't protocol for a returning agent. We're tracing the call and testing for AI. The thing is, voice recognition is a match. I need to keep her talking for another minute. Would you listen in? Thanks, ma'am."

Two rooms away, the sleepless Chief Security Officer pressed a switch and held her breath as she listened in. Captain Walker's voice was as soothing as ever.

"I'm so sorry for the wait, Joanna."

"It's Johanna."

"Absolutely. This M character, could you be more specific? I'm sure we don't need to worry about security."

"Sir Emery Ware, Chief of MI6. He works seven floors above you. At this hour, he's probably packing up to go to his club or home, depending on what sort of day it's been. He won't want dinner at the canteen. It's Wednesday and he hates steak-and-kidney pie."

Captain Walker cleared his throat. "Can I place you on hold again? So sorry." He waited for the click. "Ma'am, we've got her location. She's calling from James Bond's home. And she's right about the steak-and-kidney pie."

The Chief Security Officer felt herself go red. "I haven't had anything from the alarms we set at 007's . . . Tell her we'll send a car. Take her to 44 Kensington Cloisters."

Captain Walker returned to the line. "Ms. Harwood, if you stay where you are, a car will collect you and take you to a man called Major Townsend."

"How do you know where I am?" She sounded amused.

"Yes, well. Afraid I can't help you myself. But Major Townsend will be your man. You're most welcome."

Johanna Harwood hung up. She was sitting on Bond's front step and she counted the seconds until a Volvo XC90 with blacked-out windows swept alongside the plane trees. Two suited men with gym bodies and earpieces got out. She climbed into the back peacefully, watching London slide by. Kensington Cloisters was a dull Victorian mansion in grimy red brick bearing the brass plate of a long-defunct charity, which had a spacious old-fashioned basement, re-equipped as detention cells, with a rear exit onto an unwatched mews. Inside, a powerful-looking doorman took Harwood's coat at arm's length and hung it on one of a row of hooks. As soon as she was boxed in with Major Townsend, the coat would go for forensic analysis. She was asked to step through a full-body scanner. Before she did, she placed a lapis lazuli ring in a tray. It was returned to her on the other side.

"Follow me, ma'am."

She passed down a narrow corridor with a tall, single frosted window, behind which a camera measured Harwood's gait. The passage ended in two doors marked A and B. The doorman knocked on B, revealing a clean, light room. A table offered a vase of lilies and two cane chairs with decorative seats faced a disused fireplace. No filing cabinets, no technology, no obvious cameras. A tall man, as pleasant as the room, greeted Harwood with a warm handshake.

"Welcome home is in order, I'm told. Tea? Coffee? I understand you want to see M? Perhaps you can explain the urgency to me while we get the kettle boiled and the fireworks ready, hey?"

"James Bond has turned. He was in captivity too long and he blames M."

The man rubbed his hands together. "Goodness."

"Goodness?"

"You'll have to forgive me, 003. Yes, your fingerprint at the door matched our system and yes, your voice and your irises do, too, but you went AWOL while, ah, *medically unfit* and since that time we've suffered some serious, ah, security breaches. Now you've reappeared, shortly after the murder of Aisha Asante in Q Branch."

Harwood reached for the back of the chair. "Aisha? When?"

As he explained, she counted the days back to sending the message from Siberia. Aisha must have somehow picked up the code at source or destination and broken it. And M . . . The chair cracked under her knuckles.

"Are you quite all right, 003? Why don't you take a seat? Perhaps not that one."

She remained standing. "I know what happens in this building. If I don't give you what you want in Room B, I go to Room A, where there are no furnishings except a scarred desk with two steel chairs, and a drain for blood."

The man bounced on his toes. "As a Double O, there is no reason why you should know anything about the entrails of the Service."

"James Bond has been through the guts of this system before."

"So you've *communicated* with Bond, a man you claim is a danger to the Service?"

"If I hadn't *communicated* with him, how would I know he represents a threat?" Harwood ran a hand through her curls. "You know my file. You know I'm an expert in interrogation, on both sides. Please, save us both some time. M is in serious danger. I need to see him. Now."

The man sighed in a series of short bursts. "Would you wait here?"

It took thirty minutes for him to return. When he did, he said a car would take Harwood to see M.

"Vauxhall?" she asked. "Or Regent's Park?"

"We can't let you inside the castle until you have been cleared, you understand that, I'm sure. But M has agreed to see you."

The same car carried Harwood through the streets of London, from hotels guarded by doormen in top hats to flyover motorways with blackened terrace housing, and out into the countryside. She sat in the back, twisting the lapis lazuli ring. The lanes grew smaller, until the car was enclosed in an emerald tunnel, and then bumped up a lime avenue to a sprawling redbrick manor house. The engine quieted, leaving Harwood with the hammer of her heart. She opened the door before the driver could reach it and stepped onto the gravel. The windows of the house were so old, glass had massed at the bottom of the casements and the sun seemed to pool in the tears. The front door opened and another man with an earpiece waited for her to approach, moving aside so she could step beneath the low beam into the cool of the hall. He patted her down before beckoning for her to follow him across checkered tiles and onto a soft green carpet, which announced the library. A fire in the grate was the only light. M sat behind an Empire desk.

"003," he said. "I can't tell you how I've worried for your safety."

She stepped into the center of the Persian rug, hands behind her back, where she continued fiddling with the ring.

M looked at the security man. "Wait outside the door, would you, Jeff? Thanks. No need to stand on ceremony, Johanna. I'm sure you've earned a drink."

"Thank you, sir." She followed his gesture and sat in a deep leather chair across from the desk as he passed to a drinks cabinet and poured her a single scotch, and himself a double. He didn't move like an old man, springing in his Converse trainers. She wondered if her father would have aged like that.

M faced her over the desk. "I'm told you didn't follow protocol. But then you were always something of a rebel. I've enjoyed that about you."

"You're in danger," she said. "It's Bond. He's turned against us. He believes you . . ." She looked back at the closed door. "This isn't something you want people hearing, sir."

She watched the calculation in his face, wondering, wondering. Then he pressed the intercom on his desk, which must communicate with the security radio, and asked them to fall back to the outside perimeter.

"Where is James?" asked M.

Harwood waited until she heard the front door click and then steps on the gravel. Then she slipped the lapis lazuli ring from her finger and placed it on the green baize of the desktop. "Do you remember this?"

M switched on the desk lamp, then picked up the ring, turning it over with fingers that shook a little. "Your engagement ring."

"As Sid died, he told me you promised to give me away at the ceremony. Because I don't have a father."

He dropped the ring. "You have suffered many losses. And I'm sorry that James Bond is now on that list, too. I would have bet my life on his loyalty."

"So would I." Harwood looked to the window. "I lost my engagement ring in Russia. That's a replica made by Tiger Tanaka. The stone is coated in a nerve agent that is modified to react with your DNA. Bond has the antidote. You'll be dead in ten minutes unless you tell your security to leave the premises. No danger words, no tricks. We have overwatch and we'll know if they stay in the area. Tell them you have a guest coming and it's eyes-only."

M put a hand to his forehead. "What on earth has got into you?"

"My mother kept one of my father's cameras. It had a roll of film in it, undeveloped. I scanned the negatives."

He cleared his throat. "You're confused, Johanna. You don't know what you're saying."

"Would you bet your life on it?"

He pulled at his collar before jabbing the intercom. "Jeff, tell your team to clear out, would you? Yes. I'm expecting an eyes-only. That's right. Good night."

Harwood watched the activity through the rippling glass. "I want to know if I'm right about something. When Moneypenny decided to recruit me, I was in the right place at the right time, the child of an agent senior staff vaguely felt they owed, your *friend*—so you couldn't say no. There was no reason *not* to use me. Is that right? So you decided to use me up. Whatever you did to my father turned me into an accommodating puzzle piece for wounded men. My relationship with James helped you. And Sid. A useful distraction. But it was never a calculation to me. Never an act. It was love."

Ware rose to his feet, his fingers spread on a red leather blotting pad.

"But you used that too," said Harwood. "*See how well she fits Bond, the blunt instrument, and you, Sid, the scalpel. How fully she commits her heart. Her many talents. The thing that seems too good to be true usually is, Sid.* What a dream double agent I'd be for Rattenfänger—you practically designed me that way, just like Conrad. You made sure suspicion and doubt always fell on me. You even made me doubt myself."

"I suppose you are going to tell me I underestimated one fatal thing?"

"Yes," said Harwood. "Me."

There was the sound of drawn-out strings from the hinges as the door swung. 007 walked through the darkness and into the light.

THIRTY-ONE

The Cloud Under the Mountain

If you go to the mountain often enough, you will meet the tiger. It was a Chinese proverb but Dryden felt it deep in his bones, lying prone like a sniper beneath the shelter of the discontinued Grumman Greyhound procured by Leiter, peering through binoculars at the pyramid-shaped mountain on the distant archipelago. He passed to the square of buildings that made up Pyramiden, all seemingly empty. But Dryden knew it was an illusion. There was an army beneath the ice. Whatever Rattenfänger was planning, it relied on Zofia Nowak and a data storage center. That made destroying the cloud under the mountain his main priority. He intended to upload a virus that would crash the system. After that, he'd search for Moneypenny and Dr. Nowak. He watched the blank buildings, wondering where Mora had spun his web, and where 000 would put himself, waiting to catch flies.

The ice floe where he'd managed to land was side-on to the mountain, facing north, toward a mine shaft that had been converted into ventilation. Dryden lowered the binoculars. The main entrance was at the peak on the western flank. Cameras scrutinized every foot. He was armed with a compass, a grenade, an M16, and a Glock. Dryden slung the assault rifle around his shoulder, making sure the slide mechanism still worked. A bullet would decelerate by as much as forty feet per second faster in these conditions thanks to the denser air. But a slow bullet was still a deadly bullet. His breathing was busy in his ears, mixed with Aisha's last breath. He was haunted by imagining the look in her eyes, a problem to solve. Now, he'd solve it. As much as it could be solved.

A storm was coming, blocking radio communication. But he had brought all the backup he'd need.

Dryden scratched his chin. "I think Plan A is the best we've got. I don't even want to think about Plan B. Agree?"

Rachel nodded. "And Plan C is a *definite* no."

"Absolutely out of the question," said Dryden, taking a pill bottle from his pocket. Beta-blockers. The climate inside the belly of the mountain would be carefully monitored to protect the data servers. The human body was thirty-seven degrees Celsius. If the air spiked by more than two degrees, alarms would sound. Beta-blockers would lower their body temperature, giving them a slight edge. He tipped two blue pills onto his palm.

"Wait," said Rachel. "What if there was a Plan D, where I go in there alone?"

"And steal all the glory?" He passed her one of the pills and went to flip the other into his mouth. She caught his arm.

"Your heart," she said.

"What about it?"

"After the explosion, your pulse stopped. I was going to use a defibrillator on your chest, but when I opened your shirt and took your armor off, there were bandages over your heart. That left mouth-to-mouth resuscitation and prayer. Somebody up there likes you." She shifted in the snow. "Somebody down here likes you, too."

"I was shot, that's all," said Dryden. "000 likes to aim for center mass. Guess I was lucky."

"Lucky?"

"Lucky I have good teammates and stubborn muscle."

"Taking that pill could weaken your heart. My grandfather takes them. I called him, before we left. He's in a nursing home now. He didn't remember who I am. He was strong, until his heart gave out."

"It's my body between Britain and the blows. That's the job. You with me, 001?"

A long sigh. "I'm with you. Though with a little less flag-waving."

Dryden picked up the binoculars. The sun would not go down. There was no cover except for the ice-sharp gale and snow. He reached for the hang glider. With the wings folded, it looked like a shield. Come back with your shield or on it. Dryden checked Rachel's equipment, walked to the edge of the ice floe, looked down the hundred-foot drop, and took the leap of faith. Angling against the breath of the glacier, cross-current rattled his bones. Could this be the mission that killed him? Or did Operator's Syndrome have him in its grips for life? Perhaps he pulled the trigger because the trigger pulled him. And if so, was he all that different from 000? For once, he didn't care. As long as he put a bullet in Harthrop-Vane.

When he had woken in a body bag in Venice, rocking on the Grand Canal, it seemed the middle of a recurring nightmare, except that time it was real. Moneypenny had to convince 000 that Dryden was dead, so she had him removed from the scene zipped up in the hard-wearing PBC-backed Cordura bag whose handles Dryden had carried too many times, the weight of a friend the weight of a debt you know you can never pay. He could see them loading Aisha onto a gurney, practically feel her weight. He was rocking now, he was in his mother's arms, he was in Luke's arms, he was walking toward the light, there was sand under his feet and his nan was going to make goat curry, but Luke was asking him if he was done with the fight. Not yet. Not yet.

Dryden hit the ice clinging to the peak of the pyramid and tidied his wings.

Rachel copied his movements. She stowed the wings in the snow. The shaft was a steel mouth cut into rock. Rachel pulled ropes from her rucksack. Dryden looked over the edge. An unknown drop. He raised the night-vision binoculars. It was as Rachel had anticipated. At the base, a steel fan was guarded by dual sensors to reduce false alarms and prevent defeat techniques. On one side of the fan, a passive infrared motion detector would be programmed to catch any movement slower or faster than the fan itself. On the other side was an active microwave sensor, emitting to the opposite side of the vent. If an object bounced the microwaves back sooner than expected, the alarm would trigger.

She pursed her lips.

Dryden signed: "It's your show. Run it."

Rachel nodded. She reached inside her rucksack and pulled out a cage. It stood two feet high, and inside a dove beat its wings against the bars, entirely uncertain about this business of flying with the help of a human being. Rachel hooked her climbing rope to the side of the vent. Dryden did the same. Then she lowered the cage inside the vent and opened the door.

The dove clattered and rose, finding Rachel and Dryden blocking the way, then twisted to dive. Rachel and Dryden dropped after the bird of peace.

They could not know what to expect, except that they'd be watched. As it was, Dryden might have anticipated the design of the cloud under the mountain. It was a Panopticon. The pyramid had been hollowed over millennia into a series of caves and then over a century by mine shafts; now Rattenfänger had collapsed these caesuras to create a hollow pyramid. Black server towers, bathed in blue light, were arranged in ever-widening levels with glass floors and walls. In the center, a suspended watchtower looked out all sides on the servers.

The Rattenfänger men in the watchtower were making coffee to get them through the night shift when the infrared motion detector and microwave sensor on Vent 4 went off. Both systems triggered—that meant no false alarm.

000 turned to the screen showing CCTV of the corridor and snorted as a dove raced by the camera. "And you were saying nothing exciting happens here."

The second-in-command said, "I miss hunting pirates. You're giving me birds." He turned to the senior IT officer, who was following the direction of the dove across the screens like a ripple on the surface of a pond.

000 went to the glass, trying to find the dove with his one good eye, but the blue light was too aqueous and his eye filled with tears as if stung by sea salt, though really the pain was caused by a detached retina. The agony of his once-perfect face was as unending as water torture.

"Shut down the motion sensors," he said. "We'll guide the men using the cameras."

In the turn of both men's heads after the flight of the dove, they failed to catch Rachel and Dryden landing in the corridor.

Servers don't need sun. They don't need oxygen. They don't want heat. Their food is data. Designed to conceal, not project, this was anti-architecture. The blue light generated the least warmth and kept things semi-visible. This could be a favor for intruders dressed head-to-toe in black. However, the CCTV cameras observing the chamber were thermal, tracking the movement of anything over thirty-five degrees and feeding the footage to the watchtower. There was something curious about the watchtower. Reachable by one central lift whose blast doors opened on the western flank of the mountain, the tower had an outer ring and an inner sanctum. The outer ring was packed with security. The inner sanctum was a glowing white box. Dryden didn't have time to think about what the box might contain as he threw a space blanket over them both while Rachel used an electric screwdriver to pop the raised glass floor covering the cable system. She uncovered a four-foot space, big enough for a man to crawl through to access repairs. She slipped below. Dryden followed with a grunt, dragging the blanket after him and replacing the glass above.

The whole thing had taken less than a minute. Was it fast enough?

The dove flew north, and the guards followed its path. One officer did see a slight flare on the camera under the vent, but he took that to be a leftover signature from the dove.

Glass blocks infrared cameras, but not the human eye. Dryden and Rachel crawled on their bellies beneath the plait of wires on the lowest level, Rachel checking off Chinese characters written in the clips holding the bundles. The servers were locked into glass cages for different data blocks. They were aiming for a cage in the corner, farthest away from observers. The ground vibrated. Security officers approaching. Rachel hid her face. Dryden did the same behind her, cocking his gun. Boots pounded the glass. But the blue light was on their side. The guards ran right over them.

Dryden's muscles burned as he wormed forward. The server cages were made of bulletproof glass. But the floor panels came up with a simple screw. Rachel spun the little bit of metal counterclockwise. Then the next one. She eased the panel up. Squirmed into the cage. Pulled Dryden after her. What if there were motion sensors in the cage itself, which triggered a silent alarm? There was no way to know—the world's smallest motion sensor was one centimeter across and could be hidden anywhere in these humming machines. So move fast.

A steel door with a combination lock protected the access point to the server. Rachel put her ear to the metal and twisted the dial.

She got the combination in under a minute.

The door popped. She took a tablet from her jacket and plugged a cable into the server, attaching the devices.

"It's working," she said, smiling at him.

He scratched his right ear.

"You OK?"

"Just quiet in here, that's all."

The tablet flashed green. "All right, the virus has been uploaded. Let's go."

The answer to whether or not there was a motion sensor inside the cage was yes. One dove was a coincidence. Two were dinner.

Rachel was bending to the loose panel when Dryden saw movement through the blue. Four figures hustling down the corridor of servers, weapons raised, shouting.

The mercenaries surrounded the cage. Dryden unholstered his weapon and aimed at the biggest of them. A standoff through bulletproof glass. The guard got on his radio, but he didn't need to call for backup: 000 swept into the room with his sidearm raised, followed by ten more men.

His face seemed to have melted on one side. That left too much face intact for Dryden's liking. Harthrop-Vane smiled. Blood seeped from his teeth.

"Plan B!" shouted Rachel.

Outnumbered. Outgunned. Never outmaneuvered.

Dryden dug in his jacket. He raised the grenade.

Conrad Harthrop-Vane laughed, then bowed with a gracious arm as if to say, *Go ahead, you idiot, you're standing in a bombproof box*. One of 000's eyes was red, one blue, a siren trapped inside the man.

Rachel hauled up the glass panel.

Dryden dropped the grenade.

Rachel shoved the panel back in place.

The ground juddered, then screamed.

It was a crack, but a crack was enough. The glass floor jumped, the concrete buckled, the smoke plumed. Rachel grabbed Dryden's jacket. He wrapped himself around her and the pair slid through the aperture, plunging into smoke. Dryden landed with a smack on his back. He was in a cave with ice walls beneath the storage center, the subterranean world of the Arctic. He coughed up a lungful of smoke. "001? You with me?"

". . . Just about."

Dryden lay still, watching the smoke writhe. "This way."

Gunfire bounced between the walls. Dryden grabbed Rachel's hand and pulled her toward the light: it was a tunnel in the vast underground system that made up a hidden dimension covered by glaciers. He fired blindly. More shots replied.

Rachel was clutching her compass as if the tremulous needle might save them. She was leading them southwest, back toward the plane. Dryden wouldn't admit the thought that asked: What if the tunnel ends, what if it narrows, what if you led her here to die, gasping? He told himself it was the beta-blocker making his heart stab, plus the ear-shattering explosions. All in a day's work. The cave twisted and shrank, leaving him squeezing over boulders, until he was faced with a vertical climb up a tight shaft. He urged Rachel to go first. She reached for the handhold. Dryden followed, but his shoulders wedged. It was too narrow. He pushed, scraping his jacket, leaving stripes of blood on the ice. He could try and worm with both arms above his head, but that would mean he couldn't lay down covering fire, and below the pursuers knew they had the rats in a trap and would merely fire upward once they reached the shaft.

"Plan C!" he shouted.

"What?"

"Keep going. I'll fight my way back to the entrance."

"No way!"

"*Get going!*" Dryden pulled his feet up as fire came from below. Then he felt Rachel's hands on his shoulders. She heaved, and his shoulder moved an inch.

"You get going!" she shouted. "I won't leave without you!"

Dryden cursed and angled himself so one arm got above his head, his fingernails clawing ice. He kept the other arm down so he could keep firing. Ice filled his mouth. He pulled himself up one-handed. The shaft took his skin, exposing nerve endings with a pain that he'd cost up later. Then Rachel pulled him into a cave.

Stalagmites shone purple, orange, and green, reflecting the crystal walls. Then the reflections changed, taking on a dark shadow. Dryden pushed Rachel behind a wall of ice.

"Keep going," he told her.

"No—"

"Please."

The shadow stretched for him, coming from another tunnel. It was 000, and behind him four armed men who fanned around the chamber. Rachel hugged the ground. Harthrop-Vane hadn't seen her. Dryden stepped into 000's path, raising his weapon.

The two Double O agents faced each other, no bulletproof barrier this time.

Dryden's voice was a rasp. "She never did anything to hurt you."

Harthrop-Vane said, "You mean your pet thief? Where is she?"

Dryden gripped his temper. He heard a trickle of grit. A glance told him Rachel had kept creeping down the next tunnel. Good. "I mean Dr. Aisha Asante, you rotten bastard."

"I'm afraid the blame for that lies elsewhere."

"You expect me to believe that?"

"I suppose you believe you'll take me with you, at the very least," said Harthrop-Vane.

"I'm not going anywhere."

"Well, that's just it. We tried to capture you, but in the end all we had to do was wait for you to deliver yourself. Your efforts to find us through Trigger alerted us that you were coming. So we had Zofia Nowak create backup servers for X, our artificial intelligence system. It's working fine, despite your virus. Now all we need do is hook you up. You're the key, as much as that pains me to say, to hacking Panopticon and using your own system to blind Britain."

Dryden said, "I'll shoot myself before I let you use me as a weapon. But I'll shoot you first."

"I don't think so. I think you'll lower the weapon and let me escort you to the surface. You see this radio? The line is open to Mora, who is waiting for my word that you'll come quietly. Unless you want Mora to kill Ibrahim Suleiman. He's useful only as long as you're compliant."

Dryden's breath hitched. "Ibrahim?"

"We picked him up from Shrublands. He's waiting for you in our surgical bay with Dr. Nowak and Moneypenny, who will make sure things run smoothly. She's good at that. If you and Ibrahim don't cooperate with the surgeon, we'll kill Moneypenny, then Ibrahim, then you. We'll make sure you're last. How many more people can you stand to lose, Dryden?"

Dryden already knew the answer to that. A check told him Rachel had disappeared. He lowered the gun.

THIRTY-TWO

Fathers

This was a place for quarry. Hunters chased wild boar from the forest and pheasant and partridge from the riverbanks and scrublands, hare through sand dunes and plains, and thrush in and out of olive groves. These hunts represented ancient tradition, as did the tradition of hunting down rivals, decades of separatist bombing now indistinguishable from organized crime that turned its attention from drug trafficking toward property development. The Unione Corse bribed police and politicians, blew up properties owned by foreigners, and carefully preserved the environment in order to encourage tourism that profited their hotels and restaurants. Corsica was a modern-day fiefdom and there were no outsiders to witness the king welcome home his prodigal prince. Marc-Ange Draco's broad smile cracked his creased walnut of a face in two as he caught the rope from the boat arriving at his jetty. "Welcome home, son."

James Bond jumped out of the speedboat. "Hope you didn't wait up, old man."

"A fruitless endeavor when it comes to such a son-in-law as you."

The head of the Unione Corse and father of Bond's murdered wife-of-a-day clapped Bond on both arms, inspecting him closely before he turned to give Johanna Harwood a hand onto the slimy boards. "I am gratified to see you together. Tell me, do I have a daughter once more?"

"Careful," said Harwood, "he'll get himself captured again. I hope I didn't land you in too much trouble, sending the Russian army after you."

"Trouble is where I live," he said. "And you too, I see." He raised a hard hand to defend against the glare of the Mediterranean, studying the hooded figure in the aft of the boat.

"Thank you for this," said Harwood. "We didn't know where else to turn."

Draco bared his teeth. "M betrayed you?"

"Yes," said Bond, impassive.

"Then he is my enemy and I will bury him here, if that is your wish."

Bond and Harwood turned to M's slumped figure. When Draco's soldiers manhandled M onto the docks, Bond averted his gaze, but Harwood watched as the Converse trainers scraped over sand, then stone, then scrub surrounding Marc-Ange's castle, as M was dragged into a dungeon repurposed as a wine cellar. They tied him to a chair using hessian rope, and he whimpered in pain. Water dripped from the low ceiling, and M flinched when a drop landed on him. Bottles winked, then dimmed as Bond followed Harwood into the gloom and closed the door behind him, reducing the light to a series of stripes through the grill in the door, a barcode stamped over M's rumpled clothes. The cellar was level with the sea and smelled of damp jute.

Bond tore the hood from M's head and stood back. He said, "Why?"

Ware squeezed his knees together. He swallowed—Harwood heard his throat click—and when he tried to speak his vocal cords strangled the words. Bond's sigh was almost a growl, but he strode to the rack of bottles, chose one, and popped the cork. He let M swig until red beads stained his white stubble. Then Bond tugged on his pocket square and tended to the old man as if he were a son nursing an elderly parent.

M cleared his throat, finally grinding out: "The world is in chaos, James. You must see that. We can either direct the chaos, benefit from it, or drown in it. Do you want us to become insignificant?"

Bond stood back. "I want to stand for something. I want it all to mean something."

"What? King and Country? The West? Internationalism? *Constructs*, James. They always have been."

Bond shrugged, too heavily. "A moral force, then."

"Don't tell me. You want to be the hero."

"Somebody should be."

M shook his head. "I failed you as a teacher."

"That's your failure?" Bond stripped off his jacket, leaving him in shirtsleeves, tie, and shoulder holster. He pulled a child's stamp album from the inner pocket before tossing the jacket aside. He'd taken the clothbound album from a shelf in M's study. Such an innocent thing, for a War Book. "I kept your secret. Mora wanted the War Book. Do you know what it meant, in that place, all that time, with that man, to keep your secret?" M's gaze skittered across the floor. "Why did you even tell me about the War Book? It's supposed to be a record of essential intelligence kept between the Chief and his second-in-command. That was Bill Tanner, not me."

"Tanner was compromised," said M.

"To provide cover for you," said Bond.

"I needed someone who could never turn. A backstop in case Mora ever grew beyond my control. I needed you."

Bond looked at the ceiling. "You mean I was singled out for this painful honor because of my loyalty?"

"I wasn't wrong."

Bond flipped through the stamp album. "Mora wanted the War Book for some kind of password. But it wasn't just that—I got to know him as well as he got to know me. The War Book represented a threat to him. How?"

"Do you remember the Romeo operation in Moscow?"

Bond gave Harwood a swift glance. "No."

M followed his look. "I once told you, details will save your life. Blond or brunette, that sort of thing. Ring any bells, James, or have you screwed too many bank tellers and secretaries to recall?"

Harwood said, "If you're hoping to drive a wedge between us, know that I'll drive a stake through your heart before I let you wound mine again."

Bond thumped the stamp album into his palm. "What Romeo op?"

M shook his head like a disappointed headmaster. "Moscow, '04. You got a glimpse inside a bank account for me and discovered the owner was embezzling state funds. That was Mora's offshore account. Rattenfänger is SMERSH reincarnated as a private enterprise. And like all good capitalists, Mora has been skimming from the top, stealing money from the Kremlin in order to one day fund a coup. You must understand, James, he's my asset. I controlled him. But then—well, he started to take risks, exposing himself and me. He asked too much."

"Which Double O's life was too much for you?" asked Harwood.

M hunched, dipping his head toward Bond. It looked like he was offering his neck for a guillotine. "I saved you and Moneypenny in Tarusa. Mora wanted me to let the double kill you. I defied him to save you."

Bond ran a hand through his fringe. "Why?" This time the question was soft.

"A father's love."

Bond's breath caught.

M squirmed again. "Loosen these ties, can't you, Bond? What am I going to do? I'm old, Father William."

Bond almost smiled. He seemed to hesitate, then moved to drop to one knee at M's side, jerking the knots. M could have kissed his head from there.

Harwood said, "What about my father?"

Bond rose and retreated.

M turned on her. "See the big picture, Johanna. I reared 000 for Mora and let him wage a war of attrition from inside the Double O Section in return for intelligence that saved countless lives and kept the UK relevant to Five Eyes over *decades*. Mora and I, we are *sharks*, keeping the population under control, maintaining balance, maintaining *power*."

"I thought you were a tiger with a taste for death," said Bond. "Now you're a shark."

"Oh, *that* you remember," said M, snorting. "And what are you, if not the same?"

"I don't need a pretty metaphor for what I am. I never betrayed my country."

"I was defending my country! Mora wanted access to Panopticon when the program came online. That's why he wants the War Book. I said no. I threatened to tell the Kremlin about his embezzlement if he didn't fall in line. That's when he took you."

"What is Panopticon?" asked Harwood.

"A global surveillance program. Mora wants to control it so he can feed disinformation to Q."

"To what end?"

"I told him no."

"To what end?" asked Harwood again.

M wriggled in his binds, forearms reddening. Harwood noticed Bond wince at the sight. "He wants to cut Britain off from the Internet. Isolate us. Destroy us. He wants to change the geography of power, ruling from the icy North. That's why he tried to use Sir Bertram Paradise to melt the Arctic and gain strategic control of the shipping lanes. He intends to take over Russia. He needs the money in that account to pay off the military, whom he has persuaded to back him with the promise he will cripple the West by cracking open Panopticon. He knew that if he made a move against me before he'd made his move against the West, the War Book—the evidence of his embezzlement—was on a dead man's switch and the Kremlin would learn everything. We were at a stalemate. That's why he took you, so he could hack Panopticon and initiate his coup. But you held out against him. You didn't break. I'm proud, son."

Bond took a step forward, raising his fist, and then stopped short. His shoulders fell. "I don't want your pride. I want Mora. Tell me how to find him."

"Even with Panopticon, there has been no scent of him. What do you intend, James? He has Moneypenny."

"You say that like you care."

M said earnestly, "God knows what she's going through if Mora believes she can tell him the whereabouts of the War Book."

"God doesn't know, but I do, and I'm going to get her back," said Bond. "Panopticon is operational?"

"You have to understand, I've kept Britain at the table. I did it all for my country."

"Tell that to Sid," said Harwood softly. "You did it for you. You put yourself at the table."

"The bank account," said Bond. "You say he needs to pay off the Russian military to make his final move." He waved the book. "You once told me that I was the perfect weapon and someone was bound to use me. We have the details for his hidden offshore account, we can take his money. I drain the account and offer an exchange: the money for Moneypenny. I demand a meet. I destroy him."

"He's defeated every Double O he's ever faced," said M, "including you."

"He shot me full of drugs and chained me to a wall," said Bond, as if explaining a poor performance to his Chief. He couldn't shake it, Harwood realized. He'd be loyal to the end.

"What were you expecting," said M, "Marquess of Queensberry rules?"

"I was expecting you to be on my side."

M blinked. Harwood thought she saw a tear spill over from his red and yellow eyes. Bond looked at his shoes.

"Sid beat Mora," said Harwood.

"Mora killed Sid," said M.

"He didn't kill me. I detained him. I won't make that mistake again." Her fingers flexed on her weapon.

"You should have come clean to me in Moscow," said Bond. "I would have helped you get out from under. There's nothing I wouldn't have done for you. Do you want to go down alone, or use me one last time to take Mora with you?"

Silence stretched between them, filled by men moving about the castle, the call of birds, the rising tide. Bond's eyes were locked with M's. Then the texture of the silence changed, becoming not distance but surgical thread, knitting them together, two club members striking a deal whose terms 003 wouldn't agree with but whose outcome she'd be forced to abide.

M bowed his head. "You'll find a three-shilling stamp with an illustration of the Queen and the Post Office Tower in the Great Britain pages. The microdot with Mora's bank account details is in the crown." His eyes narrowed, just like when they discussed a problem in his office. "But going to Mora with such an offer is a suicide mission, 007."

"Not if we split up," said Harwood. "I make the offer, the money for Moneypenny, and go alone. Tell Mora you're dead. You follow and take Mora by surprise."

M shook his head. "You realize you cannot call in the cavalry on this one. 007, you have been a guest of the enemy for nearly two years. 003 is rogue. You've abducted your Chief. No one will believe a word you say."

Harwood drew her gun from her holster. She moved the safety off. "We have everything we need from you. There's nothing left but a confession."

He twisted. "A confession?"

"I want to know what you did to my father."

M looked from the weapon in her hand to the door. "It was the merciful option."

"I don't think you know the meaning of the word."

"I spared his life."

"Convince me."

M cast a desperate glance at Bond, who gave no response. M wet his lower lip. "What do you know about Operation Foot?"

Harwood frowned. "It was an MI5 mission that cleared Russian spies out of England in the seventies, leaving the KGB with no eyes inside the UK. No eyes recruited *inside* England, anyway. They recruited you in Berlin."

He seemed to ignore that. "With the loss of Russian agents in the UK, MI5 feared the KGB would seek to plant more as the Wall came down. They suspected the refugees flooding in from the East. So they sent an agent to test our outfit in Berlin."

"My father."

"I was asked to make a friend of him."

"Asked by whom?" said Bond.

"Mora made the request. He was in Afghanistan."

"Compromising Tanner to protect you," said Bond.

"Tanner turned," said Harwood. "He wasn't a saint."

"He was blackmailed," said Bond.

"So was I!" burst M.

"I'm confused," said Harwood. "Were you running Mora as an asset to protect your country, or was Mora running you because he compromised your position? You're the teacher. Help me straighten that one out."

"Maybe you don't know," offered Bond, almost gently.

M seized on his tone. "You have to understand, I had no options open to me. If I was discovered—no one would have understood, though I'd helped win the Cold War by winning Mora's trust. Sacrifices had to be made. I took to your father, Johanna, truly I did. A big Northern Irishman who liked to drink and tell stories. We got on well. He was smart—too smart. BRIXMIS was still operating. He wanted to see their files. He read through overt duties: postwar cleanup, hunting Nazi officers, finding POWs, laying memorial wreaths at Colditz Castle and concentration camps. And the rest: he wanted to know, who'd been a little too friendly with their counterparts in Soviet intelligence? And those Stay Behind slayings, who leaked the network? Yes, many of the networks were bloated and ill-managed, but still: a lot of the ammunition and explosive caches buried in the woods were now empty. Someone leaked. He was too close. Mora told me if I was in trouble I should tell his body double, an enforcer whose death I faked to keep my asset protected."

"Whose death you faked to save Mora," corrected Bond.

"And who I killed to save you," snapped M. "Would you prefer I'd let Moneypenny die in your bed?"

Bond stepped closer. "And where's Moneypenny now?"

Harwood interrupted: "Tell me what happened."

M wrinkled his nose. "I could reach the enforcer through the zoo in the West. So I watched a lion nearly take off the keeper's arm for a scrap of meat. After an hour, a tap on the shoulder. I followed the giant into the aviary. I was instructing the double to send up a smoke signal to divert Harwood's attention elsewhere when I heard the shutter release. It remains the sound of my nightmares."

Harwood tilted her head. "One day we should compare nightmares."

"It was a mistake on your father's part not to use a matchbox camera. But he'd been walking around as a photojournalist for cover. I saw his retreating back through the crowd. Charles Harwood had a photograph of me speaking with a dead man I supposedly killed in October three years before and had never seen until that day with the White Mice. There would be no way to explain the meeting and no way to explain the photograph."

Harwood thought of her father locking himself in his darkroom, printing photographs of nothing at all.

"I didn't know—could it be that Mora wanted this? Something to keep me in line? Or was I about to be reeled in by my own people? I ought to kill Harwood, I knew that. But it was one thing to kill the Nazi that killed my father, another to kill one of my own. I didn't want to see the man harmed. I considered trying to bring him round to my way of thinking, make him see that I was running my own source and getting Grade A human intelligence out of him on the future of Russia's covert plans. But there'd be no conversion. Harwood was too Protestant for that. He had his own faith, he'd made his own compromises, working for the government that starved his people. So I asked the double to make the problem go away without killing Harwood. I couldn't know he would poison Harwood with mercury, but I could see it was a logical course of action."

"Logical?" said the daughter of the man in question.

"Mercury poisoning would produce madness. No one would believe a word he said, but the man was still alive. Like I said, it was a mercy. I searched his flat after he was hospitalized, but I couldn't find the camera anywhere. I waited for the wrath of God. But Harwood never sent the film. And in case it was Mora laying down foundations for some new plan against me, I decided to do some digging of my own. I discovered his embezzlement, though I had to wait for a Romeo to get me the evidence. That's where Bond came in, years later."

Harwood said, "Why didn't you just kill my father?"

"I told you, he was a good man."

"So you thought it would be kinder to drive him insane."

"He got to live. To have a daughter."

"I nursed him as he died from self-inflicted starvation. He wouldn't eat because he believed the food was poisoned with mercury. Funny. It wasn't kindness. His death would have thrown too much suspicion on you. It was expediency."

M said, "Then show me what mercy means. I've been a father to both of you. And Sid."

"What about Aisha Asante?" asked Harwood.

M paled, his cheeks trembling, the loose skin like a rippling pond. "You may not understand my methods, but I did it to protect you. It's a frightening world and somebody has to make the necessary sacrifices. You should thank me."

Harwood pushed off the wall and lifted her weapon. She would have pulled the trigger but Bond caught her arm.

"Wait," he said.

"Don't tell me you buy his bullshit."

"We might need his knowledge of Mora. Marc-Ange Drago can keep him captive here. You'll have justice, once we kill Mora."

Harwood searched Bond's gray-blue eyes. She'd become a Double O because she wanted to stop the damage before it happened, instead of sewing up the wounds. But she was too late to do that for her father, or herself, or Sid, or Aisha, or Bond. That left something that had nothing to do with saving a life. That left revenge. But Mora was out there, and he had Moneypenny, and he was targeting innocent people who'd wake up with no electricity, no medication, no food, no water, no help. She released a long breath and took her finger from the trigger.

THIRTY-THREE

Alone and Unafraid

A nuclear submarine required one doctor. He or she was responsible for radiological and atmospheric control, supervising diet, guarding against communicable disease, conserving the hearing of crew exposed to sonar, and medical care, typically a trickle of headaches or week-two blues. Though the doctor would be trained in dentistry, he'd never see a wisdom tooth—every submariner has their wisdom teeth removed to prevent any issues that might impact the mission. The doctor aboard Rattenfänger's submarine had served with the Dutch navy, where most patrols would offer maybe one serious case, appendicitis or an abscess. It didn't keep him entertained and he was dishonorably discharged after being found to have repeatedly performed unnecessary surgeries.

Boredom was not a problem with Rattenfänger, though there was no real surgical bay on the submarine, or here in the watchtower of the cloud under the mountain. Instead, patients were bound in a canvas rescue stretcher, which was stretched now like the shed skin of a dead man on a table fashioned using trees from every Russian oblast. The canvas side faced upward with labels reading "Head," "Inside," and "Foot." The guide ropes, head strap, and restraining straps were unfastened and ready to use. It was an unusual operating room, too, a white box inside the watchtower of the hollowed-out Arctic pyramid. There was no smell except fear. Next to the table was a desk holding several computer screens and towers, with cables trundling data to the surrounding servers, an artificial intelligence system known as X. The doctor didn't understand much of that part. His job was to enter the patient's skull. Dr. Ibrahim Suleiman, gagged and zip-wired to the desk legs, would be in charge of connecting the patient's hearing aid to the computer. He was wincing over a broken arm in plaster. And Dr. Zofia Nowak, cringing in the corner, would train X to imitate the patient's brain. She was a wiry girl with purple hair and wide, vacant eyes, which she squeezed shut now as four Rattenfänger men dragged in the patient, who wasn't, in fact, coming quietly.

The doctor ducked as a set of instruments went flying, but Conrad Harthrop-Vane didn't seem worried. Rather, he appeared to enjoy himself as he barked at the guards to secure the patient. Dryden was hoisted onto the table—his kick broke a man's nose—and they wrestled with him to make sure his forehead was level with the head restraint, then Velcroed it in position. Then straps were buckled over his upper and lower chest, before his arms were dragged inside the center strap and buckled there. His feet were forced into rope stirrups and the leg and ankle straps were buckled in place. The men finally nailed the canvas into the table. They drove the last nail through the patient's shoulder. He howled.

The doctor wondered if that would be enough to restrain the man. But that wasn't for him to worry about. That was Colonel Mora's concern—and he strode in now, dragging Moneypenny by the hair, then drew up short, drinking the scene in deeply.

"Joseph Dryden, we've been expecting you. Don't go into heart failure, now."

Dryden looked to Moneypenny and said, with admirable steadiness, "Good to see you, ma'am. You OK?"

"She's been better," said Mora. He released Moneypenny. She

stumbled, hitting the tiles, where scalpels and drills lay scattered. "Conrad, make the transfer of funds to the army generals."

"Yes, sir." 000 left the room.

Mora stretched his neck. "There is a bug in your head, 004, put there by Q Branch. You represent the greatest security breach in modern times. The trouble is, we must first train X on your mind. We need a manual connection." Mora turned to Dr. Suleiman and delicately drew down the gag. "I understand you run regular checkups on 004's hearing aid."

Dr. Suleiman swallowed. "I-I-I run remote diagnostics. You can't take it out of his head. You'd need a neurosurgeon. You can't . . ."

Mora waved toward the surgeon. "He's very good at root canals. Don't worry yourself, Dr. Suleiman. You and Dr. Nowak will be on hand to make sure nothing goes wrong."

"But, but . . ." Suleiman looked toward Nowak.

"She can't help you," said Mora. "Nobody's home. You're alone, Dr. Suleiman. You have a duty of care toward 004, I understand that. Today your duty of care is stopping me from scrambling his brains and eating them. Once we've trained X to imitate his mind, we will drip poisoned data into Panopticon, and Five Eyes will believe there is a crisis brewing in the Arctic. The submarine fleet will be diverted, leaving the subsea Internet cables around Britain exposed to my shadow fleet. It's time to turn the lights off. Doctor, prep your patient. I'm told you have to remain awake during the procedure, 004." He touched a circular saw. "You'll need to lie very, very still."

Dryden said, "Ibrahim, kill me."

Mora tutted. "None of that. You'll sign the boy's death warrant."

Moneypenny rose, seemingly unsteady, holding her arm. The doctor stepped past her. The last thing he was aware of was a flash of steel.

A nuclear submarine required a single doctor. Moneypenny drew the scalpel over his jugular. His blood splashed her face and arms. Now this one was dead.

Mora picked up Moneypenny by the throat. The gleaming ruby

of his mottled tongue came toward her. This was it. But somehow, she wasn't scared. Submerged thousands of feet underwater for months at a time, a submarine crew was described as alone and unafraid; Moneypenny remembered those words from time spent around the Royal Navy's submariners. Now she wasn't alone. Now Dryden was here.

"Sir," said 000, entering the room and raising a hand, not quite touching Mora's arm, but very close to it. "Wait. The bank account is almost empty. There's three pence left: 0.03. It's Harwood. I called the bank. Even the safe-deposit box is empty, but she left a note. She'll exchange the money for Moneypenny's life. She wants to meet."

Mora dragged a sigh deep into his rattling chest and then hurled Moneypenny against the glass wall, where she bounced with the sound of a gong, before falling unconscious on the tiles. He turned to Dryden, who was thrashing uselessly against the restraints, the nail pulling blood from his shoulder.

"It appears we need another surgeon," said Mora. "If only we knew a good one."

THIRTY-FOUR

Hold On

The big gray building on Morskaya Ulitsa had occupied Harwood's imagination since Bond described his capture in Vladivostok. It was where the Russians had brainwashed him to try to kill Sir Miles Messervy. *You're a perfect weapon and someone is going to use you.* Bond had reported to the big gray building because he'd lost his memory and had the idea that Russia was important to his life. Now, Harwood traveled there of her own free will, entering the port city that connected Russia to China, North Korea, and the Arctic, coming back almost full circle as she circled in her mind to Paris, where her father would sing to her one moment and raise a chair the next moment to smash all the bulbs in the room in case of bugs; to the Barbican, where she found him living in a prison of his mind and decided to join him until the jailer let him out through the release of death; to Tokyo, and the promise of a new beginning with Bond. Vladivostok was a closed city during the Cold War, home to the Soviet Pacific Fleet, and as the fishing trawler that carried her approached the concrete skyline, she had the sense it was still closed, a pincer of police boats speeding toward her. Harwood stood in the stern, alone, and raised her hands. *Breathe.*

She was bundled into the police boat and hooded, so she didn't see the approach to the big gray building, and instead smelled the transition from oil and salt and coal to exhaust fumes and Asian spices and dust from construction. Then a door slammed shut behind her and she lost the heat of the streets and someone snapped her wrists into chains. She tugged—she was bound to a wall. Mora's voice in her ear in the Syrian mountain shuddered down her spine, but it was only in the prison of her own mind. *Breathe.*

The hood was yanked away, catching in her hair. Harwood shook her head, then winced against the glare of a spotlight emitting a low whine from the corner of the dark room. Now the smell was barbecue. She focused on 000.

"Hello, Conrad. You seem to have lost face."

He slapped her roundly. Harwood's cheek stung, but she bit back her cry.

"Where's Bond?" he asked.

She shifted her jaw. "Dead."

That stayed his next swing. "My team didn't hit him on Sakhalin."

"You think you're the only person who can kill James Bond?"

"You?"

"He never believed he could trust me. Mora saw to that. It was him or me."

"That's a scene I would have enjoyed."

His strike had loosed a tooth and Harwood spat blood at his feet now.

He stepped back with a grimace of distaste. "Where's the money?"

"I moved it to an offshore account of my own."

"That wasn't the deal."

"I don't see Moneypenny. *That's* the deal. Take me to her and I'll give you the account number."

"If that's what you want. But you might regret it." He turned to someone in the shadows. "Check her for bugs."

Hands came for her, tearing open her shirt, patting her legs. Harwood kept her gaze on 000, who eventually looked away. So he still had some shame. She wondered where his last line lay, or had he crossed it years ago? They wouldn't find a tracking device. She didn't need one. Bond had been in the aft of the trawler and would track her every movement. All she needed was faith that he wouldn't leave her or lose her.

The mercenary who had searched her nodded to 000. The hood returned. She braced herself as someone pushed up her sleeve and a needle bit her arm. *Breathe.*

She endured a labyrinthine dream—Paris–Barbican–Syria–St. Petersburg–Baikal–Tokyo–Corsica–the big gray building on Morskaya Ulitsa—until another blow reverberated through her body. She went to raise her hand to stop 000 but she was handcuffed and so cold she couldn't move her limbs. The hood was torn off. She was kneeling on a wind-blasted parade ground surrounded by huddling glaciers and confronted by a bust of Lenin, but it wasn't Lenin raising his hand to her, it was Mora. She couldn't help it, she cringed back to avoid the next blow.

"Dr. Harwood, you're right on time. Conrad tells me you ended Bond."

The gale numbed her mind, colluding with whatever sedative they'd given her, and she went under again, circling back to the conversation in the dacha, the fantasy of another life, and she almost told Mora that Bond was waiting for her. You be James, I'll be Johanna. But then the blade of wind lanced her and she said, "He believed I'd betrayed him. There was nothing else I could do."

Mora touched her cheek with his blunt fingertip. It was almost a gesture of comfort. "Sometimes the bullet takes years to arrive," he said. "It's in your power to decide whether death takes you too. I could use my powers of persuasion to force you to give me your bank account. You remember how persuasive I can be, don't you, Johanna?"

She blinked away tears that she told herself were drawn by the cold.

"Good girl. But if I do that, you will be in no fit state to perform surgery. Moneypenny isn't our only guest. We also have 004, Dr. Suleiman, and Dr. Nowak."

Harwood snapped fully into the now. That wasn't part of their calculation. What could he want with 004, Ibrahim, and Zofia Nowak? And why would Mora want her skills as a surgeon? She looked around, though all she could see was snow. Where was Bond?

"I need your tender hands, sweet Johanna. I'll let you save your team if you do me this favor in return. Then we'll *discuss* the bank account. Time for that Hippocratic Oath."

She gasped with pain as he seized her by the throat and dragged her upward, then across the parade ground floor toward broken railways snaking into the pyramid-shaped mountain. 000 followed, a smirk on half his face. A group of armed men surrounded them. She glanced skyward—prayed skyward—for Q to see her. But the clouds were the same color as the ice and as close, and if Ibrahim was here and Aisha was dead, who was on the home front now anyway?

A concrete-protected doorway let them inside the mountain, and then into a steel lift. Warmth started to creep back into her body, burning her numb hands. There was no chance of taking Mora as six more armed men and 000 followed. The lift descended. When the doors opened, it was into a watchtower suspended in the middle of a pyramid stacked with computer servers. In the center was a bright white box. The glass doors opened on the strangest surgical bay she'd ever seen: Joseph Dryden nailed in a canvas body bag to an ornate table, with Dr. Nowak and Ibrahim both tethered to a bank of computers around him. No Moneypenny. She must be prisoner somewhere. Or dead. There were blood spatters on the tiles, smeared as if someone had cleaned up a flood. A tray of polished steel instruments. Six more armed men, guns fixed on 004. There was a nail in his shoulder.

Dryden was gray and ashy. His hand twitched.

Mora clapped her on the back, driving her into the room.

"It's simply a matter, Johanna, of using these fine tools to enter 004's ear and pull out the wires of his neural implant through the canal so Dr. Suleiman can hook him up to this machine"—Mora drummed on a computer—"and Dr. Nowak can train X to imitate his mind and send messages to Q, which by her calculations she should be able to do within twelve hours."

Harwood looked around. How long would it take Bond to infiltrate the site and lay the explosives? Could he have lost her in transit?

She said, "Let me take out the nail. You're compromising the field."

"Do you not think I know when you are stalling for time?" said Mora. "Operate now, or I'll bring Moneypenny up here and kill her. It is entirely up to you."

Harwood met 004's eyes. "What do you want me to do?"

"Kill me," said Dryden. "003, kill me."

"She can't do that," said Mora. "She took an oath to do no harm and heal anyone."

Harwood calculated. If she kept Dryden alive for the next twelve hours, surely by that time Bond would be here and they could end Mora's mission before it could reach the final stage. It was one hell of a gamble. She turned to Ibrahim. "Can it be done?"

Dryden tried to shake his head, but the restraints over his forehead were too tight.

Ibrahim whispered, "Yes."

Harwood nodded. "I'm taking the nail out first. Then I'll need an X-ray of his head."

"You'll have everything you need," said Mora. "But first, I'll need my money back."

Harwood set her jaw. "After the operation. Then I'll give you the account, and you'll let me walk out of here with Moneypenny and our team."

Mora towered over her, breathing her own oxygen, his tongue rattling. "You like to live in hope, don't you, Johanna?"

"It's better than the alternative."

He grunted. "Operate. Then we'll consider your future."

"I'll need free hands."

"No, you'll need your hands bound in front of you. And you'll need an incentive not to do anything naughty with those hands."

"I don't jeopardize my patients."

"All the same." Mora nodded to one of the armed men, who stepped forward and jammed his gun against the back of Ibrahim's head. "Remember who you're playing for, Johanna."

She was returned to the magic circle in the forest. The spell was working. Her hands were moved in front of her. She was given a tray of deadly weapons. Except there were hostages, this time. A portable X-ray machine, sterilization, sedative, water. Time ticked on. Harwood studied the X-ray and then picked up the slender grip. She bent over Dryden's right ear. She murmured, "Do you trust me?"

His Adam's apple slipped up and down. "Always."

"Then hold on."

He seemed to take this as an order, because his fingers flexed in the buckles, and Ibrahim reached for his hand.

THIRTY-FIVE

Head or Heart

It's working," said Ibrahim, though he'd never sounded less happy about success. On the screen, a line shivered, representing X imitating Dryden's brainwaves in a distress signal now racing through subsea Internet cables to Q. There, the poisoned data would enter the bloodstream of Panopticon and alert NATO to divert submarines full steam toward the Arctic to intercept a Russian fleet that wasn't there, backed up by a few false reports sent by Mora's plants. In the meantime, Mora's shadow fleet would get to work: fishing trawlers, aging cargo ships, and oil tankers that would cross the convergence points of cables as thin as garden hosepipes, dispatching divers with mines to sever the UK from the Internet in one fatal stroke.

"Yes, it is," agreed Mora, looking over Dr. Nowak's head to another screen where reports from the Russian fleet confirmed the NATO subs were changing course.

"In six hours, my fleet will move. That gives us six hours to move the funds to the Russian army, who will enact my coup inside Russia as the West crumbles. All I need is that bank account, 003. Now."

Johanna Harwood sat slumped over Joseph Dryden, her hands resting on his chest, her forehead to his. She'd stayed like that since finishing threading the wires from his ear, ticking down the minutes she remained here, alone and without backup. She could hardly feel her hands or feet.

Neither could Dryden. She'd given him anesthesia, but they'd had to keep him awake to train the model. He couldn't feel the pain of her instruments tugging at his mind, but he could feel the pain of his soul being pulled from his body. One false move and she could have killed him. Should have killed him. He might as well be dead. She'd used him to end the world. He couldn't hear anything but the roar of waves, as if he were lying in surf. It might be nirvana.

But now he felt Harwood stir above him, as if bracing herself for a final blow, alone. But a Double O is never alone.

Harwood felt Dryden blink, his eyelashes brushing her skin. She sat up, checking the dressing, then the wires dangling from his ear. Ibrahim looked so pale he might well faint. Dr. Nowak was holding her breath as Mora's fingers spanned her skull with the curiosity of a phrenologist.

"The money, Johanna."

"I don't remember the account details," she said hoarsely. When had she last eaten or drunk anything? "I need water. Food."

Mora heaved a sigh. "I was afraid you'd say that. 000, bring Moneypenny in here."

"Yes, sir." 000 gave Dryden's foot a friendly shake before leaving the box.

Dryden groaned.

Harwood waited for the door to close behind Harthrop-Vane. She considered her options. There were six armed men inside the box with her and Mora. Dryden was tied down, his heartbeat on the monitor as slow as a pallbearer's step. Ibrahim had a broken arm. Dr. Nowak was somewhere else in her brilliant mind. But Dryden was blinking. That meant he was awake. And an awake Dryden was a fighting Dryden. That meant she had backup. And her hands were locked in front of her, and there was a scalpel within reach. What else have you ever needed?

Harwood said, "Ibrahim, disconnect Dryden's hearing aid from X." He glanced at Mora, hunching. She continued: "There's no need for dramatics. I'll give you the money. But we're through with the operation. So disconnect Dryden. I'm worried about his heart."

"Always worried about someone else's heart, aren't you, Johanna?" said Mora silkily. "What about your own?"

"That broke when you broke Bond."

It was what he wanted to hear and he waved his colossal hand. Ibrahim and Harwood used the three good hands between them to unhook Dryden.

"We have to reinstate his hearing aid," said Ibrahim.

"I don't think we need worry too much about that," said Mora.

Harwood told Ibrahim to tidy Dryden up as best he could. Blood crusted Dryden's neck. As Ibrahim worked he started to cry. Harwood stepped behind him. Mora was savoring the scene, and wasn't watching as she palmed a scalpel.

"Ibrahim, you might hurt him. Let me."

Harwood leaned over Dryden, then popped the scalpel and slashed the tie on his wrist. That left one hand free and she hoped for Dryden, that was enough. She spun, lashing out with the scalpel at the nearest guard. She seized the gun as it fell from his hands. Dryden reared from the table with a roar, tearing at his restraints. Ibrahim dragged the desk out of his way, then he and Dr. Nowak frantically tried to get free of their own restraints. The guards were shouting, rifles raised, but the space was so tight if they shot, they might shoot Mora, who took a single step back.

Dryden rose from the table, sending it crashing into two guards, then vaulting the thing to slam into them boots-first. He barreled under gunfire to pile into the next guard. But his balance was off. A vacuum seemed to expand inside his chest, squeezing his heart until it threatened to pop. He was blocking every blow a beat too late. Well, hadn't he always been heading toward this moment? He'd damn well take them with him.

Harwood searched for the shot to kill Mora. Head or heart? There was too much confusion in the room, innocents in the way as Dr. Nowak got free and tried to trash the computers while the guards fought her, but Mora was impossible to miss if you aimed for center mass, so she did just that.

The gun in Harwood's hand was a Pistolet Samozaryadny Malogabaritny, the same weapon Bond had raised to her in St. Petersburg. As then, the safety was already off. Mora stood six feet away. From the perspective of the bullet, Mora's chest was wide open. She pulled the trigger. In the kaleidoscope of the moving bodies in the room, it was a perfect shot. He was wearing Kevlar, but it shouldn't have been enough to stop the bullet. Not for a normal man. But he wasn't normal. The bullet drilled through his uniform, then the Kevlar, and the tip lodged in muscle, making the tattoo of the death's-head hawk moth flutter. He was driven back another step. He looked down at his chest and laughed. Mora's long arm reached for Harwood, and she fired again, but the cold had got to the mechanism and the gun jammed. He shook the weapon from her.

"Ah, sweet Johanna. You should have taken the headshot."

Then the doors crashed open.

"Allow me," said James Bond.

Part IV

Ego

THIRTY-SIX

Play Up, Play Up, and Play the Game

After Moneypenny killed the surgeon, Mora would have sucked the life out of her were it not for the lifeline thrown by 003. So he banished her to the mine shaft. Moneypenny spent the hours of Dryden's surgery and Dr. Nowak's artificial intelligence model training locked inside a cage that would descend into a black tunnel if a wheel was turned. There was no way to open the door. No light. No heat. She was certain she would freeze to death.

She thought of the prison in which she'd locked Mora. Mora's cell was at the bottom of a well, reachable via a retractable bridge, and they'd kept him in solitary confinement as if he were a communicable disease, a virus that could spread faster than a pandemic. Solitary confinement was first conceived of as redemptive by nineteenth-century thinkers, though in practice silent prayer and isolation seemed to send a man mad. Now, Moneypenny wondered if she was finally losing her own mind, dangling in the howling darkness as far above her Mora turned Panopticon against its masters to blind the West—from all-seeing, which meant all-spying, to all-blind. The everywhere war lost.

It wasn't only Mora's signal tunneling beneath the ice. Far below Moneypenny and the hollowed-out pyramid, Rachel Wolff was using a pickaxe, her bare hands, and a compass to find her way through random tunnels to the cloud under the mountain. Subsisting on vacuum-packed rations and ice melt, she was making a deal with God that if she didn't suffocate or freeze, she would use her survival for something that really mattered. She would make the most of Dryden's trust in her. She would make her life count. Just don't let me die. Please, God, don't let me die down here. Let me live to hold my grandfather's hand again.

Moneypenny was past prayer. She wanted to die.

Then the door clanked open and she heard a man say, "Miss me?"

For a moment, hope sparked inside her. But it wasn't Bond. It was Conrad Harthrop-Vane, who manhandled her from the cage.

"Mora wants you to help jog 003's memory."

She was so weak, he forgot to restrain her. Once again, she was underestimated. Three Rattenfänger men formed an escort as they entered the lift, carrying them up to the watchtower, where Harwood must now have operated on Dryden.

The lift opened. She was forced down a pavilion of black servers, like some modern-day colonnade, to the watchtower. The white box waited. Moneypenny blinked away grit, unable to believe the tableau she was seeing. The doors were blown off. Three men held Joseph Dryden on his knees. Dr. Nowak and Ibrahim were frozen mid-motion over the computer, surrounded by guards. The operating table was on its side against the wall. In the center, Mora had his arm around Harwood's throat, lifting her so her toes scraped the glass. And in the doorway, his back to her, stood James Bond, gun leveled at Mora.

The surprise on Mora's face was worth every minute of pain she'd endured.

"007," said Mora, finding a smile somewhere between ghoulish appreciation and rage. "Before you take the shot, you might want to look over your shoulder."

Bond glanced back.

Harthrop-Vane gripped Moneypenny closer. She met Bond's eyes. She said, "Hello, James."

He cleared his throat. "Hello, Penny. Miss me?"

There it was. "Day and night, James." She fought tears. "Day and night."

Bond stood between her and Harwood, between Harthrop-Vane and Mora. He gripped a Walther PPK in one hand, and a detonator in the other. He was soaking wet and blood dripped from his hands. On the floor, Dryden tried to lunge forward, but he was held back, one guard smashing the butt of his gun across his skull. He collapsed, prone on the tiles. Mora held Harwood as a shield. Ibrahim Suleiman was crying. Next to him, Dr. Nowak giggled, then covered her mouth.

Conrad Harthrop-Vane pressed his gun into Moneypenny's temple. "Drop it, Bond."

"Drop a dead man's switch wired to blow the mines beneath us?" said Bond. "You need to send this one back to school, Moneypenny."

Moneypenny tried to resist Harthrop-Vane but couldn't, dragged wide of Bond's reach into the white box. She said, "Blow the whole mountain, Bond."

Mora chuckled. "Your women love to die for you, don't they, James?"

Bond blinked twice.

Mora rumbled, "You can't even look at me, can you? Don't tell me I broke you entirely. Are you in there, Bond? Play up, play up, and play the game."

Bond's lip curled. "I'm through playing games with you."

"He speaks!" With the stump of Mora's tongue, the *s* sounded like water landing in a boiling pan.

"Unlike some," said Bond. "Cat got your tongue?"

"A kitten called Sid," he said, "before I ate him." Mora jabbed his finger into Harwood's ribs. She yelled. "I was sorry to be detained for so long. I missed our shared moments." Another jab, this one to Harwood's back. Her face paled. "As we find ourselves here, you may as well know that after all your efforts to protect Emery's book from me, the irony of it is, you were protecting the very man who wrapped you up and gifted you to me."

Bond said coolly, "So I gather."

"Now here we are. A ménage à quatre: you, me, her, and her." He shook Harwood. "I presume you had sight of the bank account too. Tell me the numbers and I'll spare Johanna's life."

Moneypenny said, "Blow it, 007, *that's an order.*"

Mora chuckled. "I'd salute if my hands weren't busy." Harwood gasped as his fingers found the nerves over her heart. "Tell me, what gave our friend Emery away?"

"Charles Harwood," said Bond.

"Hmm." Mora tilted his head. "All the way back to then."

"Yes," said Bond. "All the way back to then."

"Perhaps it's fitting it ends like this, then. Tell me, how did our sweet Johanna convince you of her undying fidelity? Got down on her knees, did she?"

Harwood stamped on his boot. He laughed.

Moneypenny was about to shout to Dryden to wake up, soldier, but then she realized his hand was moving across the floor. How long could he remain operational? She looked back at Bond, wondering if he knew what Dryden was doing. He seemed to, because he kept buying time as Harwood grew even paler, running out of breath.

"I nearly had you in Moscow in '04, didn't I?"

A chuckle. "Yes, my friend, you very nearly did. But you let Ware impress you with fast cars and cheap women. I wondered at that point if we could recruit you. However, it became clear that the angry flame burning inside you could never burn for us. Your sense of right and wrong was too old-fashioned for that. Still, Ware identified your vulnerabilities for us. Recklessness. Drink. Arrogance. Women." Here, he kissed Harwood on the cheek, and she moved to bite him, but he evaded her with another kiss on the temple. "You've spent over forty years dodging memories and dodging your conscience, conjuring up the professional to keep the human quiet. That's what you told me. Courage is a capital sum reduced by expenditure, you said. And your bank is empty."

"I've still a hand left to play," said Bond.

"I thought you were through with games?"

Bond smiled. "Never."

Dryden rose with the drill buzzing and took off the arm of the nearest guard, dousing them all in blood.

"Blow it, Bond!" barked Moneypenny.

He did as she ordered.

The explosion rose from the depths of the mines, a fireball that shattered each level of servers, turning blue light to white heat and destroying X with a force that seemed to crush the room, stealing the air and replacing it with hellfire and flood.

THIRTY-SEVEN

Killing Floor

Joseph Dryden was grateful for the cool surf on his cheek. He was swimming with Luke Luck. If this was nirvana, it wasn't so bad. But someone on the shore was crying, calling desperately for him to come back. Dryden breathed in smoke, and it wasn't barbeque. Ibrahim bent over him. Water was rising around them. The data cloud was raining. Fire extinguishers.

"What's happening?" whispered Dryden, though he could hardly hear himself over the blare of his scrambled hearing aid responding to the concussive blasts.

"The mountain is coming down! We can't get a signal out and your neural implant is offline. We need to find a plane or a helicopter and get clear of the cloud cover above to send a radio signal to London. We have to stop the subs leaving the UK coast."

Mountains coming down? That didn't make any sense, they weren't in the mountains.

"Please, Dryden!"

He was aware of gentle hands checking his head. "Aisha?"

Zofia Nowak shook her head. "I'm sorry, Mr. Dryden."

It wasn't Aisha, because she was gone. This realization sank Dryden's heart. Ibrahim shook him again.

"People are going to die," the young man implored.

The words righted themselves in Dryden's mind. He dragged himself upright. Wiped his mouth. Hauled himself onto one knee, then both feet. "Not on my watch."

Dryden took point with Ibrahim and Zofia behind him, navigating his way down black corridors, searching for an exit. He was firing the M16 so rapidly it was the back of his brain doing all the work distinguishing between Rattenfänger and friendlies. It was within the grace of a second that he lifted his finger from the trigger when Conrad Harthrop-Vane stumbled around a corner with his arm around Moneypenny's neck and a gun to her head. Dryden stood his ground on the killing floor.

Moneypenny panted, "004, remind me to give you a promotion."

"Ma'am, you'd be doing me a favor if you took one away."

Triple O tightened his grip on her. "You don't know how to stay dead, Dryden."

"Truer words were never spoken, you little piece of shit. Let her go."

Moneypenny said, "Conrad, there's one smart move here."

"Killing you and then myself?" he said, looking backward, but the way was blocked by fallen masonry.

"You won't get the chance to kill yourself," said Dryden.

Moneypenny said, "I don't want to order Dryden to shoot me to get to you, but I will. And he'll follow my orders, won't you, 004?"

Dryden felt a hand on his sweat-soaked back—Ibrahim trying to hold him up. "Yes, ma'am."

Harthrop-Vane retreated, saying: "Do you think there was ever a chance for me to be a good man?"

"Yes," said Moneypenny. "I gave it to you."

His hand fell from her throat and he gasped, his eyes swiveling. Moneypenny elbowed his gun arm aside, stumbling out of the way. At first, Dryden couldn't work out what had shocked him into relinquishing his one advantage. Then Harthrop-Vane turned around, revealing a knife in his back, and there was Rachel Wolff. She was covered in grime and contusions. She must have spent the last day and a half working her way through the mountain to find him. And now she'd stabbed 000 in the back.

Dryden sagged in relief. He beamed at her.

That was when Harthrop-Vane reached around, pulled the knife from his back, and plunged the blade into Rachel Wolff's stomach.

No.

No.

No.

THIRTY-EIGHT

Don't Look Up

As the explosives Bond had laid in the mine shafts detonated, shaking the mountain, the shudder of the floor forced Mora off-balance. Harwood felt his unsteadiness through her misfiring nerve ends. She had shot him in Syria, accurately enough to keep him alive to convince him she was turning double while convincing Sid Bashir she was pure as he hoped. She'd placed the bullet in Mora's latissimus dorsi, missing the kidney. Now she drove her elbow into the old wound and it was enough to force him to give another inch. Give me an inch and I'll take a life. Harwood tore from Mora's grip as Bond fired. But as he pulled the trigger, the glass walls of the white box shattered, a blast wave that sent his aim low and wide. The bullet buried itself in Harwood's leg.

The floor hit her. Gunfire and debris showered down on her. Adrenaline pounded, making her feel she could run a million miles a minute, but it wouldn't last. She was losing breath. An unbearable weight bore down on her. Mora was squatting on her chest, and then the stump of his tongue wriggled against her mouth, his fingers squeezing her pressure points, sending electric signals across her body that told her: danger,

danger, danger. She tried to buck him off but he was too heavy and the bullet tore at her calf. Her feet flailed, her fingertips stretched, find any option, use whatever's available. But there was nothing left.

Harwood relaxed. If there's nothing left, you may as well give in to this feeling. The floor underneath her was no longer cold, wet tiles, but a rough and closely textured carpet. She tested that with her fingertips. Yes, that's right, it's the carpet at home, and she's lying with her grandmaman, setting up a game of dominoes. Her grandmaman's hands—the color of an olive tree, soft thanks to decades of shea butter, long and fine, the bones visible like the bones of a lady's fan, the knuckles swollen, nails cleaned every day with a curved instrument like a scalpel—click-clack with the tiles. Johanna is serious, watching the dots, learning the rules of the game. She can smell the shea butter. It's just her and her grandmaman. She feels safe. So safe she's going to sleep. But she wants to play the game . . .

There was a crash and Mora was knocked from her, skidding across the floor before finding his feet like a giant spider in a storm. Bond stood over her, holding an M16 like a club. Mora bared bloody teeth at Bond. Then the ceiling moaned and an island of metal crashed between them. Bond grabbed Harwood's hand and she scrambled up, following him toward the exit as he fired over his shoulder. She heard Mora shout to his men to seize one of them alive. He needed that money. Harwood pelted down the corridor beside Bond, skidding the corner into a maintenance room. Bond tipped over a machinist table and dragged it across the door. On the other side, troops pounded on the metal.

Harwood looked at Bond. "What took you so long?"

Bond raised his eyebrow. He was soaked, icy to her touch, and his forearms were shredded with claw marks. He said, "I got held up."

"I've heard that line before."

"How's it aged?"

"Worse every time. Did you see what happened to Moneypenny and the others?"

Bond shook his head.

"004 will take care of them," said Harwood, but she didn't sound as confident as she would have liked.

"There are over one hundred men in this facility, and one way out the top of the mountain, the lift. That means a bottleneck. But the ventilation shafts open on the surface. Trouble is, they also connect with the mine shafts for air."

"The mine shafts you blew?" she asked.

The barricade broke. Glass shattered over them. Bond covered the door in gunfire. Harwood looked up at the ventilation shaft. She clambered onto a tool bench, yelling as her leg tore.

Bond stopped mid-motion. "You have damage."

"You're one to talk," said Harwood, popping the grill. She heaved herself up and then wormed around in the tube.

He climbed in after her, then turned to spray the room with bullets before slamming the grill shut after them.

"Mora has a submarine," said Bond, his voice bouncing around the steel tube. "I couldn't give Tanaka our position, but this explosion will show on spy satellites if the cloud parts. Mora will have to evacuate to the sub and run silent and deep to Russia."

"He needs the account details first," said Harwood, before stopping to clutch her leg.

Bond shredded his sleeve. He bound her calf and pulled.

Harwood punched the steel. "We can't let Mora off the ice."

Bond said, "We won't."

Harwood dragged her bleeding leg down the ventilation tunnel to a vertical shaft. The steel was superheating as the mountain boiled from the inside, melting the icy exterior. She heard more shredding, turning to see Bond binding his hands, and then he did the same for her. Through the pain, she felt the light tickle of his fingers on her palm.

"Read my fortune?" she said.

"I see a tall, dark, handsome man in your future," said Bond, the comma of his fringe falling as he drew the padding tight, so she couldn't see his expression.

"No gold?" she asked.

"Would you settle for a country estate in Scotland?"

She looked down into the shaft below. The darkness at the bottom moved, a red flicker. "If we make it out of here, I'd settle for breakfast in bed."

"Sold," he said, "to the girl with the golden eyes."

Fire. Climbing toward them. Harwood looked up at the shaft above. The glimmer of light at the top might have been an illusion, but she'd take an illusion over the idea of burning to death. There was no ladder. They'd have to wedge themselves into the barely hip-width space as the fire ate the air and spiraled up, up, up.

"You first," said Bond.

"My leg," she said. "I'll slow you down. I should take up the rear."

"Every second you argue with me is a second that fire gains ground," said Bond, "and I'm not going to yield."

Harwood said, "Did I ever tell you that you can be incredibly annoying?"

"I've picked that up from you," he said, "once or twice. Get going, Harwood."

"Stick with me, Bond."

"Wouldn't dream of missing this view," he said as she climbed above him.

"Wash out your mouth," she said, trying to keep her voice game as the heat came for her and sweat made her forearms slip on the steel. Could it be done? Harwood flexed her shoulders, gripping the sides. Her feet found temporary purchase, though they'd slip between the ridges at the joints. Her leg burned and blood was pooling in her shoe. She heard it drip-drip-drip onto Bond below. Six inches at a time, Harwood squirmed up the shaft—flex shoulders to grip the sides, lift feet, lock knees, force the feet outward, the bullet pushing the wound wider with a sickening rip, feet slipping down with her weight, flex shoulders, gain another measure of hope. But how much further could she force herself? She stopped to look up and slipped back six inches.

"Don't look up," panted Bond. "Don't worry about the light at the top. Take the inches as they come, one by one, and conquer them."

An inch was all she ever needed. Harwood yelled with the effort and pushed on faster.

When the air on her face grew colder than the heat below, she almost cried. She had to angle her body like a forward slash to extend her hand outside the shaft. She gripped hold of the lip of steel and screamed with pain as she hauled her body onto the rocky plateau. Harwood twisted and grabbed Bond's hand, pulling him out after her as the flames followed. They both rolled away from the shaft onto the ice.

"I saw a plane on my way in," panted Bond.

Harwood sat up, blinded by the glaciers around them. Then she ducked as the sound of an engine cut through the wind. She looked up to see two men coming at them on a snowmobile. Bond drew his Walther PPK from the small of his back, squared himself against the oncoming vehicle, and fired twice. Both men died instantly. The vehicle careened on its side toward them and Bond caught it like a wild horse.

Harwood gripped her calf, teeth chattering as Bond got to work, dragging oilskin coats from both mercenaries. She let Bond pull the coat around her, arranging her arms, before he did the same for himself. Then he checked the M16. The clip was empty. They were at the top of the pyramid, on a plateau cut around the ventilation shaft. She looked down at the town. Her irises shrank. Mora was crossing Pyramiden. Harwood pointed with a shaking arm. Bond took a knife from one of the dead men and pressed the blade into her hands.

"Can you move?" he asked.

She nodded. "Let's do what we came to do."

THIRTY-NINE

The Black Lights

Joseph Dryden was boxing his shadow, and his shadow was hitting back. 004 had been an army champion. 000 had boxed for Eton. The ancient Greeks told us a boxer's victory was measured in blood. It was the same for a Double O. Like a Double O, a boxer was his body, and now both men drove to exceed each other's limits. The boxer's success was his opponent's failure: his reach was his opponent's miscalculation; his speed his opponent's lag; his invention his opponent's lack of imagination. It was an illusion to picture two people in the ring. There was just one person split in half: your better self and worst, the edge of you and the shadow beyond your edge, and the contest was to see whether Jekyll or Hyde won the day. With Moneypenny beseeching Rachel Wolff to hold on, Dryden wasn't prepared to let his shadow self win today. He rained blows on Harthrop-Vane, relentless and percussive, but Harthrop-Vane was blocking and weaving. Some boxers possessed the talent of premonition, imagining a fight so many times it seemed more like a memory. For both of these men, it was a memory, both of them choosing between dealing blows or dealing with blows since birth. Harthrop-Vane fought with the viciousness of a cornered animal, ignore-and-overriding the stab wound to jab for Dryden's heart again and again, then seizing his wounded shoulder and using it as a lever to jackknife his legs into Dryden's stomach. Dryden gasped, putting a hand to his center.

Harthrop-Vane smirked. "Sure you've got the heart for this, 004?"

"More than you," said Dryden, feinting and then landing three blows against Harthrop-Vane's side, breaking his own knuckles and 000's rib.

A boxer could have no instinct for survival, or he wouldn't fight again after experiencing the first knockout blow. It was the same for a Double O. Life expectancy was so short because this breed didn't value survival. As Dryden's heart begged his head to stop, he advanced, pinning Harthrop-Vane against a bank of servers, both of them framed in flickering blue light. This man had taken the last person from his team. He wouldn't be allowed to hurt another soul. For boxers, *heart* meant fighting spirit. And Dryden was never going to lose on that front.

But then Harthrop-Vane managed to wriggle into space and caught Dryden on the right side of his head, exploding pent-up blood and sending Dryden spinning. The black lights—that's what you saw when you were knocked out, and Dryden saw them now, unconscious on his feet.

Joe Frazier once said, *I don't want to knock my opponent out. I want to hit him, step away, and watch him hurt. I want his heart.* It was the same for Conrad Harthrop-Vane: he wanted Dryden's heart, wanted to watch the moment it failed, so he didn't deliver the killing blow. He waited. He watched. But this wasn't a spectator sport. This wasn't a game. A man might play cards. He does not play boxing. He fights. And if it was a game, it was a game of endurance, betting on your body to outlast the other: the operator's last hope, *to keep going*. Dryden woke with his feet still shuffling. Harthrop-Vane's blue-red eyes wailed in his vision, unprotected. Dryden delivered a left hook to Harthrop-Vane's perfectly pointed chin, pulling 000's jawbone out of the socket, tearing at the nerve, and paralyzing the left side of his body. 000's left knee buckled and he almost went down but he stamped on the floor, splashing wildly in the rising water, trying to recover feeling as he hobbled out of Dryden's reach. Dryden pounced on him, getting 000 by the neck. The two men fell together into the tide of flotsam and jetsam. Dryden emerged first, getting his fingers in Harthrop-Vane's blond hair and holding him beneath the water.

Boxing is more about getting hurt than hurting. The body cannot shrink from it or fear it. In the ring and out of it, Dryden's body belonged to boxing: his teenage years had been a climb from welter to heavy, from middle to cruiser, to reach the point where his body alone said, *Hit me and I'll kill you—so don't hit me.* He'd been told by his father that a good big man will always beat a good little man. He couldn't afford to be the good little man. And as he drowned 000, he didn't know if he was the good big man, but he knew that when he glanced around, Moneypenny was desperately trying to stanch Rachel Wolff's blood flow, and he'd invited her into the ring, telling her it was a short life but she could make it count.

In the water, Harthrop-Vane's eyes still danced with mockery, saying, *You want the kill just as much as I do.*

Dryden let go. Harthrop-Vane rose to the surface, hacking up water. Dryden staggered back. His shadow lived, bright in the sparkling lights.

Moneypenny looked up, reached for the gun hanging limply from Ibrahim's hands, checked the safety, and shot her agent.

Harthrop-Vane clutched at his stomach. "Moneypenny?" He collapsed to his knees, staring at her. "You said . . . you said you wouldn't . . ." Then he keeled forward face-first, his arms outstretched for a crucifix.

Dryden stepped over him to reach Rachel. Her lips were moving and he read the words there.

"I should've thrown it . . . I should've thrown the knife, but my arm . . ."

Moneypenny told her to stop talking. She pressed down on the wound, but blood bubbled between her fingers. "You did us proud, Rachel."

"001. Dryden, he gave me . . ."

Moneypenny dried Rachel's cheeks. "001. Thank you."

"I wanted my life to mean something."

"It will." Moneypenny looked at Dryden. "We need to get out, reach radio signal."

"We came by plane."

"Can you get us there?"

Dryden worked his shaking arms under Rachel's legs and arms. He lifted her, tucking her warm, wet torso to his own. "Yes, ma'am."

FORTY

Bête Noire

In the snow, Mora dripped a trail of blood, which Bond covered with his own as he pursued the man. Sixty paces behind, Harwood staggered from the snowmobile, which was out of fuel, just like her. She watched Bond raise the Walther PPK and fire. He missed. Was it the concussive blast wave, the climb through the burning ventilation shaft, and now the howling wind, or was it the fact—this occurring to her now—that Commander James Bond had never actually fought Colonel Mora? He'd first met the monster while bound in a hole in Syria, and remained at his mercy for twenty-one months, forced inside his hurricane room and nearly lost there. Was he scared?

Bond's second shot chipped Mora's side. Mora twisted to face him and Bond went to shoot again, but Mora closed the gap between them and Bond flinched, retreating as Mora knocked his hand aside, sending the gun spinning. Mora's size cast Bond as a child consumed by a nightmare's shadow. Bond backed off, Mora laughing as he followed him step-by-step across the glacier. Bête noire, Harwood thought.

Harwood limped closer, clutching the knife. She felt like she was dragging her leg through barbed wire. She listed, falling into the snow, and when she went to get back up all her blood rushed to her head. Swallowing, she tried to force her throat into producing speech. If Bond had never fought Mora hand to hand, he didn't know to watch out for that gargantuan arm span and the anvil-hard fingers that Mora aimed with a surgeon's precision at pressure points, disabling your body even while you watched on, horrified, from deep inside.

But there was no need to shout a warning. Bond was pacing in a wide circle around Mora, out of reach, watching those deadly hands that had picked him apart piece by piece in that cave.

Mora's sparkling eyes flicked from Bond to Harwood on the ground. "I'll enjoy making her last when I'm finished with you."

Bond glanced back at Harwood, fear flashing across his face, and Mora used the moment to lunge forward, his fingers aiming for Bond's throat. But Bond moved fast enough, swinging back and evading the blow.

The two men orbited an invisible ring. Each time Mora lashed out, Bond ducked or faded, waiting for an opening. But no opening would come.

He had to destroy Mora's weapons. Harwood willed him: destroy his hands.

That's when Bond's foot lashed out, clattering against Mora's fingers with the sound of steel colliding. Mora reeled back, shocked, wringing out his hand. The next time Mora swiped for him, Bond ducked and rolled forward, turning and swiping with a leg, catching Mora's hands once again. The giant backed off another pace. Bond straightened, coming on with his fists ready. But he was too eager and Mora's next blow caught him in the stomach. Bond folded over Mora's coming knee, which jerked upward, catching him in the head and sending him sprawling.

Harwood squeezed the knife harder. She edged across the ice. The booms and moans of the deep shelf shifting beneath them were somehow quieter than her own ragged breathing. She could see Bond's Walther PPK in a mound of snow.

Mora landed on Bond's chest. Bond's arms were free and hammered blows at the giant's ribs. Mora's fingers found Bond's nerve endings and tried to pull them out from under his skin.

Bond didn't let go of him. He wasn't retreating inside his hurricane room, he wasn't accepting there was nothing he could do, he was standing out in the storm and fighting it. He landed blow after blow into Mora's body, and though he might not have known it he was shouting: "Die! Die! Die!" The words came to Harwood on the gale. It was a test of who would give up first, but then Mora's hand closed around Bond's face, and his fingers dug for the trigeminal nerve, putting pressure in exactly the right place to produce the most powerful pain in the human body.

Mora's mouth descended on Bond, wanting to swallow his last breath.

A gunshot on the ice is a desolate sound.

Harwood's bullet went precisely through Mora's shoulder, missing Bond by an inch. Mora snarled, then looked around. Bond struggled, blocking Harwood's next clean shot. Harwood ran, slipping and stumbling. She caught Mora's arm and hauled, enough that Bond was able to punch upward at the man's throat. Mora fell back on his knees. Harwood saw the Kevlar beneath his torn jacket had been weakened by her earlier shot. The death's-head hawk moth tattoo was waiting beneath. She raised her knife but Mora rose like a bull and the blade simply buried itself in the Kevlar as he slammed his whole body into her, sending her flying. She landed with a smack. She looked up as Mora raised both fists, preparing to bring them down on her torso.

Bond stood over her and caught the blow. From Harwood's perspective the two men weren't so much fighting as trying to hold each other up. She couldn't tell which was Atlas holding the world on his shoulders. She shook her head. What's within reach? Where was the gun? Harwood dragged herself out from under Bond's feet.

007 was wrestling with Mora, and then he was forced back and she thought he was about to fail under the pressure. Everything fails eventually. But it was a feint. He was baiting Mora to commit his full weight,

and then he twisted, leaving no support. Mora pitched forward. Bond grabbed the hilt of the knife stuck in Mora's Kevlar vest. He roared with effort. Bond forced the blade home.

Mora smacked the ice. The Arctic seemed to shudder.

Bond grabbed hold of the giant and hauled him onto his back.

Mora held the knife in place, seemingly unsure whether to pull it from his chest or leave it there to stem the bleeding.

Harwood reached the gun. She got to her feet. Her knuckles brushed Bond's and his fingers stirred, taking the Walther PPK. There was one bullet left.

"Sweet Johanna," gasped Mora. "I think I require your offices. You took an oath, remember?"

"More than one," said Harwood.

Mora shook his mighty head, as if he might be able to galvanize himself upright. He got onto one elbow, then collapsed with another grunt. He snarled. "Just who do you think you are?"

"Bond." 007 lifted the weapon. "James Bond."

Mora's skull was so thick the bullet penetrated his forehead and stayed there, like a nail in a coffin.

Harwood and Bond stared down at him, Harwood aware of Bond's chest rising and falling fast, his breath mixing with hers and freezing on the air. It was over.

Except they could hear heavy footfalls coming for them through the blur of snow, as if Mora's spirit was coming back for more. Harwood reached for Bond as a shape appeared through the snow. The polar bear padded toward them. She squeezed Bond's arm, feeling the claw marks there. They took a step back in unison. The bear was bigger than Mora. Sunlight seemed to spin through its white fur, revealing the black skin beneath in ripples. The polar bear landed a paw on Mora's ruined chest and dragged his body into nothingness.

FORTY-ONE

Sweet Sunburst

Rattenfänger were fleeing, the Pied Piper finally failing to cajole the rats. But they weren't planning to let MI6 witnesses out alive. Gunfire chased 004—clutching Rachel Wolff to his chest—and Moneypenny, Ibrahim, and Zofia across the parade ground, and then the battle ceased because an almighty blast filled the air with black cloud. The pyramid-shaped mountain had gone up like a volcano. The mercenaries and Double O Section ran for cover as chunks of ice and granite flew through the air. Dryden could hardly see, hear, or walk, but his feet were still moving as he led the way into a vehicle shed and found an electric all-wheel drive, which Ibrahim got going. Moneypenny kept her fingers pressed to Rachel's wound with Zofia in the back, as Dryden took up shotgun, literally.

"Go, go, go!"

Ibrahim picked up the radio and called all frequencies but there was no reply. Dryden stared up at the cloud cover. Part, damn you, *part*. But then he had other things to worry about as Ibrahim tried to steer them through snow with one hand. There was ragtag and then there was ragged. Dryden's teeth were chattering, he couldn't hear it but he could sure as hell feel it as the anesthesia wore off and his skull told him it was splitting apart. Dryden shouted coordinates for the plane, uncertain if he was actually whispering, the compass on the dashboard spinning as madly as his vision, every sense scrambled.

You get one miracle, Dryden used to tell his team in Afghanistan, and this was it. The plane was still there, a relic left on the moon by past explorers. Ibrahim clambered into the cockpit and got the engine going. He shouted to Dryden that he didn't know how to fly. Dryden dropped into the co-pilot's chair and told Ibrahim he'd talk him through it. Moneypenny and Dr. Nowak laid Rachel Wolff out on the worn leather. Could he see her chest stir? Her lips were blue. But then he realized they had bigger problems, as through the windshield he saw Rattenfänger on the ice setting up a surface-to-air missile launcher. He yelled instructions at Ibrahim to get them airborne.

"Where's Bond?" said Moneypenny. "Where's Harwood? We need a surgeon!"

"We have to go," said Dryden. "Now, *now*."

The Rattenfänger men fired as the twin turbine engines of the Grumman Greyhound roared and the ice floe itself seemed to bounce the plane in the air, where its thin aluminum shell rattled and screamed in two-hundred-knot wind and they jerked up-down up-down with the missile pursuing. Dryden reached for the stick, jerking the plane portside as the missile flirted with them and then fizzed, sparkling, into the white blankness of the sky.

"Wait!" Moneypenny clutched Dryden's arm and pointed at the windshield.

Harwood and Bond were limping through the mist, arms around each other, Bond waving at them, gun in his hand like a cosh. Out of bullets. Dryden looked back, past Rachel's bleeding body, to the rear window, through which he saw Rattenfänger reloading. Bond and Harwood were three hundred paces ahead. They could touch down, take them aboard, and screech up again, but it would mean decelerating to a moment of stillness. He looked at Ibrahim's watch. The shadow fleet would be moving into position to sever the UK from the Internet now. And they needed to break through the clouds, not go down.

Moneypenny said, "I know what you're thinking, but we're taking this plane down, *now.*"

"I don't know how!" cried Ibrahim.

"I can talk you through it," said Dryden, with more conviction than he felt. You get one miracle. How about two?

Ibrahim wiped frozen sweat from his face and wriggled the tension from his arm as he took instructions from Dryden and Moneypenny, dropping the nose of the plane twenty degrees and diving for the figures on the ice. Dryden hoped they understood. They did: he watched them crouch, ready to run, Bond seemingly holding Harwood up. Then the plane skipped on the ice, spitting up white cloud, pulling against the forces of gravity, and Moneypenny forced the door open—it tore off the hinges—and grabbed Bond's arm, pulling him and Harwood inside with a yell. Dryden looked out the door: another missile was speeding toward them. Ibrahim threw the throttle and two things happened at once: the glacier below cracked, opening a thousand-foot drop, and the plane sprang into the air, climbing a thousand feet and bouncing over the clouds, leaving the pyramid, Mora, 000, X, and a stranded army behind them.

Dryden levered out of the cockpit, meeting Bond in the gangway, who put out his bloody hand.

"Didn't get a chance to introduce myself before. Don't know if you'll remember me. 007."

Dryden shook his hand. "Good to have you back, Bond. Can you fly this thing?"

"Yes."

"Take over from Ibrahim. We have to get that signal out."

Bond nodded, easing the shaking technician into the co-pilot's chair before taking his position and putting on headphones. He angled the mic and recited his numbers station poem as he pointed them at the sun. His words filled the plane like a preacher's words fill a temple. "Hope on, hope ever, though today be dark, the sweet sunburst may smile on thee tomorrow: though thou art lonely, there's an eye will mark thy loneliness, and guerdon all thy sorrow. Though thou must toil among cold and sordid men, with none to echo back thy thought, or love thee, cheer up, poor heart . . ."

Dryden squeezed into the back. Harwood was telling Moneypenny her leg was nothing to worry about as Moneypenny argued. Harwood came to lean over Rachel.

"One of ours?" she asked.

"Yes," said Moneypenny. "001."

Rachel's smile was faint, but it was there.

"Can you do anything?" asked Dryden.

"It looks bad." Harwood wiped her face. "Maybe."

Zofia opened a first aid kit and arranged the meager contents. Dryden sat beside Rachel. Harwood was doing her best to sanitize her hands. She told Rachel this was going to hurt without anesthetic, but Rachel didn't seem to hear.

Bond's voice came from the cockpit, warping in and out of Dryden's hearing. "Thou dost not beat in vain, for God is over all, and heaven above thee—hope on, hope ever."

Rachel turned to face the cockpit. Her lips moved. Dryden lowered his good ear to her lips.

"Is that the rabbi?" asked Rachel. "Is he praying for me?"

Dryden's throat swelled. He nodded, taking her hand. There was no power left there.

Harwood opened Rachel's shirt with a pair of scissors, calling for Bond to keep the plane steady.

White light bathed the space, the purest dawn Dryden had ever experienced, if it was dawn. It might have been the midnight sun.

"I don't know," muttered Harwood to no one. "I don't know."

Rachel's eyes opened, sliding over Dryden, then back again, those green eyes so big she could take in the whole universe. "Did we win?"

Harwood said, "You shouldn't be talking, 001, stay quiet for me, OK?"

Dryden touched her cheek. "We did, thanks to you."

She winced.

"I'm sorry," said Dryden.

Rachel shook her head. "I can see my mother . . ."

Harwood told her again to be still. She was clearing the field of debris, readying a scalpel, repeating to no one, "I don't know."

But Dryden knew. The hand in his was cold, suddenly, irrevocably, entirely cold. You don't get three miracles. He looked at her delicate face, so small and beautiful under her short hair. He kissed her forehead. "I'll miss you, kidder."

Moneypenny put her hand on Harwood's shoulder.

"She's gone," said Moneypenny.

Harwood sagged, letting the scalpel tumble.

Bond's chant continued. "The iron may enter in and pierce thy soul, but cannot kill the love within thee burning . . . Hope on, hope ever, though today be dark, the sweet sunburst may smile on thee tomorrow . . . Yes, this is 007, come in London."

There was a switch and then someone else's voice came over the comms system. It wasn't Aisha's voice. It never would be again. But it was an English accent telling Bond they read him loud and clear.

Moneypenny stepped over Rachel to reach the comm. She squeezed Bond's arm as he passed her the headset. Moneypenny told the listener her call sign. "Shut down Panopticon. There is poisoned data in the bloodstream. Abort the NATO submarines steaming for the Arctic. Guard UK waters. A shadow fleet of Russian-owned vessels is about to attack the subsea Internet cable convergence points around the British coast. I say again, abort the NATO submarines. Guard the home front. This is Moneypenny. Do you hear me?"

"We hear you, Moneypenny," returned the voice. "Loud and clear."

FORTY-TWO

The Merciful Option

It was in Marc-Ange Draco's nature to be a gracious host. He had moved Sir Emery to a sea-facing bedroom in the turret, where M could sit at the vanity table before the window and watch a family of red kites nest in the evergreen oak. Marc-Ange entertained the spy chief at his own table. They took long walks along the cliff, where the Capu of the Unione Corse cheerfully pointed out the precipice where his men would dispose of M's body. M examined the drop without comment. Of course, Sir Emery tried bribery and blackmail, sweet talk and threats. But Marc-Ange was unmoved and M remained on the island, seeming to age another year with each day. Until the boat came in.

Bond had pointed the plane toward Japan, where Tiger Tanaka had the nation's best neurosurgeon waiting to put Joseph Dryden back together, though 004 wasn't sure even all the king's horses and all the king's men could achieve that now. The doctors saw to 003's leg and Bond's lacerations as Moneypenny—waving aside attempts to see to her malnourished frame and burnt, bruised body—coordinated with Five Eyes. The United Kingdom sparkled silver and gold at night from the perspective of spy satellites sailing overhead, the lights still on. Moneypenny told Five Eyes and René Mathis of the French Deuxième to meet her and the Double O Section on Corsica.

Another gangster might have balked at inviting half the world's intelligence chiefs to his home, or at least seen to it that he was very much out that day. But not Marc-Ange Draco. He waited on the jetty with his arms spread, relishing this opportunity to add himself to a list of big players that included, one-by-one, America, Canada, Australia, New Zealand, the United Kingdom, Japan, and France. He wasn't afraid, Moneypenny could see that much as she disembarked and accepted his kiss on her cheek. He looked to Bond with confidence. If Bond said it was OK, then it was OK. This belief was shared by the UK's allies, all of whom owed Bond a debt somewhere along the years. When René Mathis docked, he shook Bond hard, scolding 007 for making him grayer. These patricians pleased to have the heir home. She wondered if they hoped he'd become the new M. Meanwhile, they were relieved to see her, too, but the relief was more the one expressed by a scandal-ridden CEO at the arrival of a crisis manager. They hoped she'd mop up. And the attitude toward 004 and 003? Dispassionate thanks, neither Double O carrying the same decades of reputation as Bond and treated as useful if disposable objects. That, after all, was what a Double O was.

Marc-Ange laid on a breakfast in the hunting hall, but while the visiting dignitaries got to work on hair of the dog and cheek of the pig, Moneypenny whispered to Marc-Ange that she wanted to see M. He passed her a key and pointed up the stairs.

Moneypenny had to grip the iron banister for balance. Her hand shook as she slotted the key home.

M was framed in the window, blue sky riding his shoulder. The vanity had a three-paneled mirror, reflecting his overlapping selves. He turned to her and his bushy eyebrows rose a small fraction, but no more.

"Sir Emery, I've come to relieve you of your post."

M tapped the table. "Moneypenny. I must admit I never expected to see you again."

Moneypenny said, "Your friend Mora's main weakness, if I may say, was hubris coupled with a demonic appetite he prioritized over operational prudence. And yours was believing you could control him."

He cleared his throat. "A fine assessment."

"I've learned my job well. And I think I'll have yours, now."

In the hunting hall, Marc-Ange had arranged tall-backed chairs in a circle. A court, it struck Moneypenny upon reentering, and she was amused by the arrangement. She passed Draco the key. Harwood stood behind an empty chair at twelve o'clock, ready to lead, if she'd accept it. Dryden stood outside the circle at six o'clock, a man always ready to be at his teammate's six. And Bond sat inside the circle in a creaseless linen suit at eleven o'clock, his left leg crossed over his right knee, hand clasping his ankle. He rose for her, gesturing to the empty chair beside him. He'd positioned himself as Lancelot to her Arthur. Moneypenny thought that made Harwood Guinevere, and perhaps that was apt, because since touchdown in Japan, Moneypenny had watched a strain grow between 003 and 007. She wasn't sure if that strain had carried them through Russia, but she doubted it. No, it was the transition, somehow, Bond seemingly determined to bend the world around his fist, a conquering hero, not a victim. And the conquering hero always rode in alone.

René Mathis, chief of French intelligence, was explaining that a certain *awkwardness* might arise if Sir Emery was brought to public court. "We have all trusted Sir Emery for a long time. I am sure France is not alone in feeling some concerns about how the revelations contained in those microdots might reflect on our history. And it is so hard to keep secrets these days." This with a dark look toward America, France's long-held irritation at the Anglosphere alliance flashing.

Bond drew the War Book from his jacket pocket and flipped through the pages, a flash of colors.

"Let's be frank, gentlemen," said Australia. "And lady. Ladies. Sir Emery knows too much to have his day in court."

New Zealand said, "Who knows what other *insurance policies* he's kept?"

Canada said, "That's what interrogation is for."

Tiger Tanaka said, "I suggest all we need do is leave M in a room with James, Johanna, and Joseph. We will soon have our answers."

Bond shook his head. "I can't hurt him. I thought I could kill him. But I couldn't even touch him. He was a father to me, once. He still is, despite everything. Just not a very good one."

America flexed his well-defined arms. "This isn't about sentiment. We're all grown-ups here, gents. And girls. We know it can't be allowed to get as far as a court. Of course, he has to step down. But he's well past retirement age as it is. A party at the palace, a gold watch, and he can live out the rest of his days forgotten in the long grass."

Moneypenny said, "That's not justice."

America tilted his hand. "Hard to play golf in long grass."

Vallance of MI5 chuckled ingratiatingly. "That's some punishment, at least."

Moneypenny said, "*Embarrassment* isn't enough of a reason to do nothing. We tell the public they have nothing to fear from surveillance if they have nothing to hide. And then we hide when we have everything to reveal."

"I don't need a school lesson in ethics from admin," said America.

Moneypenny straightened her spine, which still burned from weeks compressed in fear. "And I don't need a school bully in a conversation for grown-ups."

America considered her through a showy squint. "A lot of bite for Bond's desk girl."

Bond clicked his tongue, then passed the War Book over to Moneypenny. "Careful," he said. "You're addressing the new M."

"When was that decided?" demanded Vallance.

"Deep in the ice," said Moneypenny, "where we stood alone, without Five Eyes, without friends, without fear, and held our ground."

America sighed. "Whatever. You can't seriously propose to drag that old man in front of the *Daily Mail*, with *his* mouth and *his* knowledge?"

"No," admitted Moneypenny.

"Then what, a deep hole?"

Moneypenny shook her head. "We've had enough deep holes. We have to find another alternative that delivers justice for his crimes without exposing us to further danger."

"Would you like a cherry on that?" snapped America.

Moneypenny leaned forward, locked in argument. Behind her, Johanna Harwood considered the circle. The room where it happens. *It* being concealment, hypocrisy, and self-serving interests. She looked ahead to a future where M enjoyed retirement as a speaker on the lucrative lecture circuit. Dinner at the club. A flutter at the races. Golf on a Sunday. A few medals in the drawer. Her father's fate didn't matter to these people. They didn't even have regard for Bond's or Moneypenny's suffering, seemingly comforted enough that Bond still carried himself with the confidence of a commander and the allure of a better version of themselves, perfectly styled, perfectly mannered, perfectly groomed, the fringe of his comma glinting with salt and pepper that only granted him more authority. And they could look past Moneypenny's brittle bones because her pencil skirt and stockings were perfectly aligned, her curls perfectly set, and her sharp words made them feel a little better about themselves, because at least they were hearing out the moral arguments. As for Harwood, she was completely invisible. The same went for 004 across from her. She could see the future. She didn't need a palm reader. It would be exactly what it always was.

That wasn't good enough.

She caught Dryden's attention, raising her eyebrows in question.

Was he also picturing Aisha's last moments and how little they mattered to the people in this room? She wagged her head toward the door. He nodded.

No one seemed to notice as they left, though maybe she felt Bond watching her—she didn't check if she was right. As she passed Marc-Ange in the hall, he gave her the key.

Harwood led the way upstairs. She'd used the main guest room when she came to Marc-Ange for help infiltrating Russia and knew he was a good host even to his enemies. She stopped outside the door, sliding her feet on the smooth red flagstones. Dryden stood close to her, the rise and fall of his chest reassuring.

Dryden said softly, "Are you armed?"

Harwood nodded.

He looked almost guilty. "I can't kill an unarmed man, even if he . . ."

She just nodded again. She knew she could, in that moment. She'd taken two oaths, for better or worse. "Watch the door for me?"

Dryden's turn to nod. She pushed the key into the door and he closed it behind her.

M stood with his back to her, leaning on a chair, watching a red kite soar alone. He half-turned, in profile to her now, the laughter lines of his face turned downward, the three panels of the mirror showing all sides to him. She pulled her gun from her holster and clicked the safety off. A sigh shuddered through him.

He said, "Is this the merciful option, Johanna?"

She said, "No."

It was a surgical shot to the heart. M pitched forward, splayed over the table, spinning the mirror, which bounced the Mediterranean sun around the white walls as baby kites exploded from the oak and spiraled in shock toward the sky. Harwood laid the gun on the table next to him, then turned and reached for the door, but Dryden opened it for her, taking her arm and gently drawing her out of the room where it happened.

She could hear commotion downstairs, chairs scraping. But she knew the back way out. A Double O always did.

She looked up at Dryden. "Tell him goodbye for me."

Dryden seemed about to ask her where she was going, but thought better of it. "It's been an honor saving the world with you, Johanna Harwood."

She shook his hand.

"Anytime you need me," he said.

"You too," she said, and then turned to leave.

FORTY-THREE

Memory

Moneypenny said, "It's technically the Survivors and Dependents Fund, but we still call it the Widows' Fund. I don't know why, it's not as if women don't . . ." she trailed off. Rachel Wolff's grandfather waited with polite concern. "Anyway, the Widows' Fund will pay for your care, so you needn't worry."

He sat with a blanket over his knees on a bench surrounded by lawn shorn to sickly stubble. The care home was wedged, with a level of irony Moneypenny thought overkill, between a university and a cemetery. The building was a converted chocolate factory, and you could tell yourself the air was still spiced with the aroma of childhood bedtimes, sugar and warm milk, though really it was the fumes of a nearby motorway that lingered.

Rachel's grandfather picked at the Egyptian cotton, a family heirloom, he'd told her. "Have we met before, dear?"

"I knew your granddaughter, Rachel. We met in your jewelry shop. My battery watch had died."

"Very easy to replace, dear. No trouble at all."

Moneypenny played with the bag of breadcrumbs the staff supplied. They said he enjoyed feeding the birds. But there weren't any ducks in the pond today. She looked around at the other inmates, accompanied by nurses dressed in medicinal shades of beige and pastel pink, as if vibrancy might kill. She thought of Rachel Wolff's bright lipstick.

"Has something happened to Rachel? I don't think she's visited lately . . ."

Moneypenny tossed a crust for a march of ants. "Are you happy here, Mr. Wolff? I could arrange to have you moved . . ."

"Oh no, all my friends have ended up here, like the old days. But I don't understand what could be keeping Rachel . . ."

The same words she used last time came automatically. "I recruited Rachel to help the government because of her courage and skills. She was very brave and she saved my life and the lives of many other people. But the damage was too severe, and there was nothing more the doctor could do. It was peaceful and she was surrounded by people who knew how brave she was and welcomed her into a family."

"But—what do you mean *damage*?"

Moneypenny realized she'd missed a sentence. She rubbed her face. Since assuming M's post, she'd taken to sleeping in her office, an hour here and there to sustain her as she tried to fix the damage Sir Emery had wrought. Yes, she'd admit it: she was suffering night terrors, and felt better in her bulletproof office with security posted at the door.

"Damage from what?" asked the old man.

She said, "History, maybe. Hope. I'm not sure. I'm very sorry."

His frown trembled. "Oh, I shouldn't worry. I'm sure you knew what you were doing. I expect Rachel will be along soon?"

Slowly, Moneypenny nodded. "I expect she will."

"Oh, good," he said, thumb drumming a beat on the bench. "That will be nice."

Moneypenny watched ants pour through a crack in the paving. "Sir, I did know what I was doing. That's the worst of it. We've failed your family twice. Your daughter came to us for help. We could have extracted her from the thieves she ran with instantly. But she was useful to us, and we let it play, and she was murdered. You raised your granddaughter to have a different life, but she was addicted to danger and wanted revenge and I used those things to get what I wanted from her. We could have left her with you. I should have left her with you. We do these things because we can, because we tell ourselves it's for the greater good, but I don't know if we can distinguish what's *good* from what's powerful anymore."

Rachel's grandfather's eyebrows trembled, a lot like M's when he was angry. He reached out and patted Moneypenny's wrist, and then his fingers probed her Nanna Ditzel–designed watch.

"New battery, was it, dear?"

"Yes. I could use a new battery."

FORTY-FOUR

Curative

A strict diet. Acts of obedience. Seek forgiveness and invoke His blessing. Pray at night. Joseph Dryden followed Dr. Akter's curative, moving with the quietness of a ghost through Shrublands. He ate the food that was put in front of him. He took the pills and did the exercises. He visited the chapel and asked God to forgive him for decisions he made and decisions he didn't. He replayed moments: If he'd trusted his mother's suspicion of the system, would Aisha still be alive? If he'd listened to his conscience, would Rachel be living a normal life in New York? Dr. Akter said he was cleared for active duty, and Dr. Kowalczyk asked him whether he wanted to quit. Quit? She asked him if he could find any meaning in Aisha's or Rachel's deaths. She told him meaning was important to his sense of purpose. He told her to go to hell. At night, he prayed beside Luke Luck's bedside, his 2ic still in a coma, and he was there now, holding Luke's hand, when a sharp breath drew his head up.

Luke's blue eyes fixed on the ceiling, then he blinked and a tear slipped down his cheek, as if it had been waiting, a pent-up grief. Dryden stood up, calling for help. Luke coughed, a sound like wind across sand.

Dryden stood back as Dr. Akter and two nurses checked Luke's vitals and gave him fluids and told him to move this way and that. Dryden watched the third miracle and wondered if he deserved it. The doctor said Luke was doing well for someone waking up from a month-long sleep and left, telling Dryden not to disturb him. But there wasn't much chance of Lucky Luke not disturbing himself, levering himself to the edge of the bed, bare feet skirting the linoleum floor, head hanging, arms dropped between his knees like a marionette waiting for string. He whispered, "Joe?"

Dryden stepped forward. "I'm here."

"Joe, I had this nightmare, there was this mad fuck, mate, I've known some mad fuckers in my time, but this one . . ." He lifted his head. "That weren't a nightmare, were it?"

"No."

Luke looked around slowly. "Honest to God, mate, I thought I died."

"Me too," said Dryden.

"When you reckon I'll be operational again?"

"Contingent on being awake."

"I'm awake now," said Luke, standing. He wobbled and Dryden caught him under the elbow. Luke asked, "Are you good?"

Those were the words Luke shouted to him after the IED in Afghanistan, as their vehicle tumbled and the blast wave passed through Dryden's body, but back then Dryden couldn't hear them. He heard them now but it was Rachel holding his hand, ready for anything, wanting purpose, wanting a family. Luke regarded him with the same expectant look.

Luke touched his face, then traced a network of scars under Dryden's right ear. "What happened?"

"We won," said Dryden. "But I lost."

Luke touched his lips to Dryden's. "You're still standing."

Still standing. Still standing, Dryden kissed his 2ic, 005, the one love of his life. Still standing, Dryden packed up his room and signed himself out of Shrublands. Still standing, he called for a car and waited with the sunshine on his face. Still standing, he entered the lift in Regent's Park and greeted Bob Simmons.

"004, I'm very glad to see you," said Simmons. "I wondered—I mean to say, you weren't at Dr. Asante's funeral."

"I was," said Dryden. "In the back."

"I didn't see you."

"That was the idea."

"You didn't want to say anything?"

"Nothing that could be said in public," said Dryden. "I said the rest to her father afterward."

"Oh. Well, that was good of you. I keep thinking, you know, what if I . . ."

"There was nothing you could have done," said Dryden. "He fooled us all."

Simmons shook his head. "Where are you going today, then? Up to the top floor?"

"That's not my office anymore. Moneypenny's looking for a new Chief of the Double O Section, now she's gone over to Vauxhall. I think she's trying to persuade Johanna Harwood."

"I must say it's a pleasure to see Moneypenny take the top spot," said Simmons.

"Yes. She'll make a good M."

"But you didn't want to stay Chief of the Double O Section?"

"I don't have the heart for it."

Simmons scratched the stump of his arm. "How is your ticker these days?"

"It'll heal," said Dryden. "I'm going to Q Branch."

"Oh—er, you are? All right, if . . ." Simmons waved his palm over the reader, and the lift descended with a lurch. "But don't tell me you've come to say goodbye? You're still 004, aren't you?"

Dryden rolled his shoulders. "Until the day I die, or I'm tethered to a desk with a thousand guy ropes."

"That is good news, sir—I mean, 004. Not that there are many of you about these days, anyway."

"005 woke up this morning."

"Did he now? Well, that'll be nice to work together again. Maybe he'll keep you out of trouble."

A smirk tugged at Dryden's lips. "I doubt it. Thanks, Bob."

Dryden hesitated at the threshold of the lab, and then let his feet carry him down the glass corridor, following the curve to the office overlooking Q's busy heartbeat. Dryden knocked on the wall.

"Careful!" shouted Ibrahim, twisting his chair. "You'll disturb . . . Dryden."

Dryden softly beat his fist into his palm. "Hey, brother. Sorry I've been AWOL for a while."

"You're never AWOL," said Ibrahim, pointing to Q. "We always know where you are."

Dryden's eyes were tugged from Ibrahim to the floor, which was spotless, and then across to Aisha Asante's desk. Dr. Zofia Nowak offered him a small wave.

"How are you feeling?" she asked.

"You wanna know something funny?"

"If you want to tell me," she said.

"I miss the voices in my head. Feels lonely without 'em."

"You should probably see a psychiatrist about that."

"I did," he said. "She told me I'd be doing myself a favor if I talked to real people, not voices in my head."

Zofia tilted her hand, as if this were only partially useful advice.

"I heard Luke's going to be all right," said Ibrahim. "Can't keep you Special Operators down."

"Not so far," said Dryden. "Maybe next time. But not yet."

FORTY-FIVE

A Brief Paradise

The graded blue waters of Shark Bay were still. The island blushed in the setting sun. The changing temperature brought the smell of evening: roasted cassava, blooming night jasmine, and damp stone. Felix Leiter watched a man-o'-war bird float over the Bahama grass. He stretched his leg, making use of the full length of the deck chair. When he heard bare feet padding toward him from the house he decided not to turn and watch Trigger cross the lawn but savor his luck for his own personal détente. But then another step joined hers, and that was a stride he knew. Felix Leiter looked around at James Bond.

"Your friend has come to take another limb," said Trigger, passing to the other side of him and surveying the pair with the hand missing a trigger finger on her hip.

Leiter rose, reaching for his walking stick as Bond drew his gun lightning fast.

"Too late," said Bond. "The angels have got you."

"You limey bastard," said Leiter, shaking his hand and then pulling him down to plant a kiss on his forehead. "Why didn't you warn me?

I would've shaken and stirred my tail feather and picked you up at the airport."

"I can't move for security in London," said Bond. "They think I'm going to vanish into thin air."

"So that's exactly what you did?"

"Well . . ." Bond grinned, and it was the let's-make-trouble grin Leiter knew so well.

Leiter turned to Trigger. "I'm surprised you didn't take his head off when you answered the door."

"I was tempted," she said. "Very tempted."

Bond bowed deeply. "My eternal thanks for resisting."

"One day I might even thank you for resisting the same," said Trigger, flexing her hand. "One day."

A half-smile. "I look forward to it."

"Hey," said Leiter. "Keep your charm to yourself. This time I got the girl of your dreams."

Trigger shook out her long hair. "Neither of you know anything about women."

Bond laughed. "No argument from me."

Leiter looked past him. "Speaking of dream girls, where's Johanna?"

The laughter faded. Bond turned to watch a hummingbird tremor in the hibiscus. "She left."

Leiter squinted. "She left, or she left *you*?"

"What's the difference?" asked Bond.

"Pretty key, I woulda thought . . ." But Leiter gave up as Bond turned his attention to Trigger, who dropped her sarong to the grass and strode nude toward the water.

"Is that an invitation?" asked Bond.

"Between her and the sharks, she's deadlier," warned Leiter.

Bond raised an eyebrow. "My kind of woman. When did you two . . . ?"

"Post-traumatic romance."

"Fun while it lasts."

"You never change, do you?" said Leiter. "How 'bout a drink?"

"How about ten?" said Bond.

They drank Russian vodka and dry vermouth. They drank rum. They drank champagne. Leiter could guess what Bond was trying to forget and didn't ask, just kept pouring. They played cards, the three of them on the veranda beneath the stars. They swam naked, Trigger holding Leiter afloat around his chest as Bond promised to ward off any sharks. They ate scrambled eggs and drank coffee, before beginning the next day with another cocktail. They fished. They told war stories, distant enough to be funny. They took a boat out to float around. They danced and got into a couple of fights with local barflies and pulled their punches and enjoyed the taste of blood. They listened to music loud enough to scare off the resident kingfisher. Bond declared his love for Trigger before passing out. She kissed his cold, taciturn face as he slept, Leiter shaking his head with a sigh. Hours later, Leiter kicked Bond awake and told him to go declare love to the right woman. But Bond told him to stop fussing like an old man, so Leiter made him Old Man's Thing, filling a cracked dish with lemon and orange skins, a bottle of cheap rum, and sugar, which he set on the stove, stirring until it thickened. Then he took Bond's battleship gray lighter and flambéed the lot before pouring Bond a glass.

"Here's to cabbages and kings," said Leiter.

Bond clinked, then shot the whole lot back. He grimaced, wiping his mouth. "That's truly awful."

"Crybaby."

"I missed you, you lousy bastard."

"You crossed my mind," said Leiter, "once or twice."

"Oh yes?"

"Just once or twice, mind."

"Of course."

Leiter sighed, stretching on the sofa, looking out through the large window at this brief paradise. "I reckon we've earned this."

Bond shrugged.

"You Brits. You bust a gut to bust the enemy's gut and then you get philosophical about it. Care to have Mora back? Bet a thousand you wouldn't. So what's eating you? You did a good job. Pest control."

"I've heard this speech before. It usually ends with you turning contrary and telling me the job stinks of lilies and formaldehyde."

"And so it does. But you always go back. It's what you were put into the world for. So what's eating you?"

Bond said nothing.

Leiter sighed. "Stay as long as you like, friend of mine. God knows I've wanted your company. But don't think I don't know what you're hiding from."

Bond stiffened. "I don't hide."

"Sure, James. Sure. Meanwhile, I've got a date and I promised the lady a fresh catch."

Leiter came back from the beach with swordfish steaks wrapped in newspaper. He walked through the palms, enjoying the sun on his face. The real world could go hang. Leiter used his prosthetic hand to nudge the door of the villa open.

"James?"

No answer. Leiter peered into the living room. There was a note on the table. It read: GONE TO SEE ABOUT A GIRL. WRITE TO ME EVERY DAY. THANKS FOR EVERYTHING.

Leiter smiled. That's my boy.

FORTY-SIX

The Sky Watches

People act, the sky watches: a proverb that used to mean the sky gods were all-seeing. Now, it was said with a glance up at the nearest AI-powered surveillance camera, never far away, even on China's porous southern border with Vietnam. Over the border, Dongxing was known as Little Hong Kong—the place you could get anything. Iron-hulled boats crossed from Móng Cái to Dongxing, where the Beilun River was ten meters wide, carrying ivory, frozen beef, cigarettes, liquor, and women. Then came the fence: China had driven the solid steel, five-meter-high electrified border topped with barbed wire into the earth across thousands of miles with cameras every couple of meters. The crossing points were heavily guarded. No one into China. No one out.

Several blocks from the pedestrianized market under neon lights and security cameras, Joseph Dryden sat with his back to the wall in the corner of a corrugated iron bar, Lucky Luke at his side. They were buying their way into China, where their mission was to discover why Dryden had seen Chinese lettering on the servers in the cloud under the mountain.

A ceiling fan stirred the humidity. The go-between was maybe nineteen, good English, long lashes that fluttered as he negotiated the price for smuggling Dryden and Luck over the river.

"Eight hundred dollars for each of you."

"That's more than an average monthly salary," said Dryden.

The boy shrugged. "I don't work in a bank. I work here. We'd get a lot more selling you."

"Eight hundred now," said Dryden. "Eight hundred on the other side."

"Twelve hundred now. Four hundred on the other side. In case we die."

Luke said, "You're not filling me with confidence, mate."

He pointed at Dryden. "Your money, your choice, American spy."

Dryden said, "I'm not an American spy."

A grin. "You're not?"

"I'm British. And I'm not a spy."

The boy shrugged. "You want us to smuggle you into China, but you're not a spy."

"I'm a journalist," said Dryden. "He's my security."

The boy looked to Luck. Then he rolled up his sleeve, revealing ivory bangles. "You want one for your sweetheart? I'll give you a bargain. Very pretty pieces."

"I'm pretty enough," said Luck.

That much was certain.

The docks were ramshackle, a remnant clinging onto a river with glowing high-rises either side. The boy left them at the edge, shining a torch onto a rowboat. Luck boarded first, keeping his hand on his gun. Dryden considered the crates in the stern, wondering what contraband they were joining. The six accompanying men were all armed, no fat on them, no quarter given. A whistle, and then they set off. Quarries, then rice paddies glinting in the moonlight. If they spilled into the Beibu Gulf, they'd see the glare of the luxury Trà Cổ Beach. But they didn't. Within minutes the boat bumped into China.

"Chuyển động, chuyển động."

The stretch of mangrove forest between the riverbank and the fence smelled like the stomach of an ancient crocodile turned inside out.

"Careful," said the youngest smuggler. "Mines."

Dryden kept his hand hooked into Luck's belt. The ground rose to the fence, barbed wire tangled up with moonlight. The smugglers cleared scrub, revealing a sewer hatch. A blowtorch flared.

The beautiful boy elbowed Dryden. "They recently installed this. Thought it would stop us."

Dryden heaved his bulk onto the streets of Little Hong Kong, pulling Luck after him. A van waited with its engine running outside a house where TV flickered in the windows. The driver jumped out and opened the back doors.

The smuggler said, "Inside."

Dryden considered the cramped interior. No windows. Locks from the outside.

"I think we'll join you up front."

"As you like."

They pulled up at a logistics company. It was busy for this hour. The driver arranged the van in a line with others that had come from the port. Dryden and Luck watched the men load the crates into the back of a lorry bound for Nanning.

"Just you and twenty tons of frozen chicken feet," said the boy. "You can't drive up front for this one. The rest of the money."

"In Nanning."

"Now," said the boy, changing his grip on his machine gun. "Or your journey ends here."

If he handed over the money now, there was nothing to keep them alive until Nanning. That said, there was not much to keep them alive right now. He had no power here.

He had no power here.

Dryden sniffed. The back of the lorry, lit by the headlights of the van, was gray with dust. He reached out a finger and sketched a death's-head hawk moth on the door.

"You know what that is?"

The smuggler shuffled back. "Yeah. Yeah. The gods are asleep . . ."

"And do not watch," completed Dryden.

The boy saluted. "You should have said. Pay there."

Dryden nodded. They climbed into the back of the lorry.

The doors closed.

Zofia Nowak's voice blossomed inside Dryden's ear. "You are now over halfway to Nanning on the toll road. You have ten minutes before the next CCTV camera. If you disembark here you can cut into the mountains."

"Copy that," said Dryden. "Over and out." He turned to Luck. "Ready?"

"To jump from a vehicle moving at ninety miles an hour?" A shit-eater's grin. "Always."

Dryden mirrored his smile. He realized—for good or bad, healthy or fatal—this was all he'd ever wanted, and all he'd ever want.

FORTY-SEVEN

Family

There was a buzz on the intercom from Phoebe Taylor, but Moneypenny had no chance to answer it before the door to her new office swung open. James Bond strolled in wearing a dark navy suit with a black knit tie and a black trilby that looked like it had been dragged through the tropics. He tossed the hat toward the coat stand, where it swung admirably. Bond came to sit on the corner of her glass desk.

"Miss me, Penny?"

Moneypenny relaxed in her chair and crossed one leg over the other. "Day and night, James, day and night."

He propped his elbow on his knee and leaned closer. "But *especially* the nights."

"That's between me and my priest," she said. "What kept you?"

"Nothing could keep me from you. Apart from Felix Leiter, a bottle of rum, and a headlong dive into forgetting. You should try it some time."

"Some of us have to keep the ship afloat."

"Dependable Moneypenny."

"Don't."

His charm cracked. "Yes. I'm sorry. About a lot of things."

Her voice softened. "Me too."

He scanned the stack on her desk. "Recruiting?"

She opened the flap of the topmost file, revealing a picture of an Asian man in combat gear. The next showed an Iranian woman. "Sometimes I feel like Ware and Harthrop-Vane won. The Double O Section down to three men and one of them still in hospital."

"Dryden?"

She shook her head. "Already in the field with 005—he's after your time."

"Where?"

"China. Intelligence suggests Mora's cloud under the mountain was built by Chinese engineers. We want to find out what they stood to gain."

"Control in Russia," said Bond. "So who's minding the shop?"

"No one. 008 is only now walking again—also after your time."

"Well, just remember 007 is taken."

"Are you back?" she asked.

"God no." His laughter petered out. "I can't come back. Not yet anyway."

"The world will always need 007," said Moneypenny. "And you, dearest friend, need the world. Now more than ever."

"What if it's not enough?" said Bond. "Maybe I'm better off buried."

Moneypenny brushed his fringe. "That's what you came to tell me?"

"I brought you a postcard."

"You know, that's what Royal Mail does, too."

"Nothing like the personal touch," said Bond.

"I'll take your word for it," said Moneypenny, brushing his fingers as she took the faded card. "What is this?"

"We wrote out the details for the bank account we used to hide Mora's siphoned funds, in case we didn't make it."

"And you sent the postcard to Harwood's home address?" asked Moneypenny, looking at the Barbican postcode.

"Don't lecture me on tradecraft, Penny, I'll go back to the bottle. We sent it to her neighbor. That's where her father used to leave messages for his imagined enemies or allies, Jo said. The neighbor would display the postcards message-out in her window. There's a small fortune in there. Use it for the Widows' Fund."

Moneypenny got to her feet, brogues sinking into the new carpet. The reflection of the Thames glittered in James's eyes. She nudged Bond's knees open with her thighs, coming to stand between his legs, and kissed him on the cheek. Bond's arm came around her waist, and they stood like that as ships passed below and the building hummed under the guidance of its new chief and nearby Big Ben ticked on.

"Don't forget you have family here," she whispered.

"Never."

Moneypenny slid her palm over his heart. "Do you remember the last time I saw you, before you were taken? You asked me if I thought you have a cold heart."

Bond said, "I remember."

"I told you your problem was much to the contrary. But I didn't get a chance to explain what I meant. I've regretted—feared—you'd die believing I thought you lacking in that department."

"As long as you don't think me lacking in any other department."

"*James.*" She swatted his arm. "What I meant was that your heart—the wounds that don't heal, the emptiness that's scarred over—would get you killed unless you held tightly to the list of people you care about. Because I knew it, and I didn't call it, when I should have. That was my job. I knew you would run into danger because you were running out of reasons to live."

Bond hummed lightly. "No regrets between old friends. That's what I came to tell you."

"No it isn't," said Moneypenny, opening a drawer and pulling out a sheet of paper. "This is where she's staying."

FORTY-EIGHT

Salvage

The irony that it was Johanna Harwood's mother's clerical job for Médicins Sans Frontières that first inspired her to set her daughter on the path to become a surgeon, before 003 alienated her mother by following her father's hidden history as a spy, and that this very choice now led her to volunteer with MSF in Liberia, was not lost on Harwood. She was the team's general surgeon, but she took on whatever job needed doing: vaccinating children, performing a C-section, repairing hernias, treating lymphoma. There were few gunshot victims because most died before they could reach the hospital; there were no ambulances. Volunteers came and went, but the mission went on.

Her days began at six thirty in the morning, when she'd have a cold shower and eat with her colleagues. It was a fifteen-minute walk through a residential neighborhood where she said hello to the same locals before arriving at the hospital for rounds before eight. Surgery began half an hour later: there was rarely if ever time for elective cases, because the night would have provided too many emergencies. She operated until one o'clock, then got feeling back into her feet returning to the house for lunch. Surgery resumed at two o'clock and lasted five more hours. Another chance to stretch her legs as she reported for dinner, then a driver would deliver her to the hospital for any additional pending cases. Both the hospital and the house were surrounded by barbed wire and travel after dark was discouraged. But Harwood often went for night walks, and the other women marveled at what they considered her recklessness.

On Sunday, she would contribute to the blood bank, which was always low. There was no central bank in Monrovia, and during surgery she had to perform red cell salvage, collecting blood from the surgical field in a stainless steel basin, which would be filtered through sterile four-by-four gauze pads into a second basin. The team did this three times, before drawing the remaining filtered blood into syringes and injecting a donor collection bag, giving the blood back to the patient through a 170-micron filter. It was field medicine that dated back to wars outside of living memory. With even the basics taking five steps instead of one, she didn't have time to think, six days a week.

It was the nurse from Germany who noticed what was beginning to show and asked Harwood to take a test before she donated blood again. After that, she stopped donating, and on the seventh day she'd run on the beach, drilling into nothingness. She didn't want to think.

A plane from Europe came twice a week, bringing mail and medical supplies. Harwood read the letters from Moneypenny, who said that the coroner had ruled M shot himself. As Harwood's fingerprints were on the gun and she shot M through the back, this struck her as an impressive level of inventiveness on the coroner's part. Moneypenny told her that if anyone in the intelligence community thought differently, they were glad to have a thorny problem solved for them, and didn't even rue the lack of interrogation, as M had left a written confession detailing his sins. Moneypenny thanked Harwood for the sacrifices she made to save Bond and apologized that she'd had to do it alone. She wanted Harwood to return and become Chief of the Double O Section. But Harwood never replied.

The UN troops she saw at restaurants in town often performed a double-take, as if there were something about her they recognized. But she ignored the practiced lines of peacekeepers. She'd heard them all before.

She wondered if she was trying to find herself, like some gap year kid. Or escape herself. Wherever I go, there I am. Until it occurred to her, one day as she scrubbed for surgery, that she wasn't aware how she appeared to the nurse across from her, nor what the nurse might want from her, or what she could get from him. She wasn't performing for an audience. She wasn't persuading a mark. She was operating but without seeking influence or force. She was, in fact, playing her part, and her part alone. Except it was a solo act. Was that what she wanted?

That evening, there was another letter waiting on her pillow. Only this time, it wasn't from Moneypenny.

FORTY-NINE

Dear Johanna

If I was laying a bet, I would have put it all on me walking out on you, not the other way around. Like you said, I have form. I suppose I can make some guesses as to why you left as you did. I doubt it was fear of repercussions. Felix Leiter—who sends you undying fealty and affection, the cad—asked me what I'm hiding from. I told him I don't hide. Much like I don't fail. But in the moments I can look myself in the mirror, I know what frightens me. That you decided you must withdraw to protect yourself from me. You might be settled there, strengthened by a purpose you can believe in. But I just need to tell you this.

I want you

I would move heaven & earth for you

I would give anything for you

Are you happy, Johanna? If you are, then I'll leave you be, and hope to see you down the road, passing me at speed. A flash of your smile, your curls in the wind, and I'll send you a salute.

Go on being as brilliant as you are. If you ever want me or need any help, wherever you are, my home is yours.

But if you want to be with someone who knows you—I know you. And you know me.

Ever,
J.B.

FIFTY

Home

Johanna Harwood pushed her Alpine A110S around the curve of the mountain, rain-specked mist sliding over the windshield, parting and then closing around her as she climbed higher. Dawn fractured into a thousand rainbows, each one caught in running droplets, painting the gunmetal road prismatic as an oil spill. The land was unforgivingly beautiful, heather and gorse the only soft spots against granite. It was a war between the light and the gray and eventually the light won, Harwood pushing through the dreck to surface on top of the world, soaring above a sea of clouds as dappled as waves. She whipped around the next bend, putting the window down, feeling the force in her hair. She saw the whitewashed building waiting for her at the end of a long road surrounded by moorland. You could almost call it a castle, though it was really a hunting lodge. She'd always wondered what James Bond could call home. A herd of deer stopped to watch her sweep up the drive, not easing on the accelerator at all. This is the race of your life. So floor it.

James Bond was leaning over the engine of his Aston Martin DB5 in the graveled forecourt of his ancestors' home. He stood in the shadow of the battlements, but at the sound of her engine she saw his shoulders stiffen and he turned, facing directly into the sunshine to watch her approach. He drew himself up. Had he meant it all? Would he still mean it? Bond closed the hood of the Aston Martin and slid one hand into his pocket, waiting. She drew the Alpine up with a splash of grit. She turned the engine off. He walked toward her with a measured step.

Harwood heard his hand land gently on the roof and then he bent down to meet her eye. There was a moment of assessment.

Then he said, "I feel better already."

"I've heard that line before," she said.

"How's it aged?"

"Better every time."

She could have opened her door herself, of course, but she was afraid. So she let him pass around the engine and do it for her. He offered his hand. She hesitated, and then took the offer, sliding out of the racing seat. Bond's hands moved down to her waist, then spanned her stomach slowly. Harwood looked up at him, holding her breath. He smiled. An answering smile tugged at her lips, which he bent to kiss.

Acknowledgments

Deepest thanks to Corinne Turner, Simon Ward, Ian Fleming Publications, and the entire Fleming family for trusting me with your legacy. It's been the honor of a lifetime.

Thank you to my agent, Sue Armstrong, for making my dreams come true.

I am forever grateful to my publishers in the UK, America, Germany, the Netherlands, and Spain, where incredible teams have given me opportunities for new experiences and new friendships. I began writing *Hurricane Room* in Barcelona while publicizing *Doble o Nada* (thanks to Roca Editorial for putting me up in a very swish hotel where it would have been rude *not* to write at the rooftop bar). I continued writing *Hurricane Room* while editing and publicizing *A Spy Like Me* and I was lucky to visit some amazing places in the process, including Segovia (which appears in this novel) thanks to Hay Festival and the British Council, and Germany (also in the novel) thanks to Cross Cult publishing. I am grateful to the centers of creative writing where I got down vast chunks of *Hurricane Room*: an icy January spent at the Literary Colloquium Berlin where 0013's chapters came into being; Cove Park on Loch Long, where the UK houses her nuclear submarines, which became a key plot point; Greenway, Agatha Christie's holiday home in Devon, where the

National Trust put me up in the garret; Arvon Totleigh Barton; Moniack Mhor; and Gladstone's Residential Library, where I finished the first draft a long way after midnight alone amidst antiquarian books. Grateful mention also goes to the Ludlow Hotel in New York, where Nick and I honeymooned, which became the meeting point for 004 and 001.

Hurricane Room is the final novel in my Double O trilogy, which I began writing in 2020. My Spotify Wrapped since then has told the story of long writing nights against deadlines soundtracked by the James Bond theme songs (I'm in the top one percent of Sir Tom Jones listeners worldwide, go figure) and *Hamilton* ("Why do you write like you're running out of time? Write day and night like you're running out of time?"). There's a not-so-subtle *Hamilton* reference in this book as thanks. The remainder of my Spotify Wrapped is Dame Shirley Bassey, and you'll also find a reference to the 2000 remaster of "For All We Know" in a line that became symbolic of 003 and 007's relationship.

Hurricane Room had many iterations and a significant turning point was discovering the work of Trevor Paglen, who makes art using spy satellites and underwater Internet cables. Visiting Bletchley Park was another key source of inspiration.

Thank you to the kind folks at Alpine and Thruxton Circuit who taught me how to drive a sports car—quite the feat as I didn't know how to drive and don't have a driving license. Rocketing around the UK's fastest track informed two chapters of *Hurricane Room* and means I can now say I *do* know how to drive, but only sports cars.

The greatest joy of writing the Double O series has been making like-minded friends. The James Bond community is passionate, creative, and inclusive, with the most extraordinary output. I owe so much inspiration to you. If you were part of my event with Licence to Queer on James Bond and travel, you were there live for my musings on James Bond's liminal lifestyle, which later became material for a scene in *Hurricane Room*. This community has dug deep into everything from Bond's fashion to the meaning of green baize (credit to Dr. Lucas Townsend for inspiring Moneypenny's line of thinking on this in *Hurricane Room*). I was especially grateful to Graham Thomas for his book *The Definitive Story of You Only Live Twice: Fleming, Bond and Connery in Japan*, which inspired 003 and 007's escape route. And of course, the ultimate credit goes to Ian Fleming himself. It was a throwaway line from Bond to M in *Moonraker* that triggered the entire novel, when Bond sprinkles pepper on his vodka and says: "It's a trick the Russians taught me that time you attached me to the Embassy in Moscow" . . . We hear no more of this period in Bond's life, so *Hurricane Room* is my attempt to fill the gap.

Hurricane Room proved the hardest novel to write in the trilogy as we suffered four bereavements as a family in less than a year. I would never have finished this book without the support and encouragement of those around me: my mum, Ellie Baker, who reread *Hurricane Room* overnight multiple times; my husband, Nick Herrmann, who never let me doubt myself; my sister, Rosie Sherwood, who spent a long weekend in Edinburgh cooking for me while I recited the *entire* plot; my godfather, Simon Latimer, my own Q; my father-in-law, Stephen Herrmann; and so many good friends along the way. Thank you.

Hurricane Room is dedicated to the memory of my mother-in-law, Vera, whose belief and pride in me meant the world and always will. The book is also dedicated to the memory of my father, Craig Sherwood, who was a production manager for rock 'n' roll and tour guide for the Double O series. There's so much of him in this book and I'm grateful I could share it with him.

Ian Fleming advised us: Always say yes to adventure. Writing these books has been an adventure like no other. Thanks for reading.

Ian Fleming

Ian Lancaster Fleming was born in London on May 28, 1908, and was educated at Eton College before spending a formative period studying languages in Europe. His first job was with Reuters news agency, followed by a brief spell as a stockbroker. On the outbreak of the Second World War he was appointed assistant to the Director of Naval Intelligence, Admiral Godfrey, where he played a key part in British and Allied espionage operations.

After the war he joined Kemsley Newspapers as foreign manager of *The Sunday Times*, running a network of correspondents who were intimately involved in the Cold War. His first novel, *Casino Royale*, was published in 1953 and introduced James Bond, Special Agent 007, to the world. The first print run sold out within a month. Following this initial success, he published a Bond title every year until his death. His own travels, interests, and wartime experience gave authority to everything he wrote. Raymond Chandler hailed him as "the most forceful and driving writer of thrillers in England." The fifth title, *From Russia, with Love*, was particularly well received, and sales soared when President Kennedy named it as one of his favorite books. The Bond novels have sold more than sixty million copies and inspired a hugely successful film franchise, which began in 1962 with the release of *Dr. No*, starring Sean Connery as 007. The Bond books were written in Jamaica, a country Fleming fell in love with during the war and where he built a house, "Goldeneye." He married Ann Rothermere in 1952. His story about a magical car, written in 1961 for their only child, Caspar, went on to become the well-loved novel and film *Chitty Chitty Bang Bang*. Fleming died of heart failure on August 12, 1964.

www.ianfleming.com

THE JAMES BOND BOOKS

Casino Royale

Live and Let Die

Moonraker

Diamonds Are Forever

From Russia, with Love

Dr. No

Goldfinger

For Your Eyes Only

Thunderball

The Spy Who Loved Me

On Her Majesty's Secret Service

You Only Live Twice

The Man with the Golden Gun

Octopussy and The Living Daylights

NONFICTION

The Diamond Smugglers

Thrilling Cities

CHILDREN'S

Chitty Chitty Bang Bang